FIELD *of* DAISIES

BARBARA HATTEMER

Kristin —
Celebrate Hope!
Barbara Hattemer

OAKTARA

Waterford, Virginia

Field of Daisies

Published in the U.S. by:
OakTara Publishers, P.O. Box 8, Waterford, VA 20197
www.oaktara.com

Cover design by Yvonne Parks at www.pearcreative.ca
Cover images © thinkstockphotos.ca: field of daisies/Elena Volkova,
119491829; girl outdoors/Oleksii Zabusik, 121618443
Author photo © 2012 Jennifer Hattemer, Dove Photography,
www.DovePhotographyFL.com

Psalm 23:5b-6 (ch. 21) taken from the King James Version of the Bible. Public domain. Psalm 121:7 (ch. 24) taken from The Holy Bible, New International Version®, NIV®. Copyright © 1973, 1978, 1984 by International Bible Society. Used by permission of Zondervan. All rights reserved. Matthew 6:25 (ch. 24), John 14:27; Matthew 28:20b; Ephesians 1:3 (ch. 28); Deuteronomy 5:29b (ch. 31); 2 Timothy 1:7; Zechariah 4:6b; Isaiah 53:5a; Isaiah 53:5b; 1 Peter 2:24c; Psalm 56:13b (ch. 32) taken from the New King James Version®. Copyright © 1982 by Thomas Nelson, Inc. Used by permission. All rights reserved. Matthew 6:34 (ch. 24) taken from the *New American Standard Bible®*, copyright © 1960, 1962, 1963, 1968, 1971, 1972, 1973, 1975, 1977, 1995 by The Lockman Foundation. Used by permission. Exodus 34:6 (ch. 31) adapted from the *Amplified Bible®,* copyright 1954, 1958, 1962, 1964, 1965, 1987, by The Lockman Foundation. Used by permission. Psalm 34:18a (ch. 34) taken from *The Living Bible,* copyright © 1971 by Tyndale House Publishers, Wheaton, IL 60187. All rights reserved.

ISBN: 978-1-60290-321-0

Field of Daisies is a work of fiction. References to real people, events, establishments, organizations, or locales are intended only to provide a sense of authenticity and are used fictitiously. All other characters, incidents, and dialogue are drawn from the author's imagination.

Printed in the U.S.A.

⌘ ⌘ ⌘

In loving memory of my grandparents,
ED AND LAURA KOCH,
whose love nourished me as a child
and whose marriage was the model I most admired.

Acknowledgments

I am indebted to two friends, Mary Lee Montgomery and Carole Currie, who read my early attempts at writing a novel, encouraged me to keep writing, and pointed out areas that needed improvement. Their good advice propelled me forward.

Along the way, all the members of my summer critique group, the Deer Isle Morning Writers Group, helped me tremendously. Without Nancy Hodermarsky's sensitive evaluation of my chapters, I might have been tempted to give up, but Nancy always appreciated the parts of the writing that were closest to my heart. D Immonen labored through *Field of Daisies* to made many helpful suggestions. I so appreciated her conviction that the book should be published.

I valued the advice of the many others who read the book and responded favorably.

The endorsement of LuAnne Wahlstrom and Marianne Troy, two professional women who worked with Alzheimer's patients, confirmed to me that I was on the right track. LuAnne said, "I smiled at every reference to the disease because it was so true, honest and accurate, capturing exactly what Alzheimer's patients and their families experience." Debbie Noonan and Anne Wood, who were dealing with Alzheimer's in their own families, were grateful to find that they were not the only ones experiencing the things I wrote about. More recently, Ann Platter helped me to keep the story moving, and professional counselor and teacher Nikka Horton monitored it for accuracy and helped me make the final changes to the story.

I am especially grateful to Ramona Tucker, Editorial Director of OakTara, for responding so favorably to my book. From the time I first met her at the Florida Christian Writer's Conference, I knew I wanted to work with her to make the book the best it could be.

Above all, I am indebted to my God, who revealed himself to me in such a dramatic and intimate way, I had no choice but to respond to him. He has drawn me closer through times of affliction and filled me with a longing to write what he has taught me. He has given me a heart to share his unfathomable love with others and to remind them that nothing is impossible with him.

1

Andrea Mulder raced up the stairs of her split-level home to answer the phone call that would change her life forever.

"Hello, Andrea."

"Hi, Dad. Is everything all right with you and Mom?"

"Yes."

"Great, I've been wanting to talk to you."

"Not now, Andrea, I need to talk business with Lans."

Andrea pursed her lips, erasing the smile from her cheerful face. How often during her childhood had she run to her father for solace and found him preoccupied with business. Leonard Collins always put business first.

"He's just come into the living room, Dad. I'll put him on." Stifling a sigh, she stretched out the phone to her husband, Lans, and perched on the wide arm of their couch. Her long legs dangled over the side like a schoolgirl's. Dressed in jeans and a matching sweater set, she looked the part in spite of her forty years.

"Hello, Leonard." Lans arched an eyebrow in response to her father's questioning. "Well, as a matter of fact, I'm quite satisfied with my job here in New York. Why do you ask?"

Andrea listened with increased interest.

"Pittsburgh?"

While Andrea studied the frown that creased his forehead, Lans rose and strode about the room. Still dressed in business attire, he appeared to be making a business decision. What could be so serious?

"That's quite an offer," he said at last. "Thanks for your confidence in me. It's a lot to think about. I'll discuss it with Andrea and the kids tonight, and we'll call you tomorrow." After perfunctory good-byes, Lans replaced the receiver and turned to Andrea, unmasked pleasure animating his handsome face.

"What is it? What did Dad say?"

Lans squared his shoulders. "Your father invited me to join his company as Executive Vice President. He promised that when he retires, the company will be mine."

Andrea sprang up and threw her arms around him. "I'm so proud of you.

1

Dad would never do that unless he thought you could handle it. Congratulations." She hugged him so hard they almost toppled to the floor. Laughing like children, they struggled to steady themselves and plopped down on the couch.

Andrea studied his expressions as he contemplated the offer. "So much to think about," she said. "You want to know how I feel about that, don't you, darling?"

"Yes," he said, brushing unruly strands of hair from her face and looking intensely at her. "But would you be willing to give up all the things you've worked so hard for? Your ministry to the women at church? The pregnancy center? The clubs at school for John and Kate? Our home?"

Andrea surveyed their living room, remembering how they had chosen each piece of furniture together. The very comfortable couch by the fireplace with its large, stuffed cushions, the glass-topped coffee table with plants growing beneath it, the over-sized piano covered with family pictures. Would it be hard to give up all the ministries she had labored so hard to start?

"I'd miss them all for sure, but they're replaceable." Her smile faded. "But do you think we could keep Mother from running our lives?"

Lans laughed.

"I'm serious, Lans." She had enjoyed being out of her mother's reach, free to establish her own identity, make her own choices. Now her mother would feel it her duty to coach Andrea on how to become an international hostess and make business contacts for Lans. She shuddered, but as she searched her husband's expectant face, she saw that he wanted this job, wanted it very much. Setting aside her concerns, she smiled at him. "Think how close we'd be to the family farm. It's just an hour's drive from Pittsburgh to Butler. That would make up for a lot."

"You're right, it would." Lans' tanned face lit up. He released her, rose, and paced about the room again. "I'd surely miss my tennis foursome, but Executive Vice President of one of the best management consulting firms in the country..." He studied the ceiling. "Your father's a great businessman. I could learn a lot from him."

"Our family comes first, Lans. Don't make our children suffer like we did as kids. You're still angry that your father was never home to play catch with you or attend your basketball games."

The lonely childhood they shared helped them understand each other.

Andrea experienced again the hollow feeling of coming home from school to an empty house eager to share her day. Her parents were in Sweden, Australia, Argentina...on business, of course. "We promised each other we'd always have time for our children."

"And we always will. Let's tell the kids tonight and see how they react."

She crossed the room to hug him once more. "Great. That will give me time to think it through." Andrea withdrew from his arms, caressed the hollow of his cheeks and searched the soft brown eyes that had won her when she was fourteen. She questioned him again. "Are you sure this is something you want, Lans? It would mean spending much more time with my parents."

"Isn't that what you've longed for all your life?" He lifted her chin with his hand and kissed her on both cheeks.

"It's what I always wanted as a child, but now..." She pictured her proud, fashionably dressed mother, blond hair stylishly coiffed, looking at her wayward child, expecting more than Andrea wanted to give. Evelyn Collins was the first woman in her circle to bleach her hair when she and Leonard began traveling to Sweden after the war. She was the first to buy a television set and invite friends to football parties on Sunday afternoons.

Andrea remembered an unending series of the best, the biggest, and the most original parties: goldfish served in finger bowls to be named and launched into her lily pond; magnificent hats required for the price of admission; husking bees in the barn at the farm. Evelyn Collins always set the pace.

"She's become so sure of herself in recent years, and she wants me to follow in her footsteps. I don't really want that. Of course, I've always longed to spend more time with Dad."

"And I've always tried to give you everything you wanted, haven't I?"

"You've done such a good job, I'm not sure I want anything to change." Was she ready to live again under the shadow of her vivacious, dominating mother?

Andrea knew her mother had had a primary role in her father's success. She had made friends with top executives who became Leonard's clients. He had always given his wife credit for growing his business. He possessed the ideas and the brains to carry them out, but he could never have forged the relationships necessary for a successful business without her help.

Her mother had other strengths. When Leonard was out of town, she handled each family crisis with grace. Andrea remembered how she had rushed to the farm to take control the day her father, Andrea's grandfather, lost his senses. Andrea sighed. Early senility ran in her mother's family, a problem she'd rather not remember.

"Let's see how the children react before we go further," Lans said. "And don't worry; I can love you just as much in Pittsburgh as I can in New York."

Andrea snuggled against his chest. She was a fortunate woman to have such an attractive, successful husband.

⌘⌘⌘

After dinner the family lingered around their circular dining table. Andrea had made a centerpiece of wild grasses and flowers to set the mood. As the children nibbled on a second cookie, Lans shared his opportunity with them, reminding them how close they would be to the farm. "But it does mean that we would have to move to Pittsburgh," he concluded.

"We would live close to Gran and Pakin. How great is that!" Precocious, ten-year-old Kate's green eyes sparkled.

"You mean we could go to the farm every weekend all summer?" John grinned exposing a mouthful of braces. Except for the wires across his teeth, he bore a remarkable resemblance to his father: straight blond hair, brown eyes, and the round, full cheeks of Lans' youth. "Can we have our own horse like you did when you were a kid, Mom?"

"Yes, one for each of you," Lans answered for her.

"My friends will be positively green." Kate clapped her hands and jumped up and down, tossing her auburn ponytail. "I can't wait to tell them."

"Kate, have you thought what it will mean to leave your friends?"

"No, I couldn't bear that, but it sounds so good."

"We could invite them to spend a week at the farm in the summer, perhaps come for a holiday. Would that make it easier? And we'll be coming back to visit Johan and Katharine." Andrea turned to her husband. "I'll miss living near your mother. She's become a close friend."

"She'll visit often when Dad's traveling. She'd be thrilled to spend time with us on the farm."

Andrea turned to the children. "Yes, she fell in love with it the summer our fathers wrote their first book together. She'll come any time we invite her." She rose from the table and put a hand on the shoulder of each of her children. "What do you say, kids? Do you need some time to think about it?"

"No," John said. "A horse of my own settles it for me."

"It's scary to think of leaving my friends, but I've dreamed about having a horse at the farm," Kate said.

"I guess the horses carry the day. I hope you have as much fun as I did on Dolly." Andrea remembered the thrill of finding her favorite horse in the barn on her ninth birthday. "She was the delight of my life. I rode her all over the Pennsylvania countryside. Remember, darling?" She smiled at Lans.

"Your mother thought I fell in love with her the summer we met at the farm, but I really fell in love with her horse." They all laughed and he drew them into a circle. "Let's ask God to show us if this is the right decision." They bowed their heads. "Thank you for this excellent opportunity. Thank you that my family is willing to join me on this adventure. Guide us as we consider all the changes it will bring to our lives."

Andrea looked forward to sharing the pleasures of the farm with her children, but what would life in Pittsburgh be like? She had never shared her parents' values. Climbing the ladder of success, business parties, traveling for months at a time; they weren't for her. She didn't want Kate and John to long for time with their parents as she and Lans had.

⌘ ⌘ ⌘

After an hour of questioning and imagining their new life, Kate and John agreed to go to their rooms to complete their homework. Lans followed them up the stairs to his office, but Andrea stayed behind to enjoy the fire. She added another log and poked its dying coals. Soon orange and yellow flames danced again. Inhaling the scent of burning pine, she scurried about the room collecting scattered papers. As she approached the grand piano, her wedding picture caught her attention. She picked it up, rubbed her fingers along the rough wood frame, and carried it to the couch by the fireplace.

As she settled into the soft cushions, she stared at the handsome young Dutchman who smiled back at her. He wore a cream-colored jacket with a daisy in his lapel and tan pants that complemented his straw-colored hair and brown eyes. She caught her breath as a titillating thrill rushed down her spine. The fire crackled and flared, mimicking the excitement that rose within her. *I, Andrea Collins, take thee, Lans Mulder, to be my wedded husband.*

She could smell the newly mown field grasses and the flowers of her bouquet. The resplendent smiles radiating from their fresh young faces warmed her so deeply she could feel the heat of the sun sparkling down on them as she pressed through the field toward Lans. Glistening white and yellow blooms bowed in the soft breeze on that summer day nearly twenty years ago. She carried an armful of daisies and wore a white organdy ankle length dress with a low scooped neck. Lans had suggested they be married at the farm in the field of daisies, the first indication that her serious young businessman had a romantic nature. Her eyes filled with tears as she remembered the thrill of that revelation.

Lans bent over the back of the couch where she was sitting and kissed her neck. "You looked like a Nordic princess coming toward me, your long hair crowned with daisies, just like I requested."

Andrea jumped and the picture dropped to her lap. "I didn't hear you come in." She reached for his hand, drew him to her side, and nestled into his arms. "Remember that incredible day, Lans? You looked so happy and confident as you stood there waiting for me."

He nodded. "It was the proudest moment of my life."

"As good as the phone call from Dad tonight?"

"Even better."

"I held onto Dad's arm with all my might, afraid I might stumble and trip on the grasses. But I remember wanting to run to you, throw my arms around you, and tell you this was even better than my dreams."

"Why didn't you?"

"Because Mother was still struggling to adjust to a country wedding. I approached you with dignity on my father's arm, just as she expected."

"And I marveled that you were about to become my wife and wondered how I could make you as happy as I wanted you to be."

"Our marriage has been all I hoped for, Lans."

"And now it's going to be even better."

She stared out the window into the darkness, wishing she could share his confidence.

2

The end of the winter of 1972 brought a frenzied reshuffling of Andrea's life. Finally the day came for her to supervise the packers as they boxed her possessions for the move to Pittsburgh. Each painting tugged at her heart as they took it down from the walls. She remembered how she and Lans had chosen every one of them, especially the one they had bargained for on the Left Bank in Paris the day before he confessed his love for her.

Two hectic days later, the moving van, loaded with their possessions, pulled out of their driveway. She took a last look at her favorite gardens, reached down to pull a few weeds, and resolved not to look back. She settled Kate and John in the back seat of their station wagon and slipped into the front beside Lans. On the way to Pittsburgh, her mind whirled with questions. Could they resist falling into the mold of her parents? Would their lives continue to focus on their family, or would they change to entertaining clients and the high social life she had been happy to leave behind?

Lans looked forward to the move with unfettered enthusiasm. Why couldn't she share his joy? She did anticipate lovely weekends on the farm. All four of them looked forward to riding through the fields and country paths together.

And Lans was right. In spite of the tensions between her and her mother, she had always wanted more time with her parents.

⌘⌘⌘

Lans started his duties at Leonard's office at once and left Andrea to set up their newly rented home. It was small. Clearly, their furniture needed more room. She set aside boxes she would not open until they were permanently settled. Every evening Lans carried more of them out to the garage and piled them high against the wall.

Within a week, Evelyn Collins hosted a party to introduce Andrea and Lans to families with children the ages of John and Kate. For this Andrea was grateful.

"Mom," she said, "that was a lovely party you had for us. The children are thrilled to have potential friends already."

"I'm glad you enjoyed it, dear. Now I'd like you to save a few more dates. Where is your calendar?"

"It's not even unpacked yet."

"Well, jot these down on a piece of paper. The Friends of the Museum are having a benefit next Tuesday, and there's a dance at the club on Saturday night. Both are great opportunities for Lans to meet Pittsburgh's top executives."

"Give us a chance to get settled first."

"I'm only trying to help you." Her mother excelled in making Andrea feel guilty when she resisted her plans.

Lans spent long hours acquainting himself with company procedures. To learn the most recent innovations in every phase of production and management, he studied the books their fathers wrote together, starting with a recent update of the one they had coauthored on the farm the summer she and Lans met. Andrea accused him of trying to absorb all the knowledge her father had accumulated over his lifetime in several short months.

Evelyn expected their presence at her dinners for a steady flow of European guests. Smothered by her mother's demands before they were even settled, Andrea felt her resolve to live a life separate from her parents slip away.

The children begged their father for a trip to the farm, but two months went by before Lans could leave business for even one weekend with his family. Spring bulbs burst out of the ground, brightened their lives for a while, then faded away. Finally when leaves began fanning out on the tips of trees, he announced he could take off a full weekend.

Expectations soared as Lans drove Andrea and the children through small country towns where flowering shrubs put a bright face on yards awakening from winter. Rolling hills of farmland spread before them; evenly spaced green blades peeped through rich, brown soil in straight rows like regiments of soldiers at attention.

"Look, Mom, I bet that's corn popping up." John's excitement grew with each turn in the road.

"Yes, they look just like Grandpa's cornfields this time of year."

"I can't wait. Do you think the farm still looks the same?"

"It's looked pretty much the same all my life, Kate, since we tore down the pigpens and diverted the creek to make the lake."

Minutes later Lans turned the car onto a small dirt road. The children devoured the scene in all directions as they crossed the bridge at the entrance of the Collins' farm. The great maple tree and tall, dark spruce still towered over the farmhouse. Those trees had caught Evelyn's eye when Andrea's parents searched for a place to board their horses. Evelyn had cried out, "Leonard, look at those trees. They're magnificent. This is the farm for us." Captivated, Evelyn sought instantly to buy the farm, ignoring its dilapidated condition, sagging porch, and hanging gutter pipes.

Kate turned to her mother. "Is it true that you swore you would never set foot in the house for fear it would fall down around you?"

"Yes, I was seven years old, and I had never seen a broken-down building that looked like it might crumble under my feet. It would have made a perfect haunted house at Halloween."

"What changed your mind?" John asked.

"Jake repaired everything—doors, windows, rotting walls, and floorboards. Two coats of white paint worked miracles, making the farmhouse look inviting rather than frightening."

"Jake still lives here, doesn't he?"

"Yes, he took my grandparents' place when he retired from Dad's company, and he's been our caretaker ever since." Andrea felt a moment of sorrow as she remembered her grandparents' last years of illness.

Lans slowed the car halfway to the house.

"Hey, isn't that where you two were married?" John pointed to an empty field.

"Yes, that's the spot where your mother promised to love and obey me forever."

"I wish I could have been there." Kate looked disappointed that she had missed the wedding, eliciting laughter from the rest of the family.

Lans stopped the car and the children jetted off to the barn. He took Andrea's hand and led her down the driveway to their wedding site. "Did we really ask all those people to drive up from Pittsburgh and stand in the middle of a hayfield?" he asked as he hugged her close to him.

"It doesn't look like much now but wait 'til the daisies bloom," she said. "And remember, it was your idea."

"I can't wait to have daisies to place in your hair. It will make me feel young again."

"There's still some romance left in my serious businessman." Andrea laughed. "Lans, this farm is still my favorite place in the world. I think I'll never come here without remembering what it was like when I was a child to jump out of the car and run into Grandma's arms. She always held me close and made me feel loved and secure."

"Hey, don't I make you feel loved and secure?"

"I could never feel anything else when I'm in your arms." She smiled at him and nuzzled her head against his shoulder. "There's something about the strength of your embrace that's irresistible."

"Dad, Mom." John and Kate galloped toward them. "There are three new horses in the stalls we've never seen before."

"Hey, slow down. What's this all about?" Lans asked.

"Gran and Pakin's horses are in their stalls, but there are three more." Kate, breathless, yanked her father's arm. "Come and see."

"New horses in the barn? Lans, what do you know about this?" Andrea turned to Lans.

"Let's take a look." He allowed the children to sweep him past the white farmhouse and up the hill toward the barn. It was a handsome two-story structure, weathered gray, but well-built and very sturdy. It looked much younger than the house. Lans slid back the wide barn door and the four of them walked over an earthen floor with a thin covering of straw. As they moved toward the row of horse stalls in the back, an array of musty smells brought a rush of memories to Andrea.

She reached out to pet Enterprise and Ladylike, her parent's horses. "Hi, Lady, it's good to see you." Next to them stood a black and white gelding and a tan mare with a beige mane. Lans put his arm around John and rubbed the gelding's nose. "How do you like this one, son? I think he suits you."

"He's a beauty. Can I ride him?"

"Yes. His name is Patches and he's yours."

"He is? He's really mine? For sure?"

"You wanted a horse of your own, didn't you?"

"You bet I did. I'll take good care of him, Dad."

"I'm sure you will, son."

Kate and Andrea stood open-mouthed looking from John to Lans and back to the horses. Lans moved next to Kate and reached up to pat the little mare. "This one is gentle and follows Patches wherever he goes. Her name is Ginger. If you like her, Kate, she's yours."

"Oh, she's beautiful. And she's mine?"

"All yours," her father said.

Kate climbed up the slats of the stall, put her arms around Ginger's head, and hugged her. "Hi, Ginger. You're just like Black Beauty's friend. I love you already."

Andrea moved to the next stall and found a chestnut mare with a white star on her forehead. As she reached out to touch the star, shivers ran through her body. She had done this before. Her other hand flew to her mouth as she caught her breath. "Dolly II," she said and started to cry. Lans moved to her side and put his arms around her. Andrea looked up at him trying to hold back the tears. "How did you find her?"

"There will never be another Dolly, but when I saw this horse, I knew I wanted to buy her for you."

"She's lovely. I can't believe it." Tears flooded her eyes and flowed down her cheeks. Lans wiped them away. Aware of his desire to please her, she rewarded him with a look of adoration.

"How did you find them, Dad?" John stopped stroking Patches long enough to ask.

"I shared with Jake that we all wanted to have our own horse and asked his advice on where to buy them. He knew of a farmer who was about to sell his farm and all his animals and suggested I start with him.

"'But you need to do it right away. They'll be gone as soon as he puts them on the market. They're good horses,' Jake assured me. So I drove up to meet the farmer and the horses and when I saw this one, I knew she was meant for your mother and the other two seemed just right for you and Kate. What do you think, kids? Was it a good deal? I hope you're not disappointed you didn't get to select them yourselves."

"Disappointed? How could we be disappointed? They're wonderful," John said.

Kate threw her arms around her father. "They're perfect. Can we ride them now?"

John took a brush from a hook on the barn wall and started smoothing Patches' mane. He turned to his father. "But where's your horse, Dad?"

"I'll exercise your grandparents' horses 'til we can look for one for me. Would you like to help me pick one out, son?"

"You bet. Wow, what a day!"

"Come, girls." Lans put an arm around Kate and Andrea and guided them toward the barn door. "Let's get settled and pack a lunch. We'll have a ride and a picnic this afternoon."

"I couldn't wait to come, but I never dreamed it would be this good." Kate threw up her hands and dashed out of the barn. "I'll be ready before you, John," she called as she raced toward the house.

⌘⌘⌘

The next morning the Mulders reined in their horses and tied them to an old-fashioned hitching post before a country inn. Eager to repeat the early morning breakfast rides she had enjoyed with her parents, Andrea wasted no time locating an inn that served a sumptuous breakfast. The smell of bacon and home fries invited them in.

"This is it, kids. As close as I could come to the inn I rode to with Gran and Pakin on Sunday mornings when I was a child. They promised me a big country breakfast. Shall we check it out?"

"It was a great ride." John's eyes danced with excitement. "Did you see how fast Patches and I went? When he broke into a gallop, I felt like a link in the Pony Express."

"Ginger kept up with Patches just like Dad said she would." Lans took Kate's hand and led her into the dining room. Waiters passed them carrying plates of apple pancakes smothered in butter and syrup, the inn's specialty.

"Look at those waffles piled high with strawberries and whipped cream." John pointed as a waiter whizzed by him.

Kate waved at the buffet. "Scrambled eggs, poached eggs, fried eggs. And look at all those muffins."

"Smell that coffee. A steaming cup is just what I need." Lans rubbed his hands.

"How 'bout a cup of hot chocolate?" John's eyes darted about the room.

"I'm sure they have that, too." Andrea followed the waitress to their table.

"I'll have one of everything. I'm starving." John slid across the bench.

"Just remember, if it's good, we'll be back. You don't have to try everything the first time." Andrea ruffled his hair and looked him in the eye. "I wish you were this eager for breakfast on school mornings."

"Aw, this is different."

"Indeed it is," Lans spoke up. "I bet I can eat as many pancakes as you can. If the meal tastes as good as it looks, we should make this a habit, Andrea."

As they returned to their horses, Lans pulled two lumps of sugar from his pocket. "A treat for your horses, kids." He handed each one a lump.

"I should have grabbed an apple from the buffet for Dolly. How my first Dolly loved them." Andrea's eyes misted over as she remembered the horse of her youth. "It's so good to have a Dolly again, Lans. You couldn't have given me a finer gift."

The inn became a regular haunt of the Mulders. Those weekends at the farm were highlights in the life of her family. Lans relaxed and gave his full attention to his wife and children. Every successful weekend left Andrea elated. Perhaps the move was the blessing they all hoped it would be.

A month later, when Andrea and Lans announced it was time to look for a home of their own, Evelyn rose to the challenge. One morning in early June, she drove up the driveway, opened the door, and walked in without ringing the bell. "Andrea," she called, "the most wonderful house is coming on the market. I heard about it at a party last night. I called the listing realtor, and she can show it to us this morning before the owners return home from a trip. How soon can you be ready?"

"Mom, it's my job to find us a home, and I plan to look soon."

"You'll love this house, Andrea. It's perfect for entertaining Lans' clients, and I can already see Kate sweeping down the staircase in her wedding gown."

"What about just living in it as a family?"

"Perfect for that, too. How soon can you be ready?"

Andrea relented. "In a couple of minutes."

As they drove up the long driveway, Andrea stared at the expanse of green lawn that surrounded the large Tudor house. "Mom, you didn't tell me there are acres of grass to cut."

The realtor spoke up. "It's on five acres of land. That far section over the hill is an orchard that's not cultivated."

"An orchard. The kids will love that, but this is too much house for us at this point in our lives."

"Nonsense, Andrea. Your father is grooming Lans to be head of the company, and you'll need a place to entertain European guests." She looked at the overgrown gardens. "Those gardens look like they could use some grooming, too. You can restore one garden at a time while Lans is learning his way."

The realtor followed the driveway that led past the front of the house and circled a towering blue spruce before they reached the main entrance in the back. A massive door of heavy dark wood featured a large metal knocker suitable for a medieval castle. It convinced Andrea the house was too large for them. When she entered a spacious foyer where French doors opened onto a large slate patio, she realized just how formal the house was.

The realtor invited them to step outside. "What a perfect place for a wedding reception," Evelyn exclaimed as she examined a large well, made of Spanish tiles.

"You're way ahead of me, Mother. I'm looking for a house for my little girl to grow up in."

The realtor pointed around the corner. "On the side yard, there's a pond and a picnic table under an apple tree." Andrea imagined Lans standing there before his favorite grill, cooking a barbecue for the children, the smell of roasting pork ribs enticing them all. The fragrance of apple blossoms lifted her spirits. She could see Lans and the children seated around the picnic table with her, the four of them laughing and relaxing together.

"This could be charming, Andrea. Let me help you design the gardens. We could make a real showplace out of this area."

"I don't want a showplace, Mom. I want a home for my children."

"The orchard is through the gate in the brick wall," the realtor said. "Through that gate on your right, there's a separate courtyard and a four-car garage with an apartment above it. But come back in and see the house, Mrs. Mulder. It has great potential."

Andrea stepped down into a large sunken living room. An oversized fireplace surrounded by floor to ceiling mahogany bookshelves dominated the room. Andrea pictured her favorite candlesticks on the ends of the long mantel and noted the massive andirons made in the form of a ship's anchor.

"How I've missed our fireplace. This one is positively majestic. I'd put a long comfortable couch on one side with a huge coffee table before it and two high-backed winged chairs on the other side. This is where we would live," Andrea said, beginning to visualize her family occupying the space.

"Wait until you see the dining room, Mrs. Mulder. It's the most impressive room in the house." The realtor moved back through the foyer and lit the chandelier in the dining room.

"Look at that Toile wallpaper." Andrea turned in a circle, awed by the scene before her. All around the room red-coated horsemen and horsewomen rode through the English countryside in pursuit of a pack of hounds.

"It's magnificent. Looks just like an English manor. Your European guests will feel right at home, Andrea."

"It's gorgeous, Mom, but not at all what I had in mind. I want an informal atmosphere where my children and husband can relax and share their daily adventures."

The realtor ushered them into a bright breakfast room with a bay window looking out on the side gardens. "Now this is more like it." Andrea smiled. "I can imagine cozy family meals in here. We could keep the dining room for special occasions." After passing through a large butler's pantry into the kitchen, her eyes lit up when she saw a cozy wooden booth opposite the cooking area. "Kate and John could have snacks here after school and tell me about their day while I work on supper."

14

The realtor led her back to the foyer and up the grand staircase. Andrea paused on the landing to imagine Kate throwing a bridal bouquet to eager bridesmaids below. Up they went to tour through five spacious bedrooms.

"Mom, look at this. The master bedroom has its own fireplace." She pictured herself dressed in a flattering negligee curled up on a couch reading until Lans came home from a late meeting. They could snuggle before a warm fire while they shared the news of the day.

"Look at the beautiful wood paneling in the room next to it. What a perfect office for Lans. He could meet with any CEO in here."

"Lans has never thought of living in such a grand house, Mother."

"Bring him over and see how he reacts. Your father will approve. He might even be a bit jealous."

The realtor escorted them into a large bright room with a mirrored wall. "Your daughter will love this room, Mrs. Mulder, and your son could have his choice of the two remaining bedrooms."

"The other one could be a guest room for Katharine when she visits. Mom's right. It more than meets our needs. We would never feel crowded or on top of each other as we are now. It's lovely, but a lot of house to take care of."

"You mustn't think of doing it yourself, Andrea. You'll have to have help."

"Let me walk through it once more on my own," Andrea said.

The realtor took Evelyn's arm and escorted her toward the door. "Let me show you the garage apartment, Mrs. Collins."

Andrea meandered through the first floor. Could she be comfortable in such grand surroundings? She descended the two steps into the living room. Her eyes swept over the furniture and hovered by the fireplace. She pictured the four of them playing their favorite games around a giant coffee table in front of a roaring fire.

She walked slowly through the house, adjusting her prior conceptions, becoming more comfortable with the large spaces. She knew the old-world charm of the house would appeal to Lans. If she agreed to it, somehow he would make it work. Kate would love the mirrored bedroom and John could play basketball in the garage courtyard, big enough to hold a whole team.

As she descended the elegant stairway, she pictured a vase full of flowers from the gardens adorning the foyer table. There was space for all their furniture, more than sufficient shelves for the contents of all the boxes piled in their rented garage. Perhaps her mother was right this time. In spite of all her arguments to the contrary, she felt she had come home.

3

Three years later Andrea rushed to answer a phone call that would change her life even more. Picking up the receiver, she heard long, choking sobs. "Mother, what's happening?"

"Leonard's had a heart attack."

"Dad!" Andrea clenched her stomach and closed her eyes. "How bad is it?"

"It-it could be fatal."

Andrea doubled over as though she had been stabbed. She steadied herself against the foyer table where the phone sat.

"The doctor hasn't given me much hope. He said Leonard wore out his body traveling the world when he was sick. He should have been home in bed." Between sobs Evelyn blurted out, "Lans will be president of the company now."

Andrea struggled to absorb the meaning of her mother's words.

"Andrea, come to the hospital. I need you."

"Yes, yes, of course, I'll come right away."

Andrea hung up the phone, sat down on the foyer steps, and cried out, "Lord, please be with him. Don't take him now." She buried her head in her hands and let the tears come.

Proud of her father and his many accomplishments, Andrea had always longed to have him home more often. The months he and Evelyn traveled for business when she was a child had left such a void in her life, she never forgot the loneliness of her growing-up years. Would she now lose him altogether?

Perhaps he would recover and lead a quiet life with his family. Was there still time for intimate conversations with him? She grabbed her purse and keys. Taking long strides out the great wooden door, she hurried to her car.

⌘ ⌘ ⌘

Outside her father's hospital room, the nurse intercepted Andrea. "Your mother is nearing hysteria. I've given her a sedative, and a nurse is sitting with her in the waiting area. I suggest you drive her home. Will anyone be there to take care of her?"

"Yes, I'll call one of her neighbors, but may I see Dad first?"

"Of course, but he hasn't regained consciousness."

Andrea peeked into the room. The slats of the Venetian blinds cast shadows across her father's tired face. The sun from the single window failed to penetrate his closed eyelids. How she would like to see those piercing blue eyes open and look at her with the pride of a doting father.

She bent over him and kissed his cheek. He did not stir. "I'll be back as soon as I take Mother home." She ran her hand down the arm that lay motionless by his side. He did not respond. "Oh, Dad," she said and fled from the room.

⌘⌘⌘

When Andrea returned to the hospital, she pulled a chair up to her father's bedside, took his hand in hers, and searched for a sign of vitality in his listless body. He had always been a good-looking man with slick black hair, manly features, and startlingly bright blue eyes. He was ever productive, creating new management techniques, writing books, managing his consulting company. He had never sat around doing nothing. It was strange seeing him so unresponsive, so still. She felt the urgency she had known as a child. *Dad, here I am, your only daughter. Stop working long enough to see me. Talk to me. I need more than gifts from abroad; I need you.* The old tapes played in her mind.

She knew her father had loved his work all his life. His success had brought worldwide recognition and material gain. But what of family relationships? All those plaques that covered his office walls, all those shelves of medals and awards in every size and shape. Had they been worth it? If he slipped away now, she knew she would go on missing him, just as she had all her life. Now she would be robbed even of the years of retirement when he might have had more time for her family.

And what would his death mean for Lans? Would he travel more? Would it bring them closer together or move them further apart? Lost in her thoughts and questionings, Andrea failed to hear the knock on the door. She looked up as Lans entered the room.

"Darling, I came as soon as the office could find me."

"Lans," she cried as she rushed into his arms, "isn't it awful? I thought we would have years with him and he would slowly turn the business over to you and spend time with us like I always wanted."

"He may recover."

"The doctors don't give him much hope. The heart attack was so severe they don't expect him to regain consciousness."

Lans pulled up a chair beside her and held her as she had longed to have her father hold her when she was a child.

When the sun sank in the sky and the room began to dim, the nurse encouraged them to go home and come back tomorrow. "We'll call you the minute he rallies," she said.

Andrea patted her father's hand and spoke softly to him. "Does he hear us?" she asked the nurse. "I've read stories of people who recover and remember conversations spoken while they were unconscious."

"Sometimes they do," she said as she escorted them out of the room and turned off the light.

⌘ ⌘ ⌘

A week later Evelyn, Andrea, and Lans still waited for Leonard to open his eyes and speak to them.

When the nurse came to take his vital signs, she noted his difficulty breathing and pulled down his blanket. The sight of his swollen legs filling up with liquid that his tired heart could no longer pump brought fresh tears to Andrea's eyes.

"What time is it, nurse?" Evelyn asked, her hazel eyes darting about the room. Usually impeccably dressed, she appeared unkempt, her well-groomed hair falling down. Andrea suspected she had not had a calm moment since Leonard's attack.

"Almost suppertime. Are you hungry, dear?" The nurse patted her arm. "Perhaps you'd like to go out for a meal."

Evelyn started to cry. "He's taken care of me since I was nineteen. What will become of me now? I've never paid the bills. I know nothing about the business. How will I cope?"

"Don't think about it now. We'll be here to take care of you and help you through the adjustments."

"I've had three years to learn the ropes," Lans said. "It won't be the same, but I'll carry on the business the way he taught me."

Evelyn's cry turned into a wail.

"You'll be well off, Mother. You can stay in your house, or we'll find you a nice apartment if that would make you feel more secure."

"Leave my lovely home? Ohhhhhhh!" she cried.

"Let's concentrate on Dad for now. We'll make plans later."

"After he leaves me," she said. "Why didn't he ever take time to teach me to pay the bills? He hasn't prepared me for this."

"We'll figure it out together, Mother."

"What time is it?"

"It's still close to suppertime. I couldn't eat a thing." Andrea turned imploring eyes on Lans.

Lans jumped up. "Come, Evelyn, I'll treat you to dinner and take you home." He turned to Andrea. "I'll go back to the office. Stay with your father as long as you like. John's in charge at home."

"Thanks, darling." She gave him a weak smile.

The nurse came back an hour later to check Leonard's condition. "His breathing is much more labored. I believe he's starting the death process, Mrs. Mulder. It's only a matter of time now. I'm so sorry."

Andrea bit her lip to hold back her grief. "Thank you for letting me know."

When the nurse left the room, Andrea pulled her chair closer to the bed. Clasping his hand in hers, she searched her father's pale face. "Dad, I was always proud that you were my father. Everyone admired and respected you. I did, too, but I always wanted more of your time.

"I remember how disappointed I was when you and Mom were away on my ninth birthday. I felt so sorry for myself. But when I found Dolly in the barn, I knew you cared and had done everything you could to make my birthday the best of my life.

"You may not have been there in person, but you gave me the feeling you would be when I needed you. Like the time I was so sick and the doctors couldn't decide what was wrong. You flew in from the West Coast as soon as you heard and got every specialist in the hospital on my case. Remember that, Dad?

"You tried never to make promises you couldn't keep, so I grew up trusting you. I guess that's why I could trust my heavenly Father when I was young, because you modeled him for me. I always thought you expected more from me than you should have, but I tried to live up to your expectations. I guess God expects a lot of us, too. I hope I can handle Mom as you would have. It will be so hard for her." She rubbed the back of his hand, hoping to smooth her own jumbled thoughts.

"But what I want you to know is that you gave me a great life. I was so fortunate to have parents I could be proud of. Travel all over Europe before I married. Grow up in a lovely home. I just wish you had been in it more."

She stroked his arm. "I feel so destitute that you won't see the kids grow up and marry. They were only beginning to know you." A smile broke out on her face. "Didn't we have fun on Sundays when we came to your house for lunch after church? How the kids loved Mom's special drumsticks and deviled eggs. They had such fun concocting their own ice-cream sundaes. But that's still not how I want to leave you."

Her voice caught. "I want you to know how much I appreciate all you did for me." She put her other hand on his and squeezed so hard, she thought he might wake up.

"I love you so much. Can you hear me? Can you take that with you when you go to be with the Lord? I always complained so much about you're not being there, but I want you to know how important you were to me. You were a good father."

She studied his face, longing for a sign of communication, some acknowledgement that he heard her. She thought she saw his eyelids flicker and the corners of his mouth turn upward. "Oh, Dad, are you there? Are you waking up?" Had she imagined it? Grateful that she had had time alone with him to say farewell, she believed he had received her message. In spite of his labored breathing, she laid her head on his chest, aware it might be the last time.

"Dad, please don't leave us. It's way too soon."

But she knew it was time to let him go. She would have to be strong now for herself and for her mother.

⌘ ⌘ ⌘

In the weeks that followed her father's funeral, Andrea discovered how much Leonard had covered up Evelyn's lapses of memory. The grief of losing her father was compounded by learning that her mother could no longer care for herself.

Leonard had made every important decision of their lives. Now Evelyn enjoyed a new freedom. She bought an expensive car she didn't need. She sold their home and moved. Not able to make friends the way she had in the past, she rattled around her big apartment and called Andrea every day.

"Andrea, I can't find my checkbook, and I need to write a check for the plants I ordered. The truck driver is about to deliver them. Can you come over?"

Andrea dashed to her car and drove across town. The truck driver waited outside her mother's apartment. Assuring him she would return with a check, she rushed inside.

"Mom, I put your checkbook in your desk. Here it is. Didn't you look here?"

"I thought it would be on the kitchen counter, dear, but it wasn't."

"What's this check for $10,000?"

"It was for a minister I watched on television. He seemed so sincere and is helping so many people."

"You're donating large amounts to little known charities all the time now. Please discuss them with me before you write such big checks. You'll run out of money in your account."

Evelyn clasped her hands on her hips. "It's my money, and I can do with it what I want."

Andrea regarded her mother with compassion. As self-centered as she could be, she had always been generous. That's why she had so many friends. Letters were still pouring in from all over the world sympathizing with her for losing Leonard.

"Here, sign this." Andrea pushed the check toward her. "I'll run it down to the driver."

"Be sure to come back. I'm lonely. Would you stay and have lunch with me?"

After lunch, Evelyn smiled sweetly. "I need to go shopping. Can you drive me? I couldn't find my car in the parking lot last time I went by myself."

⌘⌘⌘

Over the next couple of months, Andrea responded to most of her mother's summons. Soon the calls for help came several times a day.

One night after the children left the dining room table, Lans turned to Andrea. "You don't have time for me and the kids anymore."

"Lans, don't say that. Mother gets so frustrated when she can't find what she wants. I'm afraid she'll do something to hurt herself. Have a car accident. Start a fire in the apartment."

"You know I think we should hire a companion for her."

"I've suggested it, but she won't even consider one."

"You can't spend your days driving across town. Why don't we look for a first-rate nursing home for your mother? There she'd have the company of other ladies in her condition."

"You know she'd hate that. She's begged me for years never to put her in a nursing home. She's never forgiven herself for committing Grandpa to a mental hospital. I can't do that to her, Lans."

"I know how tough this is on you, darling. I keep searching for a solution, but I can't come up with one."

Andrea surprised him with a solution of her own. "Could you consider having her come to live with us for a while? We have plenty of room, and Kate is so good about entertaining her."

"I can't imagine having her here all the time."

"I know, dear. She is difficult, but I don't know what else to do." She rose from the table, put her arms on his shoulders, and bent down to hug the back of his neck. We're all so happy here, and there is Mother across town all by herself."

"And you rushing over two and three times a day to keep her out of trouble. I guess that's asking too much of you."

"Then you'll agree to it?"

He pushed back his chair and motioned for her to sit on his lap. "I guess I owe it to your father to take care of his wife after setting me up as the head of such a fine company." He squeezed her so hard, Andrea felt the urgency in his voice. "Don't let her come between us, Andrea, I couldn't bear that."

"Lans, I would never let that happen. Thank you, darling. I promise I'll make it work."

4

Weeks after her mother moved in, Andrea still searched for a routine to make her feel at home. At first Evelyn had refused to give up her independence; but by the time her apartment sold, she had warmed to the idea. She brought with her much of her furniture, crowding Andrea's well-decorated rooms with ornate pieces that seemed out of place. But Andrea, determined to make it work, marked each piece with care in case her mother ever returned to a home of her own.

Evelyn appeared on the landing. "Andrea, where are you? I can't find my glasses."

Andrea looked up from the flowers she was arranging in the foyer and bounded up the steps. "I put them on your dresser when you went down for a nap. Did you look there?"

"I've looked everywhere, and I can't find them."

Andrea put her arm around her mother and led her up the stairs to her bedroom on the back of the second floor. She and Kate now shared a bathroom, which opened onto both rooms.

"Here they are on your dresser, just where we left them before your nap."

"Well, it's hard to find things in this little room with all my things jammed into it."

"It's a big house, Mom, and there's plenty of room for all of us. Remember how you said you always loved this house?"

"Did I?" Evelyn acted surprised.

"Yes, you said you'd been coming here to parties for years, and it was one of your favorite places. Now that you're living here with your family, I hope we're your favorites, too." Andrea led her mother back down the long stairway. On the landing she pointed to the flowers she was arranging for the foyer table. "Do you like my arrangement, Mom?"

"Yes, dear, it's very nice."

"I thought you might like to take that on as a regular job. You always made such gorgeous arrangements with the flowers from your garden."

"I don't do that anymore. I'm all thumbs when it comes to putting them together in a vase."

"Well, I know you love to weed. I thought we might start on the garden by the fish pond tomorrow and work side by side. I could use some help. After having all that soil hauled up to the porch of your apartment, don't tell me you don't enjoy putting your hands in the good earth anymore."

"I do miss my garden. It was what I liked best about my apartment."

"There are more gardens here than you could weed in a lifetime. If you want to plant a vegetable garden, we'll find a spot that you can call your own." Andrea looked toward her mother, hoping she had sparked her former interest in gardening. "Oh, Mom, I just noticed your blouse is inside out again. Here, let me help you." Andrea started to remove her mother's blouse.

"I'm perfectly capable of dressing myself." Evelyn broke away and dashed across the foyer as the front door opened.

"Hello, darling, I'm home early. I've brought an old friend with me," Lans called out before he discovered Evelyn standing frozen at the bottom of the steps with her blouse hanging open.

Andrea rushed to her mother and pushed her up the stairs. "Run up and finish dressing; then come down and greet our guest." She hurried to the front door, where Lans busied himself hanging a coat in the closet. "Hello, darling," she said as she kissed his cheek and turned to shake the hand of their guest. "Eric, how nice to see you. It's been years."

"Yes, it has been, Andrea. How delightful to visit you in your lovely home. Lans said Evelyn helped you choose it." He spoke perfect English with an unmistakable Swedish accent.

"Yes, she found it for us. If you'll excuse me, I'll bring her down. She'll be so happy to see you." Andrea turned and fled up the steps to make sure she had not insulted her mother by pushing her out of the way.

She found Evelyn lying on her bed sulking. "Mother, you must come down and visit with Eric Nordstrom. Do you remember him?"

"Of course, I remember him. He was the first Swede I danced with at the ball in Stockholm."

"That's right. You made friends with him and introduced him to Dad. He was enthralled with modern scientific methods and became Dad's first and most successful client in Europe."

"Yes, he was charming."

"He's downstairs and is eager to see you. Here, get out of those old slacks and put on this dinner dress. He'll remember you dressed in the height of fashion."

Evelyn chatted about her part in building up Leonard's foreign clients, offering Andrea little resistance as she dressed her for the occasion. "There now, you look lovely. How about a spray of perfume?" She looked through the fragrances on her mother's dressing table and chose Channel No. 5. "There now, that smells delightful. Are you ready to go down now and greet Eric?"

"Yes, Andrea, if you go with me."

"Of course." The thought that her outgoing mother needed her to accompany her downstairs to greet an old friend startled Andrea. She took her hand. "Come. It will be like old times. Pretend this is your house, and you're still the 'hostess with the mostess.'"

Evelyn followed as Andrea led her down the stairs and into the living room where Lans labored to build a fire. Eric sat in a winged-back chair talking to him. He was an attractive man with a round, pleasant face. His few remaining blond strands gave his graying hair a yellow cast. When he smiled, he exuded exceptional vitality for his age.

He jumped up as they entered the room and moved to embrace Evelyn. "Evelyn, what a pleasure to see you. You are as lovely as ever. I'm so sorry about Leonard's death. He was still young with many contributions yet to make. The whole management world misses him."

"Thank you, Eric."

He took her arm and led her to the window. "What a magnificent house you've chosen for Andrea and Lans, and how fortunate you are to live here with them. It must be lonely without Leonard."

"Yes," she said.

"Remember how we danced the night we met, Evelyn? I was fascinated with you and would never have worked with Leonard if you hadn't set the stage."

Andrea, watching her mother, ready to come to her aid the minute she faltered, saw Evelyn smile as recognition of the occasion registered. "Do you remember the next evening, when Leonard played the piano and I sang? When we finished, you rose, clapping your hands and said with utter astonishment, 'He can't play and she can't sing, but they entertain us all.' Everyone laughed and gathered around the piano. Leonard played song after song in his simplistic way. You loved it, and when you sang along, all formality vanished."

"Yes, that was the beginning of a wonderful friendship and a marvelous adventure for our company. After the war, everything needed to be changed for peace-time production. Leonard revamped our assembly line and doubled our profitability."

"Come outside and let me show you the gardens, Eric. Spring is popping up all over." The old Evelyn had clicked in. Andrea's eyes clouded as she watched her mother play the charming hostess again. She turned to Lans, who

25

stood by the fire with an expression of astonishment.

"She's still there, darling. When all the confusion clears, she can still reach back and remember how it was. I'm so grateful for tonight. But what will I feed him? I had planned leftovers."

"Forgive me; I should have called. Can you drum up an elegant hors d'oeuvre or two? I've made reservations for the four of us at the club for seven. The kids can eat the leftovers."

"I'll tell Helen. She can make the hors d'oeuvres and feed the children before she leaves for the night. Do I have time to change?"

"Your mother seems to have everything under control. Go for it." He planted a kiss on her forehead.

Andrea ducked into the kitchen before she headed for her bedroom, her heart lighter than it had been since her mother had moved in with them. With Lans happy and Evelyn helping them entertain a client, perhaps it would work after all.

⌘⌘⌘

Throughout the meal Evelyn put forth her old charm and remained part of the conversation until dinner drew to a close. When Andrea saw her mother's eyes glaze over, she suggested they go home for a cup of coffee in front of the fire. When the men started to talk business, she took her mother upstairs to bed, leaving the men content with the evening and engrossed in deep discussion.

The next morning Andrea found her mother still fast asleep. Over a leisurely breakfast she and Lans rejoiced that Evelyn had contributed so much to Eric's visit. Before he left for work, Lans hugged her warmly, filling her with hope that he and her mother could exist under one roof.

At 11:30, she heard Evelyn's call and hurried to her room. "Good morning, Mom. It's a lovely day." She opened the drapes to let in the sun. "Do you feel like gardening today?"

"I feel like staying in bed."

"Would you like me to bring your breakfast up to you?"

"Breakfast in bed. Lovely." Evelyn beamed.

"You earned it last night, but don't expect it every morning."

"What did I do last night?" Evelyn asked looking blank.

"You were such a wonderful hostess to Eric Nordstrom. Wasn't it lovely to see him?"

"I haven't seen Eric for years, but I remember our trips to Sweden as though they were yesterday."

"But Mom, he was here last night. You entertained him like you used to."

"I did? Oh, I'm so tired. What did we do yesterday?"

Andrea stared at her mother. Disbelief and disappointment erased her smile. "You really don't remember? Try harder. You can pull it up. Where did we have dinner?"

"I guess here where we always do," she said, snuggling into her covers. "I want my breakfast."

Andrea hurried away, unwilling to believe that her mother couldn't remember the evening that had given her so much hope.

5

When summer came, Andrea drove her mother to the farm for a week. How she missed being there with Lans and the children. Since her mother had come to live with them, Lans claimed the demands of running the company prevented him from leaving town.

What happy, satisfying years they had before her father died. Lans escaped from increasing responsibilities at the company for days alone with Andrea and the children. They spent weekends and holidays riding together through the countryside. Early morning breakfast rides and Sunday evening services in her grandparents' country church became family traditions. Remembering how much he had missed his father during his own childhood, Lans put his family first on those weekends. As the children jumped in the hay and swam in the lake, Andrea and Lans relived the days of their courtship.

Taking a break from arguing over a dozen unimportant details, Andrea left her mother in the farmhouse and stole a short walk through the barn, over the bubbling creek, and into the north pasture. As she sat on a rock watching the cows munch grass on the plateau the creek had carved and separated from the rest of the land, she remembered how much her grandmother had loved this pastoral scene. The memory was so vivid, Andrea could almost feel her presence.

Even these short minutes of watching the cows swish their tails and pull up long grasses as they ambled along the pasture helped calm and clear her troubled mind. She longed to stay and lose herself in the beauty of the day and the scene, but fearful of leaving her mother too long, she relinquished her rock and headed back toward the house. Reaching down to pick a strand of grass, she sucked the juices of its tender end as she had often done with her grandma. The farm was a healing place for her. *Perhaps Mother will benefit from being here, too.*

Andrea returned from the pastureland through the barn. The peace she had achieved vanished as she rolled back its wide door and saw flames of fire dancing out the kitchen window. Grey smoke spiraled toward the summer sky. "Mother, Mother!" she called as she sprang toward the farmhouse.

"Help, Andrea, I need you." A troubled voice and a fit of coughing reached her as she climbed the porch steps two at a time. Once inside she saw flames rising from a sputtering skillet on the stove, one side of a curtain on the nearby window already consumed, the other just catching fire.

Her mother flailed a wet dish towel toward the flames.

"Mother, move away from the fire," she called too late. The ugly smell of singed hair reached Andrea's nostrils as Evelyn's hand flew to her head. Andrea grabbed the wet dish cloth and slammed it against her mother's hair. "Hold this tight to your head and leave the room."

Andrea pushed her toward the hall and fumbled for the oven mitts. Jamming her hands into them, she grabbed the flaming pot and flung it through the open window. She opened the kitchen cupboard and tore the fire extinguisher from its spot on the wall. Aiming it at the disappearing curtain, she pushed the button with all her strength. Sprays of foam smothered the remaining flames before the blackened wood began to burn. Her hands shook as she lowered the fire extinguisher to the floor. Horrified at the image of the wooden farmhouse aflame, she calculated how fast it would have caught fire had she not been there. Ten miles from the nearest fire station, the beloved building would have been charred remains when the fire engines arrived. And her mother. What would have happened to her mother? She shuddered.

She checked the room for lurking flames or exploding sparks and only saw a blackened window frame dripping foam. The danger over, she rushed to her mother who, still holding the wet cloth to her head, sobbed inconsolably.

"It's all right, Mom." Andrea put her arms around her mother and comforted her as she would a child. "Tell me what happened."

"You were gone too long. I was hungry, so I decided to toast a cheese sandwich. I put some butter in the skillet and turned on the stove. While I looked for the cheese and bread, it caught fire." She let out a sob. "You should have been home sooner, Andrea."

"I've never let you miss lunch. If you had waited five minutes more…"

"Don't scold me. It was a terrible experience. My hair—"

"It's okay. I'll take you upstairs and wash your face and fix your hair. You were lucky. It could have been worse." Andrea shuddered again thinking of the possibilities. "Then you can lie down while I fix your lunch." *A simple accident,* Andrea told herself. *It could have happened to anybody.*

But things like that were happening all the time now.

⌘⌘⌘

Andrea, tired and disheartened, rocked back and forth on the long porch swing that hung from the ceiling of the front porch of the farmhouse, remembering how she had rocked in her grandmother's arms as a child. How she needed that comfort now.

She had fed her mother, who seemed to have forgotten the fire, but Andrea couldn't forget it. Why did she have such an uneasy feeling? Why did her once safe and secure life seem so difficult, so uncharted?

"There you are." Her mother interrupted her thoughts. "I seem to have misplaced my book. Can you help me find it?"

"Mother, I found it for you ten minutes ago."

"I changed my blouse and put it down somewhere. Where was it last time, dear?"

"Right on your dresser where you left it. Your buttons are out of line again. Here, let me help you."

Why doesn't she try a little harder? She always dressed with perfect style. I can't believe she's so careless about her appearance.

"Don't criticize me. You forget things, too." Evelyn wrung her hands as she scanned the room. "Where's Lans today?"

"I've told you. He and the children are in Holland on holiday with his European relatives." Each time she said the words, they hurt more. She found it easier to express her annoyance than to admit the fear that threatened to unnerve her.

"Why didn't you go with them?" Evelyn asked as they climbed the stairs to her bedroom.

"I thought it best to stay home with you, Mom."

"I'm glad you did. It's nice having only the two of us here."

Andrea found the book on the dresser, helped her mother with her blouse, and hurried back to her place on the swing. Her grandmother had been dead for twenty-eight years, but Andrea still thought of her first when she needed comfort.

When she was growing up, it was her grandmother who eased the pain of her parents' long absences. Andrea could still see her waiting on the porch. She remembered the joy of running into her outstretched arms, the feel of her starched apron against her face. She could see the love in her grandmother's eyes as she studied Andrea's face. "Your freckles are disappearing, but your blue eyes dominate your face just like your father's. I've loved them since you were a baby."

Her grandmother would lead her into the kitchen, where long thin strips of homemade noodles hung over wooden racks on every counter and tabletop. "Grandma, you're making beef noodle soup for me."

The old churn sat on the kitchen floor filled with freshly churned butter waiting to be formed into blocks and stored in the refrigerator. Two crusted apple pies, still bubbling from the oven, cooled on the windowsill, wooing Andrea with the fragrance of baked apples laced with cinnamon and sugar. Often it mingled with the aroma of roast leg of lamb, Andrea's favorite holiday meal for as long as she could remember.

Her grandmother had always assured her that everything would be all right. But now everything was not all right. Her friends thought Andrea Mulder had everything a woman could want: a loving family, beautiful home, and a lovely farm as a retreat from the rush of city life. How many times had she declared herself the luckiest of women? But suddenly her life was swirling in turmoil. Was she making the right decisions? She rose from the swing and looked out upon the daisy field.

White and yellow flowers caught the summer sunlight and swayed in the soft breeze. All her life the daisies had brought her joy and comforted her when she hurt. Today they made her sad, reminding her of relationships that were no more, relationships that even now were slipping away.

Kate had called to tell her they had arrived safely in Holland and gave her a telephone number where she could reach them. But Lans had not spoken to her. He had been gone two weeks and still no word.

Lans refused to believe she could not leave her mother. She understood that he felt neglected, but why was he distancing himself from her? He had agreed to have Evelyn live in their house, but having his mother-in-law under his roof was changing him. As Andrea found herself catering to her mother's demands rather than meeting the needs of her husband, she saw the danger, but she felt helpless to do anything about it. All her life she had longed for her mother's attention. Now there was no escape from it.

Anxiety stirred inside her like a consuming cancer. She and Lans were still together, but emotionally they were as far apart as they were physically separated.

"Andrea, where are my glasses? I can't read without them," her mother hollered to her from inside the house. Before Andrea reacted, Evelyn called in a happier voice, "Never mind, I found them on top of my head."

Hopeful her book would satisfy her mother for a time, Andrea left the swing and climbed to the second floor of the farmhouse. Drawn toward the little room she had stayed in as a child, she opened the door and peeped inside. The coziness of the room drew her in. Kneeling by the front window, she looked out on the field of daisies and prayed aloud. "Lord, when I was little, I knew you were watching over me and my loved ones and that all I had to do was bring a problem to you and you would solve it. I can't handle this one by myself. Show me what I must do. What are my choices? Lord, thank you for the answers."

The same sense of peace that Andrea had experienced here long ago settled over her and drained away her tension. She approached the little bed where she had slept as a child and stretched out upon it. Another wave of God's presence swept over her and blotted out the anxieties that threatened to engulf her. She imagined herself laying the heavy weights she had been carrying since her father's death at the foot of the cross.

"Thank you, Lord, for assuring me that you are with me even in this crisis." She felt light and the bed felt soft, as if she had fallen back onto a featherbed and been enfolded in its downy comfort. She relaxed for the first time in weeks.

⌘⌘⌘

When Andrea awoke, she knew she must take her mother to a doctor, the best neurologist she could find. Perhaps there was something he could do to help her. At least she would feel she had tried everything possible. She went straight to the phone and called her family doctor in Pittsburgh.

"Dr. Snowden. Yes, I'm fine, but mother is having a hard time. Could you recommend a good neurologist? Perhaps there's something more he could do for her. Yes, we're at the farm, but we'll be home in two days. Could your secretary make us an appointment? I'll have her there whenever he can see us."

6

ndrea and her mother sat in the waiting room of one of the best neurologists in town. His offices were tastefully decorated. Andrea could have studied the beautiful paintings that decorated his walls, but her anxiety over her mother's condition made her too edgy to enjoy them. The doctor approached her with an outstretched arm. Andrea shook his hand and searched his eyes for a softness she did not find.

"Hello, Mrs. Mulder."

"Hello, Doctor. This is my mother, Evelyn Collins."

"Hello, Mrs. Collins. How are you today?"

"You know I'm not well." she said.

"What day is it today, Mrs. Collins?" The doctor's manner, as stiff as his white starched jacket, suggested he was devoid of compassion underneath his professional veneer. Perhaps he had seen so many disturbed patients like her mother, and he kept his distance to protect his sanity.

"Tuesday," Evelyn said with confidence. "No, no, I think it must be Wednesday. Oh, I'm not sure." She began wringing her hands.

Andrea agonized with her.

"Do you know what month it is?" the doctor continued.

Evelyn brightened, "Yes, I know that one. It's September, because the children have gone back to school."

"Mom, John and Kate are in Europe with Lans. You're right that school used to start in September, but it starts the end of August now."

The doctor plowed on. "Do you know today's date, Mrs. Collins?"

"If I don't know the month, I'm not likely to know the date," she said, lifting her head high.

"Do you know who the mayor of Pittsburgh is?"

Evelyn looked at Andrea. "I don't read the papers anymore."

"I see. Who is the President of the United States?"

"I'm hoping it will soon be Ronald Reagan. I plan to vote for him."

The doctor ignored her politics but noted a satisfactory answer. "Do you know your United States senator, Mrs. Collins?"

She looked at Andrea for a hint. Andrea avoided her gaze and said nothing.

"Your Congressman, Mrs. Collins?"

"This is humiliating, Doctor. I didn't come here to talk politics; I came to find out what is wrong with me." Evelyn shifted in her chair, crossed her legs, and uncrossed them again.

"Exactly, Mrs. Collins. What did you do yesterday? Anything special?"

"The usual things. Got dressed, had breakfast, pulled some weeds in the garden."

"Mom, you remember, we told the nurse who took your vital signs that your sister came for a visit yesterday." Andrea reached over and laid her hand on her mother's arm.

"My sister. Oh, yes. She's older than I am, Doctor. We don't see each other very often now, but we were very close as children."

"I see," he said. "What meal did you have with her?"

"Dinner, of course."

The doctor looked at Andrea, who had reported that her aunt could only stay for lunch. His eyes looked sad. Perhaps he did care.

"Mrs. Collins, would you mind getting up and walking along that line on the floor?"

"Not at all." Evelyn walked along the line swaying from side to side. "There, I did it."

"Yes, Mrs. Collins. How long have you had trouble being steady on your feet?"

"I won't submit to this any longer. You insult me no matter what I do. Come, Andrea, we're leaving."

Andrea swallowed hard and looked at the doctor as her mother headed out the door. "Can you help her, Doctor?" she asked, trying to keep her voice steady and holding back tears.

"Your mother appears to have a disease called Alzheimer's. I could give her more tests, but these are the usual symptoms. There is no known cure, and it can be a long, torturous road to peace. But there are new experimental drugs that may help for a time."

Andrea had suspected it was the same thing that had afflicted her grandfather and his parents. Now the disease had a name: *Alzheimer's*. Her sympathy for her mother rose as the knots in her stomach tightened. With Lans already at the breaking point, how would she manage as her mother's condition worsened?

The doctor reached for his prescription pad. "Try her on this drug for two months, Mrs. Mulder. Then bring her in for another check-up. If she has any unusual reactions, call me."

A week after the visit to the doctor, Lans and the children returned from their trip. John and Kate bubbled with enthusiasm, entertaining Andrea with stories of recently discovered relatives. They reminisced with Lans and shared jokes about special happenings and strange customs. Andrea felt like an outsider, hurt that Lans made no attempt to include her.

Their son, John, had shown great compassion for Evelyn at first; but he, too, had become impatient with her repetitive questions. John Leonard Mulder, named in honor of his two grandfathers, had Lans' power of concentration. He could not fathom a mind that let answers fall through it like a sieve.

"John, why are you home so seldom?" Evelyn often asked him.

"Because I go to college now, Gran. Just like Kate will this year."

"Yes, I remember. You'll be a freshman, right?"

"Wrong. I've been away for two years now. I'm a junior, and Kate will be a freshman."

"Did someone call my name?" Kate bounced into the room wearing a chic tennis dress that showed off her perfect figure. She threw her racquet down before collapsing on the couch. "I played with girls a full level above me. I kept up with them, but I'm exhausted. How's it going today, Gran?"

"Not very well, Kate. I have nothing to do."

Kate jumped up, all energy again. "Would you like me to dress up and give you a fashion show?" When she was a child, Kate had entertained her grandmother by parading in her high heels and beaded cocktail dresses, which looked like evening gowns on the tiny, vibrant Kate. They still enjoyed the game. Bedecking herself in diamonds and long pearls, Kate would toss Evelyn's silver mink over her shoulders and inch on elbow-length kid gloves for a final touch of elegance. Her green eyes would beam as she sashayed back and forth before her grandmother, turning smartly as if she were strutting back and forth on a fashion runway before an admiring audience.

Kate took Evelyn's hand and led her up the regal staircase to her bedroom, which was furnished with pieces of Evelyn's furniture and far too many of her favorite art objects. Kate rummaged through her closets and drawers making her selections as Evelyn chatted and asked questions that Kate ignored. Now Kate fit perfectly into the ball gowns Evelyn had worn to entertain European nobility. She held up a black velvet sheath and admired herself in the full-length mirror.

"I wore that one when I met the King of Sweden," Evelyn said.

"No, Gran, you wore it in London when you met the queen."

"Yes, of course, I remember now. I'm so glad you won't be leaving us like John does."

"Oh, but I will. I'll be starting college in two weeks."

"My, my, all this running around. I never know who will be in the house anymore."

"Mother is always here to take care of you, Gran." Kate selected a long white dress and green earrings and began the parade over again.

Evelyn clapped. "You look stunning in my clothes. I wonder if I'll ever wear them again. I don't dress up anymore."

"If you don't want them, I'll be happy to take them off your hands."

"No, they're mine. I must hold on to my things." She folded her arms and set her jaw.

"Yes, but remember me in your will. I love all your dresses and jewelry."

"Kate, don't be so greedy." Andrea peeked into the room. "Of course Mother wants to keep her lovely things. They've meant so much to her over the years."

"I was only kidding." Kate rolled her eyes and sighed.

"I'm glad you two are having fun." Andrea retreated as fast as she had appeared.

⌘ ⌘ ⌘

That night Lans planned a pleasant family evening. He realized he had been curt with Andrea of late and wanted to make up for it. She had told him how hurt she was that he had not called her from Holland and that she had felt left out when he reminisced about the trip with the children. He loved her so; he hated to think how much he had hurt her. But every time he came home now, Evelyn interrupted their most private moments. He didn't feel like he had a wife anymore. He could never count on her to travel with him. Whatever Evelyn needed had become her priority.

But tonight he would ignore Evelyn's questions and concentrate on pleasing Andrea and the children. Since they would soon be leaving for college, he had asked Andrea to prepare a farewell cookout. As he changed for dinner, he chose to wear an old favorite of Leonard's, the blue sweater shirt Evelyn had given him after Leonard died. He hoped it would please her to see him wear it. He bounded down the steps prepared to experience a happy evening with his family.

Outside on the patio, while grilling the chicken, Lans advised John about classes he should take before he graduated. John breathed in the smoke rising from the grill and interrupted him. "Hey, that's starting to smell really good. It's been a long time, Dad, since you grilled for us."

"Yes, we'll have to do it more often. The four of us used to enjoy it so much." He stabbed the chicken, testing it for doneness. When juices spurted out, he announced that the meat was almost cooked. "John, run into the house and tell Kate it's time to bring Gran down for dinner."

"Is that fashion show still going on? Kate never tires of acting like a glamour queen."

"She keeps Evelyn entertained, and that's a great help to your mother."

"I guess I'll never understand women," John said before he bounded into the house.

Lans surveyed the yard leading up to the house as he continued basting the chicken. He and Andrea had turned the ill-kept grounds into rolling lawns and well-groomed shrubbery beds. He watched Andrea, as beautiful as the day he married her, carry out bowls of salad and vegetables and set them on the picnic table near the fishpond. Everything seemed right with his world.

Andrea walked over to Lans and put her arm on his shoulder. "It's a perfect evening for a cookout. Thank you for coming home early tonight."

Lans laid the fork down and grabbed Andrea as she turned to leave. "Not so fast, young lady," he said taking her in his arms. "You look lovely tonight. It almost seems like old times." He watched the color rise in her cheeks, then kissed her and held her close.

"Nothing will ever change between you and me, Lans."

"I wish I could believe that." He searched her eyes. "Why then do I find myself doing everything alone instead of with my wife?"

"I'll always be here waiting for you when you return from your trips."

"But I want you with me. Now that the kids will both be in college, you could travel with me and help me entertain European dignitaries like your mother did for your father. But my needs don't seem to matter anymore."

"You know that isn't true. Please don't say that."

He saw the color on her cheeks fade and her eyes fill with tears. He didn't want to hurt her anymore, but he needed her now. Why couldn't she see that her place was with him? It wasn't the first time he had told her how much he needed her on his trips overseas. He was becoming as repetitive as Evelyn, incessantly begging Andrea to accompany him.

"Hey, look at the love birds," Kate exclaimed as she led Evelyn to the party.

"A picnic? How nice," Evelyn said more agreeably than usual.

Lans' optimism returned. It was like old times. He transferred the chicken halves to the platter as Kate and John settled Evelyn on the picnic bench between them. He sat down beside Andrea opposite them and reached for her hand. They all bowed their heads as he said grace.

When he finished, Lans looked at Kate and John. "You'll be leaving us much too soon, kids, but this is a perfect night and we should enjoy it. Your mother has prepared a feast in your honor. You still prefer white meat, Evelyn?" He forked a choice piece of chicken breast for her.

"You know I do." She squinted toward him, and her eyes narrowed. Pointing an accusing finger, she cried out, "How dare you wear Leonard's shirt in my presence!"

"But, Evelyn, you gave it to me. I thought you wanted me to wear it."

"You're not half the man he was. Don't ever wear a piece of his clothing again." She struggled to rise from the table.

"But, Mother, Lans thought you would be pleased if he wore it." Lans appreciated Andrea coming to his defense. "Why did you give it to him if you didn't want him to wear it?"

Evelyn freed her legs from the bench and glared at him, "Don't even try. You'll never be like him." She turned and stumbled toward the house as John and Kate stared wide-eyed after her.

"Lans, I'm sure Mother didn't mean it like it sounded. She misses Dad, and it's hard for her to be reminded of him."

"Lots of things are hard for all of us, Andrea." Lans started to rise but felt the pressure of Andrea's hand on his shoulder.

"Don't leave. I'm sorry Mother was rude to you. She's so unpredictable these days. I'll take her a tray later. We can still enjoy our picnic together."

He said nothing but added the incident to the store of unpleasant memories mounting inside him. His hopes for a happy family gathering shattered, he retreated inside himself, leaving Andrea to struggle alone to salvage the evening. John and Kate forced animated conversation while Lans remained polite but distant, as if he were already gone from the family circle.

7

During the hectic days before leaving for college, John and Kate gave Andrea much-needed hours of respite from caring for Evelyn. Andrea insisted they maintain a respectful attitude toward their grandmother, but their impatience with her repetitions increased daily. Tense and tired of trying herself, Andrea vacillated between criticizing them and lavishing them with gratitude.

Although she knew she would miss him, a sense of relief washed over her when John began preparing to return to college. She watched him load his car, her thoughts tender toward him. Every bit as handsome as Lans, John had cheeks as round and full as his father's had been as a young man. Her heart leaped as a shock of unruly hair fell out of place. Even that was like his father. Yes, she would miss him. When John pulled out of the driveway, she felt the pain of her nest emptying, but she knew his absence would eliminate much of the tension that swirled around their home.

A week later she drove Kate to the airport. The check-in lines were long and time for a leisurely parting disappeared. They rushed to the gate where people were already boarding. "I had so much I wanted to say to you," she said as she kissed her good-bye.

"I'll call you when I get there, Mom. Pray for me to get a good room-mate."

"Oh, I will, dear, and may you love every minute of your time at college." Andrea waved as Kate handed her ticket to the stewardess and went through the gate to board the plane that would carry her both to the world of higher learning and to vast new temptations. Andrea must pray for her every day.

Perhaps now she and Lans could spend time alone together, she consoled herself as she left the airport and returned home.

But many nights Lans worked late at the office. When he did come home, Evelyn dominated the conversation with her mindless questions, forcing him prematurely into his study, leaving Andrea longing for intimacy over a shared cup of coffee.

⌘⌘⌘

One rainy day in the fall, when Lans had been out of town for five days, Andrea and Evelyn spent a quiet morning at home. As Andrea arranged a tall vase of flowers in the foyer, she mused on how this enormous entryway had awed her the first time she had walked into the house. She revisited Evelyn's suggestion as she looked up the magnificent mahogany staircase leading to the second floor and envisioned Kate, elegant and radiant, descending the steps in a formal wedding gown. The vision seemed more relevant now that Kate had left for college.

To the right of the foyer in the large sunken living room, piles of split wood lay stacked to one side of the huge fireplace. Before Evelyn came to live with them, Andrea and Lans had spent lovely evenings curled up on the couch in each other's arms, watching the flames rise and fall, sharing stories of the past and present. Starved for intimate evenings with Lans, Andrea rejoiced that cold weather would soon call for warming fires.

Andrea added the final touches to her arrangement as Evelyn paced up and down the steps to the living room, crossed the foyer to the dining room, and rushed through the swinging doors to the kitchen. Even more anxious than usual, Evelyn asked, "What time is it?"

"Ten o'clock. We have no appointments today, so you don't need to worry about time."

Wringing her hands, Evelyn sighed and left the room. When she reappeared, she carried a large plastic clothesbasket, which she placed in the middle of the foyer floor. "Andrea," she whispered, "I think someone is trying to steal my things."

"Your things are perfectly safe here, Mom. You and I are alone."

Ignoring her, Evelyn scurried toward the kitchen and returned with an armful of rags, which she placed in the bottom of the basket. Puzzled, Andrea studied her mother. What could this mean? She disappeared once more and returned with a pile of sheets and towels which she placed on top of the rags. "Mother, what do you intend to do with those rags and sheets?" Evelyn said nothing but hurried back to the kitchen. When she burst through the kitchen door again, she added two cooking pans to her collection.

Andrea's bewildered eyes followed her mother up the grand staircase until she disappeared into her bedroom. With much clanging and banging, she returned carrying a pile of plastic hangers in one hand and long strands of worthless beads in the other. Mystified, Andrea stood motionless in the entrance hall as she followed her mother's comings and goings.

"Mother, what's gotten into you?" Seesawing between disbelief and denial, Andrea felt her emotions whirling out of control.

"I'm gathering my most important belongings to hide them, so no one can find them." Evelyn continued wringing her hands as she glanced into the living room. "I can feel them in that room all the time. They're watching me and waiting until they can rob me again." Her eyes flicked to every corner.

Under other circumstances, Andrea might have laughed, but at this moment she wanted to cry. Such frightening behavior made forgetfulness seem trivial.

Tender and compassionate now, Andrea took her mother in her arms. "Mother, you mustn't worry so. There's no one here to steal from you. There's not a soul in the house but you and me."

"They're sitting on the couches and chairs all around the living room. Can't you see them?"

"No, I promise you, we're all alone."

Evelyn broke loose, grabbed her basket in a huff, and fled the room. Tears blinded her eyes as Andrea watched her mother scuttle away. Fumbling for the phone, she dialed Evelyn's doctor.

"This is Mrs. Mulder. I must speak to the doctor at once, even if he's with another patient. My mother is hallucinating, and her actions are totally inappropriate." Tempted to confess her mother had gone mad, she could not bring herself to say that word aloud.

After several minutes the doctor came to the phone and asked how her mother was.

"Not at all well, thank you. In fact her behavior is bizarre. She thinks people are staring at her and stealing her possessions. Could it be the new drug you prescribed for her?"

"The medical profession is still struggling to understand this disease, Mrs. Mulder. Drugs affect different people differently."

As she listened to the doctor's description of a long list of possible side effects, she groaned. Her hand trembled as she tried to write them down. "If that's what the drug does, I'm stopping it right now. It's not helping; it's making matters worse." She knew her voice sounded shrill, even held a touch of hysteria, but she no longer cared how she sounded.

The doctor offered to change the prescription. She could pick up the new one at the drugstore in a few hours.

⌘ ⌘ ⌘

That night at the dinner table Evelyn told Lans about the people who sat all day in his living room staring at her and waiting for a chance to steal her belongings.

Lans glared at Andrea before turning to Evelyn. "You're quite safe here, Evelyn. No one is here but Andrea and me, and we have no intention of stealing your things."

"You don't believe me either." She pushed back her chair and fled from the room.

Andrea let her go. Lans rose and threw his napkin on the table. "Andrea, we simply can't go on like this. I come back to town after a hard week on the road, and this is what I get. A man needs a little peace in his own home."

"I know you do, darling. But what can I do about Mother? I can't desert her when she's like this. She can't cope on her own."

"Well, we can't cope with her, either. Whatever happened to the idea that a man's home is his castle?" He paced back and forth, his fists clenched at his sides, reciting for Andrea her mother's endless disruptions to their home life. He stopped and turned to face her. His brown eyes, dark and defeated, searched hers. She felt him begging her to stop him from what he was about to say. "I'm so tired I can't think straight. I'm moving into the Duquesne Club for a few days to think this through. If you can find a sitter, have dinner with me there tomorrow evening."

"Lans, don't leave me. I'd much rather take care of you than Mother, but I can't abandon her while she's like this. You wouldn't respect me if I did."

"What about a nursing home?"

"You know she made me promise never to put her in an institution."

"I remember the promises you made to me twenty-five years ago."

"You know I love you. Haven't I been a good wife to you all these years?"

"You don't have time for me anymore."

"It's terrible for me, too. And it's terrible for Mother. The fact that she had to put her dad away has haunted her all her life. She's feared the same thing would happen to her. Now it has, and it's breaking my heart. It's like living through Grandpa's decline all over again."

Lans resumed pacing while Andrea searched for words to tell him he was first in her life and always would be. He stopped, braced his hands on the table, and gazed into her eyes, pleading like a little boy desperate for something he had set his heart on. "Who is most important to you?"

"Don't do this to me, Lans." She could no longer hold back the tears.

She jumped up and threw herself at him. His arms embraced her, and he buried his face in her hair. "I can't take it any longer, Andrea. Come with me."

"Leave Mother alone here, in this condition? You can't be serious." She drew back and searched his face. The veins at his temples bulged. She had never seen him so distraught.

"I see where your loyalty lies. My suitcase is still in the car. I won't bother you further."

Andrea stared at him in disbelief. As the door slammed behind him, she ran to it. "Lans, Lans, don't leave me." Over her sobs she heard the roar of the motor and the screech of tires as he careened out the driveway and sped down the street. She fell against the massive door that separated her from her husband. "Lord, Lord, don't let this happen," she cried as she poured out all the agony of the past weeks and months.

Nearly spent, she stumbled back up the entry stairs, through the foyer, down the two steps into the living room, and collapsed on the couch. This was what she had been dreading, the disintegration of her marriage. How could this be when they loved each other so much?

Within minutes Evelyn appeared in the doorway. "Is it time for dessert, dear?"

⌘ ⌘ ⌘

"Where's Lans?" Evelyn asked at the breakfast table.

"So you remember he came home last night?"

"Didn't he, dear?"

"He's away again."

"Why don't we go to the farm for a few weeks?"

Andrea froze. Weren't things bad enough? Being isolated at the farm with her mother was more than she could bear right now. Pictures of her happy, promising wedding; the close family weekends she and Lans had enjoyed there; the present state of her marriage flashed before her. Pain pierced her heart. She would feel it even more at the farm. What would she do if Evelyn began hallucinating there?

"I'm sorry. I can't leave now, Mom. We were there a short while ago."

"I still own the farm. It's mine, and you're trying to keep me from going there. Dad told you to take me whenever I wanted to go."

"Dad never said a thing to me about the farm, Mom. He knew I'd take care of you the best I could, but the farm is out of the question right now."

"You're trying to take it from me." Evelyn grabbed onto the thought like a drowning man clutches a floating log. All morning she followed Andrea around, demanding her way. "You always wanted the farm for yourself. Now you think you can have it by keeping me from it." Her voice, railing and accusative, lashed out at Andrea just as her grandfather had turned against his beloved Laura when she had done everything in her power to help him.

Andrea cradled her mother in her arms. "Mom, I love you. I'm doing everything I know to take care of you and help you through this."

"Then take me to the farm."

"Not now, Mom. You'll be taking new medicine, and we don't know how you'll react to it. We have to stay close to your doctor. Maybe a few weeks from now." Why had she mentioned the possibility? Her mother might forget everything else, but she would retain this single thought. "Why don't you go out to the yard and pull some weeds? You enjoy that," Andrea forced a smile.

Evelyn glared at her and slammed the door behind her.

Having a moment to herself, Andrea called a friend of her mother's who had nursed her husband through Alzheimer's disease. He had died eight months ago after a long decline.

"Jane, Andrea Mulder here. How are you?"

"Hello, Andrea. I'm fine. How is your mother? Or should I ask, how are you coping?"

"Okay, I guess, but I have a huge favor to ask you. If you have no plans, would you have dinner with Mother tonight and stay with her until I come home? I have an important dinner to attend with Lans. I'll make her favorite stew, and I know she'd love to see you. She misses her friends so much."

"Yes, I'm free, and I'd be happy to give you a break."

"I know you understand. Did your husband ever turn against you and start accusing you of things?"

"Of course, it's part of the disease. They don't understand what's happening, so they turn against the one who's closest to them."

"She acts like I'm her worst enemy. She thinks I want to take the farm away from her. It's so much harder to have her there, and it's so far away from her doctor. We were there a couple weeks ago, and she wants to go back."

"Just do what you think best and try not to be hurt by her attitude. She can't help it and she doesn't know what she's doing to you."

"Thanks, Jane. I needed your perspective. And thank you for tonight. It means more to me than you can imagine. If you could drop in late this afternoon about 4:30, Mom won't know it's been planned. I'll invite you to stay for dinner, and that will give me time to get dressed and meet Lans."

⌘ ⌘ ⌘

Andrea checked the backyard. Evelyn was down on her knees, singing a favorite hymn, tearing up chunks of lawn and throwing them into careless piles. Working in the "garden" had become her favorite activity. Andrea suspected it connected her to her past and helped her feel normal and useful.

Andrea trudged up the stairs to her bedroom. All the people she loved were sinking into a deep pit just out of reach. Or was she the one who was sinking? Drained of energy, she flopped onto her bed. As she lay there, the words she had spoken to Lans the night before played through her mind. *"It's like living through Grandpa's decline all over again."*

A familiar ache riled her stomach and the old longing for her grandparents returned. She closed her eyes, drifted back in time, and saw her grandfather leaning on his pitchfork in the barnyard. He lifted his cap and wiped his face with his big red handkerchief, and suddenly she was there.

8

Ten-year-old Andrea ricocheted past Jake and jumped off the side of the porch as he carried her luggage into the farmhouse. She ran toward the barn, her blond pigtails bouncing behind her. Passing the pigpen and chicken coop, she greeted the occupants: "Hi, Porky. Hey, Henny Penny. Do you have any new chicks?"

A black and white Sheltie bounded out the sliding barn door and lathered her with affection. "Hi, Skip," she said, turning her face from side to side, laughing as he licked her cheeks. "Come on. Let's find Grandpa."

As she ran into the barn, a brown mare with a white star-like patch on her nose whinnied and bobbed her head up and down. Andrea rushed to the horse stalls, reached out to pet Dolly's warm muzzle and traced the star with her finger. "Hello, my wonderful Dolly. Can you hardly wait to take me for a ride? I'm sorry it took me so long to come up this spring."

Dolly poked her nose against the bulge in Andrea's pocket. "Yes, I have an apple for you." She placed it on her flattened hand and lifted it to Dolly, who wasted no time accepting her offer. "Oh, that tickles," Andrea squealed as Dolly's lips claimed the apple.

"Well, look who's come to see us." Her grandfather appeared through the back barn door. "I thought you'd never get here this year." His brown eyes twinkled under his thick, dark hair that was beginning to gray at the temples. Fritz Klinghof swept his granddaughter into his arms, kissed her, and whirled her around as he had his beloved Laura when he returned home from work in the early days of their marriage. "It's about time you came to visit us. That horse has been missing you something fierce and so have your grandma and I."

"Me, too, Grandpa." She threw herself against his chest as he chuckled and gave her another hug. "I'll be here lots this summer, you'll see. I just wanted to say 'hello.'" She turned on her toes, leaving him as abruptly as she had arrived. A swirl of energy followed her down the driveway.

In the kitchen she sampled the delicacies her grandmother had prepared for her dinner before climbing the stairs to her bedroom. Andrea could still stand almost anywhere in the room, but adults could stand only in the middle where there were no eaves. Thick carpet, heavy drapes that kept out the morning sun, and a down quilt piled high with pillows and stuffed animals made the room a cozy haven. Andrea enjoyed it more than her spacious room in Pittsburgh.

Two small windows looked out on large hayfields; one field disappeared into the woods, the other ran down to the creek that circled the farm.

After unpacking her clothes, she put them in the little chest of drawers. She placed her church dress on a hanger and hung it on the hook on the wall. Her parents seldom attended church, but her grandparents never missed a Sunday. They felt at home among the country people of German ancestry who worshipped at the one-room Lutheran church. Andrea failed to understand why it was so important to them. Her parents seemed to do very well without it.

⌘⌘⌘

Enticed by the rich smells of roasting lamb, carrots, potatoes, and onions, she returned to the kitchen as Fritz came in from the barn. He set pails of warm milk on the floor, took off the red kerchief around his neck, and wiped his brow. "Hello, darling," he said, capturing Laura in his arms and planting a loud kiss on her cheek.

"Hurry and wash up, Fritz. The roast is ready to be served."

Andrea chatted happily with her grandmother as she made gravy and scooped mint jelly into a crystal dish usually reserved for guests. In the dining room miniature ballerinas leaped over baskets of candy and balloons soared upward from the centerpiece. Leftover napkins from last year's birthday completed the décor.

"Grandma, the table is as beautiful as my birthday last year."

"We missed having you here this year, so I thought we should celebrate it tonight."

"You make every visit special, no matter when it is." Andrea hugged her hard.

Fritz, having shed his farm overalls, reappeared in dress slacks, a soft-collared shirt, and his favorite gray cardigan. Andrea, anticipating an evening ride on Dolly, had slipped into her favorite riding pants. Laura removed her white apron, and the three of them sat down to the table. Reaching for their hands, Fritz bowed his head and asked the Lord to bless the food and to bless Andrea's time with them.

"Seems like we get the best meals when you come to visit, Andrea," Fritz said, his dancing eyes teasing as he studied the roast. He grounded the leg of lamb with a fork and inserted a knife slowly into the succulent meat. Passing

Andrea a plateful, he whispered, "Let me in on your secret. How do you get Grandma to cook such feasts?"

"Now, Fritz, a visit from Andrea is a special occasion."

"Try being her first grandchild, Grandpa. Maybe that'll help," Andrea whispered back as though she were entrusting him with an important secret.

"Ah, is that it, young lady? I'll have to work on that."

⌘⌘⌘

The next morning Andrea awoke early, dressed without washing, and dashed down the stairs. Halfway down she stopped.

"You've never given me such short notice," she heard her grandfather say in a distressed voice. "Why the hurry today? New developments? What new developments? Can't you tell me over the phone?" He paused. "All right, I'll come, but it's anything but convenient."

"Why today, after all this time?" her grandmother asked.

Andrea wanted to protest, but hearing the agony in her grandmother's voice, she stopped in the doorway.

"They're trying to harass me. Break me down. That family thinks nothing matters but their own hurt, and they're determined to make somebody pay for it." Andrea had never heard her grandfather speak in such serious tones. Always teasing, he joked and tried to make people happy.

"Maybe this time they'll understand you had nothing to do with that man's death."

"I suspect they already know that. They're merely conniving to see how they can profit from the accident. They want money from someone. They don't care that I sold the car to the man who killed their son."

"If only we could find the bill of sale, Fritz."

"There's no place left to look."

"If they win the case, how much could they sue us for?" Laura's voice quaked.

"The lawyer says thousands of dollars. If only we had more insurance."

"Where will the money come from?" Laura started to cry.

Andrea heard a chair scrape back from the table and then, "There, there now, Laura honey. It'll be all right. I can't believe the good Lord would let them put an old man in jail for something he didn't do."

Andrea rushed into the kitchen and put her arms around them both. "Grandma, Grandpa, what's wrong?"

"There, there, child. No need for you to worry about our problems. We'll get through, like we always have, won't we, Fritz?" Laura dabbed her eyes with her morning apron and tried to smile, but with no light in her eyes, the wrinkling of her cheeks looked more like a grimace.

"You can explain it to me, Grandma. I'm old enough to understand. I know it's something terrible, but I don't know what. Did Grandpa kill somebody?"

Between sighs, Laura told Andrea the sad facts about selling their car, the loss of the bill of sale, the collision by the new owner, who had not changed the license plates. Both drivers had been killed, and the police had traced the license plate back to Fritz.

"Finally the two families brought a case against your grandpa charging him with negligence in maintaining the car and demanding compensation for their losses. The case has been in process for three years. I think their lawyer knows there isn't a shred of evidence that Grandpa is guilty; and he's trying to scare us so we'll settle out of court, but we don't have the money to do that."

"Dad would help you."

"We don't want to put that burden on your father."

"But he can help you, Grandma. I'm sure he can. He can fix anything."

"Andrea, your father has already made it possible for Grandpa to leave the store and come here on the farm to live. We don't want to ask anything more of him."

"All right, Grandma, but what will happen to Grandpa?"

"I don't know. We wait months and months to hear what the next step will be. It's hard to live with this hanging over our heads."

"But you and Grandpa always seem so happy, Grandma."

"We are, dear heart. Your Grandpa is a good man, but this trial could send him to jail. It hurts me when I lie in bed at night."

Andrea, troubled by her grandmother's frightened expression, brought out the egg basket. Hoping to distract her, she said, "Let's gather eggs today, Grandma."

The two swung it between them as they headed for the chicken coop. Once inside, Andrea reached into the deserted nests, picked up one egg at a time, and laid it in the basket. Poking under the sitting hens, she snatched their eggs when they stood. The hens clucked excitedly, objecting to her stealing their eggs.

"There, there, now, little Mother. You'll have other chances to have babies. Come now, Matilda, don't be so selfish. Everyone appreciates the delicious eggs you've made for us. Oh, Henny Penny, the sky may indeed fall today. Off your nest. Go and make sure we're still safe."

Henny Penny, squawking loudly, scurried out the henhouse door.

Even Laura had to laugh. "That's a great imitation of me, Andrea. My, it feels good to laugh. I'm so glad you're here today, dear."

Back in the kitchen, Andrea washed the soiled eggs and placed the largest in empty cartons for her grandmother's customers. Laura kept the egg money in a jar in the cupboard. "You never know when a rainy day may come. That might be just the amount I need," she said, as she dropped the change from a recent sale into the jar and listened to it clink against the other coins.

The chores completed, Andrea tugged at her grandmother's arm. "Come for a walk in the pasture, Grandma. Let's go see the new baby calf."

⌘⌘⌘

Laura and Andrea marched hand in hand through the barn. As they entered the pasture, Laura grabbed two pieces of tall grass, pulled off their outer shafts and handed one to Andrea. They sucked the tender end of the blade, savoring its juices as they walked.

A tributary of the creek circled the lower pasture, separating it from the hillside. The cow pasture was a grassy, flat plateau cropped short by slow-moving, munching cows. Laura found it pleasing that the little creek encircled the whole lower pasture before rushing into deeper waters at the edge of the hayfields. She loved the way the shallow waters sparkled in the sun as they cascaded merrily down shelves of slate coated with copper-colored sediment. The gurgling of the falling waters soothed her troubled spirits.

She sat on a fallen tree while Andrea ran her fingers through the cool spring water. "Most of the cows have moved up the hill, Grandma. I see Florida with her mother halfway to the top."

"Run along and greet her. She's nearly a month old now. I'll stay here."

Laura watched Andrea dart from rock to rock as she climbed the high hill and marveled at the energy of youth. Laura was only fifty-five, but today she felt old and tired. *Will this terrible trial ever end? Will we ever be carefree again?*

No longer having to put on an act for Andrea, she allowed the tears to fall as she visualized the trial when at last it came. She shuddered as she imagined a sour-faced judge peering down on her and Fritz, accusing them of the death of two drivers.

⌘⌘⌘

The upper pasture, sparsely covered with tall maple, poplar, and sycamore trees, was dotted with outcroppings of gray rocks. Scampering up its face, Andrea came upon Florida sucking milk from her mother's teats.

She waited for Florida to finish and approached her with caution, stroking her forehead as she licked the last bit of milk from the end of her nose. "Hello, Florida. You've grown so big." Florida pushed at Andrea's hand as it went up and down her long nose. "Your hide is as golden as your mother's. Hi, Annabelle, what a good job you did. Florida is a fine calf." She petted them both. Annabelle swished a fly with her tail, threw Andrea a stern look, as though warning her not to interfere with her baby and nudged Florida to move along. Andrea seated herself on a large rock and surveyed the farm below.

A barbed-wire fence ran between the pasture and a planted hillside that would soon produce crops of oats, barley, and corn. Tiny green corn stalks erupted from the brown earth. Behind the farmhouse seed packages on sticks marked the rows of Laura's vegetable garden. Laura had started tomato plants inside on the kitchen windowsills, planning to plant them in the garden as soon as weather permitted.

Andrea looked forward to late summer when the ripened corn had golden tassels and tomato plants resembled Christmas trees adorned with red balls. She especially liked the small tomatoes that she picked from the vine and popped into her mouth. Still warm from the summer sun, they were far superior to those her mother bought in the grocery store and stored in the refrigerator.

Andrea's eyes followed the creek that meandered along the northern and eastern boundaries of the sixty-acre farm. At the southeast corner of their land, it disappeared into the deep woods that she and her grandfather had so often explored together.

⌘ ⌘ ⌘

After lunch when her grandmother lay down to rest, Andrea tramped through the hayfields to the path in the woods where fern unfurled and skunk cabbage leaves grew high. She found spring violets on long stems, growing much taller than at home. The violets bloomed in a myriad of colors: white, yellow, light purple, deep purple and rosy red. She picked some of each color, adding green heart-shaped leaves to make a beautiful bouquet that she hoped would bring a smile to her grandmother's sad face.

Clutching her violets, she wandered deeper into the woods, searching for the delicate white blossoms of the trillium plants, but they had not yet bloomed. She felt a tug at her heart as she thought of the fine walks she had shared here with her grandfather. This worry had been with him for three years, but he had always smiled and looked happy for her.

⌘⌘⌘

Laura glanced at her watch: 7:00 p.m. and no word from Fritz. Twisting her hands as she wandered from window to window, she lifted the lace curtains and peered out, searching in vain for the Dodge truck. The violets smiled at her from the kitchen table. Her face had brightened when Andrea burst through the door and thrust the flowers into her hand. "A present for my favorite grandma." Laura hugged her and arranged them in her prettiest cut glass vase, but her pleasure in them had waned.

Now every passing hour added to her discomfort. Knowing she could not eat until she heard from Fritz, she waited for his return but didn't want to spoil Andrea's dinner, knowing that, next to leg of lamb, beef noodle soup was her favorite meal.

Laura sighed as she turned from the window. Her shoulders were stooped and her head bowed. "It will be dark soon. You must be hungry, Andrea. I'll heat up the soup once more, and if he isn't here by then, we'll eat anyway."

Both of them jumped as the blast of a horn broke the silence. Laura dropped the ladle into the soup as she rushed to the window for a closer look. Fritz's truck rumbled up the driveway.

"He's here. You see, Grandma, he's home to have dinner with us." Andrea, out the door in an instant, jumped off the porch and ran full speed toward the truck. She opened the door as he turned off the ignition. "You're home, Grandpa. We waited dinner for you. It's beef noodle soup."

"I've been tasting it all the way home, honey," he said with his usual good humor. Andrea jumped onto the running board and threw her arms around his neck. "Did you take good care of Grandma today? It must have been a long day for her." He looked past Andrea to Laura standing on the porch.

"I did, Grandpa. This morning we gathered eggs and took a walk in the pasture to see Florida. This afternoon I picked a bouquet of violets from the woods to cheer Grandma, and tonight I helped milk the cows. All the chores are done. and your dinner is waiting."

"I see you have everything under control. It's a good thing you were here today." He let go of Andrea as they reached the porch and took Laura in his arms.

Laura started to cry. "Did they drop the case, Fritz?"

"Nothing's changed, Laura honey. We met with their lawyers. They asked me the same old questions, and I gave them the same old answers. They offered to settle out of court. I turned them down. That's all I can tell you, sweetheart." He planted a loud kiss on her cheek. "You put dinner on the table, Laura. I'll wash up and join you."

⌘ ⌘ ⌘

Andrea surveyed the table to make sure nothing had been forgotten. A large steaming bowl of beef noodle soup sat on her grandmother's best dinner plates at each place. To the left a smaller plate held a large piece of soup meat. A loaf of homemade bread sat beside newly churned butter. Andrea set a bottle of catsup beside Grandpa's place. He never ate noodle soup without putting catsup all over his meat.

"That's the only way to have it, honey. Doesn't everyone serve it that way?"

"Nobody I know serves beef noodle soup like Grandma makes. Noodle soup at our house comes from a can of Campbell's."

"Well, let's dive in," Fritz said, rubbing his hands together and bowing his head for a blessing.

⌘ ⌘ ⌘

Sprawled in front of the living room fireplace, Andrea stroked Skippy's back while her grandparents played Double Solitaire. Andrea studied her grandmother's sweet face as she concentrated on the game. How she loved her. Her graying hair lay in flat waves about her head while glass spectacles perched upon her oversized nose. Stout at forty-eight, she wore a belted floral print dress with a plain V-neck. In later years Andrea would brag that her grandmother looked like a grandmother should look. She had never considered restraining her appetite. An accomplished cook, she enjoyed her culinary delights with the rest of the family.

"That was just about the best dinner I ever ate, Grandma."

"Too bad you had so much soup, little lady. You won't be able to join us for apple pie."

"Grandpa, you know I can always eat Grandma's apple pie."

Her grandparents never missed a night having dessert and coffee at the kitchen table before going to bed. They stayed up talking and sipping coffee

53

long after she was asleep. Andrea loved the bedtime snack, sharing intimate moments at the end of the day with her grandparents. She wished her parents had a custom like that. They never sat alone together talking about little things. Instead they entertained clients and planned long trips.

"I'll get ready for bed and cut the pie while you finish your game, Grandma." Minutes later she surveyed the plates of pie topped with hunks of yellow cheddar. The violets smiled back at her from the center of the table. Satisfied, she called from the kitchen, "It's all ready. Come and get it."

"Now that's a sight to bolster a man's spirits." Grandpa chuckled as he sauntered into the kitchen with his arm around his wife. "We sure trained our granddaughter right, Laura. She'll make a good wife for some lucky man."

"Now, Fritz, she's only ten years old...much too young for you to be talking like that."

"At the rate she's growing, it won't be long. It seems like just yesterday I could carry her all day in my arms and here she is, already preparing the meals." Grandpa squeezed her as he took his place at the table. He always made over people like they had done something special for him. He was the kindest man Andrea knew.

They bowed their heads as he blessed the food. Then he said quietly, "The good Lord has blessed us, Laura. He'll see us through this, too."

"Fritz, it's hard to think of anything else." The worry lines sank deeper into Grandma's brow like beautiful grains in a choice piece of wood.

Andrea chatted as they ate their pie. "You don't have to come with me, Grandma. Stay with Grandpa. I'll put myself to bed." She kissed her grandparents. "It'll be all right, Grandpa, God will take care of you." She saw them turn toward each other with surprised expressions. Smiling broadly to reassure them, she turned and scampered up the stairs.

As she entered her bedroom, a peaceful presence she had never experienced before overcame her. Kneeling by the side of her bed, she talked to God about her grandparents and the trial, asking that it come quickly, that it be decided in her grandfather's favor.

"Does he actually hear my prayers?" she asked the ceiling when she finished.

A quiet contentment settled over her. Satisfied that her prayers had been heard, she climbed into bed feeling safe and secure, like being in her grandmother's arms, but the muted voices coming up through the heat ducts told her that worry still hung heavily over her grandparents....

9

Andrea sat upright in her bed. Where was her mother? She rushed down the hall to Kate's room and searched the side garden where she had last seen her mother pulling grass. Evelyn was nowhere in sight. A now-familiar panic took hold of Andrea.

She hurried down the stairs and through the French doors. "Mother, where are you?" She looked to the right and to the left. No sign of Evelyn. How careless she had been to let so much time pass. How could she live with herself if her mother had wandered off and been struck by a car? Her heart pounding, she called louder, "Mother, can you hear me?"

"I'm here, Andrea. Just resting a minute."

Andrea turned and ran toward the voice. Rounding the corner of the house, she found her mother sitting on the ground, leaning against the wall of the house, her muddy gloves dangling from her hands. "I'm thirsty. Could you bring me a glass of lemonade?"

Relief flooded her. At that moment Andrea would have brought her mother anything she wanted. "Sure, Mom. You stay here."

Andrea hurried to the kitchen. When had her mother become the demanding child? How had Andrea so easily slipped into a maternal role, catering to her every need? Was it too late to apply a measure of correction to their relationship? Andrea had no idea where to begin.

She returned with two glasses of lemonade. Setting them on the picnic table by the pond, she reached out a hand to her mother. "Come, I'll help you up. You must be tired after all that work." She glanced at the pile of pulled grass in the middle of her once-beautiful lawn.

Andrea had acquiesced to the systematic destruction of her lawn. Evelyn could not cope with the challenge of the flower beds, separating weeds from flowers. Finding such decisions taxing, she contented herself with weeding the lawn, pulling up everything in whatever spot she chose to tackle that day.

As they sipped their lemonade, Evelyn chatted as aimlessly as she pulled weeds.

"You seem happiest when you're gardening, Mom. Would it be fun for you if I planted a vegetable garden? We could come out every day and watch it grow."

"My vegetables won the most ribbons at the Garden Show."

"Yes, shall we try it again? Would you enjoy entering something in the next show?"

"Mine always were the best."

"And they could be again. If you don't want to do the work, you could tell me what to do. How 'bout it?" The doorbell rang. "Wait here and think about it." Andrea jumped up and ran inside to answer the door.

"Jane, how good to see you. Thank you for coming. I'm so grateful for your help."

"I'm a bit early, Andrea. I thought you could dress in peace. How's it going?"

"Not at all well. Lans can't take her bizarre behavior. Even I get irritated with her unending repetitions. She's been accusing me all day of trying to steal the farm from her. She'll probably tell you all about it."

"Don't worry. I know it isn't true."

"How can I help her, Jane?"

"There isn't anything you can do about what's happening to her brain. I knocked myself out trying to get George healed, trying to help him keep things straight. Nothing worked. Meet her physical needs. Accept it and love her anyway. Just don't blame yourself."

"Did his personality change?"

"You bet. He was such a kind, loving husband, but I couldn't do anything to please him as he got worse."

"I keep thinking if only she'd try harder, surely she could remember."

"She really can't."

"Mother was so confident. She had so many friends. She entertained all the time and made people feel happy. Now she thinks only of herself. I hardly recognize her. And she's so unsure of herself."

"That's because she's disoriented. She can't trust herself anymore. It's easier merely to withdraw. But it can work the other way. A jolly person can become ugly and demanding, but a tyrant can become quite docile. It's all such a mystery."

"Thanks, Jane. It's good to know what's happening is normal when it seems anything but. Before we let Mom know you're here, let me show you what I've fixed for your meal. I have it on simmer, so all you have to do is serve it whenever you're ready to eat."

"It smells delicious, and you've made it so easy. Thanks."

"Thank you, Jane. I'll be forever grateful that you could give me this evening with Lans. He needs all my attention."

"Then give it to him and don't worry about a thing."

"Pray for us that it will be a good evening, Jane. We need it desperately. Now come. Mom's out in the garden."

Evelyn seemed pleased to see Jane and happy that Andrea planned for them to dine alone. Andrea slipped out while they were deep in conversation and listened inside the door to make sure Evelyn maintained her good mood. Confident that Jane could handle the evening, she retreated to her bedroom to dress and turned all her thoughts toward Lans.

She called his secretary to tell her she would be able to keep their dinner date. Rummaging through her closet, she selected her favorite black dress. Except for the color, it was much like the one she wore the night of their reunion in Paris. *Lord,* she thought, *if this evening works out half as well as that one, I'll be satisfied.*

If it doesn't? She mustn't think like that. She mustn't cry again. She began to hum a love song, then another, the songs they danced to during their courting days. She made a special effort with her makeup, brushed her hair until it bounced. Everything had to be just right.

When Andrea took the final look in the mirror, she braced herself for whatever the evening would bring. No matter how frightened she felt, she would appear relaxed and confident. Not her adversary, Lans was her husband and she needed his support, his strength. She couldn't face this terrible thing alone. She must convince Lans not to leave her, to search for a solution together. They must begin at dinner tonight. She would not argue; she would just listen. Surely he would change his mind about leaving her.

She gathered her purse and her evening wrap, the one he had bought her for her birthday, found her keys, and descended the stairs. She went to the side window and peeked out. Evelyn was pouring her heart out to Jane, probably telling her how Andrea was stealing from her. No matter: Jane could handle it.

On her way to the car she realized that the farm not only represented the decline of her grandfather but the beginning of her romance with Lans. As she turned the key in the ignition, her thoughts focused on the summer she was fourteen, when she first met Lans.

10

On a sunny day in June Andrea threw open the car door, and, without a backward glance at her father, rushed to the barn to greet Dolly. Having lavished her with caresses, she ran to the back barn door and called to her grandfather. "Hi, Gramps, we're here. I'm going for a ride on Dolly as soon as I change," she said as she gave him a quick hug.

She had not seen her grandfather since Easter. As she started to leave him, she realized his hair had turned prematurely white well beyond his temples. It must be the trial. How selfish she was to think only of herself. She turned back to him and surrounded him with her arms.

"I've missed you, Grandpa, but I'll be here for five whole weeks. We'll have lots of time to spend together."

"Now that's my darling," he said, beaming. "I thought for a minute you were too grown up to care about your old grandpa."

"I'll always care for you, Gramps," she said. "You know you're my favorite grandfather in the whole world."

"I'll forget I'm your only one and cherish the thought, honey." Andrea had no grandparents on her father's side. They had both died by the time Leonard was thirteen.

She looked at her living grandfather with more compassion than most fourteen-year-olds and hugged him a second time. "See you later, Gramps."

Running back toward the house she passed what used to be the pigpen and the front pasture. She had cried when her grandfather tore down the pigpens, butchered some of the pigs and sold others. She had watched in awe as the great shovel scooped out the earth where the wet fields lay. In the spring, the detoured creek flooded the land and filled the hole.

"The lake is finished," she called to her father. "It looks wonderful." A new wooden dock pushed away from the shore toward the center of a small lake the size of a baseball field. "It looks bigger than I thought it would. Can we buy a boat for it? Have you stocked it with fish?"

"Yes, on both counts," Leonard Collins said. "It's stocked with baby bass that will have to grow up before we would want to catch them. But I thought we could go into Butler tomorrow to look for a rowboat."

"Could we buy a kayak, too? They're really fun."

"We'll see what we find tomorrow."

"Thanks, Dad. This place gets better all the time."

Andrea raced up the porch steps into the kitchen. "Grandma, where are you?" She lifted the lid from the large pot on the stove and sniffed familiar aromas. "You've already made noodle soup for me."

Warm apple pies filled the windowsills and a vase of white and yellow daisies graced the kitchen table. Laura appeared in the hallway, her crisp white apron tied around her ample waist, her arms wide open. Andrea rushed into them and felt the familiar comfort of her grandmother's embrace. Looking into her smiling face, Andrea could see that worry had permanently etched the lines in her forehead. She looked older. The anxiety of the ongoing trial and years of uncertainty had exacted a toll. Though her smile was warm and real, something inside her was dying.

"Oh, Grandma, I love you so much. You're the most special grandmother in the whole world." Andrea crushed Laura with her hugs as she tried to express years of appreciation for things she had taken for granted. A tear rolled down her cheek as she thought of all the years her grandmother had labored selflessly to give her everything she wanted.

Andrea dared not ask about the trial. The answer was always the same. It still hung over her grandparents like a cocked shotgun ready to fire. There was no relief from the specter of ruin.

Last fall, after six years of threats and delays, the trial date had arrived. Wearing their Sunday clothes, her grandparents made the trip to Pittsburgh early in the morning. Of the ten cases scheduled, the judge heard only four. Her grandparents were still waiting for theirs to be rescheduled.

"Grandma, it's so good to see you. Easter seems such a long time ago."

"I can't tell you how I've been looking forward to these weeks with you, Andrea."

⌘⌘⌘

Andrea climbed the stairs two at a time and found her suitcase sitting on the trunk at the foot of her bed. Throwing it open, she pulled on her riding pants and boots and glanced out the window. The field of daisies blazed with blooms. A thousand yellow circles bowed in the gentle breeze while the pure white of the slender, surrounding petals caught the brilliance of the sun.

How she looked forward to the summer. If only that dreadful boy weren't coming. Her parents had insisted she would enjoy his company, but she wanted things to stay as they had always been: her grandparents, long rides on Dolly, the woods, the fields, the creek, and now the new lake. When her parents returned with the Dutch family, everything would be different.

Leonard had not been drafted during the war. The country needed his expertise to convert peacetime manufacturing plants into wartime assembly lines. With the war over, he had begun to travel overseas and help European manufacturers convert to efficient peacetime production.

Dr. Mulder, his Dutch colleague, and he planned to collaborate on a book on international business. While the men spent three weeks writing at the farm, Leonard expected Evelyn to entertain Katharine Mulder and Andrea to keep their fifteen-year-old son occupied. She groaned at the thought.

"But that's two weeks away, and Dolly needs exercise," she said aloud as she rushed down the stairs and ran to the barn.

Guiding Dolly down the hill behind the cornfields into the woods, she found the leaves full grown and the woods darkly shaded. Lush growth and the abundant fullness of summer replaced the freshness of spring and the excitement of new birth, but the path still beckoned and the dense foliage created a sense of mystery.

When they emerged from the woods into full light, Andrea sensed Dolly's impatience to move faster. "Now," she cried and dug her heels into Dolly's sides. As Dolly broke into a canter, the breeze hit Andrea's face. Exhilarated by the horsepower rippling beneath her, she turned Dolly sharply to the left, "Again, Dolly, faster." Her heartbeat kept pace with the pounding of Dolly's hoofs as they sped through the daisies again and again. Holding the reins with one hand, she raised her other hand toward the sky. "It's beyond wonderful!"

⌘⌘⌘

After a morning's shopping in Butler, Andrea and her father arrived back at the farm with a small white rowboat inside the wooden station wagon. In the top rack a red and green kayak flashed in the sun like blinking neon lights. They had so much fun equipping the new lake, Leonard had granted Andrea's every wish.

After launching the boats, they tied the rowboat in deep water and the kayak on the shallow side of the dock in case it overturned during boarding.

"They look just like they belong here, Dad." Andrea pirouetted across the dock in joyous animation.

⌘⌘⌘

Having eaten Laura's turkey sandwiches on homemade bread with her own dill pickles, the family lingered over apple pie for dessert. Andrea jabbered about the new fishing tackle she and her father had bought until the phone rang inside the house.

"I'll get it," she said, jumping up and racing to the steps.

"It's for you, Grandpa," she called back a minute later.

"Now who would want to interrupt a fellow having lunch with his family on a nice day like this," he muttered as he disentangled his legs from the picnic bench and made his way toward Andrea on the porch.

"It's your lawyer, Grandpa. He said he has something important to tell you."

"It's about time he has something important to tell me," he said, disappearing into the house.

Andrea stayed on the porch hoping to glean something from the one-sided conversation. Fritz listened. When he spoke, he repeated a date. "Yes, yes, we'll be there," he said and put down the receiver.

Andrea rushed up to him. "What is it, Grandpa? Is it the trial?" A chill ran through her.

"Yes, honey, it is," he said, putting his arms around her. He sounded tired. "We've been waiting for months to have the court date rescheduled. It is, for three weeks from today." He looked at her with sad, defeated eyes.

"Grandpa, may I tell Dad about it now?"

"Not until I tell Laura. She's having such a nice time with your family. I'll tell her later."

As Andrea watched, he trudged up the stairs with his head bowed, the bent silhouette of a broken man.

⌘⌘⌘

Andrea sulked upstairs in her bedroom. The Mulders would soon arrive and her freedom to do what she wanted would be over.

Her mother knocked on her door. "Andrea, they should be here any minute. We expect you to come down to greet them."

"Yes, Mother, I will," she said, resigned to her dreadful fate.

"And be cheerful about it. You're always complaining that you're an only child. You might enjoy his companionship."

"Yes, Mother." Andrea refused to be encouraged, certain it would be a miserable three weeks. She had helped her mother make beds for the guests all morning as Evelyn lectured about doing things because they needed to be done. She knew Evelyn did everything possible to help further her husband's business. Andrea envied her mother's gift of small talk. Conversations with strangers were difficult for Andrea, but Evelyn moved among important people with ease, as though she had been born to it. No one would ever have guessed she was the daughter of a hardware salesman.

Andrea thought her mother's confidence came from being secure in her parents' love. Always there for her, they had attended her every performance in school. But Andrea had to compete with work for her parents' time. When she starred in the Christmas play, they were out of town. They missed Awards Day when she received many of the top prizes. As her parents traveled more and more, Evelyn parroted that her place was with her husband, as though her daughter was not important.

Three weeks at the farm with her parents should have been a time of rejoicing, but they were there for the Mulders, not for her. She wished she could saddle Dolly and ride off into the distance, not to return until the Mulder boy had departed.

Looking in the mirror, she picked up her hairbrush. She no longer wore pigtails. Last year's permanent had produced an ugly mass of crinkly curls that stuck straight out from her head, but the remaining perm was just enough to make the ends curl when she rolled her hair in socks overnight. When she styled it in the morning, it became an attractive pageboy. Her royal blue blouse brought out the blue of her eyes. Her figure had improved during the past two years. She knew her father would never again kid her about wearing a chubby size jacket.

The rumble of a car on the dirt driveway broke into her thoughts. "They're here. And so it begins," she said to the image in the mirror.

"Andrea." She heard her mother's summons.

"Oh well, it's only three weeks." Taking one last look, she pinched her cheeks to add color and marched out her door. It was time to meet the enemy.

⌘ ⌘ ⌘

Andrea watched the introductions through the kitchen window. Dr. Mulder had a thick foreign accent, brown eyes that were almost black, and unruly dark hair that was thinning. Andrea thought he must once have been better looking to have attracted such a pretty woman. Mrs. Mulder had been educated in the States. Her accent was more subtle and she had Americanized her name to Katharine. Soft-spoken, warm, and reserved at the same time, she appealed to Andrea.

Out of the huddle emerged a tall young man. With the possible exception of his full round cheeks, which reminded her of a picture of Hans Brinker on the cover of one of her favorite books, he looked like an all-American boy. His straight blond hair, stylishly cut, crowned attractive features.

Andrea watched him shake hands with her grandparents, who welcomed him warmly. As he broke from the group and walked toward the porch, Andrea left her post and met him at the kitchen door. His brown eyes sparkled as he saw her. His high forehead and firm chin gave him a confident look. Andrea stared at the most handsome enemy she had ever encountered.

He put down the suitcases he carried and extended his hand. "I'm Lans," he said. "You must be Andrea."

"Yes," she said. Finding a measure of social grace, she added, "Welcome to our farm. I'll show you where to take your bags."

She turned from those bright, brown eyes that were looking her up and down. Did he like what he saw? An awkward silence hung in the air as she led him up the steps. At the top, she turned around and faced him. "If you like horses, I'll show you mine as soon as you unpack."

"I love to ride. Do you have your own horse?" He set the bags down in the rooms indicated. "I can unpack any time."

"Then let's go," Andrea said, smiling at him for the first time. Leading him through the kitchen, she grabbed an apple from the wooden bowl on the sideboard.

On the way to the barn, she came face to face with Dr. Mulder. Behind his horn-rimmed glasses, his dark eyes were warm and welcoming. In spite of the deep creases in his face, he appeared to be a kindly man. Andrea thought he must be much older than Mrs. Mulder, who was even prettier up close than from a distance. Andrea took her extended hand. "I hope you enjoy your stay on the farm, Mrs. Mulder. I'd be happy to show you our woods. They're very beautiful," she said surprising herself as well as her parents.

"I hope that goes for me, too," Lans said.

"I'm taking Lans to meet Dolly. Come on. She's in the barn."

⌘⌘⌘

As Leonard led their guests into the house, Evelyn stayed behind and watched Andrea and Lans disappear into the barn. Whatever happened to all that resistance? "He is a good-looking boy," she said aloud. "If I were fourteen, he'd be like a dream come true."

She joined Leonard in their bedroom as the Mulders unpacked. "Did the meeting of Lans and Andrea bring back any memories?"

"Like what?" he asked as he straightened his many piles of papers.

"Can't you think about anything other than that book you're writing? Lans is as handsome as you were when we were introduced at the picnic on the Allegheny River."

"But a good deal younger."

"Yes, but did you catch the change in Andrea's attitude? I think she likes him."

"That would be a great help to all of us."

⌘⌘⌘

"Here, hold this apple up for Dolly, so she can get to know you. It's her favorite treat. Open your hand like this, and place the apple on top of it."

Lans chuckled and moved his hand away when Dolly's lips pressed against it. "She tickles."

"Don't tease her. Hold it still."

He winced as Dolly tried again to take the apple. "What a funny sensation."

"Haven't you ever fed a horse?"

"No, I've only ridden at birthday parties," he admitted.

As Dolly finished eating her apple, Andrea stroked her mane and patted her long neck. "My father gave her to me for my ninth birthday. She was my favorite horse at the riding stable. I rode her on breakfast rides in the country on Sunday mornings."

"Didn't you have to go to church?" Lans seemed surprised. "I have to go every Sunday."

"No, Mom and Dad don't go very often, but I always go with my grandparents when I'm here at the farm."

Lans spotted the Western saddle hanging on the wall. "Hey, this is sharp. Something like Roy Rogers would put on his horse. Is it yours?" He rubbed the tooled leather.

"Yes, I used to ride English saddle at the stables, but Dad thought this one would be safer if Dolly stumbles in the fields."

"Do you think I can ride her?" Lans asked.

"Yes, she's gentle with new riders. I'll ride Dad's horse, Merchant. He's younger and a bit skittish, but Dad trusts me with him now. We'll have to wait 'til after lunch, though. Grandma's been fussing over a welcome meal all morning."

"Your grandmother seems nice," he said.

"Yes, she's the best grandmother in the whole world. We'll see you after lunch, Dolly. Bye now." Turning to Lans, she suggested, "Would you like to see the upstairs of the barn? It has a wonderful place to jump in the hay."

"Sure."

They walked out of the barn and up the road to the back entrance of the second story. Andrea pulled up the latch, slid open the large wooden door, and ushered him in. Climbing up a ladder to the loft, she called, "We start here. We run from the back wall and jump off into space. It's almost like flying. There's plenty of hay in the loft to catch us."

He scrambled up the ladder after her. She met him at the top. "You don't have allergies to dust, do you?"

"Not that I know of. Hey, this is great. I've never been in a real barn before."

"That's good." Andrea looked relieved. More than one of her friends from Pittsburgh couldn't jump in the hay because of allergies. "Go back down and I'll show you the granary."

After climbing down the ladder, Andrea led him into a side room filled with large bins of grains. She stopped by one that was almost empty.

"Well, look at that," Lans said, his big eyes growing bigger as he saw several field mice scampering around in it. He grabbed a pitchfork and struck three times into the midst of them.

"Got one." He held up the pitchfork for Andrea to see. A tiny mouse pierced through by one of its prongs writhed in agony.

Andrea raised her arms to shield her eyes from the pitiful sight. "Lans, how could you!" she cried. "The mice are my friends."

"I never heard of a woman who liked mice. My mom hates them. She acts like those cartoons where a woman sees a mouse and stands up on a chair screaming."

"Well, I'm not like those women, and I'll never be like them." Andrea stiffened and gave him a look of disgust. "I thought you were nice. Now I don't want you to ride Dolly." She ran from the barn and raced to the house past the adults standing in the doorway. Bolting up the stairs, she slammed her bedroom door and threw herself on her bed, sobbing.

11

From her bedroom Andrea heard the conversation at the foot of the steps.

"Where is she?" Lans asked the adults standing there.

"Upstairs in her room. What happened?" Leonard's voice was stern.

Lans ignored the question, jumped up the steps two at a time, and knocked on her door. "I'm sorry, Andrea. I won't do that to your friends again."

"Go away. I don't want to see you."

"Lans, will you come down here and tell us what happened? You started out together so cheerfully."

"Yes, Dad." He came down one step at a time and faced the adults, who stared up at him. "We fed Dolly an apple," he began.

"Yes, yes," his father said. "Then what happened?"

"Andrea took me to the second floor of the barn and showed me the hay loft. It looks like a great place to jump...."

"And," his father prompted.

"And then she showed me the granary. They have big bins of different kinds of grains in there, Dad. You should see it."

"I expect I will," his father said.

"And there were little mice running around in a bin that was almost empty."

"Mice. Ugh." Katharine grimaced.

"And there was this pitchfork hanging on the wall." Lans stopped. "You know how you hate mice, Mom. I'm always killing them for you."

"And," his father said.

"I picked it up and stabbed a mouse. Andrea told me they were her friends, and now she hates me," he blurted, sounding bewildered by the unexpected turn of events.

"I see," Leonard said. "It doesn't sound too serious. I think we can overcome the problem." Andrea could hear the relief in his voice that the attack had been against the mouse and not against her. "It wasn't the best start for a girl like Andrea," he said to Lans. "She loves all the animals on the farm, including the crickets, the crayfish, the fireflies, and the frogs. Better watch your step when it comes to practicing your manly skills in front of her."

Everyone laughed.

"I'll go up and comfort her," Andrea heard her grandmother say. "Go into the living room. Lunch can wait a few minutes."

⌘⌘⌘

Andrea lay on her bed, shuddering at the thought of the little mouse wriggling on the end of the pitchfork. She heard the knock on the door and turned to the wall.

"May I come in, sweetheart? It's Grandma."

"Yes, Grandma," she said, letting out half a sob.

Laura sat down on the bed, and Andrea threw herself into her grandmother's arms. "Oh, Grandma, it was a cruel thing to do, but I made such a scene. I'm so embarrassed. What must he think of me?"

"There, there now, child." She stroked Andrea's hair and held her close. "He's a fine boy, and you'll have a good time with him. He won't do anything like that again."

"I heard him tell everyone. They all laughed, and I'm mortified. I don't want any lunch." She pulled the quilt at the bottom of her bed over her head.

"I made your favorite potato salad, and the hamburgers are plump and juicy. How about carrying them out to the picnic table for me? You can sit on one end by me. We'll put Lans on the other end by his parents, and you can start all over again after lunch."

"I don't want to talk to him ever again, Grandma."

"I know, dear, but it will be easier later on. Come now, I need your help. Your mother is busy entertaining our guests." She squeezed Andrea's hand and led her into the bathroom where she wet a cloth and wiped her red eyes.

⌘⌘⌘

Lunch was a success for the adults. Andrea avoided looking at Lans and pretended to listen to the adult conversation. Having planned their book for months, the men talked about reviewing the latest management theories before finalizing the format of the book and the sequence of chapters. The men would take over the glassed-in sun porch. The women would play bridge with Laura and Fritz in the living room.

Their fathers agreed they would relax for the afternoon and have a swim in the lake with their families. Thereafter, they would adhere to a strict work schedule during the day and socialize with their families in the evenings.

When everyone had finished dessert, Laura rose to clear the table. "Andrea, will you help me clear the dishes?"

"Yes, Grandma." She jumped up, happy the ordeal was over.

"Lans, please help Andrea and her grandmother," Dr. Mulder prompted his son.

Lans took an armload of dishes into the kitchen, meeting Andrea coming back for more. "I'm sorry about the mouse. Will you forgive me?"

"I guess, but it was a nasty thing to do." She glared at him. Seeing his distressed look, she relented. "Have you ever paddled a kayak?"

"No," he said brightening. "Is it fun?"

"You bet. Change into your bathing suit, and I'll meet you by the lake after the dishes are done."

⌘ ⌘ ⌘

"Lans can have the first turn in the kayak," Andrea announced to the gathered families, everyone but Laura dressed in bathing suits. "You place the paddle on the dock," she instructed him, "untie the rope, step into the middle of the boat, and slide in. Then pick up the paddle and you're off."

"Sounds like fun." Following Andrea's advice, he shifted his weight onto the boat, but as he lifted his foot off the dock, the boat began to roll. He bent over and grasped the sides, but the unsteady kayak dumped him into the lake.

Andrea smiled as he surfaced. "Try it again. You'll get the hang of it."

"Hey, the water's great. You should join me."

Lans succeeded in placing both in the boat, but as he tried to push his leg forward to slide into the bow, the little boat wobbled from side to side and rolled over a second time. Holding her sides, Andrea tried to stifle her laughter as the athletic, competent Lans plunged into the water headfirst. This time the adults laughed, too.

"I have one more strike before I'm out," he announced, undaunted, as he righted the wobbling boat. "There must be a way to master this thing."

The third attempt failed as well. Andrea laughed without restraint, both families laughing with her. "You did that to me on purpose," Lans called to her as he popped up the third time. Grabbing the paddle from the dock, he splashed water in her direction and managed to soak everyone at once, including Laura, who was sitting on a chair watching the fun. "I'm sorry, Mrs. Klinghof, I was aiming at Andrea."

"Don't worry; the water feels good," Laura assured him.

"Okay, Miss Superior, you've had your revenge. Now show me how to do it," he said as he climbed back onto the dock and handed her the paddle.

"You did look funny." Andrea giggled. Deftly she righted the kayak and, holding on to the dock, slid first one leg into the hole in the center of the boat and then the other. It wobbled from side to side, but clinging to the dock to steady it, she managed to get into the kayak without tipping over. Picking up the two-sided paddle, she plunged it into the water and raced into the center of the lake and back again. She had spent two weeks practicing every day and was now adept at mastering the kayak's unsteady ways. "I did exactly the same thing the first day, Lans. It took me forever to figure out how to do it."

"Now I've got the picture. Let's forget the boats and race across the lake."

"Sure."

They dove in together, but Lans soon pulled ahead of Andrea and reached the other side first to the cheers of his parents. Andrea joined him on a rock on the shore. "Let's catch our breath before we swim back to the dock."

"Are you still angry with me? We could have a great three weeks."

"I've forgiven you. Seeing you go overboard the third time in a row wiped the memory away. You took it very well. I did have the advantage."

"This is a great place." He looked around in all directions.

"There's much more to show you."

"I didn't want to come, but my parents made me. I wanted to take a summer job, but Dad said to wait 'til I'm sixteen and enjoy family time this summer."

"Do you think we'll see much of our fathers? It sounds like they'll be out of bounds all day."

"Yes, but they're planning to spend every evening with us. It could be the makings of a great family memory for both of us. I don't see my parents for weeks, sometimes months at a time," he added. "Dad works overseas a large part of the year."

"Mine, too." Andrea knew how it felt to be left alone at home with just the housekeeper for company. Forever hoping to win more of her parents' time, Andrea worked ceaselessly to please them and brought home superior report cards, even though they took her good scholarship for granted. "Dad's never home when something special happens at school. We won the state softball championships this season and he didn't see a single game. Mother was with him most of the time and didn't see many more," Andrea said.

"This was my first year on the varsity basketball team and Dad saw me play just once." They looked at each other with understanding for the first time. "But I guess we're lucky to have successful fathers. I just wish they could be around a little more."

"What do you want to do when you grow up, Lans?"

"I haven't decided yet, but I'm going to college for sure."

"Have you picked a school yet?"

"Probably one of the Ivy League schools in New England. That seems to be important to my parents."

"I know what you mean," Andrea said with sympathy. "I've talked about going to a coed university because I've gone to an all girls' school all my life, but Mom always says, 'If you love your father, you'll go to Smith.' That's in Northampton, Massachusetts, where my father grew up." She turned to him. "I didn't want to be here these three weeks either."

"It'll be fun. You'll see." Lans plunged back into the water. "Come on. I'll beat you back to the dock."

⌘ ⌘ ⌘

Andrea sat high on spirited Merchant, her father's tall, strong polo pony, as he pranced about the barnyard, eager to be let loose in the fields. Lans succeeded in mounting Dolly, whose docile nature was more forgiving. Andrea led him through the back barnyard into the pasture area, up the hill where the cows congregated in the shade of the large oaks, and down the road to the entrance to the farm.

Andrea thought it best to start slowly. No more tricks; riding a horse was serious business. She kept a tight rein on Merchant as she guided the horses along the creek, giving Lans a running commentary on her favorite haunts and summer activities. After they had walked the boundaries of the farm, she led him back to the field of daisies and told him to hold tight and grip the saddle with his knees. She gave Merchant, who needed no persuasion, permission to go faster and Dolly followed his lead. Andrea slowed Merchant until they were riding side by side.

As he bounced in the saddle, Lans looked as expectant as a young boy about to step onto a roller coaster. She liked the way the breeze ruffled his hair. He'd make a perfect model for advertisements.

The horses picked up speed as they trotted through the field. "This is great," he called to her, joy lighting his face.

"Next time, we'll go even faster. Are you okay with this speed?"

"You bet."

This was the first time Andrea had ridden with a boy her own age. She wondered if she could be as happy in the future riding with her grandfather.

❁ ❁ ❁

Andrea scrambled up the ladder to the second-story loft. After backing against the wall of the barn, she ran and leaped over the edge, her arms spread wide as if she intended to fly. As Lans watched, she sailed through the air and landed with grace on the hay. Bouncing up, she called, "Want to try it?"

"Sure." He grinned in her direction. Following her example, he took a flying leap into space and landed next to her. "Wow. That was great. I always wanted to fly." They laughed and plopped back onto the hay. "No one ever told me about a sport like this." His eyes danced with a sense of adventure.

"It's fun to share it with you. I always jump here alone because my parents and grandparents say they're too old. Come on," she said, reaching for his hand and pulling him up. "Let's both jump at the same time."

"I bet you I can jump the farthest."

"Probably. Your legs are longer than mine." As competitive as she was, she experienced pleasure when he showed himself stronger than she. She had enjoyed having the upper hand on the dock, but, much to her surprise, she liked it better when his athletic skill surpassed hers.

They stumbled through the hay and scrambled up the ladder to the loft. Hugging the back wall, they cried out together, "Ready, get set, go!" Rushing forward, they leaped into the air at the same time. Lans landed two feet in front of Andrea and fell back on top of her.

"Sorry, Andrea. I didn't hurt you, did I?"

He looked so concerned she burst out laughing. "Not at all, silly," she said, reaching out to ruffle his hair. He caught her hand and held it in mid air. They looked deeply at each other for a moment. Still holding her hand, he fell back in the hay beside her. "Gosh, I'm glad I don't have allergies. I must have been nuts, wanting to stay home."

❁ ❁ ❁

Many jumps later, they joined the gathering around the dinner table. They all bowed their heads as Fritz asked the Lord's blessing on the meal, the writing of the book, and the three weeks they would spend together. As he started to carve the roast lamb, Mrs. Mulder spoke. "What a perfect day this has been. The weather is lovely. I don't know when I've enjoyed a swim more."

"You're making it hard for us men to put our noses to the grindstone tomorrow," Dr. Mulder said.

71

"I don't know about you, Johan, but I can't think of anything I'd rather do than sink my teeth into this book." Leonard rubbed his hands together.

"Yes. I look forward to writing, too, but I did enjoy a needed day of rest."

"Working is rest for Leonard," Evelyn said. "He's always happiest when he's working."

"I think it's important for a man to spend time with his family." Lans looked at Andrea.

Laura changed the direction of the conversation. "You and Andrea had a full day."

"Yes, Mrs. Klinghof, we had a great day. Swimming and boating, riding the horses, jumping in the hayloft. It'll be hard to beat that tomorrow."

"I'm sure Andrea will come up with something, won't you, Andrea?" Laura turned to her granddaughter.

"There's lots more of the farm to see," Andrea agreed.

"Still want to look for a job back home, Lans?" Dr. Mulder's eyes twinkled.

"Guess it's going to be a successful three weeks." Fritz chuckled as he finished serving the last plate.

⌘ ⌘ ⌘

An hour later, Andrea slipped into the kitchen and took two empty peanut butter jars from the cupboard. After poking holes in the lids with an ice pick, she called to Lans, "It's nearly dusk. Time for the fireflies to come out."

"So?" He raised his eyebrows.

"So, it's time for another experience. Have you ever caught fireflies?"

"Not that I'm aware of."

"Well, come on. This is fun."

She led him outside into the back yard and sat down on the porch steps. "In just a minute or two, you'll begin to see them light up."

"See flies light up?"

"Not flies, silly. Fireflies look like black ladybugs. They belong to the beetle family."

"Then why are they called fireflies?"

"Because they fly around and their tails light up like tiny flames of fire. There's one." She pointed to a small blinking light over the flowerbed. "See its light go on and off?"

"It looks more like a small light bulb than a ball of fire."

"In a few minutes they'll be all over the place," she said with rising excitement.

Dusk fell fast, covering the gardens and fields with a blanket of gray. "Come on." She grabbed his arm. "Let's catch some."

He jumped off the porch and opened his jar. She swooped hers under an unsuspecting firefly, covered it swiftly with the punctured lid, and held it up for him to see. The little firefly went right on lighting up inside the container.

"I like to catch a bunch of them," she said. "Try it."

He followed her example. Soon they were running from one light to another, swooping the little creatures into their jars.

"That's enough. If you put too many in a small space, they'll die from lack of oxygen. Now come up to my room." She ran inside and bounded up the steps.

Lans followed behind her. "What next?"

She placed her jar on the big trunk at the foot of her bed, motioned for him to do the same, and pulled the switch on the wall. The little fireflies gave off enough light for them to see each other's eyes glowing with excitement in the near dark. "I used to go to sleep with them beside my bed, but in the morning they'd all be dead. Now I free them to fly away and come back another night."

"Where do they go in the day time?"

"They're nocturnal. They sleep in the flowerbeds and field grasses, I guess. They wake up and fly about when dusk falls."

"Do you think you can show me everything in three weeks? If I'm a slow learner, maybe I could come back some time."

"If the book is successful, maybe our fathers will want to write another one," she said, thrilled at the thought that he wanted to return. She picked up her peanut butter jar. "I guess it's time to free our little friends."

They held up their jars like candles lighting the stairway to the first floor. Once outside, Andrea opened her jar and turned it upside down.

As the fireflies tumbled out and flew away, she whispered, "Good-bye, little friends. Thank you for lighting our way tonight."

Lans freed his and turned to her. "This has been one great day, Andrea." Reaching for her empty hand, he squeezed it.

The crickets chirped in the grasses and the frogs croaked along the lake. Andrea smiled back in the silence, glad he could not hear the thumping of her heart.

12

Still filled with the wonder of her first day with Lans, Andrea pulled into the parking lot and looked at her watch. Fifteen minutes early. That would give her time to step into the restroom to refresh her face.

"Good evening, Mrs. Mulder. Mr. Mulder left a message that he would be delayed twenty minutes."

"Thank you, Harold." He was coming...one hurdle passed. She entered the ladies' room and, unhurried, studied her image in the mirror. A stunning dress. A figure that belied her forty-five years. She moved her face closer to the mirror. She could detect the first signs of wrinkles. Frown lines deepened between her eyes and tiny crow's feet formed a half circle like parentheses at their sides. But, since she had not permitted herself to resort to tears all day, the puffiness of last night's cry had disappeared. Her cheeks glowed from the memories of introducing Lans to the farm. A few dabs of powder covered small blemishes. Grateful the light in the restaurant was soft and flattering, she reviewed her reflection for the final time. She felt he would be pleased.

In the waiting area she reached for a magazine, rustled through its pages. Still ten minutes before their date. Her eyes refused to focus on the written words. Nothing on the pages held her interest like those exhilarating days with Lans the summer she was fourteen. Delicious memories. The daisies sparkling in the sun. The ring of eager young voices in the hay loft. Reliving that first day had renewed her spirit. She would greet Lans tonight with reawakened love. How would he respond? She shuddered as she remembered the hard look on his face when he left her.

She also remembered the rush of emotions she had experienced that summer. She had not wanted to be there. She had not wanted Lans to come. Think what she might have missed! Seeing again his eager young eyes searching hers, the intervening years fell away, and she was there at the farm once more.

⌘⌘⌘

As she lay in her bed in the farmhouse, Andrea could still feel his touch. She raised the back of her hand to her cheeks. A tingling sensation shuddered down her spine. It was the first time a boy had held her hand.

As awake as if the night had already passed, she climbed out of bed and knelt by the window, the place where she had first experienced the presence of God, where she felt most secure. "Thank you, Father, for such a wonderful day." An unknown joy, even better than hitting a homerun in a softball game, overcame her.

A half moon smiled in the sky outside her window. The stars seemed brighter than in the city and the white petals caught their light as she relived the joy of riding with Lans through the field of daisies.

She listened as her parents said good night to the Mulders in the hallway outside her door. She pictured her grandparents setting out a piece of pie and sharing the pleasantries of the day over a cup of coffee. With no hope of sleep, she bade the moon and the stars good night, tiptoed across her room, opened her door, and slipped out into the hall. The second floor had quieted, but she could hear the muffled voices of her grandparents in the kitchen. Creeping down the stairway, she sat on the bottom step, preparing to listen to their thoughts of the day.

Instead she heard her grandmother stifle a sob. A low groan escaped from deep inside her. "Fritz, is it really upon us? Will the judge hear the case at last? I don't know whether to cry with dread or rejoice that it's almost over. Or will there be one more delay? I don't have confidence in anything anymore."

"There, there, now, Laura. It'll be all right. Don't lose your faith." How many times Andrea had heard her grandfather comfort her grandmother. She ran into the kitchen and put an arm around each of them.

"It's going to go well for Grandpa. You'll see. I just know it will."

"Child, what on earth are you doing up at this hour?" Her grandmother looked alarmed. "And what do you know about this? Your grandpa told me about it this very minute."

"I took the phone call three weeks ago, Grandma. He didn't want to worry you too soon."

"I wish my faith were as strong as yours, Andrea. Mine has been worn down by the long years of waiting." The furrows in Grandma's brow had grown deeper, making her look older than Andrea could remember.

"Just one more week and we'll know," Grandpa said.

"It was a wonderful day, wasn't it?" Andrea looked from one to the other. "The Mulders are ever so much nicer than I expected."

Her grandmother smiled and her grandfather jumped at the opportunity to tease her. "That gleam in your eye wouldn't be for that tall, lanky young fella that you put to shame on the dock this afternoon, would it?"

"He deserved it. Killing that poor little mouse was a terrible thing to do."

"I guess he's like most of us men. We never do learn to understand our women." Grandpa sighed as though it were an impossible task.

"I don't believe you, Gramps. You always know what Grandma is thinking and the two of you always think alike."

"Never did understand her, but I always loved her. That's one thing you can write on my tombstone: *He always loved his Laura.*"

"And she him." Grandma reached over and patted his hand. "We've had a love that lasted a lifetime, which is more than most people can say."

Andrea felt good. She had distracted them from the looming trial.

⌘ ⌘ ⌘

The next morning she wasted no time telling her father about the trial. Up and dressed early, she intercepted him before breakfast, drew him outside onto the porch and laid out the full agony of the last seven years. "Dad, there must be something you can do to help Grandpa end this nightmare."

"I've been aware of the trial, Andrea, but I don't believe he's in danger. The case against him is weak."

"But all these years he's lived in fear, waiting for the verdict that could put him in jail. Dad, why did it take so long for the trial to be scheduled?"

"Probably because neither lawyer was paid enough to push the trial."

"Grandpa thought it was because they didn't have enough evidence against him and they were trying to get him to settle out of court."

"They'll never convict him," he said.

Andrea hinted once more that he could do something to help, but he seemed to think it unnecessary. He failed to understand the toll it had taken on her grandparents' well-being. Because she had promised her grandmother not to ask her father for money, she dropped the subject.

⌘ ⌘ ⌘

After breakfast Andrea and Lans saddled the horses. Evelyn and Katharine had gone shopping and their fathers were working in earnest, leaving Andrea and Lans free to wander the farm wherever they wanted. Andrea led Lans through most of their sixty acres, remembering to stop before he became sore. After lunch, she asked him to change into his bathing suit and meet her on the front porch.

"Where are we going?" Lans asked as they trudged through the high grasses.

"Down there." She pointed beyond the field of daisies.

"What's there?" He looked doubtful that it could be anything special.

"You'll see." She called Skippy to her side and surged ahead.

Lans threw his towel around his shoulders and with a couple long strides caught up to her. As he walked beside her, he reached for her hand. She allowed him to hold it as they walked on in silence. Still holding her hand in one of his, Lans reached down with the other and picked a large daisy. He turned to her and placed the flower in her hair behind her ear. Leaning back to admire his work, he said, "That looks good. It suits you."

Andrea smiled but remained speechless. They continued on, their arms swinging as they strode through the fields to the creek bank.

"What's this?" Lans asked, surprised. He looked at the rope dangling over the water's edge, the deeper water and the lack of obstructing rocks. "Ye olde swimming hole, I do believe. It looks like something straight out of Mayberry."

"Not bad for a city boy." Andrea laughed. "Come on, I'll show you how it works." She dropped her towel and took the rope in her hands. As Skippy wagged his tail and barked, she pulled the rope back up the shore, gave a great push with both feet and hurled herself into the middle of the swimming hole. When Andrea let go and plummeted down, Skippy jumped into the water and swam to her. "Want to try it?"

"Sure." Lans grabbed the rope and pushed off with all his strength. He landed beyond Andrea with a resounding splash and came up laughing. "Hey, that was great."

The daisy fell from Andrea's hair as she bobbed up and down. Lans reached out to catch it. "Looks like we'll have to pick another one for the trip home," he said.

They jumped in again and again, Lans playing Tarzan. As he pounded his chest and let out bloodcurdling jungle cries, Andrea squealed with delight. "Jane terrified of bellowing jungle man." She feigned horror, short-lived as she burst into laughter. "Come, Tarzan, let Jane show you more of jungle," she cried, taking his hand and starting off along the creek.

When she came to the great oak tree that hung over the creek, she climbed to the top and inched her way out on the overhanging limb. As Lans followed, she leaned back against upright branches strong enough to support her weight. "This Jane's tree home."

"Tarzan like. Jane...full of surprises." Changing identities, he became serious. "Nowhere in the neighborhoods of Long Island have I met a girl at home in the treetops."

They both laughed. The creek bubbled beneath them, singing a joyful song, and the birds flitted from branch to branch chirping cheerfully. Andrea felt that all was right in her world.

⌘ ⌘ ⌘

By the end of the first week, Lans cantered across the fields with such ease their parents granted them permission to pack a picnic lunch and tour the countryside. On a hot and muggy day, they set out at ten o'clock in the morning with lunches hanging from their saddlehorns. Walking the horses along a country road, they looked up at a cloudless sky.

Andrea led them to a nearby summer camp where they could see campers taking archery lessons and practicing canoe strokes on a man-made lake. "It looks like the campers are in class and the trails are empty. I have permission to ride them when they aren't being used for camp instruction."

The horseshoes had made a loud clopping on the blacktop. Now the horses stomped the soft dirt of the riding trails with a quiet thud, allowing Lans and Andrea to take in the new sights and enjoy the shade of the wooded hillsides. When they emerged from the woods and followed an open dirt road, the horses became skittish, prancing from side to side, nervous with pent-up energy.

"Let's give the horses some exercise," Andrea called to Lans as she allowed Merchant to pick his own speed. Dolly followed his lead. As the horses stretched their legs and pounded faster and faster, they enjoyed the wind cooling their faces and the freedom of the open road. After a good run, Andrea reigned in Merchant and Dolly slowed behind him. The horses plodded along, satisfied now to let Andrea and Lans enjoy the scent of pine trees and discover inviting scenes along the roadside.

"Look, Lans, there's a brook going into the woods. Let's leave the horses here to graze and follow it in. I bet we can find a lovely spot for lunch."

They dismounted, took their lunches, and dropped the reins so the horses could graze. The water in the brook, crystal clear, cascaded from rock to rock down a gentle slope until it leveled out and bounced merrily over longer, flat stretches of shale. Here and there deep pools of swirling water looked like they might be home to a resting trout. Andrea ran her fingers through the golden sediment that covered the layers of shale. As the sparkling nuggets caught the sun's rays, she said, "It looks like you could pan for gold."

"There must be hidden treasure here that no one has ever discovered.

Should we expose it and tell the world?"

"No, we don't want all those city slickers to overrun our countryside. Let's keep it a secret between the two of us." Andrea smiled, enjoying their moment of intimacy. Lying back on the bank of the brook, she looked up at the sky. Large white cumulous clouds had formed; dark spots warned that they might become thunderclouds.

"Well, look at that. There wasn't a cloud in the sky when we started. We better have lunch and start back." Surveying the terrain, she found a dry, flat rock that rose above the water. Just behind it was a taller rock, a perfect backrest. "Let's sit there and cool our feet in the water while we eat."

"Sounds great."

Andrea freed her feet and squealed as the cold water climbed up her ankles. Lans explored the contents of his lunch bag. "Looks like your grandma packed a super lunch. You're lucky to have her. My grandparents are in Holland, and it's often years between visits."

"I can imagine how hard it must be to have living grandparents too far away to visit."

"You seem happy and comfortable together, like you've shared secrets between the three of you. It's rather stilted when I see mine. We have to get reacquainted every time they come." As he spoke, Lans took off his shoes and placed his feet in the cool water beside Andrea's. "Hey, this feels great."

"Have you been to Holland, Lans?"

"No, but Dad promised to take me the summer I graduate, before I start college."

"How wonderful. I can imagine you in wooden shoes and Dutch breeches. I thought you looked like Hans Brinker when I met you."

"I don't even know how to skate."

"You'll have to come to the farm in the winter when the lake is frozen. It will be a great place to skate."

"I suppose you already know how."

"Yes, Mom and Dad gave me skates and lessons to go with them for Christmas two years ago. It's fun. You'd like it. It's like riding fast on a horse, only the blades underneath you provide the speed."

"I better learn before I come in the winter. I wouldn't want you to be embarrassed by a stumbling Hans Brinker. How about lunch? I'm starving."

She handed him two sandwiches, homemade dill pickles, and dessert.

"I see your grandmother didn't skimp on the apple pie. It's tops."

The brook bubbled by them, rushing relentlessly on, singing its cheerful melody. "Do you hear the tune the brook is playing? I wonder what it's singing? Wouldn't it be nice if we could understand the sounds of nature and communicate with the brook and the birds and the flowers?"

Lans paused before taking the next big bite of his sandwich and looked at Andrea with surprise. "I've never thought about it," he said. "But I like the ideas you've introduced me to. When I figure it out, I'll let you know."

"Thanks, I can't wait to hear." Andrea watched Lans devour his second sandwich and reach for the apple pie. She wondered what he was thinking. She went to an all girls' school and had spent little time with boys except to play softball or ping-pong. She had heard them talking about cars and guns and gangster movies. She imagined they were oblivious to the sounds of rushing brooks and fields of wildflowers. He liked the speed of the horses, flying through the air on the rope swing, and jumping in the hayloft. Like her, he longed for family time.

A clap of thunder interrupted her thoughts and took her gaze skyward where growing patches of dark gray covered the formerly white clouds. "It looks like a summer storm. We better return to the horses before they get frightened."

"We didn't even tie them up. I'm with you," he said, downing the last of his pie.

Leaving hers in the sack, Andrea dried her feet and slipped into her shoes. "It's such a lovely spot. I'm not ready to leave it."

"Just hope the horses aren't either," Lans said, tying his shoelaces as fast as he could. "I'll run ahead if you take my lunch bag."

"Be careful not to scare them. Just go up to Dolly gently. Merchant won't run off if he sees you with her. But leave him to me. He's much more temperamental than Dolly."

Lans was on his way, following the brook back to the road. Andrea picked up the scattered papers and followed. She could see him patting Dolly as she came into the clearing.

"Here now, Merchant. That's a good boy. Don't worry. The thunder won't hurt you." She approached him with caution, raising her hand to rub his nose. With the other hand she picked up the reins and pulled them over Merchant's head. "There, there now, boy. Everything is fine. Thank you for waiting for us." She patted his mane as thunder pealed in the near distance. Merchant jerked up his head and pranced about uneasily. "Let's mount and head home," she called to Lans.

They started down the road at a good pace. The horses seemed to know they should hurry. As they came out of the woods, large drops of water pelted their faces. Andrea urged Merchant forward, but the asphalt road became slippery, causing Dolly to stumble behind them.

"Hey, Dolly, good girl. You can do it. Just take as much time as you need," Lans encouraged her.

The rain increased, soaking Andrea's hair and clothes. She slowed Merchant and beckoned to Lans to come beside her. "There's a deserted barn around the next corner. I think we should stop in there. It's raining so hard it shouldn't last long. I don't like going fast on these slippery roads. A speeding car could spook Merchant. Then we'd be in real trouble." She led Merchant off the road and into the shelter of the barn. Dolly followed close behind. The open back door made access easy, but no one could see them from the road.

Andrea found some hay on the floor and a few handfuls of grain in an old manger. These she offered to the horses and rubbed them down with her hands. "Good boy, good girl," she went from one to the other. When they seemed content, she turned to Lans. "I'll share my apple pie with you," she said as she washed her hands in the spout of water that was pouring off the barn roof.

"Hey, great. Thanks."

She tore it in half, keeping the back crust and giving him the paper with the front portion. His grateful smile was worth more than half a piece of pie.

⌘⌘⌘

Fritz drove through the pouring rain looking in all directions. *Now where would those kids be,* he asked himself. *It's no use. I can't see a thing.* He left the road and turned his car into the driveway, stopping when he neared the front porch. He shook his head back and forth to the ladies, who were all looking in his direction. "I looked on every road we've ever ridden," Fritz said, "all the way to the camp and in every other direction. I couldn't see them anywhere. Of course, it was raining so hard, I couldn't see much of anything."

"What shall we do?" Evelyn turned to her mother. "Has Andrea ever been out in a storm like this?"

"She always gets home before the rain starts in earnest," Laura said. "But she's a smart girl, and she'll know what to do. Don't worry, Mrs. Mulder. I'm sure they'll be here soon."

"We never should have given them permission to go so far. How far did we say they could go?" Evelyn had a second thought.

"We sent them off for the day with packed lunches and told them to have a good time," Laura said. "Andrea's gone so many times alone, I didn't hesitate once Lans learned to ride."

"Well, we should have been more aware of the weather," Evelyn fretted.

"The report was pretty good this morning." Fritz lifted his hat and scratched his head. "There were no clouds in the sky when the kids left. Now it's raining so hard, you'd think it's been storing up for a month."

"We can't do them any good standing here looking at the road. Come in, and I'll fix you a cup of coffee. We never did have dessert with lunch. I just made a pineapple upside-down cake. That ought to cheer us up." Laura dried her hands on her apron and forced a smile.

Fritz chuckled. A freshly baked dessert was his wife's solution to most problems.

⌘ ⌘ ⌘

"You're shivering, Andrea. Let me warm you up." Lans started rubbing her arms. "Does that feel better?" His hands moved to massage her back. "What's good for the horses is good for us. They seemed to feel better after a good rubdown."

"I can almost feel sparks of fire warming me," she said, tossing her dripping hair. She had wrung it out several times, but it persisted in dripping down her back. "Thanks, that feels wonderful."

"Any time. I'm at your service. I took a survival course once, and the instructor said the best thing to do when you're fighting cold is to stay close together." He stopped rubbing and slipped his arm around her back and held her against his side.

Andrea didn't move. Grateful for his warmth, she shivered more from excitement than from the cold.

"Thanks, that does feel better," she said in little more than a whisper as she laid her head on his shoulder.

They sat on the floor of the old barn without moving, watching the rain fall until, as suddenly as it had come upon them, it began to lessen.

"Look," Lans said. "It's stopping. It's little more than a drizzle now."

"We should probably start home. Our parents will be worried."

"We probably should," he said.

Neither of them moved.

"Lans, the sun has come out, and there's a beautiful rainbow coming out of the mist." Andrea jumped up and ran to the barn door. "It's perfect, and it covers the whole area."

Lans joined her. "Hey, let's follow it and see where it leads."

"Mom and Dad would have my head if we don't go straight home and let them know we're safe."

"Mine, too. They'll be imagining all kinds of things by now."

He held Merchant steady as Andrea mounted. When she had settled into the saddle, he looked up at her. "It was a great adventure. I'm not sorry it rained. It made the day even better."

Andrea's smile beamed down on him. "I'm not sorry. either. It was a wonderful day." She turned Merchant toward the door so Lans wouldn't see her eyes mist over. Her eyes had a way of filling up when she was happy.

13

With the trial only two days away, dinner conversation centered on serious matters. Oblivious to Laura's discomfort, the men offered Fritz advice, convinced he would prevail. Evelyn insisted on accompanying her parents while Andrea agreed to stay home with Mrs. Mulder.

After dinner Laura waved everyone away from the sink. "It helps to keep busy," she said. "You girls clear and dry the dishes. I'll start washing. It's better to do familiar tasks than think about what's ahead."

"I know, Mom, it's the uncertainty. After all these years, anything could happen."

"That's just it." Laura sighed. "It's hard to imagine the court deciding against Fritz when he's never hurt a soul in his life. But what the court has already done to him makes anything seem possible."

"It's the fear of the unknown that's so difficult," Katharine sympathized. "We'll look back and see that it was not nearly as bad as it seems now."

Laura rested her soapy hands on the rim of the sink. "I'm sure you're right, Katharine, but my stomach tells me otherwise. Forgive me if I'm not quite myself tonight."

"Mom, I'm sorry you have to go through this. It's so unfair." Suddenly Evelyn's face lit up. "Why don't I drive you to Pittsburgh tomorrow? You can spend the night with your friends, Kitty and Bill. You haven't been together in years and I know they'd love to see you. I'll go to our house and check on things there and pick you up first thing in the morning."

Laura's face brightened. "That's a lovely offer. I'd be so happy to talk to Kitty, and seeing Bill would give Fritz strength. They're our best friends and we never see them now that we live on the farm."

"Then it's settled. I'll call them right away." Evelyn rushed to the phone.

Andrea put her arms around her grandmother's back as she labored over the dishes. "I'll be praying for you the whole time you're gone, Grandma."

"Thank you, child. Only the good Lord can see us through this."

"He will, Grandma, he will." Andrea held her grandmother tight, remembering all the times the older woman had been her source of comfort.

Laura removed her hands from the dishwater and gave Andrea a soapy hug. "Pray they don't put your grandpa in jail for something he didn't do."

Katharine moved toward the sink and took over the dishes. Evelyn bounced back into the room all energy and smiles. "They're delighted to have you stay overnight. They've missed you both. You'll have so much to catch up on, you won't have time to think about the trial."

Laura pulled away from Andrea and turned to her daughter. "That was very thoughtful, dear. It will be comforting to spend the day with Kitty."

⌘⌘⌘

The day of the trial Andrea lay in bed talking to the Lord, entrusting her grandparents to his care. She had fallen asleep the night before as she read the Psalms. Surprised at how many times they spoke of God's lovingkindness toward his people, she pictured her grandmother in His loving arms and imagined God imparting strength to her grandfather. She prayed that God would prepare the heart of the judge ahead of time and give her grandfather favor with him.

She jumped out of bed and knelt by the front window. As she responded to the brightness of a beautiful day, she felt a rush of warmth. That wonderful presence pulsated through her body and left her feeling confident and peaceful. She could not talk of these things to anyone, though she would have liked to share them.

⌘⌘⌘

Lans was listening to a radio program while assembling a model car and an airplane. Not knowing one car from another, Andrea could not share this interest with him. Cars and airplanes were merely a matter of transportation to her.

After she and Katharine had worked in the kitchen all morning, Andrea dicing potatoes and onions and Katharine preparing a sumptuous meal for her grandparents' return, Andrea took her for a walk over the hills and low lands. The pasture reminded Katharine of the countryside in Holland. "It looks like a pastoral landscape from one of the Dutch masters," she said. Andrea enjoyed her company and found her gentle demeanor comforting.

As they walked toward the woods where the violets and trillium grew in the springtime, Katharine noted each wildflower, from the delicate Queen Anne's lace to the bright yellow buttercups. Andrea entertained her with stories of how the farm had appeared when her parents first bought it.

Conversation flowed between them, tempting Andrea to bring Katharine into her confidence.

"I'd like to make a daisy chain to put around Grandpa's neck when he comes. However the trial comes out, I want him to know that he's a hero to me."

"That's a lovely idea." Katharine, the source of Lans' good looks, radiated like a Madonna when she smiled, soft and compassionate.

"Have you ever braided daisies together, Mrs. Mulder?"

"No, not daisies, but I wove flowers together in Holland. We used to make decorations for banquet tables during tulip season."

"Then you know how to do it. I've never braided anything but daisies."

"I've enjoyed the fresh bouquets in the house. Your grandmother said you picked them."

"Yes, and in the spring I pick different colors of violets and arrange them." Andrea led her into the woods.

"I thought all violets were purple," Katharine said. "My, these woods are lovely. The dense growth makes them dark and mysterious. I can imagine them being inhabited by elves and fairies."

"I've always thought so, too. I used to talk to them when I was younger. They were my playmates. I spent hours alone here imagining that they built homes and tended to the wildflowers. This is where the violets grow. You can still see the plants." Andrea pointed to an abundant growth of long-stemmed, heart-shaped leaves.

"I've always seen them as little plants close to the ground." Katharine seemed surprised at their size.

"They grow taller here than anywhere I've ever seen them. And they come in many colors."

"How lovely." Katharine clapped her hands. "I'd like to see them in bloom."

"Then you'll have to come back in the springtime." Andrea warmed at the thought.

"It won't be difficult to get Lans to come next time. He'll be begging to join us."

Andrea felt herself blush. "Maybe Dad and Dr. Mulder will write a series of books so you can experience it in every season." They both laughed. Andrea felt she had never been so comfortable with an adult outside her family.

She studied her watch. "It's 11:05. Grandma and Grandpa must be in court waiting their turn. I have such a strong urge to pray for them right now." She looked shyly at Katharine. "Would you join me in a prayer for them, Mrs. Mulder?"

"Why certainly, Andrea. I'd be honored to pray with you."

"Let's sit here on this log. I'll start, and you finish." She patted the log, encouraging Katharine to sit beside her.

The passage of time slowed and the woods, dark and cool, evoked the essence of eternity. The tall trees guarded the woods like giant pillars around an exquisite temple. Katharine spoke her thoughts. "It's easy to believe in a great God when you see the magnitude of His creation."

"Yes, I know He's watching over them. No problem is too great for Him, even if it seems overwhelming to us."

"That is wisdom beyond your years, Andrea." Katharine took Andrea's hand in hers and bowed her head.

Andrea prayed aloud for favor with the judge and expressed her simple trust that God would take care of her grandparents. She asked that he bring the case to a close and not let anything delay the hearing this time. Katharine took up Andrea's thought that no problem was too difficult for him and thanked him that he knew the end from the beginning and that he was directing the proceedings to bring about his good will. She squeezed Andrea's hand when they finished.

Katharine jumped up from the log. "Let's fix lunch for the men and start making that garland of daisies. I have a feeling God has it all under control, and they'll be back long before we expect them."

⌘⌘⌘

Lans joined Andrea and Katharine in the field where they worked on the flowers. "Hi! What are you two up to?"

"We're making daisy chains to honor my grandparents when they return. Do you want to help?"

"Sure, if you can teach a guy."

"This is the way you do it." Andrea illustrated how she placed one stem over another. "Have you ever braided hair or a rope?"

"He never had the good fortune to have a sister whose hair he could braid." Katharine sighed.

"A rope then?"

"No, just show me. I'll catch on."

"You take three stems of daisies and cross them over like this. Then you keep adding another one and weaving it into the others."

"This is what it looks like." Katharine held up a chain already a dozen flowers long.

"I see you do know how it's done." Andrea admired her work.

"I've got the idea," Lans said. "Just go ahead and do what you've planned and leave me to my own devices. I have to go to the house, but I'll be right back."

As Andrea worked on a long chain to go around Fritz's neck, Katharine made a crown for Laura's head. Lans worked in silent determination, throwing a flower away now and then when it didn't fit to his satisfaction.

"Hey, what do you do with the end of it when it's long enough?" He held his up and looked at the awkward stems sticking out the bottom.

"May I help?" Andrea asked.

"Sure." He gave his creation to Andrea and watched as she cut off the awkward ends, tucked the braided stems under the flower heads, and tied them in place with a green thread.

"There." She handed it back to him. "But it's rather short. What do you plan to do with it?"

"Come here," he said, leaning toward her. He took the braided daisies and placed them across the top of her head. Then, reaching into his pocket, he brought forth two of his mother's bobby pins and fastened the chain to Andrea's hair just above her ears. He sat back on his heels. "Now that looks great. You should wear flowers in your hair every day."

He enjoyed Andrea's blush, as if he had crowned her with gold.

"That's beautiful, Lans," his mother said, "and you look wonderful wearing it, Andrea. What a lovely idea this has been. I can't wait for your grandparents' return."

"But what happens if it's bad news?" Lans said.

Katharine spoke with confidence. "The Lord is bringing about a happy ending, isn't he, Andrea?"

Katharine and Andrea smiled at each other as though they were good friends sharing a secret.

⌘ ⌘ ⌘

The three of them returned to the house and laid the crown and garland on a shelf in the refrigerator. Katharine sprinkled the daisy heads with water to keep them fresh. Soon Evelyn's car came roaring up the driveway. As it approached the house, Evelyn tooted the horn wildly.

Andrea looked at Katharine, and Katharine looked at Andrea. "It must be good news!" they said almost in unison.

"Quick, get the flowers." Andrea's heart beat fast, and she felt like laughing and crying all at once. "Oh, may it be so."

Katharine thrust the garland into Andrea's hands, took the crown, and opened the screen door. Andrea galloped through it and over the side of the porch, reaching the car just as Fritz opened the door. She searched his face until she caught the twinkle in his eye.

"You won, you won, didn't you, Gramps? Hail the conquering hero," she cried as she put the garland over his neck. Fritz took her in his arms and whirled her around like he used to do.

"Yes, honey. The judge said they had no case against me whatsoever. It's over. It really is over at last."

"I told you God would take care of you, didn't I?"

"Yes, you did, Andrea, and you be sure to thank him for us, will you? We've been praising his name all the way home."

"It would have been nice if he'd done it a little sooner," Evelyn said as she helped her mother from the car.

"Now, Evelyn, we're just grateful it's over. Don't think about anything else on such a happy day," her father reprimanded her.

Katharine held out the crown toward Andrea, who took it and rushed around the car to her grandmother. "Grandma, Grandma, it's so wonderful." She hugged her hard. "And here's a crown for you for standing with Grandpa all that time. You're to be the guests of honor at a Dutch feast tonight."

Lans came forward to shake Fritz's hand. "Congratulations, Mr. Klinghof. I can't wait to hear what the judge said. Mrs. Klinghof, what great news." He took the liberty of giving Laura a hug.

"We walked into the courtroom at nine sharp. When I saw the judge in his black robe pound his gavel, I was numb. I couldn't concentrate on anything. I was glad Andrea was praying for us because I couldn't. After two cases he called out *Ferucchi and Hasselbach vs. Klinghof.* I jumped and my heart almost stopped," Fritz said. "It was approaching 11:00."

Andrea looked wide-eyed at Katharine, and Katharine smiled at Andrea and nodded, her face lighting with the realization of the timing.

Laura carried on the story. "He read over the case and asked a few questions of Fritz's lawyer. He looked back at his papers a minute, stared hard at the Ferruchis and Mrs. Hasselbach as though he were reading their minds, took off his glasses with one hand, and reached for his gavel with the other. 'I see absolutely no case against this man.' He struck his gavel and said, 'Case dismissed.' And it was over. Just like that." Laura crossed her hands over her heart and let out some involuntary sobs. "It's over. It really is over." She went from one to the other, giving everyone a hug, stopping before Leonard and Dr. Mulder, who had come out while she was reciting the facts of the trial.

"You were right, Leonard, they had no case against Fritz, but why did it take them so long to find it out?"

"Incompetent and underpaid lawyers, I imagine. No one pushed for the trial. Your opponents must have thought time was on their side, but justice prevailed." He accepted Laura's embrace and reached out his hand. "Congratulations, Fritz. I'm happy for you."

Had her father any idea how great a toll the long wait had taken on her grandparents? He had been so sure there was no case, had not offered help, believing there was no need. Should she have broken her promise and told him years earlier?

Too late for such thoughts. She turned her full attention to her grandparents. Taking each of them by the hand and half dancing, half marching, she led them into the house. "Hail the conquering heroes. Justice has been done," she chanted.

14

"Hey, Andrea, look at this. I just figured out how I can jump farther out in the loft. If I start in this corner and run on a diagonal across the platform, I can gain more momentum." Three days before the end of the Mulders' visit, Andrea and Lans competed to see who could jump the farthest in the hayloft.

"Be careful you don't land against the wall," she cautioned as he took a flying leap over her head and succeeded in landing farther out than either of them had before.

"Gosh, you were right," he admitted. "I could see that wall coming at me. I guess I better adjust the angle."

"That makes sense to me," Andrea said in a superior voice. "Anyway, I don't know whom you're trying to impress. You already have my undying admiration."

"I'm not trying to impress anyone, Miss Know-It-All." He bounded over to her and grabbed a handful of hay and stuffed it down her back.

"Help, I'm being attacked," she screamed as he stuffed another handful down her shirt.

Andrea wasted no time in defending herself. She picked up an armful of hay and threw it directly into his face.

"Hey, dirty dog," he spluttered and choked as the hay dust entered his mouth and nose. "If that's the way you want to play, try this." He scooped up all he could handle and hurled it at her.

Andrea saw it coming and spun, successfully ducking but falling into the hay. Lans rushed over and tackled her like a football, even though she was already down. Suddenly on top of her, he held her arms behind her back.

"Lans, I'm neither a football nor a football player. Remember, I'm a girl and I'm breakable." She looked up into his face, wondering what he would do next. She was not afraid of him. But, uncertain where this was going, she thought it should stop.

Lans dropped his hold and let her fall back in the hay, still standing on his knees above her. His warrior mood vanished. "I'd never hurt you, Andrea. You know that, don't you?"

"Yes, I think so," she said, staring at the warring image towering over her.

He fell back at her side and took her hand. "You're a great sport, Andrea. I forgot for a minute that you're not a guy. Most of the time, I'm all too aware of that."

They lay beside each other for a time in silence.

"I'm going to miss you, Andrea. Our time is almost up."

"I'll write you if you'll write me," she said in a soft voice, hoping she wasn't being too forward.

"Of course, I'll write. Wouldn't it be great if we lived in the same city? I wonder when we'll see each other again."

"I told your mother about the violets in the spring, and she said she'd like to see them. The fall colors are great, too, and remember you're going to learn to ice skate so you can skate on the lake in the winter."

"It all sounds great, but we're kidding ourselves. Our dads don't even have enough time to attend our games. They're not going to be hauling us across the country to see each other." A now familiar note of bitterness sounded in his voice.

She rolled over and stroked his arm. "Don't sound bitter, Lans. It doesn't become you. You have great parents. I respect your dad, and I really love your mother. She's sweet and sensitive. I could be best friends with her."

"I was surprised how well you two hit it off, but I guess I shouldn't be. You're a lot like her."

"That's a compliment. I'd like to be like her when I grow up, but I think I'm not nearly so kind and considerate."

"You are when you want to be."

She smiled at him and reached out to touch his forehead and wipe away the frown that had settled there. He pulled her down against him and gently kissed her cheek. "We'll see each other again, Andrea, I promise."

"I'll always remember that promise," she whispered. Her heart raced. She felt light-headed, as if she might faint, but taking control of herself, she jumped up and tugged at his hand. "It's time for us to shower and get ready for dinner. Remember, the men are stopping early tonight so we can play Canasta and it's my turn to win."

"It's too early for dinner." His eyes pleaded with her not to end this special time together. Andrea's head spun and her heart pounded. Not knowing what to do, she retreated.

"It was a great afternoon," she said, consoling him as they descended the ladder. Jumping the last few rungs, she turned and ran toward the house.

⌘⌘⌘

The next day Fritz planned to harvest the hay and store it in the barn. Up and dressed early, Andrea accompanied him to the barn to help with the chores.

"You two going to help bring in the hay today or make it harder?" Fritz asked as he opened the gate for the mooing cows.

"We're going to help, of course," she said, offended that he would doubt it.

"I thought you were more interested in riding the hay wagon with your fella," he teased.

"He isn't my fella, Gramps, and you know it."

"Really? With the way you two are always together, you could have fooled me." A bemused expression suggested he knew more than he was letting on. "In here, Rosemary. You take this one, Jemima Lady." He prodded the cows into their proper stalls and reached for the milking pail.

"I'm looking forward to riding the hay wagon with Lans. It will be the first time he's ever experienced anything like that."

"Seems like he's experiencing one new thing after another this summer. He'll never be the same."

"Neither will I."

Fritz stopped tugging on Rosemary's teats and looked at Andrea. "No, I don't guess you will. Won't ever be satisfied with just your grandpa around the farm again."

"'Course I will, Gramps," she protested, but she knew he spoke a measure of truth.

"It's okay, honey. I can still remember what it was like when I first met Laura. Why, she was the prettiest thing I ever laid eyes on. It wasn't long 'til I knew my life would never be the same again. She was the only person in the world I wanted to be near."

"Tell me about it, Grandpa. What was it like when you first met Grandma?"

"Well, we were a bit older than you and Lans. I was nineteen, and she was seventeen. She was shy and didn't say much, but she was pretty as a picture. I knew right away that inside her was a heart of gold, and she'd never let me down my whole life long."

"Was it love at first sight?"

"Yes, it was, sweetheart. I came to call on her every Sunday afternoon after that. We used to sit on the big front porch at her parents' home, rock back and forth on the swing, and talk. There weren't any movies to go to in those days and no one did anything on Sunday after church but eat and visit.

She started asking me over for Sunday dinner and I always said yes. Her mother, as good a cook as Laura, would bake an extra apple pie for me to take home. She knew the way to a man's heart, she did.

"On Sunday evenings Laura would play the piano and we would all gather round and sing. Sometimes it was hymns, sometimes popular songs. She could play them all. Other young men came to call, some for Laura, some for her sisters. She had three of them, but she was the closest to my age and the only one that caught my fancy. I never looked at another woman once I met my Laura."

"You've had a really happy life, haven't you, Gramps?"

"Yes, child, we have. I never made a lot of money like your father, but we had a good life, and I was always there when my children needed me."

"I wish my father was there more often for me."

"I know, dear heart, but he's a mighty important man, and he's in demand all over the world. You give up one thing and you gain another," he said philosophically.

"How long did you visit Grandma before you asked her to marry you?"

"Seems like it was about nine months. It was in the springtime. We were walking home from church one beautiful day, smelling the blossoms in bloom, and I couldn't stand it any longer. I took her hand and got down on my knee right out there in the middle of the lane and said, 'Laura, honey, there isn't another woman in the world I want to spend the rest of my life with but you.' She looked down at me with her hazel eyes, and her face lit with a smile.

"'Laura, honey, will you marry me? I'll spend the rest of my life trying to make you happy.' She just continued to look me over for the longest time. Finally, she said, 'Yes, Fritz, I will.' I got off my knees and jumped up and threw my cap into the air and shouted, 'Woweeee!' Then I scooped her up in my arms and whirled her around right there in the middle of the lane. When I set her down, I kissed her for the first time. I'll never forget it," he said as he stopped milking and looked upward. "The sky was blue, the birds were singing, the blossoms smelled so sweet, and my girl loved me back."

"Gramps, I never knew you were so romantic."

"I wasn't born old, sweetheart. And I feel the same way about her now that I did then. Only I know her a whole lot better. You never know when you marry what a person is really like. Some people wake up after the honeymoon and find out they've made a terrible mistake, but for my honey and me, it just got better."

Meows of hunger from the mother cat and her three kittens broke his reverie. Fritz picked up his stool and pail, poured fresh milk into the cats'

94

bowl, and moved on to the next cow, still shaking his head at the wonder of the life he had shared with Laura.

⌘⌘⌘

On their final night together Andrea and Lans sat alone on the porch swing, marveling at how bright the moon was even though it was beginning to wane. Andrea leaned back against the side of the swing for a better view of Lans' profile.

"I don't think I'll ever be as happy living in the city again," he said, "especially in summer. I'll remember racing through the fields, swinging on the rope, plunging into the swimming hole, rowing on the lake, jumping in the hay, chasing fireflies at night. I'll be working in an office, going to the movies at night, and thinking of you doing all those things here on the farm, Andrea."

"You'll come again sometime, Lans. I know you will." She gazed at him, imploring it to be so. Being an only child, Andrea had learned to entertain herself. In fact, she rather enjoyed her solitary adventures here on the farm when she could enhance the woodlands with magical qualities. But now that she had experienced them with Lans, could she ever be content to be here alone again? "Good-byes are so hard. There's so much running through my mind, yet it doesn't need to be said."

"Maybe not," he replied, "but say it anyway. I don't want it to come to an end." He took one of her hands in both of his. "Andrea, I never liked a girl before, not like this."

"I'm glad," she said, relieved. "I was afraid you had a lot of girls. I can imagine them flocking around you after a basketball game."

"Yeah, they do. We go out in groups, and there are lots of girls to kid with, but not one on one."

Andrea saw a picture of girls cheering for him when he made a basket and rushing up to congratulate him when the game was over. Cute girls, more sophisticated than she, in short cheerleader skirts. Jealous even though he denied caring for them, she imagined them sliding into a booth next to him at the local hangout after the game. She struggled to hold back tears.

"Would you like to take a walk? It's a lovely night."

"Okay, sure," he said.

They walked around the lake hand in hand. The moon sparkled on the water. "It's a great little lake, Andrea. I never had so much fun on so small a body of water. Tell your dad it was a great idea to build it."

"I will. Let's sit on the dock and dangle our feet in the water." Pulling his hand, she led him to the end of the dock. Slipping out of her sandals, she sat on the edge. "It's warm compared to the night breeze," she said, kicking water into the air.

Lans removed his shoes and plunged his feet into the water next to hers. "Yeah, it feels great." His foot brushed hers and a shiver of excitement ran through her. When his foot found hers again, she didn't withdraw it. He put his arm around her shoulder and held her close, his feet playing with hers under the water.

They sat in silence enjoying the night sounds, the frogs croaking, the chirping of the crickets in the fields around them, the hoot of an owl in the distance. Andrea didn't have the words to communicate all that was on her heart. It was so new, so fresh, first love they would never experience again. She knew it and sensed Lans knew it, too. She believed he wanted time to stand still as much as she did.

The clock ticked the hours away. Lans kept his arm around her. When Andrea found the courage to lay her head on his shoulder, it felt good and natural, like it was where she belonged. He stroked her hair with his other hand. No longer afraid, she wanted to stay there forever.

Lans held up his watch to the moon. "It's almost midnight, Andrea. Are you tired?"

"No."

"Me, neither. Are you cold?"

"No, but your arm feels good around me."

"Our feet will look like prunes," he observed.

"I don't care," she said, rubbing his feet once more with hers.

"Me neither."

They lapsed into silence again, a comfortable silence. Neither felt it necessary to think of something to say. It was just good to be together.

After a time, he spoke again. "Andrea."

"Yes."

"We will see each other again, I promise."

Her heart leaped as a longing deep inside stirred. "I'll be waiting," she whispered. Tears formed in her eyes until she could no longer hold them back. When they spilled over, she reached her hand to wipe them away, alerting Lans.

He turned toward her, put his hand under her chin, and lifted her face to his. "Andrea, don't cry. This isn't the end. You'll see." His voice sounded choked as if he, too, wanted to cry. He kissed away the tears falling from

Andrea's eyes and held her in his arms. Neither of them moved for several minutes. Nothing more was said.

Deep in thought, they did not hear approaching footsteps or see the light from her father's flashlight.

"It's tough, kids," he said. "I remember how hard it was to part from Evelyn when her smile invited me to stay, but it's time to go to bed. Lans has a long trip ahead of him tomorrow."

"Yes, Dad. Thanks," Andrea said, grateful that he was not angry. They pulled away from each other and reached for their shoes. Leonard waited until they had collected themselves and followed them to the house.

At the foot of the steps, he hesitated. "There's still tomorrow morning. Good night."

"Good night, Dad."

"Good night, Mr. Collins."

Leonard disappeared into his room and left them standing in the hall. Andrea faced Lans. "Good night, Lans. It was a lovely evening." She turned to go, but he reached out, took her hand, and drew her to him.

"Good-bye, Andrea," he whispered, "'til next time." He bent down and kissed her on the lips, hugged her once more, and turned and disappeared into his room.

Andrea staggered toward her door. She opened and shut it behind her, ran across her room, and threw herself on her bed, allowing the pent-up tears to flow freely.

15

The magazine on her lap slipped onto the floor. Before she could bend over and reach for it, the maître d' quickened his stride, picked it up, and handed it to her. She gazed up at him with glistening eyes. "Don't worry, Mrs. Mulder. Mr. Mulder called again and said the meeting has just finished. He'll be here in another fifteen minutes."

"Thank you, Harold. I'm not distressed. Just remembering some very happy times," she said, smiling to reassure him.

"Yes, Mrs. Mulder. Would you like me to seat you at your table?"

"No, I'm fine right here. It only seems like a moment ago that I sat down. I'll be fine."

She cast the magazine aside and reached for her pocketbook. Dabbing her eyes, she sighed. *Lans, what have we lost? No, it isn't too late. Somehow we can find our way back.*

The picture of Lans promising her that last night on the farm, all those years ago, that they would see each other again remained strong in her mind. She could still see the earnestness in his eyes as they pleaded with her to believe him. She had believed him, and it was that promise that had made the years of loneliness bearable.

She remembered feeling that she would never be the same, that her capacity to love and to care for others had expanded like a damned-up stream, released to flow unhampered. It formed a deep well inside her from which her spirit could drink. She knew even then it would affect all her future relationships. They would either suffer from comparison or succeed if they approximated that first experience. Her friends had described hasty, mushy first kisses with boys they hardly knew while playing games like Spin the Bottle, but God had given her a special gift.

The memories of the years of waiting that followed that summer crowded in on her. A year and a half later, as she prepared for Christmas, Andrea's heart still ached when she thought of Lans, but the pain of their separation had dimmed with the passage of time.

⌘⌘⌘

The winter she was sixteen, Andrea moved an iron back and forth over the plaid taffeta skirt of her first formal dress. She had been invited to a Christmas dance by one of the boys on her neighborhood softball team. Her friendships with boys, since Lans, had centered in sports.

She pressed out the wrinkles from the full skirt, careful not to touch the black velvet top with the iron. The black blouse showed off her blond hair, making her look years older and much more sophisticated. What would Lans think if he could see her wearing it?

She slipped the long dress over her head, zipped it tight, and twirled. Would she be able to keep step with her partner? In spite of Evelyn's persistent attempts to persuade her to join her classmates' cotillion, she had been too interested in sports to take dancing lessons. Staring into the mirror, she thought Lans would want to place a red poinsettia in her hair to match the plaid of her skirt. "Oh, Lans, if only I were going to the dance with you."

She stepped out of the dress and hung it in her closet. Setting out her shoes and stockings, jewelry, and undergarments, she placed the right color lipstick, compact, comb, and mad money in her new evening bag and set it on top of her white evening wrap. Running her fingers through its downy softness, she was as ready as she could be for the big event.

Settling down in the comfortable chair in her bedroom, she lost herself in her book until the ring of the phone startled her.

"Andrea," she heard her mother calling up the steps, "the phone is for you."

"Thanks, Mom." Laying her book aside, she ambled down the hall to her parents' bedroom and picked up the phone. "Hello, this is Andrea."

"Hello, Andrea."

"Lans," she screamed, instantly recognizing his voice. "Where are you?"

"I'm in Ohio with my parents, and we'll be in Pittsburgh tomorrow evening."

"Tomorrow evening. Oh, Lans!"

"What's wrong? Can't you see me tomorrow evening?"

"Why didn't you tell me sooner that you were coming?"

"I didn't know for sure until tonight. I kept asking my parents to stop on the way home, and Dad wasn't sure he could wind up his business in time, but he'll be finished after lunch, and we can drive over. We should get in around four o'clock."

"I'll cancel my date. I won't go to the dance. I'd much rather be with you," Andrea said, distressed.

"You'll do no such thing, young lady," Evelyn said from her post at the door. "You've promised Charlie the evening, and you can't break your commitment."

"But, Mother, it's Lans, and I haven't seen him in nearly two years. You can't make me go out with someone else." Crying now, Andrea felt her world spinning out of control.

"Give me the phone, Andrea."

Andrea handed the phone to her mother and threw herself on the bed.

"Hello, Lans, this is Andrea's mother. I'm very sorry, but Andrea has made a commitment to attend a formal dance tomorrow night, and it's too late for her to break it. Why don't you and your parents come here after you check in to your hotel and have dinner with Leonard and me? Andrea will be dressed, and you can spend whatever time is left together. That's the best I can do. Her date is picking her up at 6:30."

"All right, Mrs. Collins. Thank you. I'm sure my parents will enjoy seeing you and your husband. May I speak to Andrea?"

"Certainly." She handed the phone to Andrea, who struggled to compose herself.

"I'm sorry, Andrea. I was so excited about seeing you that I never considered you might be going out with someone else. I didn't want to tell you we were coming and then disappoint us both." He sounded older, a little distant. Was it just disappointment that she had a date?

"I'm the one who's sorry, Lans. I want to see you so much." She had no shame in admitting it.

"I'm at a phone booth, Andrea. It's hard to hear you. I'll call you as soon as we reach the hotel, so you'll know when to expect us. I'm disappointed, too, but at least we'll have some time together."

"All right, Lans. I can hardly wait." She hung up the phone and glared at her mother. "Mother, haven't I always done everything you've asked of me? Don't you realize how important this is to me?"

"Yes, I do, but a commitment is a commitment, and you must honor it."

"I won't be able to give Charlie a good time. I'll make him miserable thinking I could be home with Lans."

"Just this afternoon, you were all excited about wearing your new dress."

"That was before Lans called. Charlie isn't anything to me, and Lans is everything."

"I'm sorry, dear. I feel it's important for you to keep your social obligations." Evelyn pivoted and started down the steps, leaving Andrea to deal with her disappointment.

"Mom, plllease....," she called after her.

⌘ ⌘ ⌘

The clock on the landing struck five, and still she had not heard from Lans. Agitated and nervous about seeing him, she had showered and dressed. What might have been a pleasure had become a nightmare. The falling snow turned into a blizzard. According to the radio, traffic was creeping like a wounded turtle. She groaned and paced back and forth in her bedroom. What would Lans think of her in her dress? Just yesterday she had wanted him to see her in it. Now it was the last thing she wanted him to see.

The telephone rang. She raced down the hall. "Hello," she said, holding her breath.

"Hello, Andrea, we're here. The roads are terrible, and traffic has slowed to a crawl. It will take us at least half an hour to get to your house."

"Oh, do hurry, Lans. Our time is ticking away so fast."

"Believe me: I'll do the best I can."

Andrea put down the phone, thrilled just to hear his voice. She stomped downstairs in her unaccustomed dress shoes and into the kitchen, where her mother fussed over dinner.

"Mother, they're here, and it isn't too late. I can call Charlie and tell him I'm sick and I'm very sorry, but he really wouldn't want to go with me."

"Andrea, we've been all through this. It would be even worse to do it an hour before he picks you up."

"I'll have so little time with Lans. I can't bear it."

"Take him down to the game room when he arrives, dear. I've set out cokes and hors d'oeuvres. You can be with him alone until Charlie arrives." Then Evelyn paused. Crossing the room, she put her arms around her daughter. "This is very hard on you, isn't it? I'm sorry two such important things are happening to you at the same time."

Andrea pushed away from her, tears streaming down her face. "Don't you understand? There's only one important thing, and that's seeing Lans."

"Go up and wash your face and put your makeup on again. You don't want to be crying when he arrives."

Tripping over her long dress, Andrea ran up the stairs and rushed into the bathroom. She splashed cold water on her face. Greeting Lans with red eyes and a swollen face was the last thing she wanted to do.

When the doorbell rang, she draped her evening jacket over her arm, grabbed the elegant little purse, and rushed down the stairs. Evelyn opened the door, and there he stood.

Andrea swept down the remaining stairs. "Hello, Lans," she said, formally putting forth her hand.

He took it in both of his and stared at her speechless. The snow blew into the house. "Come in, come in, Lans, before the great outdoors comes in with you. Run along to the basement now, children. Well, Katharine, Johan, there you are. Come in. Come in. It's so good to see you."

Andrea led Lans down the basement steps and into the paneled game room. As promised, Evelyn had set up everything they could possibly want on the coffee table. Neither of them cared about food or drink, but Andrea played the gracious hostess and busied herself serving Lans.

Lans found his voice. "I've thought about this moment for such a long time, Andrea, but I never pictured you grown up and dressed to go out with another man. It's like you're somebody else."

"Oh, but I'm not." Andrea lost her sophistication. "Look, here are the pictures we took at the farm the summer you were there. I'm the same person you knew then." It was her turn to look at him. "You've grown up, too, Lans. You must be two inches taller and two years older."

"Something like that." He laughed for the first time and looked at his watch. "Andrea, we have forty-five minutes after two long years. I don't know where to begin." He fumbled in his pocket and extended a small package toward her. "Here, I've brought you a Christmas present."

"Oh, how sweet of you. Shall I open it now?"

"Sure."

Andrea untied the ribbon and tore off the Christmas wrapping paper. She pried open the small box and lifted a layer of cotton. There lay a silver pin of a standing horse saddled with a Western saddle. "It looks just like Dolly. I love it, Lans. When I wear it, I'll think of our wonderful days riding together. Thank you, thank you so much."

She looked up to see him smiling as happily as she. "They were wonderful times, Andrea. I'll never forget them."

"Do you ever ride now? You never mention it in your letters."

"No, we have some stables on Long Island, but no hayfields and daisies. It wouldn't be the same."

"Tell me about your life. Is it different now?"

"Not a whole lot. More responsibilities. I work at Dad's office doing research on the weekends and during summer break now. School is about the same, only a little more homework."

"Do you know where you're going to college?"

"I'm interested in Dartmouth. How 'bout you?"

"I'd like to go to a co-ed school like Northwestern. I hear good things about it, but Mom is still pulling for Smith."

"Northwestern is awfully far from Dartmouth."

"Would it make any difference?"

"It would to me."

"I bet you have all kinds of girls in New York who'd come to a Dartmouth weekend in a minute if you asked them."

"A few, but there's safety in numbers. There's never been one special one except you." He slipped his arm around her on the couch and she leaned her head on his shoulder as she had two years ago.

His arm around her again sent tingling sensations up and down her spine. They talked about everything and nothing. Time seemed in a desperate hurry, passing so fast it left her breathless.

"We don't have time to bridge the gap of two years," she said, looking at his watch. "We have only ten minutes left."

"Ten minutes. After all this time, it's like nothing."

"But I'm so glad I've seen you, Lans. I always believed your promise that we'd meet again."

"I kept it, didn't I?" he beamed at her.

"I've been thinking of writing to you that our Glee Club is doing a competition concert in Connecticut in the spring. I have a terrible voice, but I joined it this year."

Lans' expression brightened. "You mean you might be able to come to Long Island on your way home?"

"Maybe. Do you want me to work on it?"

"Hey, that would be great." He sounded like he had the summer he was fifteen.

"I'll ask my parents and find out what the schedule is. Your girlfriends in Garden City won't be jealous, will they?"

"Who cares? Gosh, that would be super."

The doorbell rang.

"Oh, no, he's early." Her good spirits sank to her feet. "I love the pin, Lans. I'll wear it all the time and think of you." She gathered up her coat and held it out to him to help her. When her arms were in all the way, he hugged her back and buried his face in the soft fur. Evelyn called down that Charlie was here for Andrea.

She whirled and looked at Lans. If the moment were not so pressured, she would have burst into tears again. She threw her arms around his neck and hugged him, pressing her cheek against his. "I'll always love you," she whispered in his ear. She reached for her evening bag, grabbed her long skirt, and ran up the steps without looking back. Lans followed behind her.

"Hello, Charlie," she said. "I'm ready."

"Gee, Andrea, you look beautiful. I've never seen you look so good."

"It beats my softball uniform, does it?" she said all smiles, determined to carry this off since she had no other choice.

Charlie caught sight of Lans emerging from the basement after Andrea. "Who's this?" he blurted out.

Lans looked Charlie over with obvious disapproval. "I'm a friend from her past."

"Charlie, this is Lans Mulder. He's the son of my father's coauthor. Two years ago our parents made us entertain each other for three weeks at our farm." She winked at Lans. "They surprised us by stopping on their way back to New York. Lans, this is Charlie Stump. We play softball together."

She left the boys to greet the Mulders. "It was good to see you if only for a moment. Next time please give us advance notice. There's so much I'd like to share with you, Mrs. Mulder."

She took the arm Charlie offered, smiled at Lans, and said, "This hardly counts. I'll still expect you to keep that promise." She swept out the door with grace, but once outside, her spirit crumbled. How could she possibly endure the evening, knowing that Lans was having dinner at her house without her?

16

Andrea stared out the window watching the snow swirl around the driveway on Christmas Eve. Heavy flakes piled high on trees and parked cars filling her heart with apprehension. Her grandparents should have arrived by four o'clock. No one answered at the farm. They must be somewhere on the road between there and Pittsburgh.

Andrea remembered the afternoon she had waited for Lans to arrive. She felt the same anxiety, but for different reasons. As important as that had been to her, this could be far more serious.

She could still feel the emptiness she experienced when Charlie closed the car door beside her. Everything in her wanted to open that door and run inside to Lans. She had acted well in taking her leave, but regrets swept over her like an avalanche of snow. Suffocating inside, she could not rise to the occasion and fill the silence with meaningless social chatter.

Charlie made snide comments about his date two-timing him for someone else. She looked at him with disgust, too overwhelmed to make light of it. The subject hung in the air between them. Failing to be the partner she should have been, she could think of nothing to say to him.

Had her mother accomplished anything for Charlie or for anyone else by insisting she honor her commitment for the evening? It still made no sense.

The clock struck six. Her apprehension rose as darkness descended and the snowstorm became a blizzard. Her aunt and uncle arrived with their families for Christmas Eve dinner. Evelyn directed the cook to hold dinner until her parents arrived.

Instead of enjoying her young cousins, Andrea barked at them to simmer down. She searched for Evelyn in the kitchen. "Mother, shouldn't we call the police? Something's wrong."

"I don't know, dear, there must be some explanation. Ask your father."

By the time she reached the bottom of the stairs, the phone rang. She grabbed the receiver. "Hello." She could hear muffled crying. "Grandma, is that you? It's Andrea. Are you all right? Where are you? What's happened?"

"Grandpa was hit by a Mack truck," she sobbed.

"Grandma, are you serious? A Mack truck? Gramps?" It was too much for Andrea to take in all at once. It couldn't be true.

"We started late. We were so busy getting ready, Grandpa never thought about gas for the car," she said between choking sobs. "We ran out on a country road. It was snowing so we waited, hoping someone would stop and take Grandpa to a gas station or call the police for help. Finally we got a ride to a station. We left the car on the roadside."

"Grandma, I can hardly hear you. Just a minute." Andrea placed her hand over the mouthpiece and bellowed, "Quiet everyone. Grandpa's been hurt. Someone put Dad on the phone." One of the cousins raced by her up the stairs.

"Grandma, go ahead, but first tell me how bad it is."

"I don't know." Her grandmother sobbed in earnest now. "They've called an ambulance. We're waiting for it to arrive."

Andrea's father broke in. "I'll handle this, Andrea. Where are you, Laura? Andrea, go tell your mother to get on the phone."

Andrea laid the receiver on the table. She was shaking all over as she ran to the kitchen. "Didn't you hear the phone, Mom? It's Grandma."

"Is she all right?"

"Grandpa isn't. Dad wants you to pick up the phone." Having delivered her message, she raced back to the phone in the hall and listened to the terrible news.

"It was almost dark when we arrived at the station. Fritz got out of the car and stepped out between the pumps. The truck driver didn't see him until it was too late. He slammed on his brakes but still ran into Fritz and knocked him down."

"He didn't run over him," she heard her father saying.

"No, but he's unconscious. The owner called the ambulance right away. No one knows how serious it is." Her grandmother started a fresh outburst.

"Mom, Mom, what's happened?" Evelyn broke in.

"Just listen, Evelyn. I'm trying to get the story. What hospital are they taking him to, Laura?"

"Allegheny General."

"You go with him in the ambulance, and I'll meet you there. Don't worry about the car. It will still be there tomorrow and I'll take care of it. Now try to calm yourself and be ready to act like he's going to be fine in case he comes to. I'll be waiting for you at the emergency entrance. Try not to worry, and everything will be all right."

"Yes, thank you, Leonard. I appreciate your help. I hear the ambulance coming now."

"Good. If you get there first, don't worry. I'll find you."

"We'll be praying, Grandma," Andrea said before she hung up the phone.

⌘⌘⌘

Christmas Eve dinner and Christmas Day were the saddest Andrea could remember. Leonard left for the hospital insisting Evelyn stay and feed her guests. Stunned by the news, the family gathered around the dinner table with solemn faces. Her uncle failed to give the traditional prayer of thanksgiving for the Christmas family celebration and begged the Lord to bring Fritz back to them. Evelyn carried on as though this were just another social dinner. When everyone was served, Evelyn burst into tears and ran up the steps to her room.

⌘⌘⌘

Fritz did recover, and he and Laura returned to the farm, but something had changed. Fritz still joked like always. He still rose early to do the morning chores, but sometimes he returned to the house without finishing them. He could no longer keep track of his glasses. Bewildered by the change in him, Laura did her best to tend to his needs.

Andrea visited them in April, when the violets peeped through the ground and the trees burst with new life. Delighted to see her, Fritz asked the same questions of her again and again. "I've already told you, Gramps. Don't you remember?" she would remind him.

"So you did," he would say, lifting his cap and scratching his head beneath the bush of white hair that never seemed to thin. "So you did, darlin'." Yet he would ask the same question again a few minutes later.

Laura fussed over Andrea as she always had. Apple pies graced the windowsills and noodles hung on racks all around the kitchen. Things looked the same; but everything was different, leaving Andrea with the feeling she had suffered a great loss.

⌘⌘⌘

In May Andrea celebrated her seventeenth birthday. The next weekend she flew with her schoolmates to Hartford, Connecticut, to enter the competition for outstanding choirs from girls' schools around the country. After the competition, she planned to take a local flight from Hartford to LaGuardia to spend the rest of the day and night with Lans and his family on Long Island.

The competition went well, and the taxi taking Andrea and one other girl to the airport picked them up at 2:10 for the 3:00 pm flight. While the driver lifted their bags into the trunk, Andrea climbed inside, checked her tickets, and chatted with her friend, who planned to visit her divorced father. The girls exchanged excitements about their respective adventures.

Soon Andrea noticed that the driver had made a good many turns. He pulled into a station and asked directions. "Driver, you do know the way to the airport, don't you?"

"Thought I did," he said, "but I guess I made a wrong turn back there aways. I got it now. Don't worry."

Andrea looked at her watch. "The plane leaves in thirty minutes."

"Plenty of time," he said still confident.

Now Andrea kept her eyes on the road. When the driver pulled off the highway and turned around, her inner alarm sounded loud and clear.

"You really don't know where you're going, do you? How could you take an important job like this and not know your way to the airport?"

"We'll make it, lady. Don't worry."

"We have exactly ten minutes," she said.

The first sign to the airport appeared on the side of the road. "There now. Look at that," he said, pointing to the sign. "Didn't I tell you we'd make it?"

"Eight miles." Andrea groaned. "We won't be there in time."

"Hold on. We'll make it." He pushed down on the gas pedal.

They arrived at the airport at two minutes after three. Andrea ran into the desk without paying the driver or picking up her luggage. "I'm here for the three o'clock plane to LaGuardia."

The man behind the desk nodded out the window. "There she is. Already boarded and moving toward the runway."

"Well, stop it." Andrea raised her voice. "Can't you please stop it? It hasn't taken off yet."

"Sorry, little lady, you missed it. Nothing I can do now."

Andrea ran toward the door as if to stop the plane herself. With propellers twirling, the plane taxied from the gate area. She stood and watched it turn onto the open runway and take off. As it rose higher in the sky and disappeared above the clouds, she despaired. Not only had she missed her plane, she remained at the mercy of the driver who couldn't find his way to the airport. Not knowing what else to do, she returned to the taxi and found her friend crying that she would never see her father.

"Now don't worry, ladies," the driver said. "Where are your destinations?" They both spoke at once, giving him the names of the towns and the addresses of their hosts.

"I'll take you there myself," he offered. "Got any money?"

They consulted their pocketbooks and their wallets. Her friend had forty dollars, and she had thirty. "I'll do it for that," he declared magnanimously.

"But do you know the way?" Andrea asked, suspicious that this would not be as easy as he indicated.

"I have a map right here," he said. "Anybody can follow a map, I guess."

"How long will it take?"

"A couple of hours for the first stop and an hour after that for the second,' he said with confidence.

"That's in Garden City, Long Island," Andrea repeated.

"Yea, like you say."

Andrea ran to the phone in the airport to call Lans at his home. No one answered. She called La Guardia and requested that Lans be paged and told she had missed her plane. She would take a taxi to his home and arrive around 6:00 o'clock.

After her friend called her father, the two of them climbed back into the taxi, congratulating each other that all was not lost. The first hour passed without a problem. The girls relaxed, and Andrea's friend went to sleep. Another hour passed, and it began to rain. An hour after that, they had still not reached New York.

"It's a little longer than I figured," the driver admitted.

"Are you sure you know where you're going?" Andrea began to worry about stopping to call the Mulders to tell them she would be late, but not wanting to waste a minute of her time with Lans, she let the driver drive on. And on he drove, stopping again and again to ask directions. They arrived at her friend's destination at seven o'clock.

"Good-bye, Andrea. I hope you make it tonight. Do you want to come in and call?"

"No, it's only another hour," she said, still believing the driver had some credibility.

Back in the taxi, as they drove on and on, she realized the driver had no idea of distances. What was he doing in this business anyway? Her stomach rigid with strain, she willed him to hurry. She pressed her foot to the floor at every traffic light, hoping he would pass the next car in their way. She sank deeper into despair each time he stopped to ask directions. If only she knew something about the layout of the area or the relationship between New York City and Long Island. He had taken the wrong bridge and driven miles out of the way.

She felt her precious time with Lans slipping away. Could this be happening again? At 11:30 the taxi pulled up to the dark house with the front light shining. They must have gone to bed. She fumbled in her pocketbook and emptied her thirty dollars and small change into the driver's outstretched hand. "I'm sorry. That's all I have. I know it's not enough, but look what you've put us through. I've completely missed my date."

Exhausted by now, she had no fight left. Feeling sorry for the man who had tried to make up for his incompetence, she realized he was far from home with no money to show for his efforts. "I hope you find your way back," she said as she grabbed her bag and ran into the rain and up the steps.

A window opened on the second floor. "Is that you, Andrea? Where have you been? Why didn't you call?"

"Lans, let me in. It's raining."

The window shut with a bang and she could hear him bound down the stairs. He opened the door, and she fell, exhausted, into his arms. The tears she had held back since two minutes after three o'clock poured out on his shoulder.

"Lans, we've missed our time together again. You could never imagine what I've been through." She snuggled against his soft wool sweater. He must have gone to bed in his clothes, just in case she arrived.

"Have you had any dinner?"

"No."

"You must be starved. Come on. I'll get you something to eat while you fill me in. But first tell me just one thing. Why didn't you call?"

"I should have, I know, but I didn't want to waste any more time, and I kept thinking we were close, but we never were. It was a dumb decision. I'm sorry for the worry I caused you and your mother."

Katharine appeared in her bathrobe and slippers at the kitchen door. She put her arms around Andrea. "Don't worry about us. We're so grateful you're here in one piece. We imagined the worst when we didn't hear from you."

"I hope you didn't call my parents," she said, fearing the answer.

"Of course we did, when you seemed to have disappeared altogether, but they weren't home, so they don't know a thing about it."

"What a relief. Dad would be lecturing me for the rest of his life about what to do when you miss a plane. Not that I couldn't have used some advice."

"If we ever try this again," Lans looked very serious, "promise me you'll call at the first indication that things are going wrong."

"Do you suppose this is a sign we'll never spend a relaxed hour in each other's company again?" Andrea looked alarmed. "I suppose we'll laugh about this in years to come, but it doesn't seem very funny right now."

Lans said nothing.

Katharine busied herself putting out food for Andrea. "I'm sorry it's not hot, dear. We kept it warm until almost 10:00 o'clock."

"What can I say but I'm sorry."

"Enjoy yourself while you can and don't stay up all night. You must be completely worn out. I'll see you for breakfast."

Andrea nibbled at the food while telling Lans the agonizing details of the wrong turns, the seven stops to ask directions, the miscalculations of time.

"It must have been a nightmare for you," he said at last. "It sounds like an Abbott and Costello movie where everything goes wrong that could go wrong, but don't forget what it was like for me imagining what could have happened to you."

"Do you think we're ill-fated, Lans?"

"Come here," he said, pointing to his lap.

She obeyed, searching his bright brown eyes. "I always did like that combination of blond hair and brown eyes. God must have been inspired when he made you."

"Hey, you're stealing my lines."

"It's way too late to play hard to get. You know how much the last two visits have meant, and they both slipped through our hands."

"Let's get one thing straight," he said. "We're not ill-fated, and it's wonderful to have you here. There are still a few hours left, and right now I don't care if I ever sleep again. How 'bout you?"

"I might fall asleep on your shoulder, but give me a poke after a few minutes and I'll revive." She studied his face. "You know, I expected it to be awkward until we got to know each other again, but all this pressure has dispensed with the formalities. We can say it like it is. I'm no good at boy-girl games."

"I like you just the way you are. Don't ever change."

"Will you change when you go to college, Lans? Will you step into another world and leave me behind?"

"Maybe for a year or so, but you'll be following right behind me. Tell me, how is the farm? How is your grandfather? Your last letters didn't say much about him."

"I didn't want to put it in writing. He's failing badly. He's never been the same since the accident. What a Christmas. It was horrible."

"I'm sorry, Andrea. What a dreadful thing for your grandmother to bear."

"Yes, it's very hard for her. She doesn't smile much anymore...just frowns all the time, as if she's worried. It started during the long wait for the trial, but it's become much worse since the accident."

"How's Dolly?"

"Doing great."

"Do you still ride her, or is Merchant more your style now?"

"Dolly is my first and only horse. I'll favor her as long as she lives."

"How old is she, Andrea?"

"Don't even ask. It's something I don't discuss."

"Okay, whatever you say. Let's put the food away and go into the living room."

They sat on the couch together and talked far into the night. Like the last evening on the farm, every minute was precious. When the clock struck two, Lans made the decision. "You're falling asleep. We have to be up in four hours."

"What time do I have to leave for Grand Central Station?"

"I'll go in with you and make sure you make it," he said. "We should be gone by 8:30 in the morning."

"Ugh, I guess you're right. Gosh, Lans, even these few hours have been wonderful."

"They have been. And this time doesn't count either. I'll still have to keep my promise."

They held each other's gaze a long time. "I wonder if I'll ever know what goes on in there," she said, pointing to his head. She ruffled his hair and he took her hand to lead her to her room.

He paused outside her door for a final kiss. "You really wouldn't want to know," he said, smiling. "Good night. I'll see you in the morning."

17

Andrea felt a tap on her shoulder and jumped. She raised her hands from her lap and looked up to see Lans standing over her.

"I'm sorry I'm late, darling."

"Actually I've enjoyed the time. I was reminiscing about our first summer on the farm and our crazy attempts to see each other again."

He laughed. "It wasn't quite that hard tonight, but the meeting wouldn't end. Please forgive me for keeping you waiting."

"Of course."

"You look breathtaking. I always did like that dress."

"Yes. I wore it on purpose."

"Thank you for coming." He took her arm and guided her toward the beckoning waiter. "I wasn't sure what I would do if you ignored my invitation."

"Lans, you're more important to me than anyone or anything in the world," she whispered as they reached their table.

The tautness of his face relaxed. He sat across from her and devoured her with his eyes. "I don't want us to talk about anything tonight. Let's just pretend we haven't seen each other for a long time, and we're having a date and getting reacquainted."

"But, Lans, there's so much to talk about."

"Not tonight. Do this for me, Andrea." His eyes as well as his words pleaded with her.

She laid aside all the things she had planned to say. Perhaps they did need a carefree evening together. "Whatever you wish. Order for us, won't you? I don't want to make a decision, and I'd like to be in communion with you. I'll have whatever you chose." She smiled at him and he smiled back. She could tell her acquiescence pleased him. It was a good start.

Lans took charge of the dinner. He ordered their favorite dishes and, for the first time, shared details of his trip to Holland with John and Kate. He spoke of how much they missed her. Hearing that he still cared comforted Andrea. She relaxed and almost forgot the turmoil that dominated their lives.

Soft dinner music played in the background, reminding her of the evening the violinist serenaded her in Paris, and she mentioned it to Lans. He searched her smile. "I have two tickets to Paris next month, Andrea. Come with me."

The challenge took her by surprise. Knowing her answer was pivotal, she struggled for the right reply. For these few hours she had been happy. But here it was again. Her smile faded. "You've broken your own rules, Lans. Give me time."

"Yes, of course. Let's have dessert for a change." He beckoned to the waitress who brought them dessert menus. "Chocolate mousse perhaps? No, here it is, homemade Dutch apple pie à la mode, just like your grandmother used to make. What do you say?"

"Sounds wonderful to me." The evening wasn't spoiled after all, and neither of them wanted it to end. Her smile returned.

The sparkle in his eyes flashed like a diamond catching the beam of the sun.

"I've never told you about my last trip to the farm, have I?"

"You haven't told me much about anything lately." The bitterness of his tone pierced her heart, but she gave no indication that she felt it.

"While you were in Holland with the children, I was at the farm with Mother. Swinging on the porch swing, looking at the field of daisies, I experienced a longing to know the comfort of sharing with my grandmother again. I felt so uneasy about us, I cried out to the Lord for help. I turned the problem over to him and asked him to show me what to do. Then I went up to the room I stayed in as a child, where we took the fireflies the first night we caught them together. Remember?" She explored his face for a hint of tenderness.

"Yes," he said, the tone of bitterness gone.

"I knelt at the little window that looked out on the daisy field. In an instant I felt the same sense of the presence of the Lord that I had felt there as a child. I lay back on the bed and all the tension drained out of me. It was beautiful, Lans. In spite of our problems, God showed me his peace."

"Did he solve your dilemma?" Lans asked, the sarcasm returning.

"Not yet, but here we are together sharing a wonderful evening."

He reached for her hands across the table. "Andrea, stay here with me tonight."

"Lans, I can't leave Mother alone. She might do anything. Come home with me. It's our house together. It's where you belong."

"There we are again. We can't resolve our dilemma by ignoring it, can we?"

"Don't spoil what we have left of the evening. Here comes our apple pie."

Lans ate his dessert in silence while Andrea tried to make light conversation. Lans said nothing. When he had finished, he put down his fork and reached across the table. She met him halfway. He ran his fingers through hers and caressed the back of her hand as it lay on the table. He studied the rings on her fourth finger, avoiding looking into her eyes. "I guess it's time to part," he said.

"Thank you. It was a lovely evening, Lans. For a little while it seemed like old times."

He crushed her hand under his, raised his head, and met her gaze. "Will it ever be like that again, Andrea?" She thought he wanted to cry. She wanted to take him in her arms and comfort him as her grandmother had comforted her, but they were in a public place.

"Of course it will. I promised to love you forever, and I do. Try to understand and have some compassion for Mother. I know she's difficult, but I can't abandon her."

"But you can abandon me?"

"Lans, I don't recognize you. You're only thinking about yourself. Don't you care that I'm torn in two every day we're apart?"

"Is it fair to let a sick woman break up our marriage, Andrea?"

"What if she were your mother?"

"I don't know. It doesn't seem right. I need you now more than ever. The demands of the company are growing every week. I don't have enough strength at the end of the day to be compassionate to forgetful old ladies. All I know is that I want my wife back."

Reaching across the table, she stroked his cheek. A part of him was still a needy little boy. His parents hadn't been there for him when he was young, and now his wife wasn't there for him when he needed her most. Understanding this, she could stop accusing him. "I'll find a way, Lans. Give me a little time."

"I don't seem to have much choice. Come, I'll see you to your car." He was in charge again, the competent Lans who could handle any problem.

⌘ ⌘ ⌘

Lans stayed away. They talked every evening after Evelyn went to bed. He said he didn't have time to come home because he was so busy at work. Andrea didn't believe him, but she let it stand.

She interviewed every potential sitter she could find. Elsa, a kind and compassionate woman Evelyn had known and liked from church, seemed the best choice. Better still, she had previous experience with an Alzheimer's patient.

Elsa sat primly on Andrea's couch dressed in an expensive suit with matching shoes and bag. "Your suit becomes you, Elsa. Where did you find it?" Andrea asked.

"I buy everything at the Consignment Shop near the church. The wealthy ladies in town tire of their outfits after they've worn them a few times. I'm glad you like it."

"Well, aren't you clever? You always look so smart in your clothes. Now I know your secret." Andrea liked her better all the time. "Elsa, I need someone to stay with Mother while I go to Paris for two weeks with my husband. We'll be leaving the second week in October. How would you like to start the first of the month? That will give you time to get used to Mother's routine while I'm still here. And if it works out, perhaps we can talk about a more permanent arrangement when I return.

"I've been thinking about fixing up the apartment over the garage. It hasn't been used for a long time, but it's quite nice, two large rooms, one for each of you and a good-sized kitchen. You could have the run of the house during the day, but it would help if you and Mother had dinner over there so I can give all my attention to my husband in the evenings."

"I'd be happy to try. I always admired your mother. It's a shame this has happened to her."

"Yes, Elsa, it is."

Just then Evelyn burst into the room, dressed in blue jeans, an old shirt, and a pair of muddy garden gloves. She no longer cared about her appearance. "Mother, you remember Elsa from church, don't you? She sat across the aisle from us. She's come for a visit."

"Hello, Evelyn, it's good to see you."

"Elsa, Elsa, yes, I think I remember you. It's nice of you to come. I don't have many visitors these days."

"I remember how much you loved to garden. It always surprised me. I thought you would have a gardener do it."

"Andrea does have a gardener, but I like to help. I pulled all the weeds from the section by the fishpond. Come and see."

Elsa looked at Andrea for direction, and she nodded in the affirmative. They both followed Evelyn out the kitchen door. Evelyn still walked with a bounce in her step. The doctor said she had the body of a forty-year-old.

"There, see what I've done." Evelyn pointed with pride to a patch of brown earth where only an occasional blade of grass remained. "I've pulled every weed in the area."

Bewildered, Elsa looked at Andrea for instruction.

"Good work, Mom. Clearly, there isn't a single weed left. Why don't you come in now and get ready for lunch? I've asked Elsa to join us."

"That would be nice." Evelyn turned to Elsa. "When did you say we met?"

"We've known each other for years, Evelyn. I always sat across the aisle from you. I worked in the book shop at church and you used to come and talk to me about all your travels with your husband."

"Oh, did I?" Evelyn looked hard at Elsa. "Well, if you say so, it must be true. Guess I better wash up for lunch. It's my favorite meal of the day." She walked jauntily down the hall, leaving a trail of mud behind her.

Elsa turned to Andrea. "She's pulling up your grass, Andrea. She's ruining your lawn."

"It's all right, Elsa. It keeps her busy and happy, and the exercise is good for her. We'll order new sod when the weather turns cooler."

⌘ ⌘ ⌘

Andrea, too excited to wait for a call from Lans, dialed his number. "I couldn't wait to tell you the good news. I've found a sitter for Mother, and I can go to Paris with you next month."

There was a moment of silence.

"Don't you want me to go?" Her heart sank.

"You're serious. You're really leaving your mother and going with me?"

"Yes, darling, I really am. I'm thrilled thinking about spending two weeks with you alone. I know you'll have meetings, and there will be lots of dinners, but we'll have some time alone, won't we?" she said, full of joy.

"You bet! Every minute I can manage. I could use your help entertaining the wives in the daytime. You wouldn't mind that, would you?"

"I'll do anything you want. I'll be at your beck and call the whole time."

"I must be dreaming. It's too good to be true."

"But it isn't. I have a great sitter. You remember Elsa Zimmer, who sits across the aisle from us in church? She's been a widow for years and needs the money. I had her over for lunch today and she and Mom got along great. She's coming a week early to learn the routine, so everything should be running smoothly by then. Lans, I'm so excited."

"Promise me, whatever happens you won't change your mind. I don't think I could handle that."

"I promise. It's all set, and if the two of them get along well, I'm thinking of renovating the apartment over the garage for them. They could be in the house and garden all day and have their dinner and spend their evenings over there. I can make it into a nice bedroom for each of them, and it already has a great kitchen. What do you think? Could you live with that?"

"Could I? Good work, darling," he said, with more eagerness in his voice than she had heard in months. "Andrea, make it work and don't find any more excuses."

"I'll give it all I've got, Lans. That much I can promise you."

⌘⌘⌘

Like children planning a birthday party, every night they made plans for their two weeks together. It would be Paris, New York, their honeymoon all rolled into one.

The week Elsa arrived Andrea broke the news to her mother. Not pleased, Evelyn accused Andrea of leaving her in the care of someone she barely knew. She pouted and chided Andrea for not caring what became of her.

Andrea summoned all her restraint not to react, to keep a semblance of peace, so Elsa would not be frightened. She decided it would be good to leave them alone now and then, so Evelyn would become used to her being gone. Perhaps when Andrea was not there to receive Evelyn's insults, she would quiet down and enjoy having the company of a woman her age.

Andrea needed a new traveling outfit for the trip. She slipped away when Evelyn and Elsa were working on the side garden. Evelyn seemed happy. She would stay away only a few hours the first time. Perhaps Evelyn wouldn't even notice she was gone. She had confided in Elsa and suggested that she make a lunch for the two of them to eat on the picnic table in the side yard.

At her second stop Andrea found a striking blue and green traveling suit that was sure to appeal to Lans. Taking her time to find the perfect accessories to go with it, she still arrived home by 1:30. Evelyn and Elsa were sitting at the picnic table engaged in conversation. She congratulated herself. Everything was going well.

⌘⌘⌘

Two days before the trip, Andrea decided to look for a dinner dress. This time she planned to stay away longer. This would give her a chance to see how

Evelyn would react when she was aware that Andrea had left her.

She returned home at four o'clock in the afternoon. "Hello, Mom, Elsa," she called as she came in from the garage. "I found the most wonderful black dinner dress. It will be perfect."

Silence greeted her. She looked into the kitchen, the family room. They must be outside. She opened the back door and looked out. Evelyn's garden gloves and weed puller lay on the ground, but she was nowhere in sight. They must both be resting.

She went to her mother's room, opened the door, and peeked in. Evelyn was lying on top of her bed in her garden clothes, pressing a damp cloth to her forehead. Thinking she was sleep, Andrea started to tiptoe away.

"I haven't had lunch," Evelyn said in a cross voice.

"What do you mean you haven't had lunch? It's four o'clock. Where's Elsa?"

"She's gone."

"You mean she left you alone?"

"That's right."

"But why?" Andrea asked, bewildered.

"I fired her, that's why."

"You what?" Andrea tried to compose herself.

"I told her she made me sick, always telling me what I could do, so I told her I didn't like her cooking and I didn't want her taking care of me and she should leave me alone. She refused to go until you got home, so I hit her with an umbrella and told her to pack her things and go and never come back."

"Mother, how could you? You two were getting along so well."

"Call her and ask her how well we got along. But fix my lunch first. I'm hungry."

Andrea turned from the room, tears cascading down her cheeks. She had planned so carefully. Just day after tomorrow she would have been on the plane with Lans. She rushed to the phone and called Elsa's home. After six rings, Elsa picked up the phone.

"Elsa, it's Andrea. What happened? You will come back, won't you? You know how pleased I was with your care of Mother. I would never fire you."

"I know how much you want to go with your husband, Andrea, and I wanted to help you, but I can't control your mother. Why, she could have poked my eye out when she came at me with that umbrella. I didn't tell you, but after the first two days, she started calling me names when we were alone and saying hateful things. I think she was trying to make me quit. Well, she succeeded. I can't come back, and that's that." Elsa hung up the receiver.

"Sweet, gentle Elsa." Andrea moaned. "This can't be happening." She paced the floor, desperate to find an alternative. She must keep her promise to Lans. Grabbing the phone, she called Jane and told her the whole story. "Jane," she started, "is there any chance you could come just this once…"

"I would if I could, dear, but Fred's sister is arriving tonight for a stay with me. We've been looking forward to a visit for months. I'm terribly sorry."

"Yes, yes, of course. I thought you might be free. I understand, Jane. Thanks," she said weakly as she put down the phone.

"Lans' mother. Maybe, just maybe Johan is out of town and she could fly over tomorrow. I know she'd do it for Lans."

She dialed Garden City. The phone rang and rang. She would try again later.

She fixed a plate of food for Evelyn. Her mother couldn't do anything for herself anymore, but she had found a way to fire Elsa and keep Andrea trapped at home.

She took a tray to Evelyn's room and found her sitting up waiting for her. Andrea set the tray on the side table by her chair.

"It's about time." Evelyn seemed to know she had gained the upper hand.

"Mother, would you let me take you to the retirement home to see how you like it for just these two weeks? Many of your friends are living there, and they love it. You could stay in one of the guest rooms and I'll get a full-time nurse to take care of you. If you don't enjoy it, we'll never do it again. But just this once, I have to go on this trip with Lans, or he'll never forgive me."

Evelyn pushed the tray aside and jumped up from the chair. "Andrea, you promised you'd never put me away. I made you promise." Her voice rose with each word.

"It's not a hospital or even a nursing home. It's a wonderful place. People pay huge sums of money to live there. There's a long waiting list to get in."

"No, I'm not leaving here. You can't make me. You're my daughter, and you have to take care of me. You promised me you wouldn't put me away."

"I promised Lans I'd go with him." Andrea left the room and tried to ring Katharine again. Still no answer.

She fumbled through the papers on her desk for her list of sitters. *I know I kept it. Ah, there it is.* She reached for the phone and dialed the number of her second choice of sitter to stay with her mother.

"Mrs. Evans, this is Andrea Mulder. I'm still interested in having you stay with…you've already accepted another job. Oh, I see. Yes, thank you. Maybe another time."

She dialed another acquaintance from church. "Louise, this is Andrea Mulder and...you've just talked to Elsa. Yes, I see. Thank you." She hung up the phone and stared at the list, unable to make out a single name as tears filled her eyes.

⌘⌘⌘

The doorbell rang as someone pounded on the door. Andrea turned on the light. Two o'clock in the morning. She reached for her robe and rushed down the steps. Turning on the entrance light, she looked through the side window and saw Evelyn in her nightgown on the arm of their next-door neighbor. She opened the door.

"Your mother came and knocked on our door—"

"At this hour?" Andrea interrupted, unbelieving. "Mother, how did you get out?"

"I unlocked the back door and walked out," Evelyn said.

"She came to us pleading not to let her daughter put her away. She said you were going to put her in a mental hospital so you could go to Paris with your husband. Is there any truth to this, Andrea?'

"Very little," she said.

"The people were in my bedroom staring at me. They kept saying you were trying to trick me. If I didn't give them my money, they'd let you put me away." Evelyn started to cry.

"Come in, Mother. You'll catch a cold in that nightgown." Turning to her neighbor, she said, "Thank you, Dennis, I can handle this. Thank you for bringing her back."

"Are you sure you'll be all right?"

"Yes, thank you," she said as she closed the door and turned to her mother.

Instead of anger, she felt pity. What terrible force within Evelyn would drive her to such extremes? Her fashionable mother, who never went anywhere without looking her very best, stood there in a torn summer nightgown, her hair disheveled, her face distraught, shivering and crying, altogether unaware of how foolish she looked and how much trouble she was causing. Andrea remembered the terrible fate of her grandfather. "It's starting all over again. I can't bear it."

⌘⌘⌘

Lans called early the next morning. "Hello, darling. I got in too late to call you last night. Is everything a go?"

Her heart sank. "Lans, is your mother in town? I've been trying to reach her."

"No, she's with Dad in Switzerland. The good news is that they'll be in Paris part of the time we'll be there."

"Oh," she said.

"You don't sound very happy about it."

She took a deep breath. "Lans, I thought if Johan were out of town, perhaps Katharine would come and stay with Mother so I could still go with you."

"What do you mean?" His voice turned to ice. "Where's Elsa?"

"Mother attacked her with an umbrella yesterday and fired her while I was out buying a dinner dress for the trip. She won't come back."

"And?"

"I called Jane, and she has company. I called everyone else on the list and they either have taken other jobs or have talked to Elsa. No one will come. I called the retirement home to see if she could stay in one of the guest rooms for two weeks with a private nurse and they're full. I'm trying everything I can think of, Lans. Will you pray with me that the Lord will send us someone?"

She waited for his reply, but he said nothing.

"Last night our neighbor brought her home at two o'clock in the morning. She had unlocked the back door and walked to his house. She told him I was trying to put her away and asked him to protect her from me."

"Andrea, you know this can't go on."

"Yes," she said, trying hard to keep back the tears. "I haven't given up, Lans, but there's so little time. Your mother was my last hope."

"Don't call me unless you have good news," he said in a stony tone and hung up the phone. She stared at her receiver. There was no compassion. He was thinking only of his own disappointment, not about her, not about the awful plight of her mother.

She dropped the phone and let it dangle as she sank to the floor and allowed long, choking sobs to break loose.

Evelyn came up behind her and patted her on the back. "There, there now, Andrea. Don't cry. We'll have a good time together while he's gone."

18

Andrea cried herself to sleep. Awakened by a bad dream, she tossed until dawn. Lans would go to Paris without her. Her mother would spoil every good plan she made from now on. It would be Grandpa all over again. The change of personality. The ugly accusations. Could she bear living through it again?

⌘⌘⌘

After the accident her grandfather deteriorated at a rapid rate, surprising even the doctors with the speed of his decline. Like a nagging child, he asked the same questions over and over.

One morning Fritz came in early from the barn. "Where's my breakfast, Laura?"

"There's still time to milk the cows while the muffins bake. There now, you have your shirt on inside out. Let me help you get it right."

"Leave me alone, woman. I can dress myself. Just get my breakfast."

"Go finish the milking, Fritz. I'll send Andrea to tell you when the muffins are baked."

"I know what needs to be done. You don't have to tell me," Fritz flared at Laura.

Andrea watched her grandfather pour out his indignation on his beloved wife. Bewildered, she ran to her room. Again and again she asked God questions he did not answer. Peace refused to come as it had in the past. She found she could no longer bring forth words of faith to comfort her grandmother. Instead she lost herself in activity: racing Dolly, paddling the boats, swimming the lake. But she couldn't outrace her discomfort about her grandfather.

⌘⌘⌘

Returning from a ride on Dolly, Andrea climbed the porch steps and found Fritz screaming at Laura in the kitchen, as usual over a matter of little consequence.

"Grandpa, Grandma tries so hard to please you. You know she's only wants to help you."

"I don't need her help, and I don't need any sassy words from you, young lady."

He had never before turned his anger on Andrea. She looked to her grandmother.

"It's all right, Andrea, run along."

"Okay, Grandma. Call me if you need me." She tore up the steps away from the ugly scene.

⌘⌘⌘

Several days later, Andrea watched Fritz move a pile of hay from one spot to another. "Why does he think that's so important, Grandma?"

"Your grandpa remembers the activities he's always done on the farm and busies himself doing them still, but he's lost the reason behind them. It's all right, Andrea. I'm glad he's active. I'll hire someone to milk the cows and do the chores I can't do myself."

Later that afternoon Andrea found her grandmother sitting on the front porch on the old wooden swing. Now and then she pushed her foot into the porch floor, giving the swing backward momentum and thrusting it forward. She said nothing as Andrea slipped into a chair across from her. Her grandmother's folded hands lay limp in her lap, not knitting or crocheting or doing anything useful. Andrea had never seen them idle.

Her grandmother stared into the fields. Sometimes her eyes turned upward into the great maple tree and the tall, dark spruce that towered over the house. Sometimes they searched the hills across the creek. Andrea knew her grandmother's search was for answers about her husband. Why the long trial that had sapped his enthusiasm and diminished his energy? Why the accident on Christmas Eve? And now, why this confusion, which tried to rob her even of her memories of the kind man with whom she had shared her life?

The doctors called his condition *early senile dementia*. Only fifty-two, Fritz acted like an old man who had lost his orientation.

"Andrea." Grandma spoke with great urgency. "I want you to remember your grandpa as a good man."

"Oh, I will. He always tried to make me happy."

"Yes." She sighed. "He tried to make everyone happy, including his wife, his children, his friends. And he always tried to please his boss. He never did anything great or important in the world's eyes. He wasn't a business success like your father. He never built a company, and he never invented anything. But he was a good man, and we always had enough. He was a success as a husband and father. I couldn't have asked for anything more in a husband. He gave me all the comfort and support I ever needed."

Andrea could see the pain, the hurt, the unanswered questions in her grandmother's sad eyes. "He was a good man, Andrea. You will remember him that way."

"Of course, Grandma." Andrea rose from her chair and crossed the porch to sit beside her grandmother on the swing. She put her arms around her and pulled her close. Her grandma laid her head on Andrea's chest. "We'll both remember him that way always."

Tears welled in Andrea's eyes and dropped onto the gray head on her chest as they sat on the swing clasped together until dusk settled. The first stars of night twinkled above them before Fritz came down from the barn.

"Where's my dinner, Laura?" he bellowed. It was the first night in their marriage that she did not have his dinner lovingly prepared and waiting for him.

⌘⌘⌘

Andrea raced back from the mailbox, flushed with excitement, waving a letter in her hand. "Grandma, Grandma, it's from Lans. It's his first letter from college."

"What does he say, dear heart?" Grandma set aside her mixing bowl and gave Andrea her full attention.

"I don't know. I'm afraid to open it."

"Whatever for? If he's written you so soon, it can't be bad news." Her grandmother looked surprised.

"I have a feeling he's stepped into a world I can't share with him," she said. "I'm afraid he'll outgrow the memories of the farm when all the enticements of college life call to him." Andrea raised clouded eyes toward her grandmother. "Oh, Grandma, I'm so afraid of losing him."

"If the good Lord planned it to be, then it will be, child."

"And if he didn't and Lans meets someone more sophisticated and worldly and is captured by her charm?"

"Where is your faith? Whatever the Lord has planned for you will be the best. You wouldn't want anything else. If Lans runs after worldly women, then he's not good enough for you." Grandma spoke with authority.

"Did God plan for Grandpa to end his life like this?"

The older woman looked startled. "Sometimes it's hard for us to understand the ways of the Lord. I don't believe he wants your grandpa to end like this." She dabbed her eyes with her apron. "But he doesn't seem to hear my prayers right now, and I don't know what to think. I don't want to talk about it just now. Open your letter and tell me what it says. Perhaps it will cheer us."

Andrea studied the letter in her hand and began to pry open the envelope. "Three pages. That's a good sign."

"Yes, go on."

Andrea scanned the letter looking for personal words of caring. "He doesn't say anything about us." Her voice fell. "It's all about his first days at college and how he wanted to share them with me."

"Well, now, that's encouraging. He couldn't wait to get a letter off to you to share his first impressions. If that isn't caring, what is?"

"Do you think so, Grandma? Am I being silly?"

"Very silly."

Just then Fritz stormed into the kitchen. "Where are my keys, Laura? I have to get something in town."

"Excuse me, Grandpa. I'm going to my room to read a letter from Lans." Eager to avoid another scene, Andrea ran up the steps.

Behind her closed door, concentrating on her letter, she didn't hear anything else until her grandmother screamed. Then Andrea rushed to open the door.

"No mere woman is going to rob me of my manhood. Give me those keys, Laura. I can still drive myself to town."

"Fritz, you're hurting me. Let me drive you. The last time you couldn't find your car, we had to call the police."

"Give them to me, woman, or I'll…"

Grandma screamed again. "Fritz, you wouldn't!" She sounded frantic.

Andrea jumped down the stairs three at a time and raced into the kitchen. Seeing her grandfather standing over her grandmother about to plunge a large knife into her chest, Andrea froze.

"Andrea, help me," Grandma cried.

Andrea's trance broken, she rushed to her grandfather. It took all her strength to hold his arms in the air while Grandma ran from them.

Confused, he turned toward Andrea.

"Grandpa, you wouldn't hurt me, would you? I love you. I wouldn't hurt you for anything." Tears streamed down her cheeks as she stared at her deranged grandfather.

Fritz stared back at her, the strength draining from his arms. As they collapsed, Andrea took the knife from him and threw it across the room. She put her arms around him.

"I love you, Grandpa," she sobbed. "I want only what's best for you and so does Grandma. We just want to take care of you."

He stepped back, dazed. Lowering himself into a nearby chair and bowing at the waist, he clasped his head in his hands. "I love you, too, honey. I wouldn't hurt you." He raised his head and gazed toward Laura, who was huddled against the hallway wall, her eyes horrified. He moved as if to go to her, but she turned and fled up the stairs.

⌘⌘⌘

Evelyn embraced Fritz and searched his vacant eyes. "It's as though the man we have known and loved is not really there," she whispered to Andrea. Evelyn led her father to his room, gave him a sedative, and put him to bed. He fell asleep without a struggle.

Later Andrea sat on the porch with her mom and grandmother, discussing what should be done. "You can't stay alone with him any longer, Mother. We don't know what he'll do next."

"He didn't know what he was doing, Evelyn. He wouldn't deliberately hurt me."

"I know, Mom, and I'm sure he loves you with all his heart, but something clouds his thinking and takes over without his realizing what's happening. It's like it was with Dad's father. Remember how Grandpa Karl changed and said such mean things when he started forgetting?"

"I remember it well, and I've thought a lot about it this past month."

"Will you ever forget the first Sunday Leonard came to call on me? I thought he'd never want to see me again after the way Grandpa Karl and Grandma Ursula carried on."

"Tell me about it, Mother," Andrea said. "I don't know anything about Grandpa's parents."

"I had met your father at a party on the banks of the Allegheny River. Leonard was seven years older than I. Very thin then, he had thick dark hair neatly combed and bright blue eyes. He talked about his job as an industrial engineer at Westinghouse Corporation and how he wanted to write novels. He had already published technical articles. I was so impressed.

"I laughed at his jokes and coaxed him to talk about himself. He seemed very shy, but I drew him out. When I beat him at cribbage, I really caught his attention. No woman had done that before. I expected him to challenge me again, so I wasn't surprised when he asked to call on me one Sunday.

"I remember swinging on the porch in front of our house, wearing a flowing peach silk dress that was especially becoming. He came bounding up the steps looking absolutely dashing, dressed in stylish white knickers. He sat down on the swing and we rocked and made small talk when a window on the third floor opened and loud voices shattered our serenity:

"'Can't you remember anything? You've asked me that question over and over again this afternoon.'

"'How would you know? You can't remember anything anymore.'

"Leonard looked startled. I explained that the voices came from Dad's parents, who had an apartment on our third floor.

"I took him inside and played the latest popular songs on the piano to distract him. I think my singing pushed the harsh voices from his mind."

"Until I started up the stairs with a tray of food for Karl and Ursula," Laura said.

"The aroma of beef and onions was overpowering." Evelyn picked up the story again. "When Mother stumbled and spilled the soup, Leonard rushed up to carry the tray for her."

"I tried to persuade him to go back downstairs," Laura said.

"And I begged him to come back to the piano."

"I didn't want him to see that we kept the door to their rooms locked, but he seemed determined to understand the situation." Laura sighed.

"Just then Karl started complaining in a loud voice that Mother had spilled the soup and wet his napkin. Grandma Ursula started singing a German lullaby to a doll she held. Karl screamed at her again and at Mother for not bringing him catsup for his beef. Leonard looked mystified. I assured him they never used to be like that, but something dreadful had happened to their minds. They were like children again.

"Then the sound of shattering glass came from the attic, and Ursula began to cry."

"I can still hear that crash like it was yesterday," Laura said. "I told them to sit still, and I'd get a rag to mop it up and bring back the catsup."

Evelyn finished the story. "I ushered Leonard downstairs and out the door. I thought he'd never return, but I gave him the best smile I could muster. He always said it was the memory of that smile that brought him back. After we were married, he joked about the strange things that went on in the Klinghof attic."

"I never heard that story about you and Dad, Mom. And now I know why Grandpa always puts catsup on his beef." Andrea laughed and for a brief time forgot the seriousness that had led to this revelation. She turned to her grandmother. "Were Grandpa's parents different before they lost their memories?"

"Of course, Andrea. They were fine people." Laura exhaled. "It was hard taking care of Ursula and Karl when their minds failed them. It never occurred to me that the same thing could happen to Fritz. But we always kept them at home with us and saw to their needs. We never sent them away."

"I know it's hard, Mom, but there's a difference. Dad isn't just forgetful and difficult; he's become dangerous."

"He's a good man, Evelyn."

"Of course he is, but something makes him violent. You know the doctor said loss of orientation affects everyone differently." Evelyn shuddered. "Oh, Mom, it's so terrible. What if I'm next?" She flung herself into her mother's arms, and they cried together.

⌘⌘⌘

Dear Lans,

Thank you for sharing your first two days of school with me. It sounds great. You must be feeling like a man of the world now. I hope your new life continues to be good. Dartmouth must be a beautiful place.

Lans, something dreadful has happened. It is worse than dreadful. It is unthinkable, but it happened. My grandfather is very sick.

Your letter arrived and before I could read it, Grandpa came in and demanded the keys to the car to drive to town. I already told you we had to stop him from driving. He couldn't find his car in the parking lot anymore, and he was ticketed for going down the wrong lane on the highway. We were grateful he hadn't killed anybody.

So when Grandma offered to take him, I ran up to my room to read your letter. But Grandpa must have felt threatened, like he wasn't really a man anymore. He started arguing with her, but I was too engrossed in your letter to notice. But when I heard Grandma scream, I ran down to the kitchen and, Lans, you won't believe this: he was standing over her with a butcher knife in his hand, and she was struggling to keep him from plunging it into her.

I felt so guilty for leaving them. If I had stayed, maybe it wouldn't have happened. I managed to stop him and coaxed him to take a walk with me to give Grandma time to recover. I helped him do imaginary chores in the barn, all the while assuring him that we both loved him and were trying our best to help him.

Finally I heard Mother's car pull into the driveway. Grandma had called her, and she drove up from Pittsburgh as fast as she dared.

We can't leave Grandma and Grandpa alone up here anymore, so Grandma is coming to live with us. Mother has had Grandpa committed to a hospital in Maryland, and we'll be driving him down this week.

Oh, Lans, I can't believe this is happening. It's like some horror movie, but it's my grandpa and my grandma who always loved each other so much. I don't understand God any more. How could He let my grandparents end their lives like this? They're such good people.

I have to go now. It's chaos around here. I'll write from Pittsburgh next time.

Love,
Andrea

19

Three years later Andrea knocked and pushed open the door to her grandmother's bedroom. "Hi, Grandma. The mailbox was full of birthday cards. Shall I open them for you?"

"Yes, dear, that would be nice."

Looking pale and tired, the once robust Laura lay in a hospital bed in her room at the Collins house in Pittsburgh. She could eat nothing. Liquids helped her down the pain medicine every few hours. She never complained, but when tears ran from her eyes, Andrea knew the pain had grown too great.

Laura had been living at Andrea's house ever since Evelyn committed Fritz to the mental hospital in Maryland. During two years of anxiety and loneliness, she neglected to tell anyone of the sore that had developed on her left breast. One day she fell stepping off a bus and severely damaged her arm. When the doctor discovered the large growth, he admitted her to the hospital and removed her breast, but it was too late. The scars never healed, and the cancer spread throughout her body. Laura endured the pain stoically, never wanting to be a problem to anyone. Now she had been discharged from the hospital and sent home to die.

Evelyn still suffered from the knowledge that she had committed her father to an institution. All she could do now was make the long drive to Maryland every month to see that he was well cared for. The first time she visited, she had taken Laura, but seeing each other was harder than either of them could bear. Fritz cried and begged Laura to take him home. When she said she couldn't, he became angry and hurled insults at her. It had taken her weeks to recover from that visit. Andrea had heard people say that heartbreak often preceded cancer. It was easy to imagine that Fritz' decline had broken her grandmother's heart and was still crushing her spirit.

Throughout her senior year of high school, Andrea accompanied her mother on the monthly trips to the hospital in Maryland. After she started college, she drove to Maryland with Evelyn only when home on vacation. At first she had been allowed to visit her grandfather. Sometimes he seemed peaceful and she could tell herself that he was content, but the time came when he had deteriorated to such an extent her mother would not allow her to see him. The last time she accompanied Evelyn, Andrea waited in the car.

During the drive home, she comforted her mother and assured her she had made the right decision.

"It's a terrible thing to commit your father to an institution and see him deteriorate and fade away," Evelyn told Andrea. "His body is as frail as his mind now, and he spends much of his time in bed rolled up in a fetal ball. I still can't believe what's happening to him."

Since then, whenever she forgot something or lost a word, Evelyn would say, "My memory is just like Dad's." Turning to her daughter, she would add, "Don't worry, Andrea. You have your father's genes. This won't happen to you." But behind her assurance lurked the unspoken fear that it was only a matter of time until it would claim them both.

Andrea, home from college for summer break, knowing these were her grandmother's final days, had decided not to take a summer job. Laura had been so lonely this past winter with Andrea at college and Evelyn and Leonard traveling, she had asked to be moved to the home of Evelyn's sister in far away Texas. Ashamed that her mother should feel so neglected, Evelyn waved the request aside and stopped traveling with Leonard, but Evelyn's home commitments kept her on the go, leaving Laura alone in her room most of the day. Living out in the suburbs, away from the few friends she had left in the city, Laura still led a lonely life.

Andrea, agonizing over the fact that all this might have been prevented, felt nothing made sense anymore. Angry with God, she raised a clenched fist and cried out, "Why, Lord?"

When Laura had been able to attend church, Andrea had accompanied her. Now that she could no longer make the trip, Andrea stopped attending as well. Her heart, no longer soft toward her heavenly Father, hardened, a crust of anger and rebellion settling over it. She could not forgive God for allowing such tragedy to befall her loving grandparents. "Why, why must they face such a bitter end?" She sobbed when prayers and pleading brought no changes.

"This one is from Aunt Dot, Grandma. It's a beautiful picture of a farm with a big red barn. There, can you see it now?" She held it up for her grandmother to see.

"It's lovely," Laura said without conviction.

Andrea read the verse that wished her a happy birthday. A note expressed her aunt's distress that she was far away in Texas and could not be there to care for her mother. Evelyn had never told her sister that Laura had requested to live with her in Dallas.

Andrea laid the card aside and opened the next. When she reached the last one, she asked, "Is this tiring you too much, Grandma?"

"No, child, please stay with me."

"I will, Grandma. I'll be here all summer." Andrea reached over and caressed her cheek. Laura had lost weight, and her skin sagged heavily on her wrinkled face.

As Laura raised her arm in slow motion, Andrea took her hand and held it, settling the frail arm back down on the fresh sheets. Evelyn did not sit by her bedside, but she kept her mother bathed and in clean sheets.

"I miss you when you're away, Andrea."

"I miss you, too." Andrea choked as she realized her grandmother would not live to see her leave for her sophomore year at college.

"Did you receive a letter from Lans, dear?"

"No, not today." She still felt a tug at the mention of his name. Dating other boys now, she tried not to think of him too often.

He had invited her to Winter Carnival his freshman year at Dartmouth. She had made the long trip with great anticipation, thinking it would be the most fulfilling weekend of her life. Lans had been glad to see her. After a tour of the snow-covered campus, they frolicked in the snow and jumped up to pull down long icicles hanging from the buildings.

Andrea lived her dream until the round of parties began. They went from one fraternity house to another where "canoe races" dominated the entertainment. The object was to determine who could down drinks the fastest. Andrea, who did not drink, found it hard to join the gala mood. Lans drank slowly at first, but when he saw that she was not having a good time, he joined in the races. When his words began to slur, she thought she could not bear it.

Realizing his mistake, Lans stopped participating. Dinner helped, and she enjoyed dancing in his arms later in the evening, but he seemed distant, not the Lans she had known. They never talked about the future or when they would see each other again. When she told him she had decided to go to Smith College and would be close to him in Northampton, Massachusetts, next year, he showed little excitement. He murmured that was great, but said little else.

Later she learned he had not wanted to spoil the weekend by telling her he would be transferring to the University in Amsterdam in the fall. His father thought it important for him to gain European business contacts. "There are no contacts like the contacts you make in your college years," he said. "They can last a lifetime." Concerned that he would soon be starting his career, Lans had agreed.

After a strained leave-taking, Andrea sensed he would not invite her to spring prom. His letters continued but with less fervor and less frequency. He had been in Europe for a year now. His parents spent as much time in Europe as they did in the United States, so there was no need for him to visit them here. The emotional gap between Andrea and Lans widened with their physical separation.

"Remember when you first came to live with us, Grandma? You would sit in your rocking chair in your room and rock and rock while we talked about the happy days at the farm."

"Yes, dear heart, remembering the good times with Fritz comforted me during the day and helped me keep my sanity, but when I lay awake in my bed at night, I couldn't avoid thinking of the last days." A pain whipped through her body. Andrea could see its effects on her grandmother's face, but, as usual, she said nothing.

"Is it time for your pain medicine, Grandma?"

"Yes, that would be nice."

Andrea took out the pill from the little bottle on her grandmother's bedside table and poured a fresh glass of water. She put in the glass straw that lay beside it and raised her grandmother's head. Laura swallowed it with difficulty.

"Thank you, dear." She closed her eyes for a minute and asked without opening them, "Have you seen Fritz since you've been home?"

"No, Grandma, Mother and I are going next week."

"I was wondering if you might be able to make me a bed in the backseat of the car so I could go with you this time. It would mean so much to me just to touch him once more."

Andrea felt a rush of emotion, all the feelings her grandmother had not put into words. She couldn't hold back the tears as she gave the expected answer. "Grandma, you know you're not well enough to make the trip."

"Does it really matter, Andrea? I just want to get there and see him once more. I'm ready to see my Maker and I have a few questions for him when I do," she said, with more spunk than Andrea had heard from her in a long time.

Andrea laughed in spite of the poignancy of the moment and in spite of her misty eyes. "When you get the answers, will you dispatch an angel to tell me, Grandma? I need to know them, too."

Grandma chuckled. The painful moment might have passed, but Andrea could stand it no longer. "Grandma, don't you dare leave me a day sooner than you have to. I'll miss you more than I can bear. You've been the best thing in my life."

"Better than Lans?" She attempted to make light of it.

"You gave my childhood its happiest moments. Without you and Grandpa I'd have grown up feeling sorry for myself all the time. The days at your house in Pittsburgh when I was little and the weeks on the farm when I was older were the best memories I have, and seeing the love relationship between you and Grandpa gave me the pattern I want for my marriage. I don't care a thing about success and climbing the social ladder. I want to sit at the kitchen table and talk over a cup of coffee and a piece of homemade apple pie." She stood up and bent over to embrace her grandmother. "Oh, Grandma, I love you so much. Don't ever doubt how important you are to me."

Laura raised her hand and stroked Andrea's hair with more strength than she had mustered in months. "Thank you, Andrea, for telling me. You were my first grandchild and, though I loved all my grandchildren, there was always something special about the way I felt about you." They embraced, their tears mingling like tributaries forming a single river as they expressed their love for each other again and again.

Laura seemed to rally for a time. There were days when Andrea could raise the back of her bed and play simple card games with her. She read to her for hours, sometimes from the Bible, sometimes from a book of poetry called *Pack Up Your Troubles* by Ted Malone, a favorite of the women in the family. Whenever Andrea came across a beautiful passage in whatever she was reading, she would mark it and share it with her grandmother.

Laura never asked to see Fritz again. Whenever she started a conversation in that direction, Andrea quickly diverted her attention.

The summer days passed in quick succession, but in early August Laura slipped away from them. Andrea imagined her having that important discussion with her Maker in heaven. The funeral was joyous, everyone dwelling on what a special life she had lived, but when they sang her favorite hymn, "Just As I Am, I Come to Thee," Andrea lost her composure and sobbed with abandon. Happy that her grandmother's long ordeal was over, she could not bear to think of life without her.

⌘ ⌘ ⌘

Only six months later, Andrea sat in the same church pew for her grandfather's funeral. Relieved that those terrible trips to Maryland were over, Andrea hoped that her mother's fears would diminish now.

When the minister talked about what a good man Fritz had been, Andrea nodded in agreement, the terrible picture having dimmed with time. She cried as she imagined his spirit leaving the frail, rotting corpse and rising to meet her grandmother in the sky. What a glorious reunion it would be! Though Laura had her questions, she had never blamed her Savior, and Grandpa had never doubted when his mind was right. From this day on Andrea would think of them, free of all problems, together now in his presence forever.

20

Lans sat rigid on the plane to Paris, his limbs numb, his body stiff, his attitude unbending. Surrounded by people, isolated in misery, he had never felt so alone. His head throbbed from pent-up anger. He ran his fingers through his hair to make sure he could still move. Life and light had vacated his world. Was it even worth going without her? How could she choose her mother over him?

She had asked him to pray with her. Why had he turned her down? *Lord, O Lord, heal this mess!* A desperate cry from deep inside him shattered his selfish thoughts like a sudden strike of lightning. He and Andrea should have been seeking the Lord together through this whole ordeal.

He considered giving in, going back to live in the house with her mother. He would have Andrea to himself every evening when Evelyn finally went to bed, like he had during their joyous telephone conversations planning the trip. He could hold her and love her. He knew she needed his strength and comfort to see her through this nightmare.

But the demon on his shoulder clamped its hands around his head and self-pity claimed him. Evelyn materialized before his eyes, seemingly unaware and helpless, interrupting their most tender moments. He suspected she knew full well what she was doing. Why couldn't Andrea see it?

An image, larger than life, of his mother-in-law, flaring mad, rushed at him. He had dared to require his wife's attention. Her incessant question, "What time is it?" rang in his ears. What did time mean to her anyway? Her childish brattle dominated dinner conversations, obliterating his attempts to share his day with his wife. Andrea replied and offered explanations over and over as to a slow-learning child. Shaking his head, he squeezed his eyes shut, dismissing the pictures and sending them tumbling out of sight.

No, he could not endure it. He had closed that door. Determined never to open it again, he resolved to live alone. With no interest in other women, he would honor the vows he had made before God. *In sickness and in health* flashed through his mind. No, Andrea was not sick; it was her mother.

He would search for an apartment, see Andrea when the children came home for vacations, endure Evelyn and act like everything was all right, but he would not move back into his house as long as Evelyn lived there.

Lans had been gone a week. Andrea had not heard from him since the night she told him that Evelyn had fired Elsa. At first she was merely defeated, beaten down. Now an angry resentment began to grow within her. Again and again she relived that final night. He had hung up on her instead of trying to comfort her. He had no thought of her disappointment, no compassion for her dilemma. He had not called her to share what he was experiencing.

In Paris without her, did he long for her as she longed for him? Did he have any idea how much she had wanted to go with him? Did he remember their magical time together in Paris when they were young?

She went to the cabinet in their living room where she kept their photographs. Running her finger down the titles she had taped on the outside of the albums, she found it: *Europe, Summer 1952*. The summer before Andrea's senior year in college. For Christmas her father had given her a map of Europe with five countries highlighted in magic marker. It included a tour of the greatest cities in Italy, a ten-day stay in Paris to attend the International Scientific Management Congress which he had founded and still led, and a tour of Scandinavia. They would stay with business friends in Copenhagen and Gothenburg, take a three-day boat trip across Sweden on the Gota Canal, and end with a taste of the fiords in Norway. For six months she had dreamed of romantic encounters of all kinds, but the prospect of dining with Lans in Paris overwhelmed them all.

She had not seen him for three years. He had stayed overseas during the summers to take language courses. They exchanged infrequent letters, only as friends.

She drew the album from the cabinet and hugged it in her arms as she settled into a winged back chair. Her first trip to Europe...Paris...Lans.... She remembered the paralyzing fear that he had forgotten her, the thrill of knowing she would soon see him, the hours of preparation. As she studied the pictures, it all came back to her in vivid detail....

⌘ ⌘ ⌘

Evelyn called through the door that separated their adjoining rooms. "Andrea, it's time to leave. Are you ready? If we don't go now, we'll be late for dinner."

"I'm almost ready, Mom. The door's unlocked. Come in."

"Your father's waiting in the lobby. If we're not there in a minute, he'll be phoning to find out where on earth we are."

Andrea emerged from her bathroom gliding in circles across the floor. "What do you think? Will he like it?"

"If he doesn't, there's something wrong with him." Evelyn gazed with obvious approval at her only daughter as she swished about the room collecting her evening bag, gloves, and light wrap. "The dress is smashing, the blue is perfect for your eyes, and your hair never looked better. Now wipe off that anxious frown and smile as though life is glorious, you've never been happier, and if Lans wants to add to that happiness, all well and good. If his affections are otherwise occupied, you couldn't care less."

"If only it were true. If you really want to know, I'm terrified."

"That may be true on the inside, Andrea, but he'll never know. Give it all you've got." Evelyn cheered her on as she turned out the light and followed her daughter into the hall.

Head of the Congress, Leonard had chosen Lans' father both to speak and to sit as a member of his steering committee. Johan and Leonard had planned many of the coming events together. Tonight the Collins family would dine with the Mulders at the Lasserre, their favorite Paris restaurant where a charm of a gourmet skillet was required for admittance. Evelyn and Leonard had been given one on their first visit to Europe and had made it a practice to have dinner there at least once every trip.

Emerging from the taxi, Andrea swirled through the entrance of the exclusive French restaurant straight into the arms of Lans Mulder. "Andrea, I can't believe you're in Paris." His voice, deeper than she remembered, sent chills up and down her spine. Trembling from his warm hug, she laughed and radiated genuine happiness.

She embraced Katharine Mulder. "We have so much catching up to do, Mrs. Mulder. May I take you to lunch one day alone? Mom will be busy helping Dad with all the social obligations, being first lady of the event."

"That would be lovely, Andrea. I'd like nothing better." Katharine smiled her sweet smile as she would have to anyone, but Andrea thought she detected an expectation of pleasure as she accepted the invitation. "Andrea, you have grown up. Let me look at you." Andrea whirled, letting her full skirt flare out for all to see. As she circled past Lans, she thought she saw the glint of admiration in his eyes.

"Dr. Mulder, how nice to see you again," she greeted his father.

"I heard all about your adventure when you tried to visit us on Long Island. I hope this meeting will be more successful."

"Oh, it wasn't a total loss. We shared some special hours in the middle of the night, Dr. Mulder." She smiled at him and stole a glance at Lans, hoping for a nod of agreement. He showed no emotion. She saw that his years away had not detracted from his good looks. His round cheeks thinner now, his abundant blond hair just a little darker, his chin stronger, he appeared much older. His brown eyes still sparkled but his boyish exuberance had turned into a cheerful confidence. Would he still enjoy riding over the fields at the farm and walking in the dark woods?

As the waiters seated the ladies, Lans pulled out a chair and motioned for her to sit. Then he turned from the table. For a dreadful moment she thought he was abandoning her, but after speaking to the violinist, he returned to her side. Hope rose within her that this could be the happy occasion she had longed for it to be.

Leonard and Johan wasted no time jumping into the details of the Congress, while Evelyn and Katharine shared all that had transpired since they last saw each other.

"Tell me, how do you like Paris?" Lans asked as he might have asked anyone.

"I hardly know yet. We arrived last night, checked into our hotel, and went out to a lovely restaurant. It being my first night in Paris, I was excited, but Mom and Dad were morose. So, after the first course, I said, 'This is silly. Why don't we forget dinner tonight?' They looked at each other and Dad said, 'What do you think, Evelyn? She might be right.' Mom agreed. 'I can't eat a thing. Let's go back to the hotel.' So Dad stopped the main course from coming, paid our bill, and we left. That was my first experience of Paris."

"What could possibly have been so serious?"

"It's quite a story."

"Tell me."

With his encouragement, Andrea launched into a long tale about her father buying a painting by an eighty-six-year-old artist in Milan and her adventure at the airport. The attendants claimed not to understand English but kept parroting, "The artist dead. You no take this painting out of country." As they argued in a circle, the painting sat rolled up on a nearby table. Her father put it in her arms, gave her a ticket, and told her to board the plane.

"I had to walk through a row of gendarmes bearing guns on their shoulders all by myself, feeling like a clandestine smuggler taking a valuable painting out of the country."

"Wow, what a position to put you in." Lans laughed.

"I was terrified, but I did it and we almost got away with it. While the attendants argued among themselves in Italian, Mom and Dad followed me onto the plane. The doors shut behind them. The three of us were ready to breathe a sigh of relief until we heard a great banging and someone yelling. I imagined the gendarmes hauling me off to jail as they boarded the plane, grabbed the painting from the top compartment, and ran back down the aisle. Dad ran after them threatening to stop payment on the check. In perfect English, the head attendant said, "Do whatever you like, Señor. This painting will remain in Italy."

"Wow. What happened after you left the restaurant in Paris? Your parents seem to have recovered. They're quite cheerful tonight."

Seeing their parents engaged in an animated conversation, Andrea resumed her tale. "We went back to our hotel, and Dad wrote letters to everyone he could think of in Italy, to the American Embassy, and to some of his business associates. This morning, he stopped payment on the check. He's done all he can do for now…but enough of that, Lans. I want to hear all about your years at the University. Congratulations, I understand you're doing quite well. Are you still glad you came here to school? And when are you coming home?"

"Hey, one at a time," Lans held up his hands to stop the onslaught of questions. Before he could reply, the violinist came to the table and stood before Andrea.

"To welcome the young lady to Paris," he said in a thick French accent, giving the French pronunciation of Paris, making it sound romantic and mysterious. With a flourish he put his violin to his shoulder, raised his bow, and started serenading Andrea with "Just the Way You Look Tonight." As all eyes turned to her, she looked down and blushed, but her expectations soared. *He still cares!*

"Compliments of the young man, Mademoiselle. Ah, to be young and the first time in Paris. I wish you a very beautiful evening." As he bowed in her direction, she nodded her thanks, clapped her hands, and turned to Lans.

"Lans, that was lovely. I will always remember tonight as my first evening in Paris."

He smiled, letting her know he was pleased.

Afterwards, in recounting their conversation to Evelyn, Andrea remembered few details. Courses were served, eaten, and whisked away. The violinist moved about the room playing beautiful, haunting music. Andrea smiled brightly but there was nothing artificial about her show of happiness. She had dreamed of such an evening for years.

As their parents ordered coffee, Lans rose and turned to them. "Mr. and Mrs. Collins, Mom and Dad, will you excuse us? There's a band playing in the

Bois de Bologne tonight. It would be a perfect ending to Andrea's first night in Paris. You needn't worry. I'll bring her back to your hotel, and I'll take very good care of her," he assured her father.

"I'm sure you will, Lans. You may go, Andrea. Have a dance for your mother and me. It's been years since we did that. Remember the last time, Evelyn?"

"Yes, Leonard. Business manages to come first now," she said without a hint of criticism. "Have a lovely time, dear."

Andrea gathered her things, embraced her parents, and said good-bye to the Mulders. "It's been a lovely evening already. Thank you all for making it so special."

"That's Lans' department." Dr. Mulder laughed. "Don't keep her out too late, son."

"I won't, Dad. Good night all." He swept her out the door. "It isn't far. Shall we walk, or would you rather take a taxi?"

"I'd love to walk. There are so many lights, it reminds me of chasing fireflies at the farm." She looked into his face to see if he reacted to the mention of the farm.

"Do you go there any more, Andrea, now that your grandparents are gone?"

"Not often. There are so many unhappy memories now. It's too painful for me. But we still have a caretaker, and we go up for special weekends. Sometimes all the relatives from Mom's side come for holidays. Other times Mom and Dad entertain business groups there. We do miss Grandma's cooking. Those were great days, Lans."

"Yes, they were," he said. "I've never forgotten my three weeks there. I always hoped to repeat them, but it just didn't work out. I'd like to jump in the hayloft again and swing on the rope yelling, 'Me, Tarzan.' How's Dolly?"

"I don't ride her anymore. She has a sore leg that never seems to heal, but I visit her and spend time in the field with her when I do go to the farm. She's very old for a horse."

"That's sad, but I'm glad you still have her."

"Look at that couple," Andrea said. "Paris really is the city of romance. They're oblivious to anyone around them."

"Yes, you'll have to get used to public displays of affection. The French are much freer than we are in the States."

Andrea started dancing down the street. "I feel free tonight, Lans. It must be catching."

"I thought you'd like to dance under the stars. It will be like the last night

142

we sat on the dock and would have talked all night if your father hadn't made us go to bed. Here we are. Let me see if I can get a table."

Andrea looked around the dance floor, open to the sky and surrounded by the trees of the woods. Tables were tucked here and there at its edges and a band sat at the far end playing foxtrots and waltzes.

Before a waiter seated them, Lans took her hand. "They're playing a waltz. May I have the honor?" He bowed before her and looked deep into her eyes. Could he be searching for what they had known together in the past?

"You certainly may," she said as he led her onto the dance floor and whirled her around to the strains of a Viennese waltz, under the stars in the Bois de Bologne, on her first real night in Paris. Andrea closed her eyes and savored every moment, happy now that she had allowed Evelyn to push her into taking dancing lessons last year. She had complained that she never felt comfortable on the dance floor, so her mother enrolled her in a class at an Arthur Murray Studio. She learned the foxtrot, waltz, rumba, tango, and the samba. Her instructor, a samba specialist, had turned it into her favorite dance.

Seated at a secluded table, they ordered tea and coffee. Before long the band played a samba. "Lans," she said, "do you samba?"

"You bet. Do you?"

"Yes, I love it." She didn't hesitate a moment. "Let's do it."

He grabbed her hand, and they started moving forward and backward, pumping their arms in rhythm to the music. Lans became more adventurous as she kept up with him. People moved out of their way as Lans threw himself into the dance and she followed. Soon couples surrounded them and clapped to their gyrations.

Andrea gave herself to the dance, flying out on her own, circling around Lans, and falling back into perfect sync with him. They smiled at each other, holding each other's gaze through it all, oblivious to the people clapping around them. Andrea thought she must be someone else, so different was this from the life she had known the last three years.

When the music stopped, the people roared with applause. They looked at each other with surprise and gave a slight bow in each direction. Lans led her back to their table, holding her hand with a firm grip. It all felt good, even being the center of attention. But dancing with Lans here under the stars was all the attention she needed. She kept looking at him to make sure he remained happy. She felt like Cinderella, expecting her coach to turn into a pumpkin and to find herself dressed in rags at any minute. Lans seemed to remember everything they had shared. He was polished in how to escort a girl and show her a special evening, but where was his heart?

They said nothing about their last meeting at Dartmouth. Neither of them apologized for the falling off of their long correspondence. Questions whirled through her mind. *How many girls is he seeing, or worse still, is there one special one? Is this just a one-evening diversion to please his parents?*

Noting joy in his eyes, she dared to believe the attraction that had first drawn them to each other still existed. The magic of their being together had not lost its power.

21

Midnight found them still clinging to each other as they danced. No longer swirling all over the floor, they swayed back and forth to the lilting rhythm of "Sentimental Rhapsody." Lans held her close. Oblivious to everything around her, Andrea would have been content to dance in Lans' arms forever. The words to a song sung in English cut into her thoughts and claimed her attention: "Years and tears ago, I dreamed I met my love. Years and tears ago imagination made you part of me. And now, at last, I know, the love that I dreamed of. You're here at last, you're here, where years and tears ago I knew you'd be."

The words expressed what she could never say to Lans. As tears misted her vision, she was thankful Lans could not see them. But just then he pushed her gently from him and stared at her face. He cupped his hand under her chin as he had years ago. The familiarity of the gesture brought forth a flood of memories. They stood still in the middle of the dance floor and Andrea, looking up at him, tried to imagine what was on his mind.

He'll see the tears and know how much I care, she thought in near panic. Struggling to control herself, she could not prevent a tear from flowing down her hot cheek.

Lans reached up and wiped it away. Then, all energy, he took her hand and escorted her from the floor to their table. "Andrea, I'm going back to school tomorrow. I was planning not to come back until the final banquet."

"Oh," she said, "I'm sorry, Lans. It was lovely to see you again." Her hopes that things were as they used to be between them crashed like a runaway elevator. It had been so good, but it was merely a one-night courtesy, probably requested by his mother and father, not his desire to renew their friendship after all. Her face wore a pleasant mask, showing no outward sign of the collapse of her dreams.

"But I'm changing my plans," he said, ignoring her remark. "I have to go back tomorrow. I have an exam the next day, but I'll come back as soon as it's over. Will you be free? Have you made plans? What has your father scheduled for you?"

She tried to sound casual, not quite adjusted to this second turn of events. "Some sightseeing during the day...many dinners with important dignitaries.

One is with the prime minister of Belgium. Dad taught me how to curtsey when I'm introduced."

"Are they part of the Congress?"

"Yes."

"Good; then I'll be able to come. I'll speak to my father first thing in the morning. We'll have a whole week together, and this time I'll show you my world."

"I can't wait to see it, Lans." The elevator inside her that had crashed to the ground began climbing back up again, carrying her spirits to new heights.

⌘⌘⌘

The taxi pulled up to her hotel. Lans paid the driver and escorted her into the lobby. She glanced up at him and smiled. "Lans, it's been a wonderful evening. I can't thank you—"

A young man rushed up and swooped her into his arms. "Andrea, your parents told me you'd be coming back sooner or later, so I waited and here you are. Imagine our being in Paris together at the same time." He lifted her from the ground and twirled her around before a bewildered Lans.

"Chico," she exclaimed. "You said you might be here, but I didn't believe you. Lans, this is a friend from college, Chico Fisher. He goes to Wesleyan and he's kind of crazy, but we've had some great times together. Chico, this is Lans Mulder. He attends the University in Amsterdam."

"And Andrea and I have had some great times together, too." Lans shook Chico's hand and looked him over.

Undaunted, Chico replied, "Any friend of Andrea's is a friend of mine." Turning to Andrea, he said, "Hey, babe, I've got two tickets to the opera tomorrow night and one of them has your name on it. Can you come?"

Flustered, Andrea looked at Lans and back to Chico. "If my father releases me from dinner tomorrow night, I'd love to."

"Great. How about a bike ride tomorrow? I'll get a loaf of French bread and some cheese and fruit. I know a great place for a picnic." He turned to Lans. "Hey, man, would you like to come, too? I can probably rustle up another bike."

"Thanks for remembering I'm here. I'll be going back to Amsterdam, but Andrea is dining with me Monday night and for the rest of the week."

"Oh, okay," Chico said, not deterred by the chill in Lans' voice. "I'll call you about 10:00 in the morning, babe. We'll have a great time." He gave her a quick hug and dashed out the revolving door.

146

"An annoying, flamboyant young man. Chico, with all that blond hair? What do you see in him, Andrea?"

"Lans, I do believe you're jealous," she said, elated at his show of caring. "His parents were missionaries in South America. He was born there. He's just a good-time guy. He cheers me up sometimes when I'm down. I met him at a college dance, and every now and then he turns up on my doorstep unannounced, like tonight."

"It sounded well planned to me. You told him where you'd be staying."

"I never thought about it again. He's rather unpredictable, so I never count on anything. But enough of Chico. It was a wonderful evening. What a perfect introduction to Paris. It's as romantic a city as its reputation, and I'll never forget dancing under the stars in the Bois de Bologne." She spun once more before him. "I'll be looking forward to your return. Good night, Lans. It's late, and Mom and Dad will be worried. I'd better dash." She turned toward the elevator and pushed the button.

"It was great seeing you again, Andrea. I had forgotten how enchanting you can be." Lans moved toward her as the elevator door opened.

She blew him a kiss and stepped inside. Left standing alone, Lans looked uncertain, his usual composure shaken. "I'll look forward to Monday night," she said as they watched the elevator door close between them.

⌘⌘⌘

Andrea unlocked her door and closed it behind her without making a sound. But as soon as she turned on the light, Evelyn appeared in the adjoining doorway. "Well, young lady, I thought you would never come in. It must have been quite an evening."

Andrea grabbed her mother's hand and drew her into the room, carefully closing the door so her father wouldn't hear them. "Mom, it was incredible. It was wonderful. Beyond anything I could have imagined. He said he had forgotten how enchanting I could be. It wasn't me; it was an enchanted evening. We went to the Bois de Bologne and danced under the stars for hours and hours. It was unbelievable." She pirouetted toward Evelyn and embraced her mother. "Thank you for the dress and all the encouragement. I felt like a princess with Prince Charming. Poor Lans, if only he knew."

"Knew what?" Evelyn wanted to know everything.

"Did you tell Chico to wait for me?" Andrea laughed, remembering Lans' expression when Chico rushed over and embraced her.

"Of course not. I just told him you'd be coming back sometime tonight. I didn't have any idea when."

"Well, he waited and rushed up and threw his arms around me when we came into the lobby and was his usual crazy self. 'Flamboyant,' Lans called him. Oh yes, and 'annoying.' He didn't make a hit with Lans. Mom, I think Lans was jealous. He'd been planning to spend the week at the university, but we had such a great time, he decided to come back the day after tomorrow. Chico asked me to the opera tomorrow night and for a bike ride during the day...right in front of Lans."

"I'm not sure I followed all that, but I've got the idea that it was a successful evening. I'm so happy for you, dear."

Andrea felt her mother had a hard time understanding her most of the time, but an evening dancing under the stars with a special young man, this she could fully appreciate. Evelyn hugged her daughter again. "You'll have to give me a blow-by-blow tomorrow at breakfast. Now get some sleep if you can." She kissed Andrea's forehead and disappeared through the adjoining door to her room.

Andrea flopped onto her bed. "Oh, Lord, I've been angry at you all these years and look how you've blessed me this night. Beyond anything I've ever dreamed." Love poured out of her in all directions. "My cup runneth over. Surely goodness and mercy shall follow me all the days of my life," she recited out loud.

Then the first negative thought stabbed her. Was it indeed too good to be true, too good to last and develop beyond a fun week together in Paris?

"Oh, what am I doing?" she chided herself. "I'm simply going to relax and enjoy it for however long it lasts." She rose from her bed and peered out her window at Paris lit up at night. "Wonderful, enchanted city, I love you," she exclaimed as she danced around the room remembering the feeling of being in Lans' arms. "I'll never, never forget this night," she said, slipping off her clothes and going through the gyrations of the samba in her nightgown. She splashed her face with water and dreamily brushed her teeth, still mentally waltzing in circles in the arms of the man she had always loved.

⌘⌘⌘

Andrea and Lans had sauntered all morning along the Left Bank in Paris, popping in and out of a long line of art boutiques and sidewalk booths. They studied the displayed paintings and thumbed through multitudes of unframed oils and watercolors that leaned against the walls. Andrea had brought $100 in traveler's checks with her. Her father encouraged her to buy something in

Paris that reminded her of her first trip to Europe. When Andrea announced that what she wanted most was a painting, Leonard commissioned Lans to escort her to the shops along the Left Bank.

Lans had returned as promised to show her the sights of Paris. Joking and laughing as if they had always been best friends, they climbed the Eiffel Tower, poked around Montmartre, and drove into the country to explore beautiful French chateaus. In the evening they dined with the important men and women gathered for the International Scientific Management Congress. Andrea's father impressed upon her the importance of these meetings and told her he depended on her to further relationships between the countries by being charming and agreeable, no matter what happened.

At one of her father's prime events, Andrea's dinner partner had been an industrialist from the French nobility who thought the oysters on the half shell the best oysters in the world. Andrea became very talkative, exhausting her French vocabulary while ignoring the raw, slimy creatures on the plate in front of her. When she paused, the Count, a man of great importance, insisted she stop entertaining him and enjoy her oysters. So much having been said about them, she could no longer ignore them and hope the waiter would whisk them away. She took a deep breath, plunged her fork into one of them and swallowed it whole, nearly gagging in the act, but her gentleman, so pleased that she had at last tried one, seemed not to notice her discomfort.

He watched and waited for her to take another and to pronounce a verdict. Lans, engaged in a spirited conversation with several Dutchmen, could not be called upon to help in her distress. Having downed one of the slimy creatures, lest she create an international incident, she tackled them one by one. With her plate empty, she declared them a complete success. Never had she tasted oysters that had given her a sensation quite like this, all the while praying that the creatures swallowed whole would remain where they were and not embarrass her by reappearing.

"Look, Lans." She pointed to a surrealist painting on the wall that featured gray objects sliding over the side of a table. "They look just like I imagined the oysters sliding down my throat last night." She shuddered.

"Poor Andrea." Lans offered her sympathy, then burst out laughing. "When I turned around and saw you turning green as you downed the last one, exclaiming in your best French that they were *bien magnifique,* I almost lost it. The Count didn't have a clue what misery he had put you through and thought you actually meant it."

"It was a moment never to be forgotten. I could hear Father's lecture if I hadn't eaten them and offended the Count."

"You're an international heroine. As far as the Count is concerned, you are an oyster-lover extraordinaire."

"May I never live through another moment like that one," Andrea shuddered a second time, turning away from the sliding gray objects. "Look at that painting, Lans," she said, pointing in another direction. "I love the way the vines fall over the bridge and complement the cattails that jut up in the foreground. I could look at that for a very long time."

A Frenchman with a beret cocked on one side of his head slid up behind Andrea. "Mademoiselle like?"

"Maybe. *Combien?*"

"Pour la mademoiselle, two-hundred-fifty dollar."

"Oh, that's too much. I'm sorry," she said, taking a long, lingering look at the painting.

"Come, it is too much." Lans took her arm and escorted her out the door.

The clerk ran after them. "Two-hundred-twenty dollar *pour la mademoiselle.*"

"Sorry, she can't afford that," Lans said, leading her on to the next store.

"Lans, do you think he'll come down any further? I really like that painting."

"Of course, he will. Just keep on going, if we don't see anything you like better, we'll go back and play his game."

Another half hour of looking and Andrea still had trailing vines and jutting cattails on her mind. "Do you think it would help if we bargained in francs?" Andrea asked.

"No, dollars are valued because of the exchange rate. Okay, if that's the one, let's go for it," Lans said, prepared to do battle for his lady.

The clerk saw them coming. "Ah, Mademoiselle, it is lovely painting, no? *L'artiste est,* how you say, very talented. *Tres bien, n'est-ce pas?"*

"Yes, it's very nice," Andrea agreed.

"Alright, alright, two hundred dollar just for you."

"Can't you do any better than that? I simply don't have that much money." Andrea shrugged and looked sad.

"One hundred-sixty, I give it to you," he said raising his hands, as though he were bereft.

Lans stepped in. "Mademoiselle has only one hundred dollars. She would like the painting. She will offer you one hundred; take it or leave it."

"No, no, Monsieur is an artist. His paintings worth much more."

"Sorry, that's the best we can do. Come, Andrea, let's keep looking."

"Hundred fifty," the clerk called after them as they left the shop.

Lans pretended not to hear him and led Andrea back the way they had come.

"Lans," she said. "I feel sorry for him. It probably is worth that much. It's very good."

"Don't be fooled, Andrea. In France salesmen respect you more if you bargain with them. They think you're stupid when you pay the first price they ask. It's not like buying something in a department store in the States. They expect you to dicker. It's part of their standard procedure."

"How much do you think he'll come down?" Andrea entered into the game. "I really would like to have it."

"It depends on how hungry he is," Lans said. "You never know 'til the deal is made. That's part of the excitement. We'll go back for our final time in ten minutes."

They walked in and out of several more shops, watching the owners bargaining with their customers. "See, everyone does it." Arriving back at the shop, Lans cautioned Andrea, "Now, watch this and don't say a word. Give me your traveler's checks."

"Ah, Monsieur et Mademoiselle. You cannot forget zis painting?"

Lans stepped in front of Andrea. "Mademoiselle has only one hundred dollars." He showed the shopkeeper the five twenty-dollar traveler's checks. She will give them all to you for that painting. Think about it while we look around once more." He turned his back and fetched Andrea. Taking her by the arm, he guided her around the shop until they arrived back where they had started.

"Mademoiselle, here is good painting for one-hundred dollar." He held up another painting of a country scene, which had none of the strength of the arching bridge she liked so much. It lacked any detail that caught her fancy. She shook her head.

Lans turned her around as if to leave again.

The shopkeeper ran around in front of Andrea. "For you, Mademoiselle, one hundred dollar."

"You mean for the one I want?" He shook his head in the affirmative. "Oh, thank you. I will enjoy it so much. Can you take the canvas off the frame and roll it up?" She illustrated what she wanted with elaborate sign language.

"*Oui, oui,* Mademoiselle," he said, clearly happy to have made the sale. She signed the five twenty-dollar checks and turned them over to him. Removing the nails that held the canvas to the frame, he rolled the painting like a scroll, wrapped it, and handed it to Andrea.

"*Merci,* Monsieur." Andrea smiled and hugged the painting to her. Lans grabbed her other hand and led her out of the shop. "Oh, Lans, we did it. Thank you for persisting. I will treasure it always and think of you every time I look at it."

"I like the way your face lights up when you're happy," he said. "Be sure to keep that promise. Hey, look at the time. We have to get back to get ready for the banquet tonight. Are you up to walking?"

"Yes, it's a glorious day."

⌘ ⌘ ⌘

Sunday morning Andrea and Lans strolled through the gardens of the Tuileries on their way to their last lunch together before Andrea and her parents boarded a plane for Copenhagen. As Saturday night had been for lovers, Sunday morning appeared to be for families. Intrigued by glimpses of French family life, Andrea watched children in their Sunday best launch toy sailboats in the ponds. At home, everyone would have been dressed in shorts and blue jeans. Here they all looked like they had stepped out of a fashion magazine.

"Look at the twins dressed in sailor suits. Aren't they adorable?"

"I can imagine you with a couple of kids like that, Andrea."

"That dressed up? Surely not on the farm."

"Maybe in church on Sundays."

"I haven't been to church in years. Not since Grandma died."

"I'd have thought you would have wanted to go all the more."

"Probably I should have, but I couldn't understand how God could allow such good people to end their lives in such misery. I still don't, but I'm trying. I'm not quite so angry about it now that I know they're together with him."

"There are many things we'll never understand, Andrea. Look at those parents playing with their children. You can see they love every minute of it. Did your parents or mine ever take time to do that with us?"

"Not very often, but we had good times on the farm."

"Your dad worked every day."

"Yes, but he was with us at night. You have to make the best of what life deals you, Lans. I've been wondering how you will be. You seem so caught up in your work at the university. Will you be just like your father? Will work be the driving force in your life?"

"Not if I can help it."

Andrea wanted to ask him what kind of a family he wanted, but she dared not discuss that subject.

"Wasn't last night fabulous?" The final banquet of the Congress had been held at Versailles in the grand ballroom. The regal surroundings, the multiplicity of courses, the excellence of the cuisine, and the service belonged in a historical novel. "I'll never forget the elegance of it." She exhaled.

"Will that be the highlight of your trip? Or was it the opera with Chico?"

"Oh, Lans, you're too funny. The highlight of the trip will have to be seeing you again on that wonderful first night when we danced under the stars. No replica of the life of kings and queens could beat that."

"Yes, I'll remember it, too. Are you hungry? To be truthful, I've had enough food this week to last me a lifetime."

"I'm not hungry enough to do a French meal justice."

"Then let's sit here for a minute and talk about the future." Lans took her hand and guided her to an isolated bench at the edge of the park.

⌘⌘⌘

After settling her on the bench, Lans faced her as if he were ready to do battle. Searching her brilliant blue eyes, he found them enchanting, the color of an ocean on a sunny day. They sparkled with sunlight in the daytime and candlelight at night. Whatever time or condition of the day, they invited him to join in her fun. Her eyes exuded a warmth he did not have. His was an analytical mind. Good at figures, at problem solving, he lacked the depth of compassion he found in Andrea. When she invited him into her world, he experienced more of life. He felt complete. Realizing he needed her, he could not let her go this time.

Andrea interrupted his thoughts. "Will you stay here after you graduate?"

"I had thought about it, but now I'm not sure. I wasn't prepared for how I felt when I saw that Chico character sweep you into his arms. Since then I haven't been able to think about anything but how easy it would be to lose you again. If I stay here, I'll leave you vulnerable to all those crazy American boys."

Andrea glanced at Lans and laughed. "You must be joking."

He studied her in complete seriousness. Did she feel what he was feeling, an inexpressible yearning that had built mysteriously inside him in all their years of trying to spend time together? A yearning he had crushed down until he thought it had gone away. "I know it's been a lot of years in between, Andrea, and we haven't spent much more than a month together overall, but there were all those letters and all those years trying to get together when we were younger."

"Yes, it seems I've known you all my life," Andrea spoke in little more than a whisper.

"I don't know what happened that changed things between us that weekend at Dartmouth. I thought you had changed."

"I've always been the same, Lans. It was you who changed. It was like you were someone else. College had gone to your head and you were trying to fit in with all the kids from boarding schools. The boy who had loved the simple pleasures at the farm seemed to have died. I was heartbroken. And when I told you I had decided to go to Smith to be near you, you didn't say a thing. You left me thinking you couldn't have cared less."

His heart panged as he thought how much he must have hurt her. He looked away. "Since you were already committed, I didn't know how to tell you I wouldn't be there. Nothing worked out that weekend, and I didn't know how to deal with it, so I didn't." He turned to her again. "I'm sorry if I hurt you, Andrea. I didn't want to."

"After this week, it doesn't hurt anymore." She smiled at him. "This week has erased all those sad memories."

The tightness in his throat relaxed, and his heart flip-flopped. He took her hands in his. Then, fumbling into his pocket, he withdrew a small box and handed it to her. "They don't have fraternities here, so I don't have a pin to give you, but I want you to wear this promise ring. It's a promise that I'll come back to the States as soon as I graduate so we can spend time with each other and explore a future together. Are you willing to commit to that, Andrea? I'm in no position to offer you anything more than that right now, but I want you to know that you're still the only girl I've ever thought about spending my life with. I can't bear the thought of losing you before we have a chance to see if it can work. Will you accept it? It means no impetuous eloping with Chico or his like."

"Oh, there's only one like him. And there's only one like you. I'd be thrilled to wear your ring and explore a future together when you come home." Her eyes sparkled as he slipped the ring onto her finger.

"I can't believe this is happening after all these years and in Paris, of all places. I always dreamed it would be at the farm."

"Then you didn't give up on me the past three and a half years?"

"No, I tried to tell myself it was over, but something deep inside wouldn't let go."

"I'm grateful," he said. Taking her in his arms and holding her close, he kissed the top of her forehead and nuzzled his face in her hair.

⌘ ⌘ ⌘

154

Andrea's heart boomeranged around the trees as she lifted her hand and admired the delicate ring. Had it been the Hope Diamond, she could not have appreciated it more.

In Lans' arms, here on the other side of the Atlantic Ocean, in a land where no one spoke her language, she felt perfectly at home. A calm peace and a rushing joy overcame her all at once. "We're just like all the French couples making public displays of affection. Isn't it wonderful? Lans," she cried out as she broke away and looked at him in alarm. "Are you sure it isn't just that romance in Paris is contagious?"

"I'm sure, Andrea, quite sure," he said as his arms enfolded her once again.

22

With a heavy sigh, Andrea closed the scrapbook. The pictures had evoked so many happy memories, her present life seemed unreal. How could she ever feel anything but love for Lans? He was the answer to her childhood prayers. Everything she had ever wanted in a man. After sharing a storybook marriage with him for a quarter of a century, how could she face the crumbling of the wonderful world they had built together?

Where had they lost touch with each another? Unlike her grandparents, they had been too busy to share their day over a piece of pie and a cup of coffee. As their problems with Evelyn grew, they failed to pray together. Hurt feelings never resolved hung in the air and turned them into adversaries rather than partners. Shocked by the thought, she struggled to understand their dilemma from his perspective. Lans needed her, and he couldn't see beyond that.

Driven by the fear of losing her marriage, she called every Employment Agency in town. She would search until she found a companion strong enough to live with her mother.

The women she interviewed held little promise. As she neared despair, an agency called to say they had just heard from a woman they had placed once before. She had contacted them to say her job would be ending in two to three months and she would need a new situation. They described her in glowing terms, insisting she was worth the wait. They would send her application in the mail for Andrea's consideration.

"Three months can be like three years," Andrea said aloud as she replaced the receiver.

"What's happening in three months, dear?" Evelyn, now in her sweet mood, had not hallucinated since Lans left for Paris.

"Someone may come to visit us," Andrea said, "but it's a long way off and might never happen. Don't worry about it, Mom. It's time for your favorite program."

Andrea turned on the television set. When it claimed Evelyn's attention, Andrea tiptoed to her bedroom. Convinced only God could help her, she spent more and more time praying for direction and reading her Bible.

Had she and Lans been in the practice of praying together daily, she felt sure this could not have happened. Lans had taken her back to church, prayed at every meal and blessed the food, but he never started the family devotions she suggested. She read Bible stories to the children. He listened when he was home but never participated.

Their relationship with God was important to them both, but it was private. Lans had never shared his personal prayer life with her.

She knew the Lord was her answer. Everything she tried to do in her own power failed. She turned to him now with determination, praying long hours, seeking his presence and his peace. Looking for guidance, she began reading books on spiritual healing. She started listening to Christian radio stations. Evelyn found them comforting, for she loved to sing. Learning new praise songs became their best shared activity, as refreshing as the stream that flowed through the woods at the farm.

Often the radio announced that healing ministries would be coming to town. Andrea, believing each one might produce the lifeline her mother needed, helped her dress and hauled her to one healing service after another. Still smart and trim in her stylish clothes, Evelyn showed no sign of how severely her mind had deteriorated. She sang praise songs with joy and allowed Andrea to take her arm and stand with her in prayer lines. Andrea's faith for spiritual healing increased as she witnessed many miracles, but Evelyn remained unchanged.

⌘⌘⌘

Andrea ran to the phone, ever hoping to hear the voice of her husband. He would have been home two weeks now, but he had not called. She decided she would not be the first to break their silence. She, too, had a measure of pride. After all, it was he who had abandoned her.

"Andrea, dear, it's Katharine. We're coming through Pittsburgh next week. I must see you."

"Katharine, I'd love to see you." Andrea started to cry at the sound of his mother's voice. "I'm sorry. I've tried to be strong. I didn't expect to hear from you."

"I can't wait to put my arms around you. I know something is terribly wrong. Lans was so excited that you were coming to Paris and we'd all be together. He didn't warn us that you hadn't come. He merely said you had stayed home to care for your mother."

"That was true enough," Andrea regained a measure of control.

"Ordinarily, I wouldn't ask, but may we stay at your house? We don't have much time, and I want to spend every minute we have with you."

"Of course. Mother and I are desperate for contact with the outside world. You can tell me about all I missed in Paris."

"Lans was unbearable, but it's you I'm interested in. Don't hold anything back but tell me what's happening between you and Lans. I hardly recognized him, his behavior was so negative."

"Didn't he even try to cover it up?"

"With other people, but not with us. It was no use. I could see he was miserable. We'll arrive sometime late Wednesday afternoon. We'll take you out to dinner."

"Thank you, but it would be easier for me if we could eat here. Do you mind?"

"Whatever's easiest for you, dear. Johan has a morning meeting in town on Thursday, and we have to be on our way by 2:00 in the afternoon. He's giving a speech in Akron that night."

"It will be wonderful to see you, Katharine. Thank you for coming. I really need you."

⌘⌘⌘

The Mulders arrived as expected. Andrea had prepared Katharine's favorite meal—roast lamb like her grandmother used to make. Conversation centered on the excellence of the meal and their trip to Paris. Johan described meetings they attended and Katharine filled Andrea in on social events. But it was the times apart from meetings and social events that would have meant so much to Andrea and Lans. Her heart ached as their presence made her realize what she had missed.

Katharine directed much of her attention to Evelyn. They had been good friends. She tried hard to find a way to connect with her, but the world of international business and social experiences meant nothing to Evelyn. She remembered when they first met and how they became friends, but she had no memory of anything after that. The places they had traveled, the experiences they had shared were jumbled and failed to come into focus. Over and over again she asked Johan what his business was, shaking him so badly, he left the table to prepare his speech.

Evelyn chatted about her work in the garden while Andrea and Katharine washed the dishes. After sharing a final cup of tea at the kitchen table, Andrea excused herself to put her mother through her nighttime routine. Evelyn found comfort in the ritual and slept better when Andrea followed every detail.

Free, at last, the two women sat down on the couch in the living room.

"Andrea, I'm so sorry. I never dreamed it was this bad."

"I'm trying everything I know, Katharine, but nothing is working. You wouldn't believe some of the things we've been through."

"Oh, my dear," Katharine said taking Andrea's hand in both of hers. "How could Lans abandon you when you need his strength more than ever? He loves you very much, you know. He was so excited that you had found a sitter and planned to make the trip with him."

"So was I. Can you imagine how I felt when everything I had so carefully planned fell through, and it was too late to make other arrangements?"

"Yes, dear, I can."

"There's really nothing you can do, Katharine, except continue to be my friend. Let me lean on you like a mother. I need a mother so much. Mom has no interest in how I feel and what my life has become. Sometimes I cry out deep inside, 'Mother, this is your daughter. Just once, care about how I feel. Mom, stop thinking about yourself and listen to me. Just this one time, hear me.' It's as though she isn't there, yet she is there all the time without stopping. Do you know what I mean?"

"Yes, I felt the same way when I was trying to help her remember all the things we shared. It seemed she really wasn't there anymore."

"I often wonder how much she knows deep inside. She still has feelings and can easily be hurt."

"Yes, she's probably more sensitive than she can convey to us."

"It's horrible to watch her lose her dignity. It's like living through Grandpa's decline all over again. Sometimes she's pathetic. Other times she's selfish and angry. At first I thought she wasn't trying, that she could do better if she concentrated. I begged her to listen to what I told her. But I've read enough about it now to know she can't help it. The pathways in her brain are all snarled and twisted. A personality change is common for Alzheimer's patients; so is turning against the person closest to them. She thinks I'm trying to take the farm from her and that I'm trying to put her in a mental institution like she did her father. I can't think of anything worse than losing your mind."

"I agree." Katharine regarded Andrea with deep concern and caring.

It helped Andrea to know that someone in the Mulder family offered her sympathy. "If Lans had a bit of your compassion, we wouldn't be in this mess."

"I'd like to tell that young man a thing or two. I thought I raised him better than that."

"Don't say anything to him. I'm sure somewhere inside he knows he should be helping me, but scolding him will only make him more defensive and harden him further."

"Spoken by a woman who's lived for years with a stubborn Dutchman!"

They laughed together. Andrea, grateful that the evening had ended on a happy note, enjoyed having someone she could confide in, someone who cared.

⌘⌘⌘

The next morning Katharine made several long-distance phone calls. When she finished the last call, she searched for Andrea and found her tidying Evelyn's bed.

"Ah, let me help you with that," she said, grabbing the other side of the bed covers. "Andrea, I have something to suggest to you."

"You have my full attention." Andrea lifted the spread onto the bed.

"I remembered a friend of mine in New York talking about going to a clinic in Georgia where they specialize in chelation treatments. She came home full of stories about people with various ailments who had been healed. I talked to her this morning and she said there were several patients there with Alzheimer's. Dr. Malcolm Henderson, the doctor in charge, was quite confident he could improve their condition. Chelation treatment isn't recognized yet by the medical profession, but it's gaining respect among those who aren't afraid to try alternative methods. She said it's being offered in major cities now, but this clinic is among the best. She was so enthusiastic, I thought you might want to give him a call and talk to him about your mother."

"What's chelation?"

"It's a process of putting a substance called EDTA and mega doses of vitamins directly into the bloodstream. It forces out the bad kind of calcium deposits, heavy metals and other impurities, and it opens up arteries. He's had the greatest success with people with angina pain. After treatment, many of them never have pain again."

"Wow. That sounds interesting. What's the place called?"

"Woodhaven Retreat."

"I've never heard of it, but I'll certainly talk to the doctor. We have nothing to prevent us from going. The children won't be home until Christmas."

The ring of the telephone interrupted their conversation. Andrea picked up the receiver to hear an angry male voice ask for Katharine Mulder. Andrea gasped and covered the mouthpiece. "Katharine, it's Lans, and he wants you." She stretched out the phone to her and clasped her stomach as if shielding herself from the shock. "I'll leave you alone," she said as she rushed from the room.

Katharine found Andrea on her knees in her bedroom, the room that she and Lans had shared. She knelt beside her and put her arms around her back.

"Let's pray together," she said. "Dear Father in Heaven, we come before you humbly asking your intervention in the lives of these two fine young people. Father, we know that nothing is too hard for you, not even Evelyn's illness. If this clinic is the answer, I pray that you will lead them there. If you have another solution, please show Andrea what it is.

"Father, reveal your loving nature to my son and soften his heart toward his wife. Oh, Father, bring them back together, whatever it takes." She raised her hand to her mouth as if to stifle an involuntary cry. Tears streamed down both faces. Andrea reached for a box of tissues and extended it to Katharine.

Katharine wiped her eyes. "Andrea, I have to leave early. He's furious that I came without letting him know. He says I'm being disloyal to him. He's sent a car to fetch me to have lunch with him and Johan. Andrea, I'm so sorry. I apologize for my son."

"No need to do that, Mother," Andrea said, still wiping her own eyes. "I understand completely. Thank you for coming. I needed you more than I realized. May I call you Mother after all these years? It will be sort of like losing a friend and gaining a mother, but that's what I need right now."

"Of course, dear. I'd be honored." They embraced and cried on each other's shoulders.

23

A ndrea wasted no time looking into chelation treatments at Woodhaven Retreat. It seemed more than coincidence that several of her fellow church members had been there with good results. One had been admitted with acute angina pain. After taking treatments for a week, he began taking long walks. Now he walked six miles a day without pain. With high hopes she made a reservation for mid-October.

⌘⌘⌘

"Tell me about your family history, Mrs. Mulder. Did anyone on your mother's side experience a loss of memory?" Dr. Henderson took notes on a legal size pad. He peered at Andrea over his glasses, which rested halfway down his nose. His rotund figure denied the healthy lifestyle advertised in the clinic brochure, but his face exuded warmth and concern. A kindly man, he soon won her confidence.

"Yes, my grandfather—that is her father—developed Alzheimer's disease at the age of fifty-two. They called it *early senile dementia* then. He died of it five years later."

Evelyn sat in the room, disinterested in the conversation but fascinated by the colorful medical charts on the walls.

"And his parents?" Dr. Henderson prompted.

"Yes, but I have no idea what their proper diagnosis was. I often heard my grandmother and mother talk about how they both lost their minds in the end. I came to believe they both had Alzheimer's."

"I see." He scribbled something down in shorthand. "Anything before that?"

"I have no idea. Mother's grandparents came over from Germany soon after they married."

"And on your father's side?"

"Nothing like that. Only heart disease, cancer, things like that. What does that have to do with Mother's history?"

"Just trying to get the complete picture," he said. "You are aware of the strong hereditary tendency of this disease, are you not?"

"I am," she said, "but aren't there other factors that influence it: stress, diet, exercise? I've even heard it related to a woman's menopausal history. I've read dozens of articles. Many mention an excess of aluminum in the system." Andrea glanced at Evelyn to make sure she was not listening to their conversation. "They all indicate the exact cause of Alzheimer's has never been proven, Dr. Henderson."

"We're all trying to learn as much as we can about the disease, Mrs. Mulder, so we can help people like your mother."

"Can you help her, Doctor?"

"We'll have to do extensive testing first to chart her blood circulation, particularly to the brain. It will tell us a good deal. May I suggest since you are staying with your mother anyway, that you take the tests as well? It is something you will have to watch."

The thought had occurred to Andrea with increasing frequency, but she refused to dwell on it as her mother had. "I guess I might as well, since I'm here."

⌘⌘⌘

Having left Evelyn conversing with a nurse and another older patient, Andrea sat in the room outside the doctor's office waiting to learn the results of the three days of tests she and her mother had taken. Although apprehensive, Andrea believed nothing he could tell her about her mother's condition would surprise her.

His nurse appeared at the door. "You may come in, Mrs. Mulder."

The doctor looked up as she entered and waved in the direction of a chair opposite his desk. "You understand that we believe we can help both you and your mother increase the length and quality of your lives."

"Yes, Doctor. Everyone I've talked to here thinks you're next to God. They're buzzing with stories about all the people you've helped. It's very reassuring."

"Good," he said. "Your mother's case, as you know, is well advanced. However, with our treatments, the disease may be slowed down. We are hopeful that we can help her measurably. You must understand, however, Mrs. Mulder, that Alzheimer's disease is much more difficult to treat than heart pain or even cancer. I can't promise you anything."

"Yes, Doctor, I understand. How long do you think it will take?"

"I recommend treatments for six weeks."

"Six weeks? That's a long time, and they're very expensive."

"Did you see the young boy whose cancer is in remission before he left this morning?"

"Yes, he was radiant and so were his parents."

"He was here for three months. Do you think it was worth it to them?"

"Yes, of course. All right, we'll do it. When can you start Mother's treatments?"

"This afternoon after lunch. Each session takes two to three hours. She can sleep, read, or watch television. She will be seated in a comfortable chair while she receives intravenous treatments."

"Am I free to take a walk during those times?"

"We haven't discussed your test results yet, Mrs. Mulder." He lifted his glasses and regarded her with deep compassion. He began telling her the results of her electrocardiogram and blood and urine tests. He read to her the flow of blood rates in various parts of her body, particularly to the brain. "The build-up of plaque in your arteries is considerable." He shook his head as he looked at each new page.

"What does it all mean, Doctor?"

"It means that your arteries are badly clogged already and that the blood flow to your brain is inadequate. Without treatment you could become acutely senile in six months."

Andrea stared at him. "I feel just fine, and I'm not at all forgetful."

"I'm only telling you what the tests indicate."

"Acutely senile in six months." The words rang in her ears. Six months? Didn't it take years of forgetfulness to become acutely senile? She desperately wanted to believe it wasn't possible. But she remembered the rapid decline of her grandfather as he lost not only his memory but his concern for his beloved Laura. Almost overnight everything he said and did was totally unlike her experience of him.

Could it really be that fast for her? An overwhelming fear and dread like she'd never known overcame her. The horror of it so terrified her that she had difficulty hearing what the doctor was saying.

"I don't want to scare you, Mrs. Mulder, but you may well be in deep trouble if you don't take the treatments. One thing we know the chelation treatments will accomplish is removing unwanted calcium, which is destructive to the nerve cells. They are also especially helpful in removing heavy metals like aluminum, which has long been associated with Alzheimer's. I was surprised myself to see your test results, but you are fortunate to be here where you can receive immediate help."

"Fortunate?" She stared at him in disbelief, until she remembered the young boy who had gone home that morning, his cancer in complete remission. This doctor was no charlatan. He knew what he was doing. He had been diagnosing and helping people for years.

"The treatments are important for your mother, but they are urgent for you. May I schedule you to start with your mother this afternoon?"

"Y-yes, I-I guess so." Andrea felt like someone had just thrown a fifty-pound weight at her stomach. Off balance, her head reeling; she couldn't think. She had to get away and be by herself. "Are we finished, Doctor?"

"Yes, if you have no further questions."

"Thank you," she said as she rushed from the room.

Andrea knew only one thing at that moment. She needed fresh air. Fear clouded her mind and built in her throat, closing it down. Her stomach churned, and everything inside her constricted. She folded her arms across her middle, trying to hold herself together.

The horror of the doctor's revelation followed her. The evil one hurled unwanted thoughts at her like a knife thrower pinning his victim to the wall. *You have so little time. There's nothing you can do. Your husband will recoil from you.* Her chaos focused on one certainty: her children must never know.

She pushed through the exit door of the clinic into a crisp fall day. The sun shone on the red and yellow leaves and warmed her, lessening the chill of the doctor's words. A solitary path invited her into the surrounding woods. Feeling the need to keep moving, she ran until she came upon a wooden bridge across a stream. Taking hold of the railing, she looked down at the water gurgling beneath her. It reminded her of the farm when she and Lans had climbed into the treetops onto the branch that reached across the creek. As carefree as the flowing stream, they had watched the water rush merrily by. They were rushing into the beautiful world of first love.

But that was then. Now she could not see the beauty. Darkness swirled around her and tried to claim her.

She picked up a stone and hurled it into the water, shattering the peaceful scene. The water splashed in all directions, then calmed and continued its steady flow.

But there was nothing steady or peaceful about her life now. She needed Lans, needed him to face this crisis with her. She would call him, but he would be at work. Not a good time to interrupt him. Should she even tell him? She had to talk to someone. Katharine. Yes, she could call Katharine. She had suggested that Andrea bring her mother here.

She stumbled back to the clinic but hesitated, afraid to reenter that strange, threatening world. Out here among the trees she felt more at home.

She stood at the edge of the woods staring at the building. Did it represent life or death to her?

Forcing herself to go inside, she crossed the lobby and closeted herself in the phone booth. Her hands trembled as she fumbled through her change. The very thing she could never allow herself to consider, the one thing she could not handle, confronted her. First her grandfather, then her mother. Was it her turn now? Why so young? Her grandfather had had all that worry about the trial. The accident had been the catalyst for his early decline. She thought of the tension she had endured the past two years. Was it playing havoc with her mind and body?

She dialed Katharine's number and counted four rings. *Please be there, Katharine.*

Someone picked up the phone. A cheerful voice said, "Hello, you've reached the Mulders."

"Katharine, Mother, I need you."

"Andrea, what's wrong? You sound terrible."

"I am terrible. I'm at the clinic where you suggested I bring Mother. We've both spent three days being tested, and I've just been told our test results."

"You took the tests, too?"

"Yes. The doctor said Mother is well advanced and needs the treatments, but that they're even more urgent for me because they could do more good."

"Why you, Andrea?"

"He said I..." The words gagged her throat.

"Yes, Andrea, go on."

"He said I could become acutely senile in six months."

"Is the man mad?"

"He's very well respected, even revered. He's helped many people. Just this morning a young boy went home completely well. He had cancer, and after three months of treatments, it's gone."

"You need a second opinion," Katharine said with force.

"Katharine, you were the one who recommended him. Remember?"

"My friend thinks highly of him. But you still must have a second opinion."

"I'm out here in the country with Mother. I can't leave her, and since I'm here anyway, I said I'd take the treatments. But it's what I wouldn't ever allow myself to think about. Mother feared all her life that it would happen to her. Now that fear is on me. Katharine, I'm so frightened."

"Don't accept it. Just take the treatments for good measure, and we'll pray that God will take this terrible thing from you."

"Yes, of course. That's what I needed to hear. I want to call Lans, but I can't."

"Why not?"

"Can you imagine what he'll think? He'll be glad he's stayed away. He can't stand seeing Mother deteriorate. He won't be able to cope with the idea of his wife's brain becoming marred with plaques and tangles. Promise you won't tell him?"

"Andrea, he should be there with you, to hold you, to comfort you."

"Yes, I want that, but I know now it would only hurt the way he thinks of me. You'll agree with me if you think about it, but I have to talk to someone. Allow me to talk to you, Katharine. I'll trust you completely if you promise you won't tell him."

"Andrea, this is much too serious to keep from your husband."

"Okay, I'll think about it; but for now, promise me you won't tell him."

"All right, but call me every day this week and any time you need to talk."

"I will, Katharine. Thanks for being there for me."

"Oh, my dear, of course I am."

Andrea hung up the phone feeling comforted. She was not alone.

⌘⌘⌘

Andrea received treatments with her mother. She sat reading every morning and afternoon as the doctor's formula dripped into her veins. She could not concentrate on her book, nor could she shake haunting thoughts that she would lose her memory, lose her dignity, watch Lans witness her deterioration. She tried to be brave and brush them aside, but they remained.

That day in the doctor's office fear planted a root. Every time she returned to the memory, another root grew until a stronghold claimed more and more power over her. She smiled less, laughed less, worried more. Sinking into a low-grade depression, she could function and take care of herself and her mother, but every thought about the future brought with it the paralyzing fear that, sooner or later, even if the treatments were successful for a time, she would become another victim of the dreaded disease.

After the first week of treatments, her mother rebelled at being restrained. She stopped eating. The doctor promised her a bowl of ice cream if she would sit through the treatment. As she received more and more ice cream, she lost her appetite for everything else.

167

Andrea argued with the doctor. "It can't be good for her, eating all that sugar with no vegetables or wholesome food."

"You're right, but the most important thing is that she keep taking the treatments. She's willing to do anything if we reward her with ice cream."

"There must be a better way." Andrea thought it foolish to have started the ice cream. Now Evelyn demanded it every day for lunch and dinner.

Andrea had looked forward to mealtime. The food, tasty and healthy, appealed to the eye, but waging the everlasting war with Evelyn and the doctor took all the pleasure from eating. Although Andrea longed to leave the clinic, fear for her mother and fear for herself kept her there.

She talked to Katharine often. "Mom, I don't know what I'd do if I couldn't talk to you. When I think how easy and happy my life was just a few years ago, I realize I didn't appreciate it nearly enough. Most people don't value what they have until they're faced with losing it."

"Andrea, don't sound so defeated. Your life isn't going to stay this way. You and Lans have years of happiness ahead of you."

"I used to think so. Now I don't know."

"Andrea, Johan leaves tomorrow for two weeks overseas. I'm not going with him. I've been thinking I would enjoy a trip to Georgia. The leaves are turning and it would be a lovely drive. Could you get me a room in the nearest motel? I'd like to visit you for a few days."

"Yes, please come. I need to see you. Sometimes I think I'm going crazy in here."

"I think I need to have a talk with that doctor," Katharine said.

⌘⌘⌘

As their six-week stay came to an end, Andrea loaded the car and prepared to start the long drive home to Pittsburgh. She still had no idea what to think of the whole experience. Katharine had come and scolded the doctor for giving Andrea such a frightening diagnosis. He had shown her great patience, answering question after question about the test results.

Katharine had met and talked to many patients who had benefited from the treatments. There seemed little doubt that the clinic was saving and improving lives. In the end, Dr. Henderson won her confidence and convinced her that the treatments were necessary for Andrea.

Evelyn's behavior remained much the same. The doctor insisted she would live years longer. Years longer, but with what quality of life? Evelyn did seem to be forming her words better and to be moving with greater ease.

Andrea hoped the expensive treatments had done some good, but her mother's memory had not improved.

Andrea felt their bodies had benefited, but they had not received the kind of miracles the heart patients and some of the lupus and cancer patients experienced. The fear that the treatments had not helped her enough to ward off the oncoming Alzheimer's remained embedded in her consciousness.

Andrea watched her mother say good-bye to a group of nurses. In spite of her stubborn refusal to eat her food, Evelyn had become a favorite of both the staff and the other patients. Known for her unusual antics, labeled the ice cream lady, she seemed to enjoy holding the attention of a group of people and making them laugh. When she arrived, she had been afraid of being "put away." Now she played the part of the social queen she used to be. It warmed Andrea's heart to see her in that familiar role.

The doctor appeared to bid them good-bye. "Ah, you're looking well this morning, Evelyn." He called them by their first names now. "Andrea, you should be grateful for the treatments. Your mother is much improved. Your final tests show improvement, but you should take local treatments once a week from now on and come back for a season of several weeks every year."

The threat remained. *Will it ever leave me?*

She thrust out her hand. "Good-bye, Doctor. Thank you for your good care of Mother and me." She turned to Evelyn. "Bid everyone farewell, Mom. If we don't leave now, they'll have us hooked up again in no time. Now's our chance to escape."

Everyone laughed and hugged Evelyn as they would a child. All the staff and many of the patients waved as they drove down the long driveway and turned onto the highway. Andrea, relieved to put the experience behind her, anticipated a pleasant drive home.

24

The first hour on the road went well. Evelyn chatted about everything and nothing. Andrea, grunting agreement now and then, focused on Lans. She had not spoken to him the entire six weeks of their stay. How she longed to see him, to feel his arms around her. Should she call him? If he knew what she had been through, would he be more caring or would their relationship become more strained?

Aware that Evelyn had quieted, Andrea glanced at her. Her mother sat upright, rigid, staring straight ahead. Her mouth hung open as if she had stopped midsentence.

"Mother, are you all right?" She looked again. Evelyn had not moved.

As Andrea turned back to the road and contemplated where she could pull off the highway, Evelyn broke loose and grabbed the wheel. "Andrea, pull over. You'll hit my dog. She's running in the middle of the road."

"Mother, let go. You're interfering with my driving." She managed to loosen Evelyn's hands from the wheel.

"Stop, Andrea, stop. You'll hit Tabitha. Can't you see her on the road?"

"No, Mother, I can't see her. She isn't there. She's safe at home. Jane is taking care of her."

"She's there, I tell you." She grabbed at the wheel again, but this time Andrea pushed her mother's hand away before her hold tightened. Pulling the car onto the shoulder of the road, Andrea turned off the ignition. She looked into Evelyn's face and saw her eyes wild with fright, her features distorted. They held not a trace of joy. Social Evelyn was gone.

Evelyn hunched over and raised her finger to her mouth. "Shhh," she said. "Your father's sleeping in the back seat."

Andrea turned and looked behind her. Except for their cosmetic cases and jackets, the seat was empty. She looked back to her mother.

"Get me home immediately, Andrea. There's a big dog at my feet, and I don't have enough room."

Bewildered, Andrea started the car and pulled back onto the highway.

"Watch out for Tabitha," her mother screamed.

Andrea jumped. "Mother, don't do that. We'll have an accident."

"We'll have an accident if you hit my dog."

They drove on in silence, Andrea trying to discern what her mother was seeing.

"Are we almost there?"

"Mother, we're just starting. We'll be driving all day. What's happened to you? You we're so happy the first hour."

"Keep your voice down, Andrea. You'll wake your father."

⌘ ⌘ ⌘

Toward evening Andrea pulled into her driveway. She had driven straight through, stopping only once for gas. She contemplated looking for a hospital along the way, thought of calling Lans for advice. Instead she kept on driving, reliving the long ride to Long Island when she was a teenager, knowing she should stop to call Lans, not wanting to shorten their time together. That drive had set her nerves on edge, but this was far worse.

Throughout the long drive Evelyn imagined her little dog running on the road just ahead of the car. "You'll hit her, you'll hit her! Pull off the road," she cried again and again. A minute later she demanded, "Faster, Andrea. Take me home, now!" She described to Andrea animal and human passengers crowded in the front seat between them and stacked in the back where she thought Leonard lay sleeping. Nothing she said made sense. Although she no longer grabbed the wheel, she asked every few minutes when they would be home.

⌘ ⌘ ⌘

Andrea braked the car and turned off the ignition. Her hands fell to her lap, shaking, her fingers curled as though they still gripped the wheel. Exhausted, wanting only to collapse, she called up resources she didn't know she had.

She took Evelyn inside to her bed and rang the doctor's office. Close to six o'clock. She prayed he would still be there. He answered. When she told him what had happened, he instructed her to take her mother to the hospital immediately. "I'll call to have her admitted and be there as soon as possible." Andrea felt the first sense of relief from the long nightmare. Soon she would receive help.

⌘ ⌘ ⌘

The doctor put Evelyn on Valium to calm her, but she experienced an allergic reaction to the drug and fell in and out of consciousness. When awake, she hallucinated more than ever. At night she awoke screaming and became so violent the nurses strapped her to her bed.

The little rain that must fall into every life now seemed to Andrea to be coming in torrents. She had slept in a chair in Evelyn's room every night for a week. When sleep would not come, she read from the Psalms, seeking the comfort that evaded her. All week she pondered the meaning of Psalm 121. "The Lord will keep you from all harm." What did that mean? She went to sleep thinking about it and considered it anew every morning. Stopping in the hospital library, she found a commentary and learned that the believer would be preserved, not that he would never suffer adversity, but that he would go through it and come out a winner.

Adversity seemed to own her. Would the Lord keep her through it all? One thing was becoming clear to her. *Only* the Lord could see her through it.

At last the doctor declared Evelyn out of danger. Andrea had been so focused on her mother; she had taken no thought of herself. Glancing in the mirror she saw eyes dull and tired, large circles beneath them, her hair barely combed. Time for a beauty rest.

At eight o'clock in the evening she gathered her things to go home for a good night's sleep. On the way to the elevator her eyes fell upon a row of telephones. Without thinking of the consequences, she called Lans and asked if she could come to his apartment to see him.

⌘⌘⌘

A strange sensation gripped her stomach as she drove up to her husband's residence for the first time. She parked the car and knocked on the door. The two-story townhouse was larger than she expected. *He must plan to live here a long time.* Having no idea what she would say, she knew only that she had to see him.

Lans opened the door. "Andrea." He looked puzzled. "What's happened? Have you been in a car wreck?"

She raised her hands to her hair. "Oh, I didn't think about how I looked."

"Come in," he said. "Tell me what's wrong."

She laid her jacket and purse carefully on a chair and turned to face him. She opened her mouth to speak but didn't know what to say. Why had she come? Not to tell him about Evelyn. Not to tell him about herself. She had nothing to say to him.

"I'm sorry I disturbed you. I must go." As she gathered her things, Lans looked at her as if she had lost her mind. Maybe she had. She hastened toward the door.

"Andrea," he said, his face stern, voice hard. She turned around, dropped her bag and coat on the floor, and threw herself into his arms, sobbing.

He put his arms around her. They felt so good. He softened, and soon he was stroking her back, trying to comfort her, saying nothing. "Thank you, Lans. Thank you. I needed that so much." It was all she could say. She sobbed again, loud, choking sobs from deep within.

When she had quieted, he said, "Now tell me."

"There's so much. And you don't want to know any of it." She left the comfort of his arms and faced him, surprised to see moisture in his eyes. "Mother's in the hospital here. We've been at a clinic in Georgia for six weeks. I left a message with your secretary in case you tried to call."

"Yes," he acknowledged.

"Mother had stopped hallucinating and was doing quite well. We thought it had helped her, but she had a stroke on the way home and went absolutely crazy. She saw Dad lying on the back seat, her little dog running on the street in front of the car. At first she kept grabbing the steering wheel to pull me off the road. I wanted to find a hospital. I wanted to call you to ask what to do. Instead I kept driving. When we got home, I called her doctor. He put her in the hospital and gave her Valium. She had an allergic reaction to it and, Lans, it's been awful. I'm exhausted and falling apart, and I couldn't think of anything but to come to you. I'm sorry."

"Don't be sorry, Andrea. I'm glad you came."

"You are?"

"Next week is Thanksgiving, and I'm going to college to spend it with the kids. Come with me."

"Oh, Lans," she cried and started to sob again.

"Don't tell me, I know. You can't leave your mother."

"The house next door has come on the market. I've been thinking about buying it for her and hiring a companion to live there with her. It would be even better than fixing up the garage. What do you think?"

"She won't stay there. She'll be pounding on our door every day, firing whoever it is you find." Bitterness returned to his voice.

"You'll see. I'll work it out, but it will take time."

"Yes, of course." He closed up again.

"Don't send me away like this. It was so good to feel you cared, even for a few minutes."

"Andrea, you know perfectly well I care. Don't torture me."

"Do you ever think what it's like for me, Lans, away from you all this time, having to deal with these terrible things?"

"It's your choice. There are homes for people like your mother where constant medical help is available and where they are taken care of very well."

"I've visited them all. They tie patients like her to their chairs all day and drug them so they haven't any fight. I couldn't do that to Mother."

"We've had this conversation before, Andrea. What do you want me to tell the children?"

"That I'm looking forward to their coming home for Christmas and that I hope to have a companion for Mother by then so we can do things as a family."

He stared at her. "You never get the point, do you? No one can live with your mother. Look what she's done to you!"

"I'll work it out this time, Lans. Trust me. I agree this can't go on any longer." She gathered her things again, kissed him on the cheek, and whispered, "Thank you. Please pray for the right person." She left him standing in the middle of the room and hurried to her car.

She could have spent the night, but this time he hadn't asked her.

⌘⌘⌘

Andrea went home and slept better than she could remember. In the morning she called a realtor and asked for an appointment to see the house. Next she called the employment agency. They had heard again from the lady they had recommended. She would be ready to take appointments in two weeks. "Excellent," Andrea said. "I'll make myself available at her earliest convenience."

Evelyn came home at the end of the week, calm now and overjoyed to find Tabitha waiting in her room. The effects of both the stroke and the Valium had worn off and she seemed much better. Perhaps she had benefited from the treatments after all.

The treatments! Reminded of her own plight, Andrea shivered the length of her body. The fear in her belly remained firmly entrenched.

⌘⌘⌘

Once rested again, Andrea made her morning Bible Study and prayer time a priority. Each morning while her mother slept late, Andrea pursued her relationship with God. She had prayed for her mother's healing to no effect. Now she turned to God with renewed vigor to seek her own healing. She

174

longed for the peace she had once known, but at each mention of the future, the phrase *"if I'm still well"* formed in her mind. Fear colored her every thought.

She heard the teaching that worry is a sin and studied the command of Jesus: "Therefore I say to you, do not worry about your life." A footnote defined worry as a "distraction, a preoccupation with things causing anxiety, stress, and pressure." Did that not describe her life? Distracted from her job of helping others, she focused on herself. Jesus told her to take no thought of tomorrow but she couldn't escape the preoccupation with her future. Determined to change, she copied Matthew 6:34 on a three by five card and taped it to her mirror. Every morning and every evening she read it aloud. "Therefore do not be anxious for tomorrow, for tomorrow will care for itself. Each day has enough trouble of its own." With this statement she heartily agreed.

⌘⌘⌘

Adele sat on the couch with her hands folded in her lap. Andrea, more nervous than she, fumbled with lists of questions to ask during the interview. Adele's auburn hair, pulled back in a bun, was beginning to gray at the temples, but she looked the picture of health. Her stylish brown suit with an orange suede collar and cuffs complimented her brown eyes and reddish complexion. Her appearance pleased Andrea.

"Tell me about yourself, Adele. How long have you lived in Pittsburgh?"

"I've lived here all my life. Started out on the South Side in Mt. Lebanon. Now I live wherever I'm working."

"Have you ever traveled?"

"I visit each of my children every year…one in Florida, one in St. Louis, and one in Denver. I always wanted to see Europe, but my husband and I never had the money. We got by nicely, mind you, but with three children, there wasn't a lot left for vacations."

"Mother has traveled a great deal. She will enjoy telling you all about the places she's been. Would that interest you?"

"Oh, yes. I love to hear about faraway places. It's the closest I come to being there."

"How long have you been a widow, Adele?"

"It's been eight years now, and I'm still not used to it. I miss Henry, but I try not to think about myself. I just care for those I work for, and that keeps me going."

"How many people have you cared for?"

"Three in these last eight years. I had short-term jobs before that when Henry was alive. The first was a woman in her sixties who died of cancer. The second was a cantankerous old man who moved to California to live with his daughter. I wasn't too sorry to leave that one," she confided. "And I've been five years taking care of a young boy who's been very disturbed by his parents' divorce. His father is remarrying, and the new wife thinks she can handle him. She has a lot to learn."

"So you have dealt with difficult situations."

"Yes, ma'am, I have. You just have to establish right off who's in command, nicely, of course. Then everything goes fine," she said with unusual confidence.

"Have you ever worked for anyone with Alzheimer's Disease? The agency told you that's Mother's problem, didn't they?"

"Yes, they did, and no, I haven't, but Henry's sister had it and he was her only relative. She died just a year before he did. I was mighty glad I didn't have to take care of both of them when he took sick."

"Well, it sounds like you've had a great deal of experience. I must warn you that Mother can be difficult, but I will work with you to make it as easy as possible. Would you like to meet her?"

"Yes, Mrs. Mulder. You and I can talk on and on, but what counts is how your mother and me take to each other."

"Good, I'll bring her in, or perhaps you'd like to come out to the garden. She was a fine gardener in her day. She had a beautiful home with a big patio that was surrounded by raised flowerbeds. She kept them weeded and as neat as you've ever seen a garden. She still loves to have her hands in the dirt, but she doesn't know the difference between weeds and blades of grass any more. She spends her days tearing up our lawn, but I let her do it because it keeps her happy. It's good exercise for her, too."

Andrea held the door open for Adele. As they walked outside, they could see Evelyn on her hands and knees pulling up the grass from Andrea's lawn.

"I see what you mean. It's a pity to struggle through all that work for nothing."

"Think of it as therapy, Adele." Andrea turned to her mother. "Mother, I've brought a special friend to meet you and I've asked her to stay for lunch. This is Adele Kransky. Adele, this is my mother. You may call her Evelyn. We're very informal these days."

"Hello, Evelyn, you pull a mighty mean weed. Looks like you enjoy getting your hands in the good earth."

"I've done this whole section of the yard." Evelyn pointed with her mud-packed nails to a large area of brown space in the otherwise well-manicured lawn. Soon I'll be starting one over there." She waved her hands toward the far side of the fishpond.

"Well, good for you, dear heart, you're doing a fine job."

The use of the endearing term her grandmother had used for her as a child startled Andrea. She hadn't heard it in years. Other things about Adele reminded her of her grandmother, too. Adele, more fashionable, had watched her figure, but there was something homespun about her, like Andrea's grandparents. She sensed she would like her.

Adele helped Evelyn up from the ground. "Will you take me for a walk around the garden, Evelyn, and show me your favorite plants?" She turned to Andrea. "You can go to the kitchen and see to lunch, Mrs. Mulder. Your mother and I will take a little stroll and get acquainted."

Andrea could see who was going to be in command of the household, but she felt they were off to a good start. Adele was all the employment office said she would be.

⌘ ⌘ ⌘

After lunch, Evelyn showed Adele one of her scrapbooks from Europe. Filled with pictures, newspaper articles and clippings about Leonard's speeches and awards, it even contained a few about Evelyn speaking to the wives of businessmen from other countries. Andrea had brought it out thinking it would be good for Adele to know that her mother had not always been helpless.

When they had finished looking through the scrapbook, Adele stood up and announced it was time for her to leave. She gathered up her pocketbook and shook hands with Evelyn. "Thank you for taking me on such a nice tour of the garden, Evelyn, and on a tour of Europe as well. Not many people are privileged to do both in one afternoon. It was nice to meet you, dear. Don't work too hard in the garden now."

"Bye," Evelyn said with unusual sweetness. "Come back again sometime."

"Perhaps I will." Adele beckoned to Andrea to follow her to the door.

"I'll walk you to your car, Adele," Andrea said as she opened the door.

When they were outside, Adele turned to her. "Your mother is a sweet lady, Mrs. Mulder. I like her."

"You do? You do understand Mother is not always so content."

"I understand perfectly. Do you want me to consider the job?"

"Why, yes, I do, Adele," Andrea said, surprised it was Adele who was concluding the interview.

"Good. I will ask the good Lord if this is where he wants me and let you know what he says."

"So you're a Christian, Adele?"

"Been a God-fearing Catholic all my life. He takes care of me, and I do what he says. It's a good arrangement."

"Indeed it is. Perhaps you could teach Mother and me a thing or two about that."

"I'll require time off for church every Sunday."

"I'm sure that can be arranged."

"You'll be hearing from me soon. Thank you for lunch," she said as she sat down in her car and prepared to leave.

As Adele drove down the driveway, Andrea raised her hands toward the sky and spoke aloud. "She just may be the answer to my prayers, Lord." Andrea felt more hopeful than she had in a very long time.

25

Three days later Adele called Andrea to say she could start the job the second week in December. Andrea hung up the phone and cried aloud, "Lord, you are so good to me." She twirled in delight, as happy as she had been dancing down the streets of Paris when she and Lans were young. "Thank you, Lord."

She would have two full weeks to establish a routine before the children came home for Christmas. Adele would occupy the bedroom next to Evelyn's until February, when Andrea would close on the house next door. If everything worked out, Evelyn and Adele would move into that house together, and Andrea would have a life of her own again. She could travel with Lans and give her full attention to the children when they were home during the summers. When Lans saw how well things were working out, he would move home, and her family would be intact again.

Andrea wasted no time starting to ready Adele's room. As she worked, she turned on a praise tape and began to sing. Evelyn heard the music, came to the door, and peeked inside.

"Hi, Mom, do you remember Adele, the lady who came to lunch last week? She'll soon be coming to stay with us."

"You're leaving me!"

"No, I'm not going anywhere, but she'll be a lovely companion for you. You had such a good time walking in the garden with her and telling her all about your trips to Europe. It will be like having a friend again. You'll like it."

"Where are my friends?"

An often-asked question Andrea declined to answer. When old friends did come for a visit, Evelyn could not remember them. They were sympathetic at first, but Evelyn's conversation was so self-centered, they sensed she had no interest in anything that concerned them. Andrea apologized and explained her mother couldn't help her self-focus; it was part of the disease. Soon they gave up and stopped coming. Evelyn hadn't had a visitor in months.

"I know why." She answered her own question. "It's because I'm a dummy now."

Andrea took Evelyn in her arms and caressed her. "You're not a dummy,

Mom. God loves you, and he's sending you this wonderful lady to take care of you."

Evelyn pushed away from Andrea and pointed a finger in her face. "I want you to take care of me."

"I'll still be here, but the two of us together can do a better job."

"You want to go away and leave me." Evelyn's voice rose to a scream. "You want to desert me, too."

"Mom, I love you and the children love you. They'll be home from college soon, and Adele will help us get ready for them. We'll have a good old-fashioned Christmas with all the traditions you started when I was a child. You'll see. It will be lovely."

"I want to go to the farm for Christmas."

"How can you forget everything but the farm? It's been years since we spent Christmas on the farm. This isn't the year for that." Andrea closed the subject.

"You won't ever take me to the farm."

"Mom, it's too cold now. You wouldn't enjoy it. We'll try it next spring when the weather is better."

"You're keeping me from the farm." Evelyn's voice rose further.

Andrea turned up the music. "Sing with me, Mom. Tell the Lord how much you love him."

Andrea began to sing as she finished making the bed. She took Evelyn's hands and moved her around the room in a dancing step. Evelyn loved the music. She soon forgot her complaints and began to hum along. "Lord, I lift Adele and Mother up to you. Bind them together in love. Please bind them together in love. I don't know when I've wanted anything so much, Lord. Please make it work."

⌘ ⌘ ⌘

At the end of Adele's first week, Andrea sat in the living room reading before the fire, the back of her neck taut, her shoulders hunched halfway to her ears. It had been a hard day. She felt like a bow stretched to its fullest. One more problem and she would let go, sending an arrow zinging through the air to pierce the next person to bring her bad news. *Stress is one of the factors I can control. I mustn't be this tense. It will bring on the Alzheimer's.*

The dreadful disease hung over her like a death sentence. The words *acutely senile* repeated in her mind as they had endless times since her stay at the clinic. Her family knew nothing about the terror that woke her at night, the unrelenting fear that was her constant daytime companion. Tense and taut, she shuddered, then made a concentrated effort to relax her shoulders.

She could hear Adele's slippers flip-flop down the hall. As the sound came closer, she looked up to see Adele with her chin raised high. "Your mother fired me today, Andrea. Would you like me to leave?" She stood erect, almost rigid, giving no other sign of emotion.

Andrea motioned to the chair opposite her. "Sit down, Adele, and tell me about it. Neither you nor Evelyn had anything to say at dinner. I should have realized that you had quarreled."

"I do not quarrel, Andrea."

"No, I mean I realized something was wrong. What happened?"

"After the nice, healthy lunch I fixed her, your mother wanted a dish of ice cream. I told her it wasn't good for her, and she left the table and went to her room. I followed after I cleared the table to check that she was taking her nap, and I found her eating a candy bar. I took it and threw it in the wastepaper basket explaining that too much sugar had given her the stroke on the way home from the clinic, and that we weren't going to eat sugar anymore. She became furious and called me names I will not repeat." She drew in her breath and held herself even more erect.

"I'm sorry, Adele. You know Mother doesn't mean anything she says when she's angry."

"She must respect me and my judgment. I know what is good for her, Mrs. Mulder. You know I'm trying to establish good habits for your mother."

"Yes, of course, I know that, Adele. But you must remember that Mother no longer thinks like an adult. If someone takes something she wants from her, she pouts like a child."

"She fired me. She told me to pack my things and to get out of this house."

"Adele, you know that I do the hiring and firing now. I'm very pleased with the way you care for Mother and I wouldn't think of firing you for such a thing. Mother will have forgotten it in the morning and I hope you will, too."

She drew herself up again. "You will explain to your mother why I am still here if she questions?"

"Yes, Adele. Now get a good night's sleep and think no more about it. I'm sure it will happen again, but please don't take it seriously. Just imagine how you would feel if you couldn't control anything in your world. It must be a scary feeling."

"I love your mother, Andrea. I can tell she was a great lady, and I'm trying my best to make her happy."

"I appreciate your efforts more than I can tell you, Adele. One day Mother will, too. Just give her time to adjust. She was a very independent woman."

"Thank you, Andrea. I'll leave you in peace now."

Peace. *Is there any peace for me when someday soon I may be just like Mother?*

⌘⌘⌘

Christmas morning Lans arrived before breakfast and talked to Andrea while she cut fruit and made the children's favorite muffins. The four of them had attended the Christmas Eve service together the night before while Adele took care of Evelyn. It was the first time Andrea had kept a promise to Lans since her failure to go with him to Paris. He arrived Christmas morning as relaxed and optimistic about the future as she was.

When John and Kate appeared, they plugged in the Christmas tree lights. "It's time to gather in the living room," John called out. Kate turned up the music. Soon enthusiastic voices rang with "Joy to the World." Andrea looked around at the smiling faces and thought her heart would burst.

When the music stopped, Kate knelt before the coffee table. As the youngest child of the family, she lit the Christmas candle. Lans indicated they should all hold hands and form a circle around her. He recited their traditional Christmas prayer and prayed a blessing over each member of the family for the coming year. "And please give a special blessing to Adele as she cares for Evelyn. We are so grateful, Lord, that you sent Adele into our midst. May the coming year be all that we hope it will be. Amen." He squeezed Andrea's hand so hard she could tell he was sincere. "Now John, it's time to read the cards on each gift under the tree and Kate, you may distribute them."

As the ritual of opening one at a time began, Adele sat with Evelyn on the couch. "Here, dear, let me help you with that bow. The card reads, *To Gran, with love from Kate.* My, this is beautifully wrapped, Kate." Adele opened the box and held it before Evelyn, who pulled out a lovely beige shawl. She pressed her fingers against the soft material and smiled. Adele laid the shawl around Evelyn's shoulders.

"I hope you like it, Gran," Kate said. "It will keep you warm on chilly nights."

"Now isn't that thoughtful," Adele murmured.

"Thank you, dear, it's lovely." Evelyn reached out her hand. Kate rushed over and embraced her.

Andrea took a deep breath, releasing some of the tension she had felt as she prepared for the holiday. How she wanted this to be a successful Christmas.

Warm family fellowship continued around the breakfast table, the children exclaiming delight over the muffins and everyone talking about their gifts. It was the first time Andrea and Lans had engaged in normal conversation since her failure to accompany him to Paris.

After breakfast John and Kate asked to be excused to exchange gifts with their closest friends and Adele took Evelyn to lie down for a nap, leaving Andrea and Lans alone with no responsibility but basting the turkey. A silent snow decorated the trees outside as the two of them settled before the roaring fire.

"This is a good Christmas, Andrea," Lans said as they sat down together. "Adele seems to have the ability to keep your mother happy and content. I meant it when I thanked the Lord for sending her to us."

Andrea liked his use of the word *us.* It was the Christmas she had hoped and longed for. Sitting alone with Lans relaxed and happy in their home was even more than she had anticipated. "It's good to see you smile again, Lans. There will be many more times like this, I promise."

"This is one promise you were able to keep, Andrea. If this honeymoon between Evelyn and Adele lasts, my hat is off to you. You said you would find a solution and you have."

Andrea left Lans and moved into the kitchen where she pulled the turkey from the oven. As she lifted the lid, the smell of the roasting bird flooded the house.

"Am I ready for one of your turkey dinners," Lans exclaimed as she returned. "Restaurant turkey just doesn't do it."

"Do you take all of your meals out, Lans?" They had never discussed his lifestyle.

"All but breakfast. I do manage to pour myself a bowl of granola," he said, laughing.

When Andrea had finished her chores, instead of sitting in the chair opposite Lans, she picked up her knitting and settled down on the couch next to him. "You'll have to come home for a meal more often."

He said nothing but reached over and put his arm around her and pulled her closer. She continued to hold her knitting, but her hands fell to her lap. She laid her head on his shoulder and savored the moment. Neither of them spoke. He searched for her hand. She let go of the knitting and gave it to him.

"I'm so grateful for this day, Lans. It's been such an encouragement to me that we're still a family, that we have a future together. Thank you for today. It's been lovely."

"And it isn't over yet. My mouth is watering for your turkey dinner." He was in better humor than she had seen him this whole year.

"Mom always did say that the way to a man's heart was through his stomach."

"Your grandmother must have taught her. She believed a good meal was the answer to everything."

"You're right. When I was a little girl, Christmas was a wonderful experience. Grandma cooked for weeks ahead, making eleven different kinds of Christmas cookies, caramel candy, and chocolate fudge. For Christmas dinner she served not only stuffing with the turkey but mashed potatoes and noodles and bowls full of gravy, and, of course, apple and mincemeat pies."

"Ugh. It sounds like an orgy," he said as they laughed together.

"All that sugar and carbohydrates, and we ate every bit of it and loved it. I can't imagine eating all that now."

"You don't look like your grandmother did either," Lans said, "for which I have always been grateful."

"She was a wonderful woman."

"Yes, but you are a wonderful woman, too, Andrea, and your figure is as trim as when you stood in that daisy field and floated toward me like an angel. I've been thinking of that a lot lately."

"Have you, Lans?" Andrea could feel her cheeks flush. She was no longer accustomed to his compliments.

"Andrea," he said, his voice turning serious. He hesitated, caressed the top of her hand and began again. "Andrea—"

Determined footsteps pounded the stairs and Evelyn burst upon them. "I will talk to my daughter, and you can't stop me." Lans separated from Andrea as though they had been caught stealing forbidden intimacies.

Adele followed close behind Evelyn. "I'm sorry, Andrea. Your mother has been complaining about not having the run of the house and being cooped up in her room on Christmas Day. I was trying to give you and Mr. Mulder some time to be alone."

"She wouldn't let me be with my family on Christmas Day. Nobody wants to be around me anymore. They think I'm a nobody without any feelings. Well, I am somebody and I'm going to prove it." Evelyn, close to hysteria, ran from the room and out the front door.

No one followed her. Adele apologized for the outburst. Andrea tried to calm Adele. Lans said nothing but looked as though his best friend had

184

betrayed him. Andrea looked at Lans' expression, and ran to him and grabbed his arms. "Lans, I'm terribly sorry. Mother will calm down. Don't let this spoil our day." She pleaded with him with her voice, with her eyes. "It's been such a lovely day and it isn't—"

A loud crash in the driveway broke her thought. The three of them looked at each other in horror. Andrea bolted for the door. She ran toward the gate that led to the garage. Evelyn's car had crashed into the brick wall that separated the garage area from the house. Andrea opened the car door and found Evelyn sobbing over the wheel. "I just wanted to prove that I am someone," she cried. "I thought if I showed you I could drive, you'd know I'm still a person."

Andrea reached in and turned off the ignition. The right fender had hit the wall but the driver's side of the car was intact. Andrea helped her mother, shaking and crying, from the car and put her arms around her. "There, there now, Mom." She comforted Evelyn as Laura might have done years ago. "Everything is all right. You don't have to prove yourself. We all know what a fine woman you are. We know you are a person with feelings, and we want you to live with dignity. Mom, we're all trying so hard to make you happy. How did you find the keys?"

"They were lying on the hall table." Evelyn sobbed louder.

Adele stood by, shaking her head.

"Adele, take Mother to her room and let her rest until dinner." Adele put her arm around Evelyn and led her, still sobbing, into the house.

Andrea turned to Lans, frozen to his spot on the driveway, his eyes blazing. "Lans, I know you're angry and disappointed, but don't run away. Don't leave us to eat Christmas dinner alone. The children will be home in a short time. This was a setback, but Adele is working out. Soon they'll be living next door, and things will be normal again."

She took his arm and led him toward the house. He allowed her to guide him but remained silent. When John and Kate returned and throughout the dinner, he acted as though nothing had happened. But Andrea could feel him distancing himself from her. He had reached out to her. They had stepped up to the door of reconciliation, but Evelyn had slammed it shut. The magic of the day evaporated as though it had never been. The chord that bound them together seemed frayed, almost severed.

26

That night Andrea lay on her pillow reviewing the day. She had opened her heart to Lans. He was about to come in when Evelyn rushed into the room. Andrea saw again the horror on his face after the crash.

Inside her, self-pity moved in to room with fear, which had taken up permanent residence. Fear saw its opportunity and put down another root.

Is this all I have to look forward to? Every time we get close, Mother ruins it. Will I be like her before Lans and I get back together? She relived the crash and the pitiful sight of Evelyn crumpled over the wheel. *"I just wanted to prove I am someone."* Would Andrea experience that feeling of being a nothing someday? Without Lans to love her, she was halfway there already.

How she longed to talk to her grandmother. She had always been there to comfort Andrea when she needed her. But her grandmother had been dead such a long time now. Andrea cried again. The loss of her dreams for reconciliation with Lans merged into fresh grief over her early loss of her grandparents. Who now could she turn to for comfort? She tossed and turned and cried out to the Lord to guide her through these desperate days. In the early hours of the morning, she fell into a fitful sleep and dreamed of her grandparents.

Laura and Fritz were chasing each other in and out of the clouds. Fritz's wide smile flashed at Laura as he ducked into a cumulus billow and popped out again a cloud away. Laura jumped to his cloud but just as she caught up to him, he disappeared again. She turned around looking in all directions with a sweet smile on her young face, not the least disturbed that he was playing tricks on her.

Andrea saw him emerge again behind Laura. He crept up behind her and grabbed her by the waist. Turning her about, he lifted her from the cloud and whirled her around and around as though she were as light and wispy as the clouds themselves.

Andrea watched in wonder from a cloud nearby. Now they were both laughing as if they hadn't a care in the world. Andrea called to them, "Grandma, Gramps. I'm over here." They turned and looked in her direction, further delight registering on their faces.

"Andrea, dear heart, come to me." Laura extended her arms wide.

Andrea leapt from her cloud into Laura's warm embrace. As she received the comfort she had longed for, Fritz surrounded them both with his arms. The three of them were together again.

Laura drew back and scrutinized Andrea's face. As her grandparents both started questioning her, Andrea opened her mouth to answer them, but the sound she heard was her mother calling. Evelyn's voice penetrated the dream as Andrea struggled to stay with her grandparents. Evelyn called a second time, angry now. Andrea jumped out of bed and rushed into the dark hall. "Where are you, Mother?"

"I'm right here, and I can't sleep."

"It's too early to get up. The sun isn't up yet."

Evelyn ignored her. "It was a terrible Christmas. She wouldn't let me out of my room. She didn't want me to be with my family on Christmas Day."

"Mother, come in and sit here on my bed." Andrea turned on her light and put a comforter around Evelyn's shoulders. Evelyn rattled on about how angry she was while Andrea, fighting to retain her dream, said nothing.

She had been robbed of a longer visit with her grandparents, but she kept her disappointment to herself, savoring every minute that she had spent with them. As Evelyn wound down, Andrea squeezed her. "Mother, I have something wonderful to share with you."

"What is it?" Evelyn stopped complaining, as eager as a child to hear something wonderful.

"I was sleeping when you called me," Andrea started, "and I was dreaming about Grandma and Grandpa." She left out the part about how much she needed the comfort of her grandmother's arms. "They were young again, younger than I had ever seen them, except in photographs. Laura's hair was long and pulled back with a large ribbon. Fritz's thick hair was as straight as ever but it was brown without a speck of gray or white. Neither of them wore glasses and the wrinkles on their faces were gone. They looked so happy. They were playing hide-and-seek in the clouds. Then Grandpa slipped up behind Grandma and grabbed her and whirled her around like he used to when they were first married."

"How did you know about that?"

"Grandpa told me," Andrea said, surprised at the sharpness in her mother's voice. "It was like having a visit with them, Mom, and it was wonderful to see them happy together."

"Did Dad say anything about me?"

"No, they both started asking me questions, but that's when you woke me up. It would have been lovely to have had a longer visit with them."

"I'm afraid to see Dad. Do you think he can ever forgive me?"

"Forgive you, Mom?"

"Yes, for putting him in that institution."

"He must know by now it was to protect Grandma. But he's not like that anymore. He's young and well and happy with Grandma. I'm sure he never thinks about it now."

"It was only a dream, Andrea. It might not be that way at all."

"Of course, but I found it comforting and I thought you would, too."

Evelyn began wringing her hands. "I've thought about it so often." She pulled the comforter tighter around her. "What a terrible thing to do to your father. He'll never forgive me."

"Mom, you know you didn't have any choice. You did what you had to do."

Evelyn sank to her knees before Andrea and grabbed hold of her arms. "Andrea, promise me you'll never put me in an institution like that. Promise me you'll keep me with you and never put me away. I know it's happening to me. I can't remember things. I'm a dummy."

"Don't upset yourself, Mom. You're not a dummy. You're still a stunning woman for your age. Just look at your figure. Most women your age would give anything to look as sharp and trim as you do when you dress up for something special."

"But I don't have anywhere to go, Andrea. Where are my friends? Why don't they ask me to play bridge anymore?"

"You've chosen to cut yourself off from many of them."

Evelyn shook her head. "It's because I can't remember the cards." She tugged at Andrea with even greater force. "Promise me, Andrea. Promise me."

"I promise to keep you with me as long as I possibly can, Mom. And maybe, if you just tried a little harder—"

"No, not as long as you can. Promise me you'll never, ever, put me into a place like that."

Andrea reached down and put her arms around her mother. She tried to comfort her just as Andrea wanted to be comforted. *Mom, Mom, how I need you to comfort me, to care about what's happening to my family. Just once, Mom, couldn't you take an interest in someone or something other than yourself?* Her yearning turned to remorse, and Andrea felt ashamed of her thoughts.

She stroked her mother's hair as she sang a lullaby Evelyn had sung to her as a child. Then she prayed aloud, "Lord, thank you that you are the God who heals. Thank you for the picture you gave me in my dream today of

Grandma and Grandpa healed and happy. Lord, I ask that you touch Mother now. Take from her the dark thoughts that haunt her. Lord, you are the God of peace. Please bring peace into Mother's life. We thank you for taking care of her."

They continued to sit on the edge of the bed, each of them grappling with the dark monster that had invaded their lives. A hungry creature with an insatiable appetite, it was swallowing up their joys and their most valued relationships.

27

Four days later the children returned from dinner with their father. Rather than coming inside, Lans dropped them off at the door and sped away. When they came into the house, they handed their mother a note.

Dear Andrea,
   Thank you for a delicious Christmas dinner.
   I have taken a six-month consulting job in Sweden and will not return until the first of June.
   Regards,
   Lans

Regards. Who sends a note to his wife and signs it *regards?* Andrea glared at the offending paper. She had empathized with Lans up to this point. Now, crushed by disappointment, she thought of him as the villain in her life. He was deserting her when she needed him most. Tired of trying to make things work, he was running away to Europe where no one would criticize him. She appreciated the check he sent every two weeks for the upkeep of the house and her personal needs. He provided for her financially, but emotional support was what she needed. She had never felt more alone than she did at this moment.

John watched Andrea's reaction to the note. "Kate, why don't you take Mother to church tomorrow? It will be good for her. I'll stay home with Gran until Adele returns from her church."

"I'd be happy to take you, Mom. It's just what you need."

"Your father is what I need," Andrea said, her voice devoid of hope.

"Well, it will be second best. Great idea, John."

⌘⌘⌘

John wondered how he would entertain his grandmother for two long hours. Although he had often spent time in her presence since the onslaught of her illness, he had never been alone with her. She could no longer play cards with him like she used to, or any other game for that matter.

"Gran, how about a nice walk in the park? Would you enjoy that?"

"Yes, John, I would."

"The sun's out, but you'll have to bundle up. It's cold."

"I don't mind."

He found her coat in the hall closet and grabbed a scarf from the shelf. "You can put this over your head." He buttoned her coat, led her to the garage, and installed her in the car. Heading for the park, he made light conversation and pointed to things he thought might interest her along the way. She chatted and relaxed until they passed the local nursing home.

"I know that place," she snarled at him. "Andrea wants to put me there."

"No, Gran, she promised you she wouldn't."

"She asked you to take me there."

"No, we're going to the park for a walk. Remember?"

"You're trying to trick me. I know what you've planned. Well, I'm not going." As the car stopped for a red light, she struggled to open her car door.

"What's got into you? Mom just needed to go to church." He reached over her and pulled the door shut. The car behind him honked as the light changed.

"You can't take me there," she screamed, grabbing the wheel as she had the day Andrea brought her home from the clinic. "I won't go."

"Gran, stop acting crazy. I'm taking you to the park," John repeated, forcing her away from the wheel.

She tried to batter him with her hands. "Take me home now."

"Okay, okay. I just thought you'd enjoy a change."

He accelerated the car, glancing at his grandmother as she scowled and brooded over her dark thoughts. When they reached home, he tried to help her out of the car. She drew back from him. "Don't touch me. I can do it myself." She rushed into the house, tripping over the threshold.

John hastened to help her. "Are you all right, Gran? Believe me, I'm not trying to hurt you."

He led her into the living room and sat her in one of the winged-back chairs by the fireplace. "I'll make a fire. Would you enjoy that?"

She glared at him, saying nothing as he crushed sheets of newspaper and piled logs on top. He lit a match to the fire and when it burst into flames, sat opposite her. She stared at him from frightened eyes as though he were a prison guard about to torture his captive.

"Do you know that she leaves me alone with all those people staring at me?" Evelyn broke the silence.

"What people, Gran?"

"The ones on the couches who are watching us now. She knows they want to steal my things, but she leaves me here alone with them."

John's eyes opened wider, and he shrank back into his chair as he looked around the room. "Who are you talking about? Mom and Adele never leave you alone."

"Your mother wants people to think I'm crazy so she can put me in a nursing home, but I made her promise never, never to leave me."

"Mom won't do that."

"Don't argue with me. Show respect to your elders. She wants to put me away. She wants to take the farm from me." She jumped up, ran to him, and grabbed his sweater. "John, John, save me. Don't let those people get me. Don't let your mother put me away." She started thrashing her arms against his chest. "The people, they're coming toward me. Save me, save me!" She collapsed at his feet sobbing.

Horrified, his eyes darting about the room, he gathered her off the floor. "Would you like to go to your bedroom and lie down, Gran?" He helped her up the two steps to the front hall and started up the long flight to the second floor. When the front door burst open, John jumped, ready to believe anything could happen next, but it was Adele returning from early church. "Am I glad to see you," he exclaimed in relief. "Gran needs you. She's seeing people coming after her, and just the two of us are here alone."

Adele took immediate charge. "There now, dear, Adele is here. There's nothing to worry about. Let's go upstairs and I'll bring you a nice cup of tea and a cinnamon bun." She turned to John. "It's all right, John. It sometimes happens when she gets frightened. I'm sure you were doing your best."

⌘⌘⌘

An hour later when Kate and Andrea came home, John rushed to his mother and put his arms around her. "I'm so sorry, Mom. I didn't realize what you've been going through until now. It must be awful."

Andrea stroked his arm. "It's all right, John. She can't help it. Don't think badly of her."

"It's you I'm worried about, Mom. You can't live this way."

Having their son understand and comfort her softened the shock of Lans leaving her.

28

Two months later Andrea lay awake listening to the wind howling through the trees. Alone in the house for the first time since Evelyn had spent a week in the hospital, she should feel relieved. Why then did she feel so empty?

She had not allowed herself to think about Lans. At first she concentrated on the final days of the children's visit, on the repair of the car, the closing of the house next door. She oversaw the remodeling, trying to make the house as pleasant as possible for Evelyn and Adele. Evelyn had complained without ceasing that Andrea was putting her out of her house while Andrea explained again and again that the move was in Evelyn's best interest.

The movers had arrived at 7:30 that morning to pack Evelyn's belongings, which were by now scattered throughout Andrea's house. Andrea returned Evelyn's crystal, her china, her silver, all of which had been mixed with Andrea's and incorporated into her kitchen cabinets when they sold Evelyn's apartment. At the time Andrea had marked every piece of Evelyn's furniture, making it easy now to separate the two households. As the movers carried each piece to the truck, Andrea felt a sense of relief. She liked space rather than clutter and looked forward to having her home sparsely furnished again.

They were able to pack, load, and unload all in one day since Evelyn's belongings were reduced to a minimum, and the distance was short. Evelyn had run around Andrea's house all morning, ordering the movers not to forget her favorite pieces, some of which had been given away years earlier. If Andrea had it to do over again, she would have sent Adele and Evelyn away for the day and handled everything herself. In the afternoon, Andrea had tried to make Evelyn feel she was in control by asking her to make decisions about where to place the furniture in the new house.

"Where would you like to put your favorite painting, Mom? This one," she said, holding up the painting they had bought in Italy on her first trip to Europe. "In the entrance hall, or how about over the fireplace? Remember how it arrived from Italy on your birthday, two months after we returned from Europe? What a wonderful surprise. I never saw you so happy. Dad was right that the man who sold us the painting would find a way to send it to us after Dad stopped payment on his check."

But, after the turmoil of the morning, such a decision was too much for Evelyn's troubled mind. "I don't know. I can't decide. Can't it wait?" She looked distraught and bewildered. The doctor had warned Andrea about the difficulty of moving a person in the advanced stages of Alzheimer's. The best thing for her was to remain in an environment where she knew where everything was. Since Evelyn no longer cared for herself, Andrea counted on Adele to put things where they would be most helpful, but that left Evelyn without moorings. Had it been a mistake to uproot her mother from all that was familiar to her?

The day had been long and Andrea lay exhausted on her bed. Sleep should have come easily, but with the move accomplished, she realized her days would no longer have meaningful purpose. She had nothing to do tomorrow but look in on Evelyn and Adele to make sure their new life started well. The children were happy at college. Lans had no need of her. Now that she could travel, go to Sweden to visit or stay with him, he was not interested. She had not heard from him since the first of January, the morning before he boarded the plane.

Waves of loneliness washed over her. Tears spilled onto her pillow. She had had so much to occupy her thoughts and so little time to think of herself. Now her future loomed before her, bleak and lonely. She had long ago relinquished all personal involvements, resigned from every board and charity that had once occupied her time, from every social group that might have given her pleasure.

Her body jumped as the wind rattled the shutter outside her window. Was someone trying to break in? She had never been afraid to be alone in the big house. It had been her home, her place of security; but there was nothing secure about her life right now.

And what would the future hold? *"Acutely senile in six months."* The offending words echoed through her head. They played back so often they had formed a groove in her mind. The slightest reminder triggered the needle of her mental recorder to fall into that groove and play those haunting words again and again. She and her mother had returned from the clinic five months ago. It would soon be six months. Dr. Henderson claimed that having taken the treatments, Andrea had delayed the onset of the disease, but the possibility that she would sooner or later have to face it stole her peace and filled her with fear and self-pity.

"My peace I give to you." The words formed in her mind. Immediately she felt guilty. The sin of worrying had claimed her again. Worry would not add a day to her life, but it might bring on the disease sooner. She turned on

the light and reached for the Bible on her bedside table. turned back to the concordance. "Peace, peace. Ah, there it She thumbed through the pages of the Bible until she found it.

"Peace I leave with you, my peace I give to you; not as the world I give to you. Let not your heart be troubled, neither let it be afraid." She the words out loud, then again to herself, willing herself to believe them.

She spoke to the Lord. "You are my peace. I trust you with my life. Whatever is left of it is yours. Lord, lead me out of this valley of despair and make my life count for something." Realizing her obsession with her own plight, she cried out, "Help me get my mind off myself, so I can be a blessing to others."

She thought she had cried enough tears, but still they flowed. Anxiety, her constant companion, gripped her body and pulsated through her veins. "I don't like the person I'm becoming. I'm so far from where I should be," she agonized as she turned off the light and lay back on her tear-soaked pillow.

"And lo, I am with you always, even to the end of the age." As the words came, a blanket of comfort smothered her desperate thoughts. "Lord, you are my hope and my comfort. I must have more of you." Andrea sat up in bed and raised her arms in surrender. This was the direction her life must take. She had tried before to know him better but had been bogged down in taking care of her mother. Like Martha, she had concerned herself with earthly cares. Now she must cultivate a Mary role, sitting at Jesus' feet and learning from him. Peace enfolded her as she sank into her pillow and snuggled into her blankets. A new challenge lay before her, perhaps the most important of her life.

⌘⌘⌘

Andrea awoke the next morning with a start as the sun, streaming in the windows, struck her eyes. The clock registered eight-thirty. She hadn't slept that late since her mother had come to live with her. She bounced out of bed with renewed energy, dressed in a rush, and walked next door to see how her mother and Adele were adjusting to their new surroundings.

Slipping into the house, she found them in Evelyn's bedroom. Evelyn lay on her stomach in her bed receiving a massage from Adele. "Good morning, Andrea," she purred. The pleasure in her voice had long been absent. Adele had made a good start.

"Good morning, Mother. You seem quite content. I trust you ladies had a good night's sleep."

served your mother breakfast in bed. She
ry day of her life."

ve it there for a long time, Adele. When she
, a live-in couple stayed in the apartment over
Mom breakfast in bed every morning and gave her
u re doing. Did she tell you?"

ought I'd make her feel special today. She liked it so much, I
ke it part of our daily routine."

nat's great. Mom, Adele is going to spoil you. You'll never want to live with me again."

"Can we take Adele to the farm?"

"Why, yes, we can." Andrea's face brightened at the thought. The two of them could handle her mother at the farm and then she wouldn't have to listen to her complaints about Andrea stealing the farm from her. She could leave them to go riding as well. "As soon as warm weather comes, the three of us will drive up to the farm." She already looked forward to new freedom.

"Since you two are happy, I'll go back to my house. Call me, Adele, if you need anything or can't find anything. I'm not sure myself where we put everything last night, but between the two of us we can figure it out." She bent over and kissed her mother and saluted Adele. "You're a genius. I haven't seen Mom so content in years."

⌘⌘⌘

Arriving back home, Andrea threw her jacket aside, grabbed an apple from the buffet in the dining room and bounded up the stairs to her bedroom. She settled into her favorite chair before the fireplace and opened her Bible. She leafed through the pages of the New Testament until she came to the book of Ephesians. *This will be uplifting,* she thought. A few seconds later the words of the third verse jumped out at her.

"Our Lord Jesus Christ, who has blessed us with every spiritual blessing." She read it several times and pondered the meaning of the footnote: "Spiritual blessing refers to divine privileges and resources available now." Lans prayed a blessing over each family member every Christmas, but it must refer to something more than that.

She needed divine resources and she needed them now. Wanting to learn more about these resources, she decided to do a study of the word *blessing.* She jumped up, jogged to her bookshelf and reached for a large volume, *Strong's Exhaustive Concordance of the Bible.* Now that she had the whole house to herself, she started speaking out loud as if God were sitting opposite her and carrying on a conversation. "Every day I'll look up verses that contain the word *blessing* until it is crystal clear what they are. Thank you, Lord, for giving me this direction. I'm excited about what I'll be learning."

She began with Genesis 12 and the blessings of Abraham. God said he would bless Abraham and make him a blessing and bless all those who blessed him. Her Bible explained that this meant not only material blessings, but God wanted to prosper him spiritually, emotionally, and physically as well. In the third chapter of Galatians, God promised to give all believers the blessings of Abraham. Intrigued, she wanted to understand what that meant.

Every morning she read a chapter of the story of Abraham and contemplated its meaning for her own family. When she came to the end of Abraham's life, she read about Isaac, the son of promise, and Jacob, who received his father's blessing. A new picture of God began to form in her mind. "Lord, you want to pass on blessings from generation to generation, not debilitating illness!"

29

Andrea delighted in her daily study, wondering why she had not started sooner. How could she have faced such a staggering problem without first turning to God?

Her Bible lay open on her lap as she prepared to look up the next reference to *blessings* in the large *Strong's Concordance.* As she stared at it, she remembered how angry she had been toward God, how distant he had seemed after the terrible deaths of her grandparents. But when Lans came back into her life, her thoughts toward God had returned to thankfulness. She was overwhelmed by the blessings he bestowed on her.

She remembered it was Lans who proposed that God be an integral part of their marriage. Lans had taken her back to church the year they were married. Once again, her mind drifted to a former time....

⌘⌘⌘

On a brisk March day in the spring of her senior year in college, Andrea waited for Lans under the clock at the Biltmore Hotel in New York City. A feisty wind blew away the remains of winter and ushered in the spring. Tulips peeped up through the ground in window boxes and park beds. The crisp air energized her. Her whole body tingled with expectancy.

The clock struck 5:30, their appointed time of rendezvous. Lans had planned to leave work by 5:00 and promised to be waiting for her, but she arrived first. She had spent most of her life waiting for Lans.

Dressed in a flattering blue and green wool suit, her long hair in a loose pageboy, Andrea looked her best. Her eyes danced as she experienced the thrill of the big city and contemplated a week with Lans. They had had a good weekend at college when he returned from Holland. Lans had been there to comfort her when the news came that her beloved Dolly had died. Today she waited for him with the assurance that he cared for her as she did for him.

Yet she still didn't know him well. He seemed so sure of himself. His years alone overseas had given him confidence that he could overcome any problem. His confidence gave her a sense of security when she was with him. When they were apart, she wondered if he needed her as much as she needed him.

As the big clock chimed six o'clock, Lans appeared on the run and swept her into his arms. "You look absolutely wonderful, darling. My boss called an important meeting at 3:00 this afternoon, and I couldn't leave until it was over. Forgive me for keeping you waiting."

"Now that you're here, it's easy to forgive you. When you look at me like that, I'd probably forgive you anything," she said, reaching up to caress his cheek. "Lans, I'm so excited about this week together. I have to tell you, my expectations are huge, and now that you're here, they're soaring."

"So are mine and, if I can help it, it will be even better than we anticipate."

He hailed a taxi and opened the door for Andrea to enter. As he settled in beside her, he took her hand. "I'm glad to see you're still wearing my ring."

"If I weren't, I'd have let you know long before now." Andrea laid her head on his shoulder as delicious feelings rushed through her and swept away the irritations and uncertainties of the long wait.

"I've found a great French restaurant that has just opened. A couple from France owns it. When I greeted them and ordered in French, we started talking. The second time I went, I was so homesick for you, I started telling them all about our week in Paris and that you were coming for a week in New York. They can't wait to meet you. I'm sure they'll give you the red carpet treatment."

"How wonderful. I didn't expect anything to be personal in New York."

⌘⌘⌘

The French couple welcomed her with old-world charm, the chef emerging from the kitchen to greet her in person, his wife hovering over them to make their evening memorable. When they sent their compliments to the chef, he returned to their table to prepare Crepes Suzette with extravagant flourish, his gift to their evening. Aware that Lans was watching her every move to make sure she enjoyed the excellent food and the European atmosphere, she relaxed. The warmth of the evening melted her reserves and chased away all her doubts. How she enjoyed being in his presence!

After dinner, they walked hand in hand around Times Square. Andrea's mood became ecstatic. As she floated down the street at Lans' side, she broke into dance. The bright lights of the billboards lit up her eyes. She flashed smiles in his direction.

"Lans, I feel like I'm on the dance floor of the Bois de Bologne. My feet won't stand still. Like I'm wearing the red ballet shoes, and they have a life of their own. Do you think I'm silly?"

"I think you're delightful. And I'm wondering if this sober businessman can keep you in ecstasy, or if I'll be so dull and boring, you'll dance right out of my life."

"Never, Lans. You dull and boring? Why, you're by far the handsomest man in Times Square, probably the most intelligent, too, and a great conversationalist. I'm sure you'll be successful at whatever you do. What more could I ask for?"

⌘⌘⌘

The Collins' family and the Mulders shared the box closest to the stage at the hit play *The King and I*. Andrea had heard such rave reviews, she expected to be disappointed. What could be so exciting about a romance between an English schoolteacher and the King of Siam? But she enjoyed it far more than she could have imagined.

Lans and Andrea started off holding hands, but once the play was in full swing, they clapped so often, they gave up. From the box in which they were sitting, Andrea felt she could reach out and touch the actors and actresses. She could see every expression. By the end of the show she felt that she was well acquainted with Gertrude Lawrence and Yul Brynner.

As they left the theater, they shared their delight in the show. "My favorite song was 'Getting to Know You,'" Lans said. "I could identify with wanting to know all about you."

"It was superb. I'll never forget the elegance of the costumes and those elaborate sets. And the song, 'Shall We Dance'…I think I'll be singing that for the rest of my life."

Ever the practical one, Leonard tapped Lans on the shoulder. "You have to be at work early tomorrow, Lans. Why don't you let me take Andrea to the hotel tonight? You go home with your parents and get some rest, or you'll be falling asleep on the job."

Lans and Andrea exchanged disappointed glances. "Yes, of course, that's the only sensible thing to do," she said, resigned as they followed the jostling crowd outside and up the street.

"I don't feel the least like being sensible tonight, but I'm sure you're right, Mr. Collins." Lans turned to Andrea. "When will I see you tomorrow evening?"

Katharine Mulder spoke up. "Andrea, why don't you come to Garden

City and have lunch with me tomorrow? Your parents and Johan must attend a dinner meeting tomorrow evening, but I hadn't planned to go. We can spend some time together in the afternoon, and then you and Lans can spend a quiet evening at home."

"That would be lovely, Mrs. Mulder. Mother, does that suit your plans?"

"Yes, dear, that would work well."

"You can spend the night and we'll go into the city together the next morning," Katharine continued. "We have tickets for Radio City Music Hall at Rockefeller Center in the afternoon. Would you like us to meet you for lunch or at the theater, Evelyn?"

"At the theater, I think. I'll have a nice breakfast with Leonard and skip lunch. Ever since I saw a picture of myself in riding britches on a ranch in Wyoming last summer, I skip meals whenever I can."

"Do you think you can find Garden City, Andrea? I wouldn't want to go through anything like we did last time you promised to come." Lans chuckled at the thought.

"I'm sure Dad can tell me the best way to get there. Believe me. I never want to relive that episode." Turning to Katharine, she said, "Thank you for the invitation, Mrs. Mulder. We never had that lunch in Paris, and we haven't been alone together since our days on the farm. We have so much catching up to do."

"Indeed we do, Andrea. I'll look forward to it. Any time after 12:00 will be fine."

Andrea and Lans shared a good-night hug. "It was another perfect evening, Lans."

"Yes, it was," he said. "But I'm already looking forward to a quiet evening at home, the one we missed when we were kids."

"I'll be there first this time." Her sparkling smile showered him with promises of great times to come. She slid her hand out of his as she backed toward her parents and blew a kiss in his direction.

He caught it and placed it on his cheek as they went their separate ways.

⌘⌘⌘

Andrea paid the taxi driver who had driven her from the train to the Mulders' house. On the short ride over, she relived the turmoil and failed expectations of her first trip to Garden City. Standing before the Mulders' door, she raised her hand to announce her arrival, marveling at how different things were this trip and how much had passed between her and Lans since then.

Before her hand reached the door, Katharine opened it. "There you are, Andrea. I see you had no trouble this time. How I'm looking forward to our time alone together." She chatted amiably as she took Andrea's jacket and ushered her into her home. "We could have gone out to lunch, but I thought it might be nice to stay here."

"Oh, yes, Mrs. Mulder, I've loved all the restaurants, but it will be great to have a home-cooked meal. Kind of like being back on the farm with Grandma," she said as her eyes clouded. "Goodness, I still can't think of her without getting tearful."

"She was a wonderful grandmother to you, wasn't she, Andrea? Come sit here a moment," she said, sitting on the couch and patting the cushion next to her.

"Yes, just about perfect. She taught me so much about the simple joys in life. Bigger and more is not always better. She and Grandpa had so little, but they had a whole lot more genuine happiness than my parents ever had, in spite of Dad's tremendous success and their bigger and bigger houses. Thank goodness for the farm. I think I'm a little less spoiled because of it."

"My dear, I would never consider you spoiled. But I remember those weeks at the farm as a very special time. Life moved at a slower pace than we're used to, but I enjoyed it very much."

"My grandparents belonged to a time that has passed. It wasn't so long ago, but it seems almost like another century. Grandma looked so much like a grandma with her rounded figure, her flat gray hair, and always her apron. I can't imagine you and Mom looking like that ever. That era is gone."

"I'm looking forward to being a grandmother, Andrea. I imagine Evelyn is, too."

"You'll make a wonderful grandmother, Mrs. Mulder. I can imagine you with a grandchild on your lap reading picture books, then making up bedtime stories."

"Do you want to have children?" Katharine asked.

"Oh, yes, I want very much to have them. And I want to be with them for all their important events, not always traveling like my parents."

"Yes, that's something you and Lans share. He's bitter about his father never being around to play sports with him."

"That's why the time at the farm was special, a heavy dose of family for both of us. Was it hard for you, Mrs. Mulder, having your husband away so much and then having to travel with him?"

"We lived an exciting life, but I disliked leaving Lans so often. I wanted a whole houseful of children, but it never happened. Johan always loved his work just like your father." Katharine sighed and rose from the couch. "I guess it's time for me to make lunch. Why don't you come into the kitchen and talk to me while I prepare it?"

⌘⌘⌘

With the dishes washed and put away, Katharine led Andrea into an informal sunroom. "What a lovely room…it's so cheerful and comfortable."

"Not very fashionable, but Johan likes it this way. It reminds him of the old country."

"The lace curtains on the windows look just like I imagine the windows in Holland. Have you enjoyed living in the States, or would you rather be living there, Mrs. Mulder?"

"We've been here so long, I seldom think about it. I guess I'm too Americanized to want to return. I'm used to all the freedom American women have and I like it."

"The girls at Smith talk on and on about their careers. Marriage isn't their first concern. They expect to marry, but they're much more excited about breaking into new fields for women."

"What about you, Andrea? How do you feel about having a career?"

"Well, until I do marry, I expect to work in the business world. I've worked off and on at Dad's office since I was twelve. He's eager for me to graduate and take a full time job with him. I guess I'll enjoy it, but it's not my heart's desire."

"What is your heart's desire?"

"That's something of a secret, Mrs. Mulder."

"I see how your eyes sparkle when you look at Lans, Andrea, and he talks about you all the time now. His father and I are so pleased that you and he are seeing each other again. If anything develops, we want you to know we would be pleased to give you our blessing."

Andrea blushed but said nothing.

Katharine continued her thought. "I was disappointed when Lans stopped seeing you when he was at Dartmouth. He had many short-term romances through the years, but none of them ever amounted to anything. He doesn't share himself easily, and he never found anyone he could open up to like he did to you on the farm. It was a first romance that never lost its magic. Even when you weren't seeing each other, he would reminisce about those days on the farm. He never forgot you."

"Nor I him."

"We were always rooting for you, Andrea."

"Why, thank you."

"I often prayed about it. 'Dear Lord,' I would plead, 'when Lans marries, please let it be Andrea.'"

"You embarrass me, Mrs. Mulder, but I can't think of anyone I'd rather have for a mother-in-law, if anything like that ever did happen, I mean." Her cheeks heated.

"Well, dear, that's just a little secret between you and me, but I wanted you to know how Johan and I feel."

"Thank you. Grandma would have liked to hear you say that. I used to read her Lans' letters and she always rooted for us, too. She said she thought the good Lord had put us together for those three weeks because he meant us for each other. Dear Grandma, everything was so simple and straightforward for her. She loved her Lord, but look how he allowed her life to end."

Katharine moved closer to Andrea and put her arms around her shoulders. "Lans used to tell us how upset you were that God would allow your grandparents to end their lives with so much tragedy."

"I never could understand it, and I still don't. I guess I never will, but I try now to focus on what a happy life he gave them and not how it ended. I don't believe it was God's plan for them to go through that long trial and to suffer such terrible illnesses."

"There's a common enemy we all have, Andrea. He does everything he can to stop that kind of happiness among humans."

"Yes, if I should be angry at anyone, it should be at Satan. He roars around seeking whom he may devour, and I have to be careful not to let him devour me with those bitter feelings."

"Have you forgiven God for allowing what happened to your grandparents?" Katharine withdrew her arm and gazed into Andrea's eyes.

"Yes, I have. When the Lord brought Lans back into my life, I knew he loved me and I had never doubted that he loved them."

"I'm glad, Andrea. You wouldn't want to build your life on a bitter foundation. Your grandparents wouldn't have wanted you to be angry at God for their sakes."

"You're right, I never thought of it that way, but that's the last thing they would have wanted for me."

Katharine wiped away the tears that were running down Andrea's cheeks and caught one on her own. The two women embraced, each aware that this afternoon's sharing had cemented the bond that formed long ago—the day they made daisy chains in the hayfield.

30

Their final night in New York Lans took Andrea to dinner at the little French restaurant where their week had started. Andrea learned later that he had requested a secluded table and confided to the hostess that this was to be a once-in-a-lifetime experience and they were not to be disturbed. She made a fuss over how well Andrea looked and kept her part of the conspiracy, disappearing as soon as they were seated.

Andrea, wearing her most sophisticated black dress and her mother's starburst diamond earrings, had had her hair styled in a fashionable New York salon.

"I'm not sure which sparkle is the brightest, your earrings, your flowing blond hair, or your beaming blue eyes. I guess I'm about the luckiest guy in New York to be sitting across from such a glamorous and sophisticated young woman. Sometimes I look at you and think, 'Where has Andrea gone?' You won't ever stop being the wonderful girl I met on the farm, will you?"

"Would you rather I had appeared in pigtails and jeans?"

"Not tonight. You look like the girl of my dreams, but don't forget how to put your hair in a ponytail and ride across open fields. That girl is part of my dreams, too."

"I'll always see you as a fifteen-year-old boy learning how to kayak, gallop on a horse, and experience a rope swing and a hayloft all for the first time."

"Tarzan like. Tarzan like Jane, too," he said as they laughed together, relaxed and comfortable in each other's presence. Could it ever be any other way?

The waiter appeared and they ordered their meal. "I'm so glad you brought me back here, Lans. It was a perfect beginning to our week, and it will be a perfect ending."

"I don't like the word *ending*. It sounds so final. I've been thinking rather in terms of new beginnings," Lans said looking very serious as he studied her face.

As she returned his gaze, she realized he was not dancing with laughter like she was. "Lans, you're much too serious for the occasion. Do you have bad news to tell me?"

He took her hand across the table. "I planned to wait until after dinner, but I can't wait any longer."

"Wait for what? Don't keep me in suspense. I'm imaging all kinds of things." By now Andrea was becoming alarmed. Was he going back to Europe? Had he taken a job in another country? Would she be left waiting for him again?

"Remember when I gave you the friendship ring the last night in Paris as a commitment to spend time together when I came home?"

"Yes, of course."

"I was thinking in terms of spending time together day in and day out, to make sure we would still have something to say to each other. I wanted to make sure the excitement of Paris wasn't the only attraction, and that we wouldn't become bored with each other."

Andrea gasped. It hurt even to hear the words. What was he trying to say? She tried to make her face expressionless, not wanting to reveal the pain she was feeling.

He continued. "I can't see when we're going to be able to do that, Andrea. I'm committed to the New York area with my job."

That was good news. The pain subsided to a slight ache. Did he no longer want to pursue their relationship? But they were getting along so well together.

"And you are committed to finishing your degree and then going home to work for your father in Pittsburgh."

"Yes."

Lans stroked her hand. Was he trying to lessen the blow? Was he saying there wouldn't be time to pursue their relationship? But it's been so good. How could he think it not worth pursuing?

"As for me, I don't need any more time with you to know how I feel. I want to spend the rest of my life with you whether we have anything to say to each other or not." He chuckled as the words poured out. "That's not what I meant to say, Andrea."

Andrea was trying to digest what he had just said and what it meant.

"What I'm trying to ask, Andrea, is, will you marry me? Will you be my wife?"

"Oh, Lans!" Her free hand jumped from her lap to cover her heart. As the full meaning of his words penetrated her mind and her thoughts changed gears, her nearly broken heart started pounding with excitement and delight. Her eyes kept searching his face, making sure it was not some kind of a joke, but that he really meant what he had just said.

Before her flashed a series of pictures of their times together: the kayak spilling him into the lake and his determination to try again; the two of them on horseback galloping through the field of daisies, his boyish face animated and excited by the speed and the challenge; the first time he put his arm around her to keep her warm in the barn that sheltered them from the storm; the night she left him and went off to the dance with another boy; dancing in his arms under the stars in the Bois de Bologne; his jealousy over Chico and his quick change of plans to take charge of her week in Paris—

Lans interrupted her flashbacks. "What are you thinking, Andrea? Is it so hard for you to give me an answer?"

"Oh, Lans," she repeated. She saw him now in the present, frowning at her for keeping him waiting. "Yes, yes, I would be thrilled to be your wife. Oh, yes, I will marry you." Her free hand found his, and they sat and stared at each other, marveling at the commitment they had just made and all that it might mean.

He withdrew his right hand from hers and reached into his pocket. "I bought this for you today, but if you don't like it, we can pick out another." He opened the little box and pushed it toward her.

She took it with both hands and said, "Oh, Lans" for the third time. "It's beautiful, and you chose it yourself?" She looked up at him and smiled. "I'd much rather have the one you chose. How did you know I would like a marquise solitaire? We've never talked about it."

He reached over and took the ring from the box and slipped it onto the fourth finger of her left hand. "I thought it suited you. Regal in its shape, simple in its design, sparkling in its personality, and a splendid example of God's handiwork." As he rolled her hand back and forth, its many prisms caught the light and sparkled like the stars dancing in Andrea's eyes.

"I didn't know you were so poetic. It's lovely." She sighed, releasing all the pent-up emotions of the last few minutes.

"There's quite a lot you don't know about me."

"And, I dare say, there's much you will discover about me," Andrea said.

"I'm looking forward to it."

"Lans, you know I'm an only child. I've had my way about most things."

"Remember, I am, too."

"Wow," she said like a schoolgirl, "when we clash the first time, promise me you'll remember this moment and not be angry."

"I could never be angry at you," he said, cupping her hands in his again.

"I'll remind you of that often, I'm sure."

Before he could reply, the chef, minus his apron and dressed in an evening jacket, appeared with his wife, who was all smiles. With a flourish, he raised a violin to his chin and serenaded the newly engaged couple. Lans smiled at Andrea with obvious pride. Andrea felt self-conscious but enjoyed the moment to the fullest.

The couple had obeyed Lans' orders until he proposed. Thereafter they hovered over him and his bride-to-be to give them a once-in-a-lifetime dining experience, compliments of the house. The chef offered his best creations, cooking many of them tableside with his usual ceremony. After they served the flaming Baked Alaska, they kissed Andrea on the cheek and shook hands with Lans, offering endless congratulations and best wishes, and promised to leave them in peace for the rest of the evening.

"Lans, weren't they wonderful? You must have told them ahead of time for them to go to all this trouble."

"No, but I did warn them this was to be a special evening and we needed to be left alone. I guess it didn't take a genius to figure out what was on my mind."

"I will never, ever forget it, not a single course. It was like being at those banquets in Paris all over again. Everything but the oysters, of course."

They both laughed.

"Andrea, I thought we might be married this summer, about a month after your graduation. What do you think?"

"I haven't had time to think, Lans, but that sounds good to me. Mother will be all in a dither, but nobody knows better how to give a good party and she'll be ecstatic planning a wedding. She'll want to invite everyone in Pittsburgh."

"What about being married at the farm?"

"The farm?" Leaving behind the picture of her and her father walking down the aisle of Shadyside Presbyterian Church, she tried to readjust.

"Yes, in the field of daisies," he said.

"Why, Lans, you're more of a romantic than I thought. What a wonderful idea. What made you think of it?"

"Rereading some of your letters about sitting in the field of daisies and remembering our good times together," he explained.

"I never told you I used to sit there plucking one daisy after another and tearing off the petals saying, "He loves me, he loves me not, he loves me, he loves me not." She raised her hand to her mouth to stop the flow of words. She was revealing how she had longed for him all these years.

"And now you know the answer. He does. I think I've always loved you since that summer. I just didn't always know it." He reached toward her hand, which was already moving toward his, like the irresistible pull of two magnets in close proximity. He caught it and held it firmly but tenderly, caressing the back of it with his thumb.

"What do you say to an outdoor wedding?"

"In the field of daisies?" she asked again, getting used to the idea. "I like it, I really do. It's only an hour's drive from Pittsburgh. Everyone could drive up for the day. The bridesmaids and ushers could stay in town at friends' houses and be there for all the preliminary parties."

"Will you make the ushers wear tuxes as they escort guests onto the field? Can't we just have a simple wedding without all the pomp and circumstance?"

"I'm my mother's only daughter. If you want to get off to a good start with her, you'll have to allow her to plan a wedding. Having it at the farm will be a challenge, but I'm sure she'll be creative and enjoy doing something entirely different."

"How do you feel about not being married in a church?"

"I'm fine with that. I haven't been attending since Grandma died. The hardest part will be thinking about her not being there. She always said she wanted to live to see me married. She would have been so happy to know it will be to you, Lans. She was as eager to receive your letters as I was. I always read them to her and she would say, 'Now he's a fine young man. He would make a good husband for you.'"

"Did she? I'm sorry I never saw her again. But don't you think she'll be there in spirit, especially if we have it at the farm?"

"Yes, and Grandpa, too, both of them young again and in love. I try to picture them that way." A tear crept down Andrea's cheek at the thought of her grandparents missing her wedding.

"They would want you to go back to church, Andrea."

"Yes, I suppose they would."

"Tomorrow will you come to my church and let me introduce you to my minister and my friends? You can take the four o'clock train back to college."

"You've thought of everything."

"Yes, and I'd like us to start going to church every Sunday after we're married. We'll need Jesus in the midst of our marriage covenant."

"Yes, of course. I always feel closer to him in my room at the farm. I remember when I was overwhelmed with his presence there when I was a little girl, before I met you. I'm sure his presence will pervade our wedding, Yes, I think we should have it at the farm."

He reached across the table and took both of her hands in his. "So it's settled. My bride will wear daisies in her hair, stroll through the daisy field toward me, and long daisy chains will hold back the guests. Then we will be there all alone together with Jesus."

"Lans, what has happened to you? Where is the serious businessman I thought you were?"

"I think they call it love. Enjoy it while it lasts, because when the honeymoon is over, the serious businessman will be struggling to make a living for his bride."

"Lans, what a wonderful life we'll have together."

⌘⌘⌘

It had been a wonderful life until something in their relationship began changing. Was it only two years ago that everything seemed right with their world? "We'll be there all alone with Jesus," he had said. *We need to be alone with Jesus now. Only he can fix this mess. Why didn't Lans pray with me when I asked him? We should have taken this problem to the Lord together like my grandparents would have done. Instead we are isolated from each other, an ocean apart.*

She closed her Bible and fell to her knees. "Lord, O Lord, bring us back together again. Remind him that it was he who invited you into our marriage. Help him draw on your strength and find the grace to come back to me." Sobbing gently, she bowed her forehead to the floor and imagined Lans on his knees in a hotel room in Sweden, asking God to show him the way home.

31

When Andrea reached Exodus 20, she studied the Ten Commandments and the laws that followed, trying to understand how God wanted her to live. Her mind kept jumping back to the fifth commandment, which promised long life to those who honored their father and their mother. She realized that she had begun to think of her mother as self-absorbed and selfish, not having any concern for other people. She had even suspected that at some level Evelyn understood that she was forcing Andrea to choose between her mother and her husband.

Certainly Andrea cared for her mother, but had she been dishonoring her in her thoughts? She remembered the good times they had had together during her teen years when Evelyn took her shopping in downtown Pittsburgh. She could still smell the enticing aroma of their favorite lunch— baked ham and dill pickles on warm toast with mayonnaise. They laughed together as they discussed what dresses Andrea would need for coming occasions. More than generous, her mother took her from one department store to another, never giving up until they found just the right outfits. Her mother had had many friends because she was equally generous with others.

Andrea remembered the fun they had contemplating her reunion with Lans in Paris and how she had waited up for Andrea far into the night, eager to see her happy. It was good to remember her mother like that. She had always encouraged Andrea's social life. She remembered her delight in all the preparations for the wedding. Evelyn wanted it to be perfect, to launch Andrea and Lans on a beautiful life together. She had cared deeply for their happiness then.

Such memories made the sacrifices Andrea had made seem right and confirmed to her the wisdom of trying so hard to help her mother through her declining years. Andrea had no choice but to take care of her mother, even in her terrible condition, and to make her last days on earth as pleasant as they could be. But was she justifying her actions, or had she indeed made the correct choices? Now that she had found a workable compromise for her mother, could she and Lans come together as if nothing had driven them apart?

⌘⌘⌘

Andrea pursued her study with perseverance and diligence. By the time she reached Exodus 34, she had come to understand the dual nature of God. He was a just God who could not tolerate rebellion and disobedience, but he loved his people and his desire was to bless them and to show mercy to those who loved him. His loving character was revealed again and again: "The Lord God, compassionate and gracious, slow to anger, and abounding in loving kindness and truth; who keeps loving kindness for thousands, who forgives iniquity, transgression and sin."

Deuteronomy 5:29 revealed the longing of God's heart to bless his people. If they kept his commandments, it would be "well with them and with their children forever."

Andrea read how he provided for his people in the wilderness with the cloud in the daytime, the pillar of fire by night, sending them manna to eat and, when they complained, quail for meat. Their shoes and their clothes never wore out through the forty years in the wilderness. God kept his promise to them and brought them to the edge of the Promised Land, even though they never stopped murmuring and complaining. Because of their continued disobedience, they were not granted the privilege of entering the Promised Land; but Joshua and Caleb, because they had a different spirit and had followed God fully, entered the land and were told their descendents would possess it.

Contemplating all this, she longed to follow God with her whole heart and to have the kind of spirit that would please him. Now that she had so few distractions, she threw herself into knowing God in a deeper way than she had thought possible.

Every night before she fell asleep, she read and meditated on the Psalms. She began having spiritual dreams in which she felt the presence of God while she slept and after she awoke.

Intrigued by how often the Psalms spoke of God's lovingkindness, she remembered how she had focused on that word the night before her grandfather's trial. Now she underlined it and counted: 139 times in the first half of the book. Often she found it mentioned two or three times in a single psalm. She now pictured a loving Father who wanted to shower his children with kindness, joy and mercy.

"He wants to bless us with his favor," she said aloud, feeling the weight that sat upon her shoulders lighten, "but when we disobey him, we open ourselves up to all the results of disobedience listed in the Bible." She was familiar enough with those but reading Deuteronomy 28 about all the blessings that would come upon those who obeyed God's commandments, she was comforted and encouraged.

⌘ ⌘ ⌘

Two months had passed since Andrea began her search. Often now she stayed up until after midnight reading her Bible and remained in bed after her alarm clock sounded. This morning at 8:30 a loud knock on the door awakened her. Throwing on her robe, she rushed to the front door to hear angry voices outside. Opening the door, she found Evelyn berating Adele.

"Mother, how could you be so ungrateful to Adele, who has done everything possible to make you happy and comfortable?" She looked from one to the other, hoping that the argument could be squelched before it produced terrible consequences.

"She thinks she can boss me around. I told her it was my house, and I would decide what was best for me."

"Your mother asked me to leave, Andrea." The words struck Andrea with the full force of a hurricane, blowing away the peace she had struggled so hard to obtain. Once again fear rushed in to fill the void.

Ushering them through the entrance hall and down the living room steps, she sat down on the green velvet couch that had once been her grandmother's and motioned to Adele to join her. "Adele, sit here and tell me what this is about."

Evelyn paced the floor wringing her hands as she had often done in the early stage of her illness.

"You know that I have been gradually reducing your mother's medicine and giving her proper nutrition and vitamins. When she stopped the medicine altogether, the hallucinations stopped. Then I started introducing one vitamin at a time to make sure she could tolerate it."

"She thinks I'm a storage box for pills. Every day there are more, and they stick in my throat. I won't take them anymore."

"Is that all this is about?" Andrea asked, relieved.

"Yes, but your mother called me all kinds of names, and I think it's time for me to go."

"Adele, you've been so good for Mother. You've accomplished miracles already, and I'm sure they're just beginning. You can't abandon her now." Without Adele, she would have no time to follow the new path the Lord had set before her. Adele had a way with Evelyn. She pampered her so much she could find little to complain about. The pills were not important enough to break up their happy routine.

Adele broke into her thoughts. "I've studied vitamins for years, and I know what's best for your mother. The doctor was killing her with all those drugs. She needs proper nutrients. If she won't take them, I won't be responsible for her."

"And I won't take them ever again," Evelyn asserted herself, making a show of folding her arms and giving Adele a defiant look.

"Mom, Adele is giving you vitamins to make you well. You've been so much better these past weeks. If Adele leaves, who will give you a massage every morning and rub your feet at night? No one will ever take better care of you."

"I can make my own decisions." Evelyn was not moved.

"Adele, stay for today and give this serious thought. You wouldn't want to see Mother lose all the progress she's made under your care, would you?"

"Of course not, but it's nice to be appreciated once in a while." Adele started to cry.

Andrea put her arms around her. "There's no way I could appreciate you more than I do. You've given me back my life. I appreciate every detail of what you do for Mother. I marvel at it every day. Whenever you feel unappreciated, come to me and I'll overwhelm you with appreciation."

"Doesn't anyone care what I think?"

"Of course, we care, Mother. You're what all this is about. I suggest that neither of you talk about it the rest of the day and see if you don't feel differently in the morning." Turning to Adele, she said, "No more vitamins for today. Let's give things a chance to work out."

"All right, I'll call you in the morning." Adele took a deep breath and squared her shoulders. "Come, Evelyn, it's time for your walk. We'll go home and get Tabitha. Spring bulbs are in bloom, and it's a lovely day."

Andrea watched them go, letting out the built-up tension with a sigh. Like a drill sergeant leading his platoon, Adele took over. Evelyn followed meekly by her side.

32

A dele rang early the next morning. Andrea's shoulders tightened as she picked up the phone. What would be her decision?

"Your mother and I had a terrible fight last night. I packed my things and planned to leave this morning."

Andrea's body tensed as she braced herself for accustomed disappointment.

Adele continued, "I said to myself, 'I'm not taking any more of this. I'm leaving.' During my prayers I asked the good Lord to find me a place where I would be appreciated." She paused.

"You know I appreciate you, Adele, and Mother does, too. Remember that all the pathways in her brain are tangled, and sometimes she doesn't know what she's saying."

"Your mother is a stubborn woman, but I have come to love her."

"I know she loves you, as much as she's capable of loving right now."

"I was praying for a new position when suddenly the Lord appeared at the foot of my bed."

Shivers ran through Andrea's body.

Adele continued. "He told me there was no one but me to love and care for your mother, and he wanted me to stay."

"He did?" Andrea's heart pounded so hard she had trouble concentrating on Adele's words.

"Yes, he did, and I promised I would. So that settles it. I'm staying until the day your mother dies, no matter what she does or says."

"I'm so grateful. That gives me confidence to face the future. Thank you, Adele."

"Don't thank me," she said, "Thank the good Lord. I'm doing it for him. He's placed a love for your mother in my heart, and I'll do everything I can to help her enjoy the rest of her days."

"I always thought you were an angel sent by God. Now I know you are." Tears streamed down Andrea's face. The Lord had heard her prayers for her mother. He hadn't healed her, but he had sent someone to care for her in her situation. She put down the phone and looked heavenward. "Thank you. Thank you for sending Adele."

That night Andrea read again in Deuteronomy the many blessings God wanted to give his people if they kept His commandments. How she wanted to deserve His blessings, but she realized she could never be good enough to deserve them. It was a matter of grace. Undeserved blessing, unmerited favor. That was the meaning of grace.

Alzheimer's must have followed her family for generations, becoming part of their genetic heritage, like those extraordinary plagues or curses mentioned at the end of Deuteronomy 28. They could result in such things as prolonged sickness, madness, confusion of heart. The chapter further detailed "fear that terrifies the heart," "fear day and night," "no assurance of life," the very fears she was experiencing. But Jesus had taken all those upon himself. Because of his perfect work on the cross, her children and grandchildren could receive his grace and live free of the fear that haunted her.

"Now, Lord," she said, "show me how this can be accomplished." She had no idea where to start, but turning the problem over to him, she felt confident that, having brought her this far, he would show her how to proceed.

✻✻✻

Three weeks later Andrea sauntered through the orchard at the back of their property where she and Lans had allowed nature to reclaim the land. Uncut green grasses and abundant daffodils, once planted there, now covered the hillside. Exceptionally beautiful this time of year, the mass of yellow blooms bounced and bowed in the spring winds. She and Lans had often come here to sit on a log, hold hands, and talk about special moments at the farm. They both loved the wildness of the hillside with its sharp contrast to the well-manicured lawns that surrounded their English Tudor home.

She remembered the happy days of the children's middle and high school years. Lans had loved building a fire in the old-fashioned fireplace. He and Andrea often sat before it in each other's arms and marveled at how fortunate they were. When the children joined them, the four of them played word games as they watched the flames dance over the glowing logs.

The gardens had been neglected before they bought the house, but little by little they had worked together on restoring them. They filled the pond with lily pads and large gold fish, which the children delighted to name and converse with when they surfaced at feeding time. Picnic lunches and grilled dinners on the large wooden table near the pool became a family tradition during the summer. In the fall they picked fruit together as a family, harvesting crops of apples, pears, or raspberries from the orchard. So many happy memories. Andrea felt a stab of pain as she relived these happy times that were no more.

How she longed to hear from Lans. She knew he had been writing to John and Kate, but she never asked about him. He would be home soon. Perhaps things would be different then.

She walked beyond their property to the little house at the edge of the woods where her mother and Adele lived. After knocking on the door, she let herself in. Adele was giving Evelyn her daily massage. Andrea saw that all was well between them and left, excusing herself so she wouldn't interrupt their daily routine. Her mother loved to be pampered, and Adele knew just how to do it.

Everything had remained quiet since the near break-up. Andrea could see that her mother and Adele were settling into a peaceful existence. Evelyn had stopped wringing her hands, and Andrea could tell she enjoyed her days more. She no longer paced the house talking to the shadowed guests who had once dominated her days. As her speech began to slow, she stopped fighting verbally. She no longer demanded Andrea's constant attention. Peace had come to their world.

Andrea walked on, praying as she went, thanking the Lord for his provision for her mother. She remembered all the healing lines they had stood in together. The Lord had not healed her, but he had sent Adele. Would there be anyone like Adele to care for Andrea when Alzheimer's struck her? "No, Lord, no. Anything but that," she cried aloud. There it was again; fear still gripped her. Would her fate be like her mother's?

But your word says that you've "not given us a spirit of fear but of power and of love and of a sound mind." She loved that scripture, had written it on a 3x5-inch card and taped it to her bathroom mirror beside the verse that she should not be anxious about tomorrow.

"I'm trying, Lord. I'm trying. Thank you for a sound mind. I am focusing on your power and love. Why then can I not overcome this terrible fear?"

On her way home she stopped at her mailbox to pick up the mail. She put it under her arm and trudged up the driveway, past the circle of red and yellow tulips that would soon unfurl. They had been a gift from Johan and Katharine from Holland. Neither the anticipation of the tulip blooms nor the joy of her visit to the hillside of daffodils was strong enough to blot out the fear that there would be no one to care for her when her time came. Ashamed of her lack of faith, she hung up her coat and searched her mail. She still longed for a letter from Lans.

As usual, there was none. She opened each envelope as she came to it, ending with a brochure about a week at a Christian family camp in Kentucky. Glancing through the list of activities and speakers, she noted that the main speakers specialized in praying with families who experienced recurring problems in succeeding generations. She stopped and read that sentence a second time. Was there such a specialty? The brochure had captured her attention. She read it from start to finish.

Have you ever wondered why generations of your family have suffered a series of happenings or illnesses that were similar or had a common thread? Come and meet Bill and Wendy Fillmore, who have prayed with hundreds of troubled families.

Prepare to gain a deeper understanding of all that Jesus Christ accomplished on the cross for you. Absorb their teaching and make a personal appointment with them for prayer. You, too, can be set free!

Once inside, Andrea read the brochure a second time. "To be set free from fear. Oh, how wonderful," she said to the kitchen walls. Here was hope. No matter how slim the chance that it would work for her, she would pursue it. She fumbled through the papers piled on her kitchen counter until she found her calendar.

"Ah, here it is. May 25 to 31. Nothing but a Memorial Day picnic, which I can miss," she said, still speaking aloud. She hugged the calendar to her breast as though it were giving her permission to go.

The phone rang. She reached for it. "Hello, Andrea here."

"Andrea. How are you?"

"Katharine. I'm doing fine." She had trouble turning her attention away from the lifeline she had just been offered. She couldn't let it go.

"Katharine, how would you like to spend a week at a Christian family camp with me?"

"When and where?" she asked without hesitation.

"May 25 to 31 in Kentucky, in horse country. You could come here and we could drive down together and stop and see some of the great horse farms on the way. Lans and I always talked about taking the kids on a trip like that." Her enthusiasm for the adventure grew with each new idea.

"Johan will be traveling. I'm free."

"Then we're going." Andrea gave her no opportunity to refuse. "Won't we have fun? There are classes in writing, dancing, crafts of all kinds, and there will be Bible Studies and lectures every day. It sounds like just what I need." Her voice rose with excitement. "Katharine," she said in a more sober tone. "I need to do this, and I probably won't have the guts to do it alone. I need you to do this with me."

"Then it's settled. We'll go."

"Hallelujah!" Andrea exclaimed. "The Lord must have planned for you to call at this moment, before I had a chance to throw the brochure away. Katharine, I have so much to tell you. I've learned so much in the past two months."

"It sounds like you've had some time to yourself. How are Adele and Evelyn enjoying the new house?"

"Just fine. Adele is like a drill sergeant one minute and a fairy godmother the next. She's taken control of Mom's daily routine, tells her what to do, what to eat, what vitamins to take, when to take a walk, and when to sit still. Most of the time Mom does what she tells her because in between Adele pampers her excessively, gives her a massage every morning, rubs her feet at night. Keeps her moisturized in oils and skin creams. Cooks wonderful meals and makes special treats for her. Mom doesn't realize what a godsend Adele is and fires her every now and then, but Adele won't go."

"What keeps her there?"

"She had a vision of the Lord standing at the foot of her bed when she was all packed and ready to go. The Lord told her that there was no one else to love and care for Mom, and He wanted her to stay. That did it. She'll stay now as long as Mother lives. Can you imagine being that fortunate in this day and age when it's next to impossible to find live-in help?"

"Something had to break for you, Andrea. You've done everything humanly possible to take care of your mother."

"I don't think this is a human thing. It's a God thing. The Lord didn't choose to lift this cup from Mom, but he surely is taking care of her. I'm so grateful. It's like he's sent us an angel."

"And you can get away to take a trip?"

"Yes, I'm sure I'll be able to by then."

"Have you written to Lans to tell him?"

"No, I haven't heard from him since he left, Katharine."

"Not anything?" Katharine registered disbelief. "Well, I'm going to let him know. You should be taking a plane to Sweden, not driving to Kentucky."

"Katharine, please don't say anything to Lans. If this trip is as important as I think it is, it has to happen first. Just trust me in this. I'll explain it all to you on the way to Kentucky. And thank you for going with me. You're a true friend. Somehow I always think of you that way rather than as my mother-in-law."

"I am your friend, Andrea, and I would do anything to help you and Lans bring this separation to an end."

"Great. I'll send you a copy of the brochure and I'll make reservations for two. To prepare you for this, Katharine, be sure to read the first fourteen verses of Deuteronomy 28 before we go. Concentrate on how much God wants to bless us if we will only obey Him. I'll try to explain all I've learned on our way there, but I need you to be praying. I think the Lord is directing this and it's going to be a life-changing experience."

"I can't wait. We'll have a lovely week together."

⌘⌘⌘

Andrea continued to devour the words of Scripture. She read that God told Ezekiel and Jeremiah in the Old Testament and John in the New to eat his words. To all of them, the word tasted as sweet as honey. A note in her Bible suggested that the message must saturate the personality of the one who proclaims it.

The concept excited Andrea. She would ingest the word until it became a part of her. Studying the word gave Andrea new optimism. For some time now it had been her main source of joy.

She prayed, "Lord, prepare me for this encounter." As she rocked back and forth in the chair in which she had nursed her babies, flipping through the pages of her Bible, the Lord spoke to her heart. "Not by might nor by power, but by My Spirit." By this Andrea understood that it would be the presence of the Holy Spirit that was important. God, himself, would do the work through his Spirit. In fact he had already done it. Isaiah said, "He was wounded for our transgressions" and "By his stripes we are healed." The second chapter of 1 Peter took it further. "By whose stripes you were healed." It was already done.

David spoke of walking "before God in the light of the living." Alzheimer's was like a living death. The body still lived but the mind drew inexorably closer to death. Andrea wanted to walk in the light of the living. "Lord, let me live every day of my life!"

33

Excited, energized, gesturing as they walked back to their cabin, Katharine and Andrea talked about the evening's teaching by the Fillmores, the couple Andrea had come to camp to meet. "That was powerful," Andrea exclaimed. "How could we have missed it all these years?"

"It changed my picture of our heavenly Father." Katharine gazed at the star-lit sky. "Look at the moon and the stars. He must be smiling down on us."

"It's a glorious night, and the week's forecast is good. I'm so excited to be here. Weren't you surprised that there are six hundred references to blessings in the Bible?"

"It's such a positive approach," Katharine said. "I had no idea God's desire to bless his people is so pervasive in Scripture, especially in the Old Testament. We hear so much about his being an angry God, a jealous God."

"That's because he loves us so much," Andrea said, raising her hand skyward. "Didn't you like their description of how strongholds are developed? How Satan plays upon our insecurities and fears with nagging thoughts, suspicions, and doubts that build and build. Mother has entertained them all for years. I did, too, though I never expressed them. Dr. Henderson's diagnosis seemed to confirm them all and invited Satan to fill my mind with paralyzing fear."

"The mind is where the spiritual battle takes place. I was happy to hear them say it is easier to keep from getting an illness than it is to receive healing after it has taken hold. That's encouraging for you, Andrea."

"What caught my attention was that God doesn't interfere in the normal course of your life unless you ask him, but you have to ask in faith believing. That's the part I've been working on."

Katharine finished the thought, "And when you do ask, it allows him to change your life, even the results of your genetic code."

"Now that's powerful," Andrea said, as she held the cabin door open for Katharine. "And while much remains a mystery, the important revelation is that I can be healed."

"We're at the right place this week. I need to hear these things as much as you do."

"I think everyone needs to hear them, Katharine."

Three days later Andrea opened the door of their cabin, threw her pocketbook on the chair, and collapsed on the couch.

Katharine came running from the bedroom. "Andrea, how did it go? I've been praying ever since you left."

Andrea's face lit up. "Thank you, Katharine. I knew I could count on you." She roused herself from the couch and threw her arms around Katharine. "It worked. The fear is gone. I'm free of it at last!"

"Oh, my dear, I'm so happy for you." Katharine held Andrea in her arms as tears trickled down her cheeks. As they parted, she wiped them away. "Tell me all about it. But first let me get you a glass of iced tea. I made your favorite, cinnamon rose with apple juice and lime."

Andrea, her countenance serene, sat down at the table and waited until Katharine poured the tea. "I knew this was the day," she began as Katharine joined her, "from the first thing we did this morning in writing class. Our instructor asked us to write a story about something that had frightened us. I wrote about someone struggling with the prospect of becoming a victim of Alzheimer's.

"When we had finished, the instructor asked us to read our stories aloud. After I read mine, a young man in his thirties jumped up and said he had written about the very same fear. His father had lost his memory and he had just placed him in a nursing home. Keith was haunted by the idea that the same thing would happen to him. I watched beads of perspiration break out on his forehead as he described his feelings.

"I told him that I thought today was my day to overcome that fear and invited him to sit in on my prayer time with the Fillmores. After class we were able to make appointments back to back at 3:30 this afternoon. We met at their cabin. I thought sitting in on my time would build his faith."

"How fortunate you were able to help someone else at the same time."

"I came back here for lunch and when you didn't come, I figured you were involved in ministry of your own, so I left the note and went for a long walk."

"I came back after having lunch with a lady who was all upset about her daughter marrying a European. I think I helped ease her mind. I read your note and I've been praying nonstop ever since."

"Dear faithful Katharine." Andrea laid her hand on Katharine's arm. "Thank you for your prayers. I needed them." She smiled at Katharine, grateful to have a mother-in-law she loved who loved her.

"As I walked and talked to the Lord," Andrea continued, "and thanked him for this opportunity, I felt enveloped in his peace. I didn't hear a loud voice out of heaven, but I sensed him speaking to my spirit and telling me that he had many plans for my life, that it was far from over. Encouraged, I walked through the woods, sucking on a piece of field grass like Grandma and I used to do on our walks at the farm. I enjoyed fellowship with the Lord for almost two hours and ended up at the Fillmore's on the dot of 3:30."

Katharine nodded with approval.

"Keith was waiting for me, rubbing his hands together as though he were trying to keep warm while beads of perspiration still dripped from his forehead. He made me a little nervous, but I tried to appear calm for his sake.

"We went in together. After greetings and a little chitchat about how great the camp was, the Fillmores suggested we start. They were lovely people. Wendy had a sweet spirit and Bill exuded strength and confidence. They asked me to tell them my story and what I hoped to accomplish by seeing them. I kept it as brief as possible but hit the high points from what happened to Grandpa and his parents to what I've been through with Mom, and my frightening diagnosis at the clinic.

"I explained that fear still gripped me whenever I thought of the future. I told them about receiving the brochure in the mail and your calling me at the very time I was reading it, about Keith's and my writing on the same subject this morning and that I felt God had directed everything about my being there. I told them I believed this was my time to be freed from the fear that Alzheimer's would claim me and future members of my family.

"They were pleased with my optimism and laid out the scriptural position for what Jesus accomplished on the cross for us."

"Tell me everything you can remember," Katharine said eagerly.

"I can't remember it all, but I wrote some of the Scriptures down so I can help others." Andrea took a slip of paper from her pocket. "Deuteronomy 30 tells us that God sets before us life or death, which in my case is Alzheimer's, and the choice is ours. God tells us to choose life so we and our descendants may live. We do that by loving him, obeying his voice, and realizing he is our life. In the book of John, Jesus said he is the way, the truth, and the life, and he came to give us life abundantly, not a life of fear but of abundant blessing.

"The Fillmores said what happened on the cross is pivotal. A divine exchange took place. Every evil that was due us was placed on Christ, that every good thing due to Christ could be placed on us. He was wounded that we might be healed and punished that we might be forgiven. God judged him in our place. He treated Jesus like rebellious men and women deserve to be treated so that now he can treat us like Jesus deserved to be treated. God was just. Someone had to be punished for centuries of disobedience, so he took the punishment upon himself through his Son, so he might show mercy and goodness to his people."

Andrea walked around the room as she recounted all that she had learned. She leaned over the table and looked into Katharine's eyes. "I'm so grateful that before Lans and I were married you encouraged me to mend my relationship with the Lord. If I had remained hardened and angry about what happened to my grandparents, think of all I would have missed."

"You would have found your way back, dear. The beautiful faith you had as a child had deep roots. But go on. Tell me everything that happened."

"They went through how easy it is for us to be disobedient. Man wants to be self-reliant, and when he thinks he is, he gets puffed up with pride. That separates him from God and diminishes how much God can bless him.

"The requirement for blessing is in Deuteronomy 28. It's so simple. He wants us to listen to his voice and do what he says. That means listen to what he says in the Bible, his guideline for our lives, and follow his commandments. When we stay humble and depend on him, he'll bless us, but when we become self reliant and disobedient, we open ourselves to the dark things of this world."

"Doesn't this have a much broader application than just Alzheimer's?"

"Of course. The Fillmores told us about families with problems of addiction and child molestation, even things like divorce. For some families they keep happening in generation after generation.

"Some of my friends have stories like those," Katharine said.

"I hope I'll be able to help people realize what Jesus has done for them, so they don't have to live in fear."

"But how did they pray for you?"

"When they told us to get comfortable, I sat in my chair, closed my eyes and relaxed. When Wendy and Bill started praying, I felt ushered straight into the Father's presence and when they invited his Spirit to guide us, I knew he was there and would do just that. I didn't have to try to believe; it was like God gave me a gift of faith.

"Bill asked him to break the stronghold over our family and to release me from the fear of Alzheimer's. He prayed in a calm voice, confident God was doing the work he asked him to do. Of course, the Holy Spirit made it happen, not Bill, but he was faithful to ask and we both believed the Holy Spirit responded.

"Wendy said I should claim my release on the basis of what Jesus did on the cross for me. I closed my eyes, and the sense of his presence pervaded the room. I felt I could reach out and touch him.

"'Lord,' I said, 'in the presence of these new friends, I thank you for all you suffered on the cross for me. I thank you for your provision for me and for giving me an understanding of how much you want to bless me and my family. As I thank you, Lord, I choose the life you offer me. I claim complete release from Alzheimer's disease for me, for my children, and for future members of my family. I claim release from the fear that I will lose my memory and my mind. I thank you that my children won't have to witness my mental decline as I have witnessed the decline of Grandpa and Mother. I look forward to living according to your word to the best of my ability for the rest of my life.'"

"That was beautiful, Andrea," Katharine said, eyes misty.

"Afterwards Bill said that I should live expecting all those in my family to experience blessing. He said the Lord is good and his love endures forever. He showed me Psalm 119 where the Bible says that his faithfulness continues through all generations. I will pray for my children and coming generations to honor God. If they do, I believe he will be faithful to bless them.

"Isn't it wonderful, Katharine? I truly believe that my children won't have to watch me deteriorate like I watched Grandpa and Mom, so they won't fear it happening to them. Of course, they must choose to listen to God and do what he says. Each of us has that choice to make."

"I'm so happy for you, dear." Tears ran down her cheeks.

"It's over. They prayed, I prayed, and I believe it's been done." Andrea stretched out her arms toward Katharine.

"And I believe it, too." Katharine hugged Andrea as hard as she could. "God is so good. I believe with all my heart that he wants us to call on him to change our misfortunes and to walk in his blessings, and you and Lans are going to do that from now on."

Andrea registered alarm. "Not a word to Lans about this, Katharine. You promised."

"Not a word. But things will change, you'll see. I think the Lord simply wanted you to be alone for a time, so you'd have to depend on him for the solution."

"At least I feel I have something to offer Lans now, instead of years of illness and difficulties. I know we'll have trials, but I believe we'll walk through them together and God will be with us. Best of all, the children will be spared. If I don't succumb to Alzheimer's, they won't ever fear it like I did."

34

Andrea had been home from camp for over a month. She knew that Katharine had met Lans at the New York airport and taken him home for the Fourth of July weekend. He would be returning to Pittsburgh tonight.

Katharine promised she would say nothing to him except that she had spent a lovely week with Andrea at a camp in Kentucky. Andrea was well and Evelyn and Adele were living in harmony in the house next door. Would Lans care enough to question his mother further?

She longed to know that he still cared, but as she considered his state of mind, a thought struck her with the force of a thunderbolt hurled from heaven. She must not be in Pittsburgh when Lans returned. She could not bear the suspense of waiting for a call that might never come. She had been lighthearted and free of worry since their return from camp. She must remain optimistic now.

She rang Adele to tell her she would be driving to the farm this afternoon and suggested she tell Evelyn only that she had left town but would be back soon. The three of them had spent a week at the farm in early May and again during the middle of June. Both weeks had been successful. Thrilled to be there, Evelyn stopped complaining to Andrea about taking the farm from her, and Adele rejoiced that Evelyn had fresh country air to breathe.

In less than twenty minutes, Andrea packed a suitcase and phoned Jake, who had retired from the company and moved to the farm as caretaker. He and his wife lived in a separate home on the property. "Jake, I'm on my way out the door, and I'm coming to the farm for a few days. Sorry to give you such short notice."

Andrea sang as she drove. Rather than running away from her problems as Lans had, she was running to something.

She arrived late in the day and prepared a light supper to eat on the picnic table in the backyard. In no hurry, she lingered at the table, inhaling familiar country smells, watching the blue sky morph into crimsons, oranges, and yellows. Had she come upon the scene suddenly, she might have been frightened, seeing burning flames consuming the pasture hills. Instead, a feeling of well-being rose inside.

After washing the dishes, she settled onto the porch swing and, with the same fascination she had experienced as a child, listened to crickets chirping in the fields and watched fireflies blinking in the darkness. Reliving the night she introduced them to Lans touched off a stream of happy and sad memories. But something in her attitude had changed. No longer haunted by past tragedies, she found her memories comforting, like visiting old friends. She looked forward to the future with pleasure.

⌘ ⌘ ⌘

The little room where she slept as a child welcomed her. Its friendly familiarity hugged her and bestowed on her the love and security she had always felt in her grandmother's arms. She opened an old copy of the Living Bible and searched until her eyes fell on a well-marked verse in Psalm 34: "The Lord is close to those whose hearts are breaking." That verse sustained her during her separation from Lans and drew her closer to the Lord than ever before. She believed he had always been waiting for her, but until her world fell apart, she failed to give him her full attention.

Perhaps one day she would thank Lans for leaving her alone and pushing her toward the Lord. Otherwise she would not have been able to appropriate what Christ had done for her on the cross.

As she thanked God for her new freedom from fear, waves of the Spirit washed over her and shot through her body. They brought perfect peace one minute and feelings of ecstasy the next, like sinking deep into the water of the lake, at the same time being lifted up by its buoyancy. Relaxed and restful, yet expectant and alert, she lay awake far into the night enjoying the presence of God.

Overcome by a strange stillness, she felt a sense of surrender beyond anything she had yet experienced. With all the fight drained from her, all the striving to work things out in her own power, she surrendered her life to God. She surrendered her mother. Her marriage. If God wanted her to go it alone, she was willing. If he wanted her to resume her marriage with Lans, to work at restoration and healing, to work at a deeper communication than they had known, she was willing.

She fell asleep in the early hours of the morning, as though she were falling into her heavenly Father's arms.

⌘ ⌘ ⌘

In the morning she awoke rested, still at peace. She knelt before the front window to watch hundreds of daisies, rustled by a summer breeze, bow on graceful, swaying stems. Masses of yellow centers shone like tiny suns; white petals sparkled. The atmosphere was electric making Andrea feel alert and exceptionally alive. With eyes wide open, she saw herself running toward the flowers. A white-robed man materialized in the middle of the field. Encouraged by his warm smile, she ran toward him. He stretched out his arms to her. Strong, yet tender, his face broadcast love and compassion. His flaming eyes focused on hers and bade her come to him. Just before she reached him, she called out, "Lord, Lord, it was you all along!" She had always thought it was Lans she had sought there, but it had been Jesus all along. Only he could satisfy the deep longings of her heart.

She had expected Lans to fill her every need, but Lans had needs and deficits of his own. At that moment she saw her preoccupation with her mother's condition from his point of view. She should have tried harder to balance his needs with her mother's. When things started going wrong, she could have shown him sympathy rather than expecting him to agree with her priorities. Had her priorities been right or was her first duty to her husband as Evelyn had taught her all her life? The Bible said that a couple should leave their parents and cleave to each other. She had given in to her mother's demands and expected Lans to do the same. Should she have been more understanding?

Suddenly she knew that Jesus wanted her marriage to continue. She and Lans were not meant to struggle alone, but to witness to others how good a marriage could be with Jesus at the center of it.

She arose, turned from the window, and made her way to the phone on the landing. Lans had arrived home last night. Though Monday morning, this was a business holiday. He would be planning to go to the office to catch up on his mail but might not have left his townhouse yet.

"Father, don't let me be too late. Lans, please be home."

She picked up the phone in the hall and dialed. "Hello, Lans, it's Andrea."

He returned her greeting in a noncommittal tone, but she thought she detected a spark of pleasure in hearing her voice.

Her heart flooded with love for him. "I'm alone at the farm. The sun is shining and the field of daisies is magnificent." She decided to be bold. "How soon can you meet me here?"

She held her breath through the silence, longing to be comforted by his gentle, deep voice. "Give me," he said, with no hint of emotion, "three hours." Another long pause as though he were trying to figure things out in his head.

"And have the horses ready."

She put down the receiver and ran to the field. He still cared, and he was coming to her. She plucked the largest daisy she could find. "He loves me, he truly does love me," she cried out to the heavens as she pulled off one leaf after another. Whirling around in sheer delight, she hugged the little daisy to her heart. "And he's coming to me here at last!"

⌘ ⌘ ⌘

Andrea dressed herself with great care, choosing her most stylish jeans and a blue blouse that complemented her eyes, making them look twice as big. She brushed her hair until it danced and crowned it with a daisy chain like the one Lans had made her the summer they met. Looking into the mirror, she was satisfied that he would see an energetic, radiant woman, confident and at peace, in the prime of her life. The tired lines had diminished, and the thought of Lans driving to meet her here at the farm made her smile. The picture of the frazzled, distraught wife he had carried since the last time he held her at his townhouse would be replaced with the welcoming smile of a vibrant woman eagerly waiting to please him.

Backing away from the mirror, she glanced at the clock. Ten minutes short of the three hours he had requested. She must remember to thank Jake for keeping the kitchen so well stocked and for leaving a defrosted leg of lamb in the refrigerator. Having made good use of the three hours, she ran down the stairs and through the kitchen where the smells of roasting lamb and baked apple filled the air. She looked with satisfaction at the apple pie cooling on the windowsill and the centerpiece of daisies on the kitchen table. She would show Lans that he had a wife who not only cared about his needs but would see that they were met.

She jumped over the side of the porch like she had as a child and hurried to the barn to saddle the horses.

⌘ ⌘ ⌘

Lans pulled into the driveway and crossed the bridge over the creek. Noting that Andrea had launched the boats, he saw himself as a boy of fifteen turning over in the kayak for the third time and emerging from the lake to see a young girl laughing at him. He proceeded down the driveway until he saw her standing in the field of daisies holding the reins of two saddled horses. Opposite her, he stopped the car and turned off the ignition. The reserved greeting he had planned and the emotional distance he had meant to maintain vanished when he saw her radiant smile and daisy-crowned hair. He ran toward her as eagerly as he had when they were courting.

As she took a step toward him, he gathered her in his arms, held her close, and buried his face in her hair. The smell of shampoo mingled with freshly cut daisies reminded him of the terrible void in his life during the past year.

"Andrea, I've missed you so much. I've hungered for you at night. I don't ever want to live without you again."

"Lans, I love you. I've always loved you. I wanted to be with you more than you can imagine."

His long, passionate kiss swept away the months of turmoil, contention, and penetrating loneliness. As they broke apart, he took her face in his hands and studied it as though he were seeing her for the first time. Her beaming eyes promised everything he wanted.

He watched her search his eyes and gave her the assurance he knew she needed. "Lans, we're going to have a wonderful marriage!" he heard her exclaim.

Then playing the coquette, she thrust the reins of his horse into his hands, mounted, and dug her heels into her horse's side. "I'll race you to the woods," she cried.

He threw his leg over the saddle and followed her. Sensing the excitement in the air, the horses broke into a gallop, and the daisies blurred beneath them.

Epilogue

The romance characters in this story are fictitious, but the theme of generational Alzheimer's disease, the afflictions of the characters, and the diagnosis given the main character are based on the personal experience of the author. The diagnosis, made by a doctor whose reputation remained solid, was given in 1979. At this writing, in 2012, over thirty-two years later, the author still has a sound mind and has lived free of the fear of Alzheimer's since 1981.

About the Author

BARBARA HATTEMER, educated at Smith College and Harvard Business School, worked for a management consulting firm before marrying and raising four children. For fifteen years she fought for high community standards at home and throughout the country, giving hundreds of Radio and Television interviews and debates. Featured in *Christian Herald Magazine* and Focus on the Family's *Citizen*; recipient of *Christian Herald's* first James 1:22 Award, she appeared on *The Today Show* with Bryant Gumbel and on Dr. James Dobson's Radio Program.

In addition to many magazine articles, she wrote a chapter, "New Light on Daycare Research," in Phyllis Schlafly's *Who Will Rock the Cradle* (Word Publishers). Her book ~~Don't~~ *Touch That Dial: The Impact of the Media on Children and the Family*, an analysis of social science research on the harms of sexually explicit and violent media, was published by Huntington House.

Now Barbara writes inspirational fiction. As a teenager, she summered on a Pennsylvania farm caring for animals, picking wildflowers, and riding her horse through hayfields bursting with daisies. She chose this setting for *Field of Daisies* and, drawing from personal experience, wrote a fictional story that offers hope to families experiencing Alzheimer's disease in successive generations.

Barbara is uniquely qualified to write this book because she experienced firsthand the deteriorating effects of Alzheimer's disease on her loved ones and the fear that it would soon come upon her. The love story is fiction, but the generations of Alzheimer's are drawn from her own family.

http://www.BarbaraHattemer.com
www.oaktara.com